WALL STREET NOIR

EDITED BY PETER SPIEGELMAN

AKASHIC BOOKS
NEW YORK

Published by Akashic Books
©2007 Akashic Books

Series concept by Tim McLoughlin and Johnny Temple
Map by Sohrab Habibion

ISBN-13: 978-1-933354-23-1
ISBN-10: 1-933354-23-2
Library of Congress Control Number: 2006938154
All rights reserved

First printing
Printed in Canada

Akashic Books
PO Box 1456
New York, NY 10009
info@akashicbooks.com
www.akashicbooks.com

WALL STREET NOIR

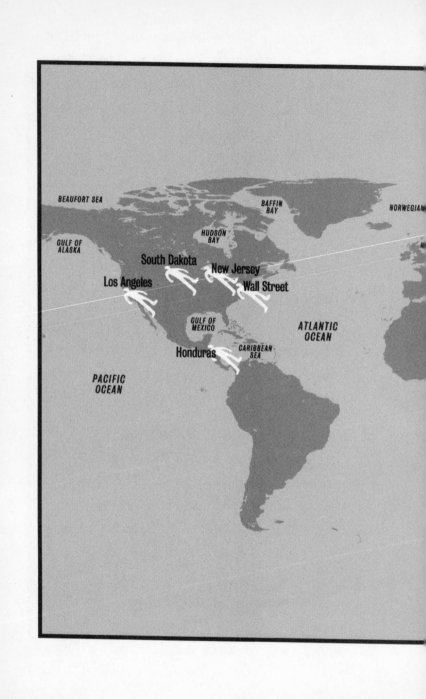

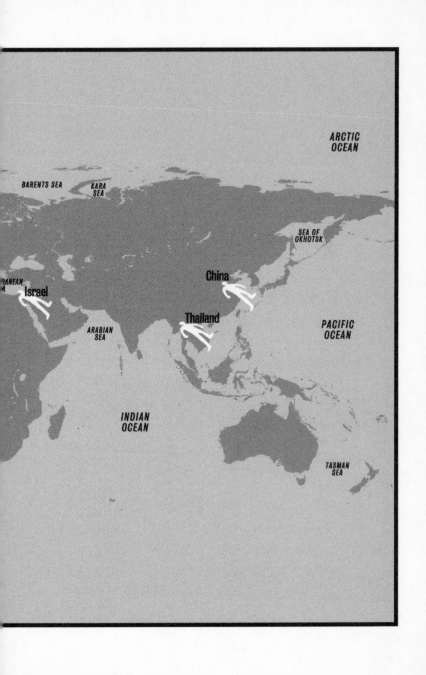

For Alice

Acknowledgments

All books are collaborative efforts, but none more so than anthologies, and so I owe many thanks to many people: first and foremost, to all of the contributors, for their talents, time, good humor, and professionalism; to Johnny Temple, for seeing the possibilities; and to Reed Coleman, for a good eye and sound advice.

TABLE OF CONTENTS

PART III: MAIN STREET

PART IV: GLOBAL MARKETS

INTRODUCTION
TRADITION

W all Street is long on tradition. The opening bell, the floor traders' vivid jackets, black Town Cars at curbside, long nights spent hunched over spreadsheets, helicopters to the Hamptons, lap-dance tabs that run to five figures—these shared rituals and experiences bind generations of money folk one to the other, and so preserve and propagate the culture. But there's one link in that chain more tarnished than the rest, and less fondly regarded: crime.

Financial crime has a history much longer than Wall Street's—by several thousand years at least. Conflicted interests, insider trading, and outright fraud are as old as the first marketplaces—as old as the first swap of flint chips for bearskins, no doubt—and they've been part and parcel of Wall Street since the days of the old Dutch barricade. Just as Wall Street has raised finance to high art (or at least, to expensive spectacle), so has it done crime bigger and flashier than its Old World antecedents. Sure, there was the South Sea scam, and that business with the Vatican Bank, but Wall Street has given us Robert Vesco, Ivan Boesky, and the Hunt brothers, not to mention playing midwife to Enron, Adelphia, and Qwest. And unlike some traditions (floor traders are an endangered species at the NYSE, and the bean counters are ever more skeptical about receipts that come dotted with glitter), crime on Wall Street actually has a future.

Caveats about past performance and future results notwithstanding, I feel pretty safe in this prediction. The news gives me comfort. Every day seems to bring more stories of front-running, insider trading, and cooked books, and some business blogs (the more ironic ones, to be sure) even offer travel tips for white-collar bail-jumpers. Crime endures on Wall Street through cycles of boom and bust, and waves of regulation, deregulation, and re-regulation—a constant in an otherwise changing world.

This persistence and bright future of crime stands in marked contrast to the public image the Street projects these days. Viewed from a distance, on the cable business channels, say, it seems like such a clean, well-lighted place. The sort of place where investment decisions are guided by careful formulae and subtle strategies, by dispassionate consideration of all the facts and figures; the sort of place where cool reason prevails. The information is out there for all to see; you just need to interpret it correctly. It's as pure a meritocracy as one could ask for, so get some software, open a margin account, and knock yourself out. It's a comforting notion—but it doesn't hold up on close inspection. Close up, you see distortions in how the information flows (remember that suspicious trading activity before the merger announcements?). You see the sheen of sweat, and you can almost smell the fear and greed.

News reports of Wall Street crime don't often focus on the gritty parts. Not surprisingly, they're usually more concerned with the nuts and bolts of a scam—the who did what when, the mechanics of the money laundering. The human details get lost in the numbers and technique. But it is in those details—in the textures of fear, greed, envy, and paranoia, in the class, race, and sexual frictions—that Wall Street is revealed as a very noirish place indeed, a place that is far more Jim Thompson than Warren Buffett.

Beyond the buying and selling, the dealing room is a theater of outsized, often dysfunctional personalities, banging heads (and other body parts) in sometimes ugly, sometimes entertaining, and usually noisy and fascinating ways. And always there's money at stake—big money. Of course, as the cliché goes, that's just for keeping score. To many of the players, money is a proxy for more desperate stakes: the sense of self is on the line. Who has the biggest, brassiest pair? Whose is longest? It's a zero-sum game, and if he's the Man (or she is), then you are not. Step onto any trading floor, anywhere in the world, and watch the action for a while—you'll get what I mean.

The writers in this collection get it, and that's no surprise—many of them are industry insiders or refugees, and all are keen observers of the Wall Street scene. Their stories are dark (sometimes darkly funny) tales of hungry egos, cut-throat competition, cultural dislocation, sweaty suspicion, not-so-innocent bystanders, and desperate deals with a variety of devils. And while these tales offer not a shred of advice about what to do with that 401k, their cautionary aspects are unavoidable.

Hard to miss also is that many of these stories are not set on those short, crowded blocks between Trinity Church and the East River. This too should not surprise. In the past couple of decades, Wall Street has decamped from its historic home in lower Manhattan and—riding a wave of globalization and deregulation—conquered vast new territories around the world. There are stones from the old Dutch wall in Midtown Manhattan; Greenwich, Connecticut; London; Moscow; Mumbai; and in the shining sci-fi skyline of Shanghai, too. Today, Wall Street is everywhere—the undisputed capital city of money—and these writers explore its neighborhoods old and new, from its downtown roots to its glossy uptown digs, from Main Street, U.S.A. to the wider world beyond. It's a shadowy landscape, to be sure, but they are savvy guides.

Peter Spiegelman
Ridgefield, Connecticut
April 2007

PART I

DOWNTOWN

AT THE TOP OF HIS GAME

BY STEPHEN RHODES

40 Broad Street

O n the day they conspire to put a bullet in my head, I experience an epiphany.

My epiphany is this: a fourteen-year career on Wall Street wears away at your soul, as assuredly as a stream against limestone. It pushes you to a place where you don't fully recognize who you are, or how you got here. Everyone around you becomes a stranger, including—no, *especially*—your own wife. Working sixteen-hour days in those glistening glass towers in Manhattan, engaging in mortal combat with some of the planet's brightest and most power-obsessed bastards who have trained their full concentration on destroying you and stealing the business you've built up over the years—well, it hardens you. Wall Street eats its young, and today the beast has a particular appetite for a certain thirty-six-year-old maverick with seventy-eight people reporting to him (which would be me).

So today they plan to execute me. How do I know this? Well, last night at 9:30 p.m., an urgent BlackBerry message instructed me to report to Howard Ranieri's office at 7:30 a.m. sharp for a mandatory meeting. That particular e-mail was no surprise; a head's-up had come from a friend in HR that my employment would be terminated during this impromptu meeting.

My response: *Bring it on, jerkweed. Bring it on.*

Ranieri is now more than forty minutes late for his own meeting. Typical move for this passive-aggressive, hair-challenged, beer-gutted, no-talent clown. I should mention that Ranieri is my co-head in the Equity Structured Products group.

Outside Ranieri's office, the phones on the trading floor twitter relentlessly. This morning, Goldman Sachs has issued a dire report on certain Latin American economies. As a result, the overseas financial markets are getting walloped.

The twentysomething stress addicts that populate the trading floor gaze into their Bloomberg screens seeking divine guidance. I hear the voices of my people reporting losses in the overseas markets like breathless wartime correspondents witnessing heavy casualties from the front lines. *The Footsie is getting whacked, hammered, slammed, smashed, crushed, drilled, smoked, spanked, roasted, sewered, bashed. Beaten like a red-headed stepchild, clubbed like a baby seal.* Boom boom, *out go the lights.*

Ranieri's tardiness is driving me to distraction. It's Friday, for chrissakes. I've got a dinner party at the Honeywells' tonight. And I've got a wife who may have been cheating with a kickboxing instructor for God knows how long. Do I really need to have Ranieri playing with my head in the moments before he gleefully fires me?

Abruptly, Howie breezes through the door of his office. "Sparky, glad to see you're here," he burbles as if he's five minutes late for a tennis game. "I'm really truly sorry about this, but—"

"No, you're not."

"Come again?"

I pronounce each syllable slowly. "I said, 'No, you're not.'

Meaning, no, you are not sorry. You are the polar opposite of sorry. You kept me waiting on purpose."

"*Touché*, Sparky." Ranieri's laugh is a brutish grunt. "Maybe you're kind of right about that."

"Not a problem. I passed the time by reading all your e-mails."

Ranieri inspects me to see whether I'm serious, but my poker face is inscrutable. *Backatcha, jerkweed.*

"Anyhoo," Ranieri says with narrowed eyes, "let's move on to the reason we're here. You know Brian, I presume."

I turn around and see Brian Horgan, a VP from HR, skulking in the doorway, craving invisibility. Brian is a good guy in my book; he was the one who gave me the head's-up about this meeting. I take note of the thick Redweld tucked under his arm—my personnel file, no doubt.

"Um, good morning, Mark." The poor bastard winces as he says this. It's obvious this is anything but.

"*Of course* I know Brian," I say breezily. "We've worked together for what . . . six years?"

"Yeah, six years," he confirms.

"Six long years recruiting the best structured products group on the Street, from the ground up."

Ranieri steers the conversation away from my accomplishments. "Well then, I hope we can make this as pleasant as possible for everyone concerned. Given your contribution to the firm, we've moved heaven and earth to be generous." *Translation: You need to sign this piece of paper promising not to sue us, or you walk away with nothing for fourteen years of service.*

I wheel around to my friend from HR. "Your work is done here, Brian."

"It is?" There is a look of palpable relief on Brian Horgan's face.

"Go back to your office, check your e-mail for further instructions."

Ranieri erupts. "Just what the hell are you trying to pull—"

"It's not my doing. Sanderson has taken an interest in this—"

"Bullshit. He's in Hong Kong."

"Exactly. And Sanderson says stand down. Nothing is to happen until he returns to London on Monday."

Ranieri scrutinizes me. "Does Becker know about this?"

"Why would that matter?"

Ranieri scowls venomously, then wheels his Herman Miller Aeron chair over to his flat-panel computer screen. His lips move as he reads the fresh e-mail from Sanderson. Then he slams his open palm on the surface of his desk. "Sonuvabitch!"

I turn to Horgan. "Like I was saying. Until this gets sorted out, you're free to go."

Ranieri grumbles with a dismissive wave. "Whatever." With a surreptitious wink, Brian Horgan reassembles the file and departs.

My co-head makes a big show of closing the door and sealing us off from the rest of the trading floor. "Swift move, asshole. You knew I was leaving for Barcelona with my family tonight, didn't you?"

"Guess you'll just have to postpone your victory dance."

"Maybe . . ." Ranieri regards me with a feral leer, "but you can postpone the inevitable only so long, Sparky."

I lean back and give him a smile that's . . . well, yes, call it *self-satisfied*. "Let's recap, shall we? Four months ago, you pull some strings in London with Ian Becker—your Harvard roommate—to conjure up some do-nothing job that suggests to senior management that you're not utterly useless. Lucky me: Since I happen to drive the lion's share of revenue in the U.S., Becker drop-kicks you into *my* sandbox as a co-head. Says you've got a lot to learn and you're 'here to help.' Instead, what happens? You steal my ideas, my team, my business, my *revenues*. You systematically bad-mouth me to Becker and the rest of senior management as 'redundant' and 'not a team player.' You and Becker wait for my mentor to be incommunicado somewhere so you can pull this lame-ass coup d'état." I shake my head in disgust. "You're not even worth keeping around to order lunch for my people."

Ranieri leans back calmly. "On the one hand, screw you for messing up my vacation. At the same time, I commend you for pulling off that last-minute clemency from the powers-that-be. Very creative." A slow smile spreads across his face. "But guess what? Turns out your guy is getting a bullet to the head himself from senior management. So looks like we have a do-over first thing Monday morning."

"We done here?"

"For now."

"Good." I bolt upright and regard my mortal enemy with utter contempt. "You'll excuse me, I'm going to go back to the desk and make some money. I'll leave you to whatever it is you do all day."

Bite me, jerkweed. And I'm out of there.

Moments later, I experience an emotional cocktail of mild embarrassment and genuine euphoria when the entire derivatives trading floor erupts in a standing ovation. On the Street, information is the ultimate commodity, and the news that I survived Ranieri's savage assassination attempt causes spasms of joy among the all-star team I've assembled.

"Okay, okay, all right!" I shout over the sustained applause, whistles, and catcalls. "A for effort, but this show of loyalty won't necessarily have a favorable impact on year-end bonuses."

The cheering tapers off into an admixture of laughter and mock boos. I hear a muffled thud behind me as an apoplectic Ranieri kicks his office door shut. I love these people. *Love them.*

"All right, people, show's over. Let's pump it up and make some money for the Brothers."

As if a switch is turned on, the trading floor becomes electrified, crackling with high-voltage activity. The discordant brays of traders fill my ears:

"I'm choking on micro-gamma decay on my long-vol position, and unless they rally I'm gonna be achin' like there's no tomorrow—"

"Johnny Meyer, pick up the double-donuts!"

"I called Tommy at DB for a chinstrap in the double-Monday nasty; the bid's gone to a bad neighborhood—"

"I took the bid up a noogie from 10.2 to 10.25 and oh-fived a sweet-one pick-off of the crowd. Am I a hammer or what?"

This is in my blood, the thrill and agony of trading derivative securities. There's no Betty Ford clinic for this addiction, nor would I voluntarily twelve-step myself away from this high. Come Monday, if Ranieri succeeds in taking this world away from me, I will wish him a particularly painful strain of testicular cancer.

I slide into the Aeron chair at my trading turret. "Morning, Terri. Any news on your mom?"

"She's getting much better, thanks for asking." My assistant is Terri Aronica, a sweet-natured girl from Staten Island.

Her freckled presence on the trading floor is akin to a gazelle amongst lions, so I'm highly protective of her. In return, her loyalty is beyond question. "She's coming out of the hospital this weekend."

"Good. That's great to hear." I try to sound casual. "Hey, listen, Compliance is all over me to do my semi-annual supervisory thing. Can you pull all the personal trading records of Howard Ranieri for the last two years? And tell the back office I need it over the weekend."

"Sure thing." When Terri says it's a sure thing, I know she means it.

☘

To: *All Equity Personnel*
From: *Howard Ranieri*
It is with deep regret that we announce Mark Barston's resignation from the firm, effective immediately. As Mark steps down as co-head of Equity to spend more time with his family and pursue other opportunities, please join us in wishing him the best and thanking him for effectively teaching me everything I know, which kindness I repaid by stabbing him in the back . . .

It is six hours later, and I'm mentally composing my resignation announcement. It's customary on Wall Street to extend the courtesy of ghostwriting the memo announcing one's involuntary departure, but I'm finding little joy in my imaginings.

Having escaped the offices of Fischer Brothers, I'm on the 4:36 p.m. Metro-North train out of Grand Central to Greenwich. I'm unaccustomed to the brightness that floods the filthy confines of the bar car; for over a decade, my profession has required me to keep coal miner's hours. I've rarely left the office before nightfall. Still, I'm somewhat surprised that the bar car is so well-populated. Must be advertising types.

With their game faces off, the commuters look positively miserable. They are die-hard junior execs with their eyes still on the prize, feverishly making love to their BlackBerries and Dell Inspirons and Motorola RAZRs. I make my way up to the bar.

"Two Absoluts in a cup, straight, wedge of lime."

Just as I get my cocktail, the train pitches suddenly to the left, and someone collides with me, nearly upending my double shot.

A striking blond girl in a pastel sundress murmurs an apology around a dazzling smile. "So sorry."

I'm taken aback. This is a radiant burst of genuine friendliness, and I have an instant attraction to this girl—and not all of it sexual. It's more that she seems a beacon of positive energy on a suddenly very hostile planet. She makes me think of lemon meringue pie.

"It was my fault, actually," I offer.

"I suppose it doesn't matter much either way, does it?" The girl holds my eyes for a moment while I try to place the accent. Australian, I guess, with the vanishing r's. I'm intrigued.

"My name's Mark," I say, surprised at my own cojones.

"Fiona."

"Ah. Can I get you a drink, Fiona? A Coke?"

"I'd much prefer a Foster's, actually. With a vodka chaser." With that, Fiona flips open her cell phone to smile-and-dial.

When I return with the drinks, I tune in to bits of her conversation. It is peppered with an exotic slang, putting me in mind of *A Clockwork Orange*.

"It's choice . . . That's spot-on . . . Did you dip-out for a moment? What a complete saddo she turned out to be . . . Ah, Viv, Ranieri can be such a drongo sometimes."

Ranieri. Could it be?

And now I realize I've seen her somewhere before—on the trading floor, maybe . . . ? Fiona accepts the shot and the beer and slugs down four quick throatfuls—*we have a party girl here.*

"*Kia ora*, baby" she says. She snaps the cell phone shut and turns to me. "That was my mate Vivica. She's my cozziebro. I trust her with my deepest secrets." Fiona hoists her beer in a toast. "Thanks for your kindness. I'm not used to that, especially in New York."

"It's nothing really. Are you from Australia?"

"Australia? How insulting."

"I didn't mean any offense—"

"No worries. I'm from New Zealand originally. But for the last year, I've lived in Greenwich."

"I live in Greenwich also." I struggle to sound casual. "I couldn't help hearing the name Ranieri. Would that happen to be Howard Ranieri?"

"Yes," she says in amazement. "I live with Mr. Ranieri."

"You what?"

She choke-laughs, and a geyser of imported beer spews forth, making her laugh even harder. "That came out completely wrong. His family, I should say, I live with his family. I'm an au pair. The Ranieris are my host family in America."

Ranieri's au pair! This makes perfect sense—the trophy nanny to go with the trophy wife. It was all *so* Ranieri.

"And you just dropped his children off in the city."

"Right," she says.

"At Fischer Brothers. For the family vacation in Spain."

"Which got canceled, thank you very much, and screws up

all our plans. Wait a minute—how did you know that . . . ?"
Her voice trails off as she tries to decide whether I'm a clairvoyant or a stalker.

"So happens I work with Howard Ranieri."

"Bloody hell!" With a mock-naughty face, she hides the
beer behind her back and giggles. "Don't tell him you bought
me a beer. He'll flip out."

"Deal," I say conspiratorially. "That is, if you tell me what
you meant when you called Ranieri a *drongo*."

Fiona draws in a sharp breath. "Ah, yes. A drongo. Well,
the American equivalent, I guess, would be dickhead."

I double over in laughter. Things are definitely looking
up.

So, for the next forty minutes I'm treated to a private performance of Fiona Hensleigh's one-woman off-Broadway show
that might well be titled *The Greenwich Nanny*.

She riffs animatedly about her adventures since being
plucked from Christschurch, New Zealand and plunked
down in Greenwich, Connecticut, U.S.A., the very vortex of
history's most excessive bull market. And she dissects the
archetypes of the Connecticut Gold Coast in deliciously
bitchy detail: the beauty-shop-addicted, Prada-obsessed
prima donnas, whose sense of entitlement is without limita-
tion; the insecure, cigar-smoking Master-of-the-Universe
wannabes, whose self-worth is measured by the girth of their
Range Rovers; and their worshipped, fretted-over, unlovely
offspring, spoiled beyond belief and taught at the youngest
age that viral disrespect for authority is a virtue.

As Fiona speaks, I'm picturing the Ranieri household,
and it's a fascinating insight into my rival's secret world. Mrs.
Ranieri, apparently, is something of a bitch on ice. And

Ranieri himself is no candidate for sainthood, prone to moodiness and shouting matches with his better half. I bide my time, awaiting an angle, a vulnerability to use against my blood enemy. Fiona tantalizes me with the possibility that she has some juicy tidbits about Ranieri that she wants to share, but she doesn't trust me enough to give up the goods. Smart girl.

Now, I cannot say this with absolute certainty (for I am admittedly out of practice in such things), but I think this Fiona Hensleigh finds me attractive. There is a certain tilt of her face, a certain way she lets the gleaming wisps of her blond hair tumble over her eye. Then, in an instant of startling clarity, I suddenly realize how the distance between our bodies has shrunk. A chill prickles my skin with each incidental contact between us. Unless this is purely my imagination—and I'm willing to concede it might be—there is an unmistakable electricity between me and Ranieri's nanny.

Fiona is telling me how much she misses some dreadful-sounding Kiwi delicacies—Minties, Jaffas, Moro bars, Wattie's tomato sauce, and Vegemite—when the Old Greenwich train station rolls into view.

"My station," I say, and feel a genuine pang of regret that this encounter is coming to an end.

"Well, it was very nice talking with you, Mark."

"Likewise, Fiona." I offer my hand and the New Zealander's equivalent of *aloha.* "*Kia ora.*"

She glances at my wedding band, then locks up my eyes with hers. "And what about tonight?"

Flustered, I manage: "Tonight? What about it?"

"We were planning to have a piss-up at *Chez Ranieri,* but now it looks like it's moving to the beach. You ought to pop on by."

"A piss-up?" I stand immobilized as other commuters pour around us to the platform. Pressed up against me, her breath is warm on my cheek, and sweet with the tang of lager. *One Night Only—The Nanny's Ball—Live at Greenwich Point Beach.* The thought of me in the midst of a gaggle of out-of-control drunken au pairs? Tempting, but a tad self-destructive. "That's not in the cards, Fiona. I've got a dinner party I'm obligated to attend."

She rolls her eyes in a deliciously feminine way. "Oh, I'm *so sure* that will be loads more fun than our ten-kegger."

"Ten-kegger, huh?"

"Anyway, you change your mind, come by the beach?"

"Yeah. I'll keep it in mind." I walk off the train backwards, nearly stumbling into a heap on the platform. They say crack cocaine is instantly addictive. I totally get the concept.

Okay, I know this is sick, but I'm in tell-all mode, so here goes: My BlackBerry has been programmed to tally up the number of days Susan and I have gone without having sex.

It tells me we're at seventy-eight days and counting.

Wait, there's more: Just recently, I have discovered that my wife is also surreptitiously keeping track of this ignoble hitless streak. She pencils tick marks into the kitchen calendar, and by her count, we've been on the sex wagon for seventy-seven days straight.

I own up to it: The demise of our relationship is mostly my fault. My struggle with Ranieri over the last months has turned me into someone other than the person she wed in sickness and health so many years ago. And her infertility problems have weighed heavily on us for even longer. In our calibrated attempts to conceive, we've followed to the letter the clinical manner in which teams of doctors have instructed us to copulate, and have spent the last thirty-six months not so much making love, as conducting laboratory experiments.

It's taken its toll.

To wit, I'm convinced that Susan no longer loves me. I suspect she is in love with at least one, if not two others in the Greenwich vicinity, and I often lay awake nights going over likely candidates. Is it Adam, the wacky New Age martial arts expert at her yoga center on the Post Road, the kid with bad teeth who teaches her Tae Bo and promises to launch her on a spiritual journey to discover her inner self? Is it Dr. Lauren, the collagen-lipped lesbian physician who wears no undergarments when she prescribes migraine treatments at Norwalk Hospital? It could be both, I suppose, or neither. Maybe we've just encountered one of those rough patches that couples therapists are always going on about. One of those things we're supposed to traverse together, before the next phase of our lifelong partnership.

The appearance of Peter I. Tortola's name in my checkbook register suggests otherwise.

This Friday night, I find my wife in the small childless bedroom designated as the Quiet Room. My wife is strikingly pretty, even as the chiseled angles of her face are softening with time, but just now she's an unsettling sight in the darkened room. Susan has an ice pack swirled over her forehead and eyes. On the bureau next to the trundle bed, a spent Epi-Pen and bottles of migraine medication are arranged in a neat row. Susan—God help her—is in full-blown aura mode with bursts of colors. With her head tilted back and her arms along the armrests of the recliner, she appears to be clamped in an electric chair.

"Susan, you all right?"

"Migraine," she murmurs tonelessly.

"Need anything?"

"Solitude."

Though she can't see me, I nod in the darkness. I realize how my Friday night will play out, and it ain't a pretty picture. But I can't hold myself back.

"Susan?" My tone is the most delicate I can manage.

"Mm?"

"We need to talk about something—but only when you're up for it."

"What is it?"

"It can wait."

"If it can wait, why bring it up? Just tell me, Mark."

I sigh. "A canceled check came in from Citibank. Made out to Peter Tortola."

Susan has no immediate response to this.

I push. "We need to talk about your intentions, Susan. I need to know what that check means."

All is silence. I'm aware of my own labored breathing. Peter I. Tortola? He's Greenwich's most obnoxious pit bull, a vulture, a shark, the lowest of snakes—a high-powered divorce attorney who specializes in going after Wall Street husbands, with the tenacity and teeth of a moray eel. His quarter-page ad is a weekly fixture in the otherwise-good-news pages of the *Greenwich Time* community newspaper. *IT HAPPENS TO THE BEST OF US: D-I-V-O-R-C-E.*

"Susan, we can talk about this later if—"

"You heartless bastard!" Her voice soars to a blood-chilling volume, and I am transfixed by the fury. "You sadistic son of a bitch. Why would you torture me when I'm in this condition? What's the matter with you? Get the hell away from me!"

I dutifully comply. There is little doubt, after this exchange, that we will be more than a little unfashionably late to the Honeywells' dinner party.

Wealth whispers.

For generations past, this was an unspoken code in Greenwich, the humility of old money. After all, darling, living in this town, how shall we say? *Res ipsa loquitur.* But the relentless tsunami of urban barbarians descending upon the Connecticut Gold Coast with fat Wall Street bonuses has killed off any vestige of subtlety here. Now Greenwich is just another brand name to accumulate.

The McMansions roll past as Susan and I wind our way along treelined Round Hill Road. It's nearly 8:30 and we have not said a word to each other since our chat in the Quiet Room. I now believe that our conversations are inexorably headed for the same fate as our sex life.

My Aston Martin approaches the Honeywells' seven-bedroom mansion on Larkspur Lane. Rich Honeywell is yet another Greenwich hedge fund asshole, one of those Wall Street guys with marginal talent and a nine-figure chunk of someone else's family money behind him. A once-in-a-lifetime fluke—a federal deregulation of pension plans—has made him obscenely wealthy in his own right, and kept an endless convoy of Brinks trucks dumping mountains of money on the doorstep of his Steamboat Road office.

Rich's house is an eat-your-heart-out monument to his new wealth, a dramatic custard-yellow contemporary with Hudson Valley stone veneer set on five acres of what was once a fertile onion farm. And it's equipped with all the usual accoutrements: four-car garage, tennis court, THX-certified home theater, mahogany wine cellar, and an Olympic-sized pool. There are two backhoes in the front yard, suggesting further expansion is imminent.

The Honeywells' Belgian-bricked drive is jammed with probably $3 million worth of luxury automobiles, and I wedge my convertible into a space between a Porsche Cayenne and a yellow Hummer with personalized plates: *183 IQ.* I turn off the car, and the ensuing silence is deafening. I crave a talk before we go in, a clearing of the air. Perhaps it's naïve, but I still hope that we can turn this around before we pass the point of no return and head down the path of mutually assured destruction. As a prelude, I clear my throat—and get no further.

"I want out, Mark. I'm done with this." Susan delivers this statement in a flat, lifeless tone, as she might say, *Looks like rain.* She opens the vanity mirror to check her makeup. "I want sixty percent of everything, and the house as well. You keep the cars and the retirement accounts. I'd like to file the papers next week."

She snaps the mirror closed and exits the convertible. And just like that, it's official: My marriage has begun its slow-motion spiral to the first circle of hell.

We approach the front door wordlessly, trying to assemble a convincing facsimile of a happy and centered Greenwich couple. Rich Honeywell opens the door with a flourish. He's dressed in a pair of black Ted Baker slacks, a charcoal Armani shirt, and Donald Pliner loafers.

"Hey, it's the Barstons!" Honeywell says theatrically, as he hugs Susan (a bit too warmly for my comfort). "Word up, Barston? You get lost on the way or something?" This offhand dig is a passive-aggressive notice that we are the last to arrive, but it's the unintended irony that makes me blink. *Yeah, I got lost on the way, all right.*

"Jennifer's been asking all night, 'Where're the Barstons, where're the Barstons?' She'll be psyched you're finally here." Rich says this breezily as he shepherds us through the palatial, antiseptic interior of his McMansion-in-progress. Like the homes of most of our friends, the design has a predictable look and feel. The furnishings bear the fingerprints of a particular interior designer who specializes in a bland, WASPy décor that appeals to new money clients with absolutely no sense of style of their own. She's booked up for six months in advance. "Jen, come say hello to the Barstons."

Jennifer Honeywell curtails her lecture to the waiter on how to serve the platter of jumbo Gulf shrimp, and wheels around with exaggerated delight. "It's the Barstons!" she squeals like a teenager, and I remember something I'd heard about her trying out a new antidepressant.

We apologize for being late, then I give Jennifer a kiss, Jennifer and Susan kiss, and Rich takes advantage of the pleasantries to try to score a kiss on the lips with Susan (which she successfully evades). I take note of Jennifer's new body—it has been honed and shaped by spinning classes and Pilates into a rock-hard leanness that teeters on the verge of masculinity. The excessive athleticism has introduced an asexual coarseness to her face. Too bad; she used to be among the most attractive of my friends' wives.

Rich makes a sweeping gesture toward the French doors. "The bartender's got a bottle of Grey Goose with your name on it, kimosabe."

"Let's have at it," I say.

Honeywell directs us to the open-air patio overlooking an exquisitely manicured backyard of Kentucky bluegrass— an emerald carpet gleaming under a full moon. Predictably, Susan and I peel off in different directions. It will be this way for the entire night, but I'm cool with that. The blast of communal energy from the party lifts my spirits.

At the bar, a pimply-faced Greenwich High School kid gives me a double shot of Grey Goose on the rocks. Duly fortified, I meld into a nearby amoeba of acquaintances. They interrupt their debate about Robert Trent Jones golf courses to slap my back, shake my hand, and high-five me.

"I was just saying," Ford Spilsbury says, "that the Lido course on Long Beach is as close to eighteen-hole nirvana as you're ever going to get. The sixteenth hole is the ultimate par five, and you have an eagle opportunity if you can survive the double-water carry."

The five of them—Spilsbury, Foster, Brightman, O'Clair, and Cantwell—are clubhouse friends, and, like me, they are all Wall Street jerks: bankers and brokers and traders and lawyers. The Ivy League degrees on this patio cost millions in tuition dollars, but they were worth every penny. The diplomas our parents bought for us are a license to steal. Collectively, we siphon off a disproportionate chunk of the country's GNP, and trundle it north to our trophy wives in Greenwich. We buy expensive cars and homes and boats and pools, and go on obscenely expensive vacations, all of which is meant to inform everyone just how much we're taking out of the American economy for ourselves. Our nine-year-olds are infected with this zombie-like consumerism, and are as tragically conversant with the iconic symbolism of Tiffany and BMW and Prada as their parents. We confuse wealth with class; we think they are synonymous, when they most assuredly are not. Inevitably, we will pass the former on to our children, but not the latter.

In this particular fishbowl, we wrap ourselves in an aura of effortlessness. We are expert at concealing the fears that haunt us at 3:00 in the morning: the TMJ-inducing toll our careers take on our stomachs and our mental health; the slow decay of our marriages; the warning signs that our children might not end up at an Ivy League university; the velocity at which our spending is outpacing our income. We hide behind the breezy accomplishment of breaking eighty on the course at the Stanwich Club, pretending everything is right in the world when we've come to know that the pursuit of this life is a cancer to the soul. I gaze up at the moon in the star-studded sky and heave a sigh. Maybe my spirits aren't so lifted after all.

I'm mildly surprised to find my glass is empty. I break away from the group for a refill. As I'm waiting at the bar, a call lights up my cell phone. I flip it open. "This is Barston."

On the other end an uncertain pause, then a soft fumble of the handset. A hand slips over the mouthpiece. Heated whispers, shushing, and the musical laughter of drunken young girls—a live feed directly from Fiona's piss-up at Greenwich Point Beach.

I say nothing, just listen. More giggles and whispers, all unintelligible. Her nanny friends put her up to this, I realize, and it is so juvenile, so immature—a slumber party prank, for chrissakes—and then, the act of chickening out; the curt click of the line going dead. I'm staring at my phone, waiting for . . . I don't know what.

I'm jolted from my reverie by the underage barkeep holding out my replenished drink. I take a greedy slurp, my temples throbbing with the pulse of curiosity over this au pair Lollapalooza taking place just a few miles away.

The night wears on, booze is consumed in disturbingly large quantities, and the conversation becomes edgy. The subject matter is friendship, fidelity, and minding your own damn business. *Would you tell a friend if you knew his wife was cheating?*

Foster says, "No fucking way, it's not my business."

Cantwell says, "Of *course* it's your business. It's your buddy."

Foster: "I can't be the one to tell him something like that. It's too . . . heavy, man. I'd be ruining his life."

Rob Brightman chimes in: "So you'd keep it to yourself? How would you sleep at night?"

O'Clair says: "I get Foster's point. Why is it his responsibility to break the news that the wife is banging the tennis instructor?"

I jump in. "He's your best friend, Chris, that's why. You couldn't look him in the eye at a party like this if you knew his wife was being unfaithful. You're duty-bound to tell him, and let *him* take the appropriate course of action. Case closed."

The passion with which I deliver this point brings the debate to an abrupt end.

Brightman breaks the uncomfortable silence: "So any of you assholes have something to tell me?" The group explodes in laughter. Everyone, that is, but Ford Spilsbury, who has kept conspicuously out of the conversation.

Forty-five minutes later, when a preoccupied Spilsbury quietly approaches me during the Chicken Kiev dinner and asks to speak to me alone, I feel my stomach knot. I somehow know what's coming.

"I heard what you said on the patio," he says, avoiding my eyes. "About friends."

I nod.

Spilsbury almost whispers it. "I think I'm the kind of guy who *would* tell a friend about that."

"You have something to tell me, Ford?" I reply, my voice warbling. But I already know he does.

Friday evening has segued somehow into Saturday morning. Newly armed with the knowledge that my wife has been having an affair for the last six months with her college friend's husband, I plunge through the darkness of the Backcountry, heading to the other side of the looking glass. I recognize this quest can only end badly—scandal, ruination, utter self-destruction—but it no longer matters. I'm powerless to stop the forces that have overtaken me.

A fantasy torments me: *I arrive at the beach and she spies me . . . She pulls away from her friends and comes so close that I can feel her breath on my cheek. "I knew you'd come." She locks up my eyes in hers as she says this, a note of triumph in her voice. She is such eye candy, I can barely contain myself. We are intoxicated— not just by alcohol, but by the electric danger of being so close. I spirit her away to a secluded beach at the ass-end of Sound Beach Avenue. With the languid hiss of low tide in our ears, the au pair steps forward. She kisses my neck, puts her hot hands up my shirt. I grab her apple-bottom ass and pull her toward me. She responds with a tongue-loaded kiss. I can taste the salt on her skin and smell the soap in her hair.*

This is going to happen, I convince myself. *This is redemption. This is revenge. This is justice.*

I punch the accelerator and push on toward Greenwich Point Beach.

I arrive within minutes, and the scene is surreal. Kid Rock's "Bawitdaba" throbs in the background, and yet the Nanny's Ball has come to an undignified end. Five Greenwich police cars have pinned down at least a hundred stoned kids, all tongue-studded, belly-ringed, lip-pierced, and tattooed. Blinding blue-and-red strobes light the beach in psychedelic hues, and the squawk of the radio dispatcher says backup is on the way. The acrid smell of pot is heavy in the salt air. Six half-naked, soaking-wet party animals are led by in cuffs. I'm numbed by the commotion, but amidst the crowd, I see the object of my desire. *Fiona.* Ranieri's au pair is in the epicenter of this frenetic scene, crying her eyes out. She looks scared and vulnerable and . . . *oh, so incredibly young.*

I swing the Aston Martin into a dark corner of the parking lot and kill the headlights. I don't take my eyes off Fiona's face as I begin to formulate a daring rescue mission. *How far away is she? Thirty yards? Forty?* I could edge up on the far side of the crowd, grab her by the arm . . . then a short sprint back to my car, and we're home free. I can almost hear the sweet relief in her voice. *"I knew you'd come."*

I open my car door and step out. And nearly fall.

Just then I realize how intoxicated I am. My head is swimming in Grey Goose, my legs are jelly, and I'm now bathed in a panic-induced sweat. I climb back in my seat and grip the wheel. Static blasts from a nearby police radio, and I jump. I can't make out the words, but when I squeeze my eyes shut, they become clearer. The words are my own:

Where you going with this, Barston? You put yourself in the middle of this—to what end? So you can wind up in the police blotter for DUI and God knows what else? And for what—some chick who chatted you up in the bar car for less than an hour? This is your grand plan to get back at Ranieri—fucking his nanny?

Another squawk of static and I realize it's coming from the radio of a Greenwich cop glaring my way. As he strides toward my car, I fumble the door closed. The cops is shouting something, but somehow I get the vehicle in gear and kick up a cloud of sand, which I pray obscures my license plate.

Miles from the beach, I pull over. I'm sweat-soaked and shaking, and I rest my head on the steering wheel and gasp for breath. And suddenly I'm pounding the dash in fury and self-loathing.

What were you thinking, you pathetic, sorry-ass sonuvabitch?

It's nearly dawn when I get home and stumble to the front door. On the third attempt, I jam the key into the lock. At first I don't see the white envelope propped up against the door, and I kick it across the foyer. I stagger toward the stairs and almost leave it there on the Kashan rug, but something catches my eye and pierces the alcoholic fog around my brain: the Fischer Brothers logo.

I have to sit to retrieve the envelope, but I manage. Crosslegged on the floor, I thumb-wrestle it open and look inside. And I know instantly.

It's nothing short of a miracle: the last-ditch Hail Mary pass thrown desperately with seconds to go, the game-winning homer in the bottom of the ninth, the sudden-death eagle on the eighteenth hole at the Masters—impossible victory from certain defeat. It is the life preserver that will save me from going under for the last time, that will save me from myself.

"Terri," I whisper reverentially, the papers trembling in my hands. I say my loyal assistant's name over and over.

I enter Ranieri's glassed-in corner office on Monday morning, and I am ready to bite the ass off a bear. For his part, my enemy is bouncing a blue rubber stress ball off the windowed wall. He receives me exuberantly.

"Happy Monday, Sparky. How was the weekend?" He resumes throwing the ball against the glass.

"Must you do that?" I ask pointedly.

"You mean *this?*" He sidearms the ball again and smirks. "Why? Does it bother you?" I decline to engage in this lame banter, and silence prevails.

Moments later, Brian Horgan arrives with my thick personnel file. Sauntering in right behind him is Senior Managing Director Ian Becker. Becker is Ranieri's ultimate boss, and mine too—here to see that I'm officially terminated, and that the empire I've created is handed over seamlessly to his Harvard roommate.

"Guess this is show time," Ranieri says. We lock eyes for a moment and he quickly looks away, shoving the door closed. He ceremoniously circles back to his chair, slouching into an elaborately casual posture. "Let's pick up where we left off on Friday. Ian, you care to kick things off?"

Becker clears his throat and speaks in an authoritative British baritone. "Let me start by saying we commend you for the contribution you've made to this firm. You've gotten us off to a respectable start, a decent standing in the league tables. But, candidly, you've developed something of a reputation for not being a team player, especially when it comes to matters involving your co-head. So, it's the consensus of senior management that we need to have a single focal point for the future of the business. Regrettably, that means that one of the two co-heads needs to move on. It's nothing personal, Mark, but—"

"Not true, Ian. It absolutely is personal."

"If that's how you feel about it, then fine."

"That's exactly how I feel about it. As for my people, let the record show that they consider Ranieri to be a rodent-faced, backstabbing, Mickey Mouse amateur who will crash this business into the ground within a year. By which time they'll be poached away by our competitors."

Ranieri's eyebrows climb his forehead in offense, but he holds his tongue in check.

Becker's face softens in saccharine compassion. "Be that as it may, Mark, you should know that there will be a formal announcement about a restructuring shortly, possibly as early as Wednesday. I'm working to find a proper place for someone with your skill set, but we've got headcount pressures from upstairs. If these efforts fail, well, we're committed to ensure proper protocol is followed with regard to your termination. We've all pushed hard to be fair—no, to go way beyond being merely fair—and we're—"

I yawn theatrically.

Becker draws back in outrage. "Am I boring you?"

"Matter of fact, yes, you are. Even worse, you're wasting my time."

Becker sputters, furious at this insubordination, when a sharp rap sounds at the door. The cavalry has arrived, and right on time. All heads turn as David Rosenman, the firm's Associate General Counsel, opens the door and leans in.

"Ian, I need to see you," he says.

Ian Becker is annoyed by the disruption. "We should be done here in about fifteen minutes, David. Can we circle up at 8:15 a.m.?"

"It wasn't a request, Ian," Rosenman says sternly. "Step out of this meeting *now*."

Becker is puzzled, but there's no mistaking the seriousness in Rosenman's voice. He mumbles something under his breath, rises from his chair, and disappears around a corner with Rosenman.

"What the hell was *that* about?" Ranieri says to no one in particular.

"Oh, that?" I say. I produce a cigar from my jacket pocket and light it. "That would be about the Eagles Mere III CDO. The 'kitchen sink' collateralized unit."

Ranieri freezes, color draining from his face. The transformation is astounding: He ages ten years in an instant—exhausted, pallid, scared. *He knows exactly what I'm talking about.*

I push on. "According to a routine compliance check on personal trading that was run over the weekend, both you and Becker have sizable positions of these Eagles Mere III units in your personal trading accounts. *Sizable* positions."

"You fucking son of a bitch," Ranieri whispers hoarsely.

"So I imagine right now Rosenman is asking Becker how it is that a security that cost him $50,000 a unit is throwing off $11,568 in interest—a *month*. That would be about $140,000 a year, risk free—"

"You're *so* going to regret this, asswipe."

"What kind of security pays nearly three hundred percent interest a year with zero risk? I don't know, I've never heard of such a thing." I exhale a luxurious cloud of smoke. "But maybe—and this is just a theory, mind you—maybe it's a dummy security concocted by you. And maybe—just maybe—it's a little something you cooked up to divert hundreds of thousands of dollars a year from the firm's institutional clients to you and your greedy-ass butt-buddy. Now, why would you do such a heinous thing? I don't know—perhaps as a quid pro quo for Becker naming you to a certain co-head position in equity derivatives? It's just a theory, of course."

"This conversation is *over*."

"You're goddamned right it's over!" I yell. "Sun Tzu is

required reading at *Hah-vahd* b-school, isn't it? You must know *The Art of War* by heart. *A mortal enemy must be crushed completely. More is lost stopping halfway through than through total annihilation: the enemy will recover and will seek revenge. Crush him, both in body and spirit.*"

Ranieri regards me with a superhuman loathing. He remains mute.

"Hey, Brian?" I say, getting up to leave. "I'll be at my desk if you need me."

Brian Horgan is open-mouthed with awe as I shut the door.

Checkmate, motherfucker.

My head is spinning. Events have been set into motion that will be impossible to stop. There will be lawyers and compliance officers and regulators piling onto this situation in the hours, days, and weeks to come. Both Ranieri and Becker will pay an enormous personal price for fucking with my livelihood. There's even a good shot that they will be thrown out of the industry. So be it. *Kill or be killed*—that's Wall Street in its purest form, isn't it?

As I cross the trading floor, I receive another standing ovation. Apparently, Terri Aronica has spread word of the Eagles Mere scandal among the trading floor personnel, and I am acknowledged as the undisputed heavyweight champion of the world. This time, though, I don't bask in the adulation. There is little sense of accomplishment in my Machiavellian maneuver, because with this second bullet dodged comes a second epiphany: *This is no victory.*

I have crushed Ranieri, but his voice is playing in my head: *You can postpone the inevitable only so long, Sparky.* And I know he's right. How many more Ranieris are even now lining up to take what I've built? How many of them are in this room, smiling and clapping for me? And if not one of them, then it will be Susan and her cadre of lawyers. How many more bullets can I dodge?

There are handshakes, back pats, light punches on the shoulder, as I make my way to my seat. The applause subsides and the normal trading room chatter rises. Random static from a speakerphone fills my ears and I think of the other night with Fiona. Even if I'd whisked her off that beach, she too would have turned on me eventually, gotten lawyers of her own, tried to pick my bones clean. Maybe it's destiny or some law of nature: Once you're at the top of your game, everyone becomes your enemy—rivals, friends, lawyers, lovers, superiors, subordinates. They plot and scheme and come after everything that matters to you, everything you love and care about.

Terri puts a steaming latte on my desk. Her freckled face beams and her eyes meet mine. It is an intimate moment: Together, we triumphed over the forces of evil against great odds. Yet at this moment, absolutely no one is beyond suspicion. *Et tu, Terri?* I force myself to smile back, even as Rich Honeywell's mocking voice unexpectedly fills my head.

You get lost along the way, Barston?

A TRADER'S LOT

BY TWIST PHELAN

1 North End Avenue

E very morning for the past nine months, David Sherwin had disembarked from the Hoboken ferry and joined the flow of people on the walkway to the New York Mercantile Exchange. Chewing on an antacid from the roll in his pocket, he would shuffle along with the crowd, his mind on his meager market positions.

But today, David didn't reach for the tablets. Instead, he tilted back his head and inhaled the faint saltiness of the river, barely discernable under the stench of diesel fumes from the ferry. The flat gray strip of water stretched away to the horizon, where it merged into the overcast sky. For an instant David was back five years, to when he'd first met Malia and other things weren't so important.

Heedless of the heavy mist, David walked with an almost forgotten energy—dodging concrete barricades and posts topped with security cameras, threading through knots of traders, clerks, and Exchange employees—toward the fifteen-story concrete and marble box that housed the world's most important trading floors for metals and energy. Everyone he passed was talking about the same thing. "It'll be there in two hours" . . . "The Hub was evacuated this morning" . . . "Already Category Four." David walked faster.

He passed three homeless men crowded under a concessionaire's canopy, driven there by an earlier downpour. Propped up against the storefront, one of them wore a discarded trader's jacket, the splash of yellow garish against the otherwise unremitting gray. Although he usually didn't give to street people, David stuffed a bill into the offered cardboard cup and wondered if the man was the jacket's original owner.

I'll stop at Cartier on the way home. Malia had always wanted one of those watches, the kind with the twelve little diamonds around the face. *Maybe I can get to the Porsche dealership before it closes.* David pictured a low-slung convertible—red, her favorite color.

"Up for this afternoon's game, Dash?" The familiar voice jarred David from his daydreams. "They're playing the Dodgers." Mike Vigneri, a fellow trader in the natural-gas pit, came up beside him. When things were slow, Vigneri sometimes ducked out before the closing to catch an afternoon game at Shea.

"Sure, if it's quiet," David said, knowing no trader would be leaving the Floor early today. Vigneri grinned at the joke.

David pushed through the revolving doors of the main entrance and strode across the marble lobby. He inserted his ID card into the turnstile slot and walked through the metal detector.

The Exchange was located less than two blocks from where the towers had stood, and security had been substantially increased since the attacks. In addition to the metal detector in the lobby, surveillance equipment had been installed on the Floor and around the building perimeter, public tours had been discontinued, and cops in flak jackets accompanied by bomb-sniffing dogs patrolled the premises. On elevated terror-alert days, a Coast Guard gunboat armed with missiles sat offshore in the murky Hudson.

"This hurricane is sending gas to the fucking moon!" Vigneri said as they changed into their trader jackets in the locker room. He rubbed his thick hands together. "Gonna be some serious money made today."

"Yeah," David said. If Vigneri only knew. He stuffed his pit cards and trade pad into a pocket of his bright blue jacket. Except for the color, it looked like a med student's lab coat. He clipped a yellow badge to his collar, just above his photo ID. The bright plastic pin was engraved with four letters derived from the initials of his name: *DASH*. Traders called each other by their badge symbols and used them when writing up trades.

The badge meant David had a seat on the Exchange. Not an actual place to sit—on the Floor, only the clerks did that—but rather the right to buy and sell commodity futures on the trading floor. Exchange seats sold for two million dollars, or were leased for upwards of twenty thousand a month. The seat David traded on was owned by his wife.

At least it had been until two days ago.

David popped an antacid and closed his locker. "I'll see you up there," he said.

Although he usually took the elevator, today David bounded up the stairs, reaching the Floor five minutes before the opening bell. Crude oil, heating oil, gasoline, natural gas, propane, coal—the Exchange set the prices for the fuels that ran the world's economies. Out of breath from the unaccustomed sprint, David pushed his way to his usual place in the natural-gas pit.

While other exchanges were going all-electronic, and overnight energy trading could be done by computer, during business hours the New York Mercantile Exchange still transacted business as it had for over a hundred years—buyers and sellers announcing bids and offers at the top of their voices.

As a rule, only a handful of natural-gas traders were usually in the ring this early. But today the pit was packed, the mélange of garish polyester jackets turning the space into a kaleidoscope. Traders who normally worked crude oil or gasoline pushed in next to the natural-gas regulars to get in on the action.

The room had a musty, damp-clothes smell, despite the cold drafts pouring from vents in the ceiling. As the electronic clock moved toward 10 o'clock, David could feel a surge of anticipation roll through the pit, more intense than usual.

His eyes went to the flat-screen television suspended overhead. The station was tuned to the Weather Channel instead of the customary Fox or CNBC. The news crawl across the bottom of the screen read, *Category 5—175 m.p.h. winds*. David stared at the computer graphic, a swirl of neon red against a blue background. After Malia had gone to sleep, he had spent most of last night at his computer tracking the swirl as it moved across the Gulf. The tension in his shoulders eased as he saw the storm was still on course.

The seconds on the digital clock slowly ticked by. 9:58:17 . . . 9:58:42 . . . David balled his hands into fists and jammed them into his pockets so no one would see them trembling. 9:59:36 . . . 9:59:53 . . . 10:00:00. The opening bell rang, and two hundred voices and two hundred arms were raised.

"Hundred Deece at eleven even, hundred Deece at even!" . . . "Take 'em all!" . . . "Fifty Deece at thirty!" . . . "Buy 'em!" . . . "Fifty Deece at eleven fifty!" Traders screamed, waved their arms, bounced up and down—anything to get noticed and make the trade.

Yesterday, natural gas had closed at ten dollars per contract. Overnight on the electronic market, the price had shot up a dollar. Now, seconds after the opening, it had jumped another fifty cents.

David saw a pair of glasses knocked from a trader's face by an errant elbow. Their owner was unfazed. "Two hundred Novy at twenty!" he shouted, his hands moving as if he were throwing down gang signs. *Novy* and *Deece* were slang for delivery months November and December.

Instead of joining in the frenzy around him, David simply watched the quote board, where orange, green, and red numbers flickered against a black background. Natural-gas contracts were priced in dollars and cents, and normally moved up or down in one-cent increments. Today the price was increasing twenty, thirty cents at a time.

A hurricane was heading for the Henry Hub, the gas-processing plant in Louisiana where over a dozen of the country's major natural-gas pipelines converged. The Hub had been shut down the night before as a precautionary measure, squeezing supply and driving up the price. If the pipelines were damaged by the storm, natural-gas delivery would be held up for weeks, possibly months, resulting in default on billions of dollars' worth of delivery contracts.

According to the National Hurricane Center's computer model, the hurricane would collide with the Hub in less than two hours. As the red swirl moved across the TV screen, the pit became a seller's market, the price of natural gas soaring as the big producers bought back their outstanding contracts and the speculators who had sold short scrambled to cover their positions. The only question was, *How far up will it go?*

The rubber floor and acoustical padding on the walls did little to blunt the clamor. The din of the Exchange washed over David. Closing his eyes, he reveled in the sound of wealth being created. *Mine and Malia's.*

Beside him Vigneri completed a sale. Trading jacket straining at the seams, he scribbled down details on price, quantity, and delivery month, and the badge symbol of the trader who had bought from him on a pit card before frisbeeing it toward a man sitting behind a low counter at the center of the pit. Wearing a baseball hat and plastic goggles as protection from the flying pieces of cardboard, the pit card clocker frantically collected and time-stamped the cards. They were then rushed to the data entry room for transmission onto the wire services and entry into the Exchange's permanent records.

We could go to Europe. Malia had studied French in college. David imagined the two of them sitting in a Paris café. Sunlight sparkled off the diamond trim on Malia's new watch, and she was laughing like she used to.

Vigneri nudged him. "What's up, Dash? Don't you want in on this?"

"I'm already long." David paused. "A hundred contracts."

Vigneri's jaw dropped. "Well, fuck me."

Maybe I'll fly Malia to Paris, give her the watch there. She couldn't be mad at him then. He imagined her pink and glowing among the rumpled bedclothes in a romantic hotel. Perhaps they could finally start their family.

Malia's father had been a natural-gas trader, too, doing well enough to retire to Bermuda after Malia left for college. He had kept his seat on the Exchange, though, leasing it out to various traders over the years. When he died last year, Malia had inherited it. Her father's second wife had gotten the house and bank accounts in Bermuda.

After her father's death, Malia had planned to continue

leasing out the seat. But David knew the extra few thousand a week after taxes wouldn't be enough, not if they were to have children. He wanted kids, but Malia claimed she wasn't ready. Their discussions had become arguments, worsening each month. Malia's parents, though distant, had provided her with a comfortable childhood—piano and riding lessons, nice house, trips abroad, private school. David figured his wife's reluctance stemmed from not wanting less for their own kids. But that took wealth—real wealth—the kind her father had made. The old guy had never said a word, but David was sure that Malia's dad thought his daughter had married beneath her.

"This is our chance, Malia," he had said. After a few weeks she had given in, and David quit his job at a brokerage firm and became a trader in the natural-gas pit. That had been nine months ago.

But things didn't work out as David had planned. Floor trading for his own account was worlds away from sitting at a desk taking telephone orders from clients. Although he had mastered the skills of buying and selling on the Floor, David wasn't a "natural." He didn't have a feel for the market, and couldn't anticipate its ebbs and flows. Before long, he had burned through their nest egg. With barely any capital left, David had been reduced to trading one and two contracts at a time, eking out less than his former salary.

But David was convinced more volume could improve his returns. "To make money, you have to spend money," he had told Malia. But they had no access to additional funds—unless Malia borrowed against the value of her seat. A million and a half dollars of trading capital, the clearing firm rep had told him. But Malia wouldn't hear of it.

"It's all we have for our retirement," she had said when

David raised the subject. Despite his entreaties, this time she stood firm, and David had resigned himself to an existence as a one-lotter. Until the phone call from his brother last week.

In love with the ocean, Thomas Sherwin had dropped out of college with the aim of spending his life on the deck of a ship. He currently ran a fairly successful fishing charter business out of a small port town in Louisiana.

"Got the boats out of the Gulf yesterday," Tom had told David. "All the signs point to a big one coming our way—warm water, cold mass descending, no wind shear. Even the old timers are leaving. Looks like it's going to hit around where those pipelines are."

Tom knew weather, especially hurricanes. His livelihood depended on it. When he said a tropical storm was headed through the ocean toward the Henry Hub, David believed him.

After hanging up the phone, David had been overcome with a peculiar sensation. A hunch, a gut reaction. The other traders talked about them all the time, but David had never really understood before now. It was an awareness of having arrived at an unmarked intersection in life, the sense that if he didn't act, he would forever suffer the misery of what could have been.

Getting the money turned out to be easier than he had thought. David merely slipped the signature page of the loan documents into the stack of tax returns waiting for Malia's signature. As usual, she scribbled her name without reading anything. His clearing firm accepted it without question.

The Exchange required all members' trades to be backed by a clearing firm. To secure the guarantee, members pledged collateral—usually cash, sometimes a letter of credit or the deed to an Exchange seat.

David liked his clearing firm rep. Earl Kinder was a tall, middle-aged man with the dry understanding of someone who had heard too many lies and witnessed too many traders undone by the pits. Though a bit too cautious for David's taste, he was one of the few who did business with one-lotters.

Kinder's fingers had hesitated over the keyboard. "There's no shame in being a one-lotter, Dash."

A photograph sat on the clearing house rep's desk. It showed a round-cheeked woman and two boys with Kinder's red hair, standing among piles of leaves in front of a modest white house. David had studied it for a moment.

"I'll be fine," he said.

Kinder had started typing, pushing back from the computer less than a minute later.

"There's your one-point-five, Dash. You know the drill. If you fall below your margin, start liquidating, or I'll do it for you. Lose it all, and I have to pull your badge and sell the seat."

David briefly clenched his jaw. A million and a half dollars was in his trading account, secured by Malia's seat. *At last I'm holding size.* It was like holding dynamite. He could feel the power—and the undercurrent of danger, too.

"I'll be fine," he repeated. "There won't be a problem."

After leaving the clearing firm's offices, David had gone downstairs to the Floor. At an unattended computer, he had logged onto the National Hurricane Center's website. The tropical storm was following the path his brother had predicted. *We are not concerned about the Gulf Coast and we expect little if any impact on the oil industry,* read the latest bulletin. But David hadn't been swayed. Tom always called storms right. His gut told him there was no reason to doubt his brother now.

With twenty minutes left before the close, David had

commenced buying. Ten, fifteen contracts at a time, working his way up. Some of the traders had been curious about such volume from a one-lotter, but David explained he was doing a favor for a broker friend.

After the closing bell rang, David had flipped through his trade pad, slightly astonished. He owned a hundred natural-gas contracts. Every ten-cent change in price meant a loss or gain of a hundred thousand dollars.

On the ferry ride home, David had paced the deck, restless and jumpy. He wouldn't be riding the slow, fat boat much longer. Maybe he and Malia would move to Manhattan, or better yet, Connecticut. Malia and their kids would have their own leaf-strewn yard.

Now, thirty-six hours later, that life was within reach. All David had to do was watch the numbers go up as the red swirl moved across the screen. The hurricane closed in on the Hub, and the fifty-cent opening bump in price became sixty cents, then seventy-five.

"Thirty Deece at eighty-five!" someone yelled from the other side of the ring. David did the math in his head. *Up a million and three-quarters.* Caught up in the calculations, he didn't hear the quiet voice right away.

"Looks like you made a good call, Dash," Kinder repeated.

Because a trader could buy or sell ten-dollars' worth of contracts for every dollar's worth of security posted, the clearing firms kept a close eye on their customers' positions. If the market changed direction and a firm didn't pull a trader's badge in time, the clearing firm had to eat the loss. David had seen Kinder physically hustle a busted trader off the Floor so he couldn't do any more damage—not to himself, but to the clearing firm's credit line.

"Remember, the market gives, and the market takes away," the clearing house rep said. "Don't you think it's time you covered?"

David checked the quote board. The December contract price had hit twelve dollars, up twenty percent from yesterday's close. He'd made two million dollars in less than an hour—and the storm still hadn't hit the Hub.

"Not yet," he said.

But watching the clearing house rep walk away, David wondered exactly whom he was trying to convince. If he sold his position, he could pay back Kinder, redeem the seat, and be left with more trading capital that he had ever imagined, his one-lot days forever behind him. *Malia would want me to get out.* David stretched up on his toes, preparing to shout his offer, then hesitated.

To make money, you have to spend money. His own words came back to him, and he felt a sense of certainty, destiny even. There was two million dollars' profit in his account, enough to buy another hundred gas contracts. David glanced at the television screen. The hurricane was still bearing down on Louisiana.

Successful traders all had a story about their Big Day— the moment on the Floor that had defined them, the day they made the trade that launched them into a new place. This was his Big Day—David was certain of it. At last Malia would respect him.

"A hundred Deece at twelve!" shouted the trader in front of him.

David bent down and spoke into the man's ear. "Buy 'em."

The trader frowned at him. "A hundred at twelve? You're sure?" His tone made clear he knew David was a one-lotter.

Hearing the other man's doubt, David felt something rise

up inside him. He jerked his head in a nod. "Write it up."

As the trader scribbled the details of the trade on a pit card, someone called, "Dash!"

David glanced around the ring and spotted Vigneri's bulky frame on the other side. His friend cupped his hands around his mouth and shouted, but David couldn't hear him over the hubbub. Vigneri made a slashing motion across his throat, then gestured at the quote board.

David looked up. December gas had dropped a nickel. As he kept watching, the number changed again. *Ten cents down.* His stomach churned. The market was turning against him.

He calculated his loss—two hundred thousand. A *temporary slide*, he told himself, like a car skidding across an ice patch, then regaining traction before it hit anything. Small when compared to two million. But as he watched, the numbers dipped again, and the two hundred became two hundred and fifty.

David felt as if he were in a pool of rising water. He craned his neck to see the television. *Breaking News* read the crawl at the bottom of the screen. The red swirl was still there, but the dotted line showing its projected trajectory had shifted. According to the graphic, the storm would bypass Louisiana altogether. *The hurricane is going to miss the Hub.* David's heart banged against his ribs. He flicked his eyes back to the quote board just as the gas number began to nosedive in earnest.

Around him, shouts became bellows as the market fell. A few feet away a trader held his head in his hands and moaned, while another threw up. Transfixed, David watched the price grind down, taking his dreams with it.

The house was the first to go. "Eleven seventy-five." *Kiss the place in Connecticut goodbye.* "Eleven forty." *There goes the red Porsche.* "Eleven twenty." *Au revoir, trip to Paris.* "Eleven ten." *No more Cartier watch.* David winced at every downward tick, the plummeting number like a finger poking him in the chest.

"Eleven dollars!" yelled the trader beside him. All of David's profit was gone. The realization jolted him from his stupor, and he raised his hands to join the cacophony.

"TWO HUNDRED AT TEN EIGHTY! TWO HUNDRED AT TEN EIGHTY!" he shouted.

There were no takers. Abandoning the hand signals, David screamed ever-decreasing offers. "Ten sixty! . . . Ten forty! . . ." It was like trying to find someone to catch a falling knife. No one answered.

By now the spread between buyers and sellers was so huge, it was practically unbridgeable. One by one, would-be sellers stopped shouting. Instead they stared wordlessly, watching the price of gas plunge too quickly for the quote board to keep up. The ground was littered with discarded pit cards. In the middle of the ring the clocker gaped at the traders, eyes large behind his goggles, bewildered at having nothing to do.

At last the number slowed, finally stabilizing at its pre-hurricane level of ten dollars per contract. David stared at the quote board, the neon colors blurring. Two million dollars gone, like water through his fingers. All that was left was—

Realization burned through him. It wasn't only a watch or a car that was gone. He owed the clearing firm two million dollars for the two hundred contracts. *I lost Malia's seat.* As if reading his thoughts, Earl Kinder materialized on the other side of the pit and headed toward him.

David tasted bile in his mouth. He whirled and began shoving his way out of the ring to the exit. He couldn't face the clearing house rep. Not until he figured out how to save the seat.

He burst through the Exchange's revolving doors and into the cold air. Reporters from the financial press hovered near the entrance, looking for first-person accounts of the carnage. They surged forward at the sight of David's trading jacket. Dodging the photographers' zoom lenses, he sprinted down the walkway that led to the ferry. Once he was north of the pier and onto the rocks, the journalists abandoned their pursuit.

Reaching the river's edge, David propped his hands on his knees and took several deep breaths, waiting for his heart to slow. A pair of pelicans trundled along the shoreline, like two old men on their way to the corner bar. There was no one else around.

David sank to the ground, heedless of the damp rocks. Raindrops stung his skin and the air was sour with exhaust and brine. He could hear the hum of traffic behind him on the West Side Highway.

Tomorrow he would talk to Kinder, work something out. Even as he formed the idea, he knew it was ridiculous. The Floor was like Vegas—you had to pay to play.

Two million dollars. He'd had his Big Day, and already he couldn't really remember what it had felt like. One thing was certain: Getting what you wanted and losing it was worse than never having had it at all.

"Dash." The soft voice startled him out of his reverie. A hand dropped onto his shoulder. "I'm sorry, but it's over."

Kinder. Wiping the sweat and tears from his eyes, David pushed himself to his feet, a litany of *if onlys* running through his brain.

If only I hadn't borrowed the money against the seat . . . If only I had sold out instead of buying more . . . If only I hadn't believed red cars and trips to Paris would make things right between Malia and me again . . .

"Did you cover before you left?" Kinder asked.

David shook his head, then shivered as the wind knifed through his thin trader's coat. The sky was low and opaque.

"After I sell out your position, we'll go upstairs to turn in your ID." Kinder nodded at the square of plastic on David's lapel. "I need you to give me that."

"Mr. Kinder, please . . ." David covered the badge with his hand. "Spot me fifty," he begged, his voice cracking. "I'll pay you back."

"You know I can't do that. Give me the badge, Dash. The sooner you do, the sooner this will be behind you."

David tightened his grip on the plastic pin. Kinder reached out as if to pry his hand loose. David twisted away, stepping into the water and shoving the rep with his shoulder. Kinder gasped as he lost his footing on the slick stones. He started to topple forward.

In that split second, David knew he could reach out and catch the falling man. But he didn't move. Instead, he watched Kinder strike his head on a sharp rock and land face-down in the river.

The clearing house rep lay still, save for one hand undulating in the current as though it were waving. Blood leaked from his wound, clouding the water before it was swept downstream.

Ankle-deep in the icy water, David stared at the scene in disbelief. Then panic overtook him, propelling him out of the river and back onto the walkway, where he tried to collect himself.

He was alone. No gunboat, no security patrol, no pedestrians or loitering homeless. Even the pelicans were gone. Unable to think of what else to do, David began walking toward the Exchange. As the building loomed in front of him, he slowed his pace and looked toward the Hudson.

Maybe I should . . . He had a decent term life insurance policy, enough so that Malia could start over. David veered off the walkway toward the water, his shoes squishing on the gravel.

"Hey, Dash!"

David turned to see Vigneri lumbering toward him, a cigarette dangling from his fingers. Almost unconsciously, David reached into his pocket for an antacid tablet.

"Christ, I hate these stupid smoking laws." Vigneri exhaled a stream of smoke through his nose and eyed the roll of antacids in David's hand, though he didn't seem to notice his wet feet. "The Exchange should have bowls of those on the Floor for days like today." He barked out a laugh. David flinched at the sound.

"Jesus, you're twitchy. That's what holding size will do to you." Vigneri dragged on his cigarette. "So, did you catch my signal and get out in time? That reporter I used to date told me about the 'cane missing the Hub right before it went out over the air. I got short, made a little money."

David's mouth was so dry he could barely speak. "Not exactly."

Vigneri grimaced. "Ah shit, Dash." He dropped his cigarette onto the gravel and ground it out with his shoe, then glanced at his watch. "Close is in thirty minutes."

For a moment, David watched the river slide past. He thought he could see tendrils of red in the water. "Let's go."

They walked back to the Exchange, David's wet pant cuffs flapping against his ankles. David dully watched his ID pass through the card reader at Security, then followed Vigneri to the elevator.

The natural-gas pit was in full cry, as frenetic as it had

been that morning. Out of habit, David glanced at the quote board, then looked again. Gas was trading at thirteen, up three dollars from the opening.

His eyes flicked to the television monitor. The red swirl had been replaced by a blaze of flames leaping into the sky. David stared at the image, struggling to make sense of it, as a roar went up from the pit—the signal that the price had hit another new high.

Vigneri broke off talking with another trader. "Can you fucking believe it? When they evacuated the Hub, someone left a valve open at the gas processing plant. The whole damn place blew up! Gas is going through the roof!" Vigneri punched David on the arm. "You're making a killing, you lucky bastard."

David was stunned. Because Kinder hadn't sold the two hundred contracts, his account was up four million dollars. And Malia's seat was safe.

His heart beat faster as he mentally replayed the scene at the waterfront. He and Kinder had been alone. Vigneri had chalked up his nervousness to holding a big position. Hope spread through David's chest. *My Big Day.*

Against Floor rules, he pulled his cell phone from his pocket. Punching in Malia's number, David checked the quote board again. As soon as he told her the good news, he'd sell. No way was he making the same mistake twice.

Underneath the electronic display, a security camera slowly panned the area. Just like the ones posted along the riverbank.

RICHARDS WAS *IN THE MEETING* WITH NORCO SUPPLIES, HE'D STARTED ON THE OFFER FROM CAISSON.

THAT'S WHEN NORCO TOLD HIM ABOUT THE COUNTER OFFER FROM ANOTHER COMPANY THEY SUPPLY ...

HAMMOND.

CHRIST!

HAMMOND HAD TO KNOW ABOUT OUR MERGER PROPOSAL.

CAISSON AND HAMMOND BOTH USE NORCO FOR MATERIALS, BUT THAT'S WHERE THE OVERLAP ENDS. THE LEAK HAD TO HAPPEN HERE.

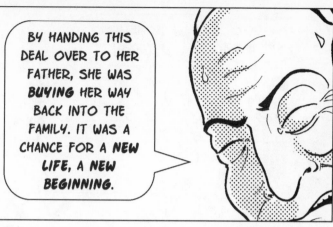

A TERRORIZING DEMONSTRATION

BY JIM FUSILLI

23 Wall Street

An aptitude with higher mathematics earned him an enviable position at the nation's most powerful bank, but he soon lost it to petulance. "No good will ever come of you," said the paymaster as he tallied his severance, wagging an ancient finger. "Not by half are you as clever as you believe."

With a smirk on his lips, the young man departed the bank's gray, bunker-like offices. By the time he stepped into the bustle of Broad Street, he decided the events that had led to his dismissal required redress.

He told himself neither the prissy clerk who declared his work ill conceived nor the secretary who deemed his advances untoward was worthy of his consideration. The creaking paymaster was a cross-eyed dolt.

Soon he realized not even the attenuation of J.P. Morgan himself would compensate for the unwarranted assault on his character.

By the time he reached Cortlandt Street, he knew that only the institution itself would merit the full force of his intellect in the service of his sense of Justice. Taking the Sixth Avenue El uptown, he began his withdrawal into what would be a lengthy period of unwavering purpose.

When he returned to the corner of Wall and Broad streets twenty-one months later, on the third Thursday of September 1920, it was to execute a plan that, in his mind, was perfect.

Mauro sat on the brownstone steps, elbows on scuffed knees, and gazed doe-eyed into the summer evening, his ten-year-old mind all but unoccupied by thought.

The slight, round-headed boy was unaware he had been judged insufficient by the nuns, who recommended to his mother that she return with him to Terracina. Paterson teemed with Italian immigrants, they explained carefully, and only the brightest among them would find purchase in America.

Stunned, Mauro's mother took her son by the hand to the public school. The sympathetic vice principal, a Mr. Piatti, *un Milanese*, was made to understand that the boy was the family's future, the reason they had come to northern New Jersey from southern Italy. Mauro was placed in the third grade class for slow learners. When September arrived, he would be the oldest among his new classmates.

Widowed by a trolley accident, Mauro's mother took in laundry and repaired garments for her Essex Street neighbors, many of whom considered use of her services an act of charity. Among her customers was the man who moved in three floors above her basement apartment, the rare American in the Italian quarter. She saw him as quiet and respectful with a dash of charm, despite his angular face that dry skin had reddened at the nose and pale eyes of a peculiar aspect she could not identify.

Each Tuesday, he left a plump pillowcase outside her door, a crisp dollar bill atop his soiled clothes.

One afternoon, she found in his shirt breast pocket a crinkled deposit slip from the Morgan Bank of 23 Wall Street. Eager to return it to him, she instructed her son to sit outside and summon her when the man approached.

Mauro wiped his nose with a slender arm as he watched an orderly row of black ants enter a narrow breech in the steps where, earlier, he had inserted a pignoli nut.

"Mama," he shouted, "*sta venendo!*"

Removing her apron, Mauro's mother scurried to the wrought-iron fence and held out the slip, her hand trembling with nerves.

In greeting her, the man removed his boater, revealing hair lighter than the color of straw.

Mauro watched incuriously.

The man thanked her and buried the paper in a side pocket. Returning his hat to his head, he said, "Perhaps the boy would profit from a visit. Wall Street, the financial capital of our country, and the New York Stock Exchange, of course."

She smiled in agreement.

He tussled the boy's hair as he climbed the steps, soles scraping brownstone.

He rented the apartment in Paterson after learning the city was the anarchists' capital of the United States, home to La Questione Sociale, a weekly newspaper whose circulation at one time exceeded fifteen thousand, roughly the equivalent of the daily distribution of *The Wall Street Journal*. Its publisher was Errico Malatesta, a proponent of violence as a means to social change.

Another Paterson resident, Gaetano Bresci, returned to Italy in 1900 and killed its king, Umberto I.

And a third Italian anarchist, Luigi Galleani, also lived in Paterson for a while, until he was deported. His admirers, known as Galleanists and largely comprised of laborers of Italian descent, absorbed his philosophies. A few had bombed police stations, creating the infernal weapons by following Galleani's instruction manual that bore the title "*La Salute è in Voi*," a crude translation of which is "To Your Health."

"The irony of it!" said the man who had dyed his hair the dark color of a Mediterranean native. His tittering laughter drew the ire of the people at an adjoining table in the library's reading room. He quickly gathered his notebooks and blue prints, leaving the Galleani manual in plain sight.

In fact, he had no real need for the Italian's instructions. In the Yorkville section of Manhattan, there were Germans, some of whom had served the Fatherland in the Great War, who knew how to build bombs far more sophisticated, and devastating, than those the Galleanists deployed.

Using the name Errico Bresci, the man purchased a wagon built in 1893. At a stable on Paterson's Mill Street, he bought a ten-year-old harness for the dark bay he kept under the Brooklyn Bridge.

T.J. O'Neal Jr., a resident of Nutley, New Jersey, transported himself to lower Manhattan via the Tubes from Newark. He did so daily, endeavoring to complete the crossword puzzle of the *Newark Star* before arriving at the Hudson Terminal.

The twenty-minute ride was inevitably uneventful, for Mr. O'Neal traveled after the morning rush had ended. From his window, he saw the great concrete and sandstone towers of Wall Street, one rising higher than the next, as if climbing each other in competition for a gold ring hidden among the clouds. Though he had been a waiter at Ye Olde

Chop House on Cedar Street for more than a decade, he still felt a jolt of amazement at the sheer audacity of the district, the intensity of its activity and its presumption of success.

Today, a man carrying a tennis racket assumed the seat next to Mr. O'Neal, arriving at the moment the train slid to the underground.

"Hello," said the black-haired man, who introduced himself as Fischer.

Mr. O'Neal nodded politely, but in such a way as to discourage further conversation. The puzzle beckoned.

"I've seen you," said Fischer, adjusting his tennis racket. "You are amiable."

Mr. O'Neal gripped his pencil and edged against the train's sidewall.

"September," the man said, "in this, the year of our Lord nineteen hundred and twenty, on the day you read in your newspaper that many police of the Old Slip Station have been reassigned . . ."

The waiter frowned, but did not turn away. He had heard rumor of a pending action by the New York Police Department against Communist agitators marching at Brooklyn Rapid Transit Company headquarters and its assorted car barns.

"On that day, you are best served to remain at home." The man nodded knowingly. "A dastardly deed. Chaos."

The train eased its speed as it entered the Hoboken terminus.

"I am in the employ of the Secret Service," he continued, "and I know whereof I speak."

He stood as the train came to a halt, reaching high for a leather strap.

Mr. O'Neal watched as the man tucked his tennis racket under his arm and departed.

Mauro's mother ironed her son's white cotton shirt, his brown short pants, his brown knee socks, and polished his black shoes with diluted vinegar, also replacing the newspapers that had covered the holes in their soles. After she bathed him, she watched as he dressed, and admonished him to remain as neat as he was at that moment.

He grimaced as she dragged a comb through his thick curly hair.

She handed him her last handkerchief. "Use it," she said.

"*Sí*, Mama," he replied.

She tugged him toward the living room, tapping the sofa as she sat.

The boy nestled into the plump cushion at his mother's side. His feet failed to reach the floor.

"*Grazie*," she said.

"Thank you," the boy replied in singsong, his accent thick.

"*Sì, por favore.*"

"Yes, please," he recited.

"*Non, por favore.*"

"Ah, Mama! *Arresto!*" he whined, jutting his bottom lip, thrusting his hand in the air. "*Sì, non. Non, sì.* No, yes. *Sono parlaro inglese*—"

She grabbed his earlobe. "You listen to me," she said in rapid Italian. "This man . . . You know where he's bringing you, this man? You think there you walk around like they dragged you out of the straw?"

Straw?

"*L'America*," she said, letting go.

"*Sì*, Mama, *ma*—"

"*Dovete essere il la cosa migliore?*"
"Be the best," Mauro replied dutifully.
"*Ah.*" She nodded in triumph.

The man bought, separately, red ink and a set of rubber stamps. Last night, after rinsing the black dye from his hair, he pressed the same message onto five sheets of coarse paper:

> *Rimember*
> *We will not tolerate*
> *any longer*
> *Free the political*
> *Prisoner or it will be*
> *Sure death for all of you*
>
> *American Anarchist*
> *fighters*

It had cost him fifty dollars and the price of a meal at the Hotel Marguery to learn from a postal inspector the precise language the anarchists employed in previous threats. During the supper, the man told him of the troubled tennis pro Fischer and his postcards bearing predictions of doom.

Now, as dawn beckoned, the man whose hair was once again lighter than the color of straw, folded the sheets of paper and slipped them into an inside pocket of a blue suit that had once belonged to his late father, a builder of solid repute, a diminutive man who had been as dedicated and self-effacing as his wife was disdainful and superior.

As he examined the tiny room, the man thought of the after-event and the comeback of those who had been humbled. To no one, he said, "Eager to blame and thus they will, and it will be those whose culpability best serves their interests. For they know only of opportunity."

He packed the ink and stamps into a brown paper bag and deposited them in a trash bin a block south of the offices of *La Questione Sociale*.

As he crossed a dim, litter-strewn alley on his return to Essex Street, he repeated what he had said, adding, "But in their heart of hearts, they will know they have been taken down."

Mauro was studying his parade of ants on the brownstone steps when the man emerged precisely at 8 o'clock.

"Ready for adventure, Mauro?" he asked, and offered the boy his hand.

"Good morning," Mauro said, as instructed.

"Let us proceed then, shall we?"

The man brought a finger to the brim of his boater when Mauro's mother came into view.

"Thank you," she said, her hands anxiously clasping the fleur-de-lis pickets of the wrought-iron gate. "Thank you very much. Thank you."

"Yes, this will be a day to remember," said the man. "A day for the ages."

She didn't fully understand, but when he looked to the September sky, she did too. It was flawless, the lightest blue with downy clouds.

"*Ciao*, Mama," Mauro said, his voice cracking with sudden nerves.

"Be a good boy," she replied in Italian, and then repeated what she had told him last night and again this morning. "Listen to the man."

Clasping her hands in front of her breasts, she watched as

they walked along Essex Street, her son skipping to match the man's confident stride.

Mauro opened and closed the stable door, and was engulfed quickly by overwhelming scents and unexpected heat. He stayed close to the entryway, taking sips of cool air as he peered through the vertical space between the red doors.

Though the snorting horses behind him seemed mammoth and mice scurried near his freshly polished shoes, the boy was more baffled than frightened. His mother had told him of streets of gold, towers that kissed the sky, and the world's smartest men. Now he wondered if he had misunderstood.

As Mauro watched, the man emerged in green overalls from a barn on the other side of the narrow thoroughfare, dragging an old rack wagon, its yellow bed enclosed by poles and rails covered by ragtag canvas. The man grunted as he brought the wagon to a halt, then chucked the wheel against the curb.

The man approached the stable, mopping his brow. Mauro retreated, backing into a weather-beaten barrel, blinking in the sudden wash of light.

"Come," the man said to the boy as he marched past.

With Mauro lingering behind him, the man deftly harnessed a dark bay mare, affixing blinders the old horse accepted without protest.

Responding to a clicking sound the man made with his mouth, the horse left its station, albeit without enthusiasm, its long tail hanging limply.

"Follow and shut all doors," the man said, as he tugged on a strap, leading the animal toward fresh air.

As Mauro reached up to close the stable, he tried to

make the same clicking sound, but could not. He shrugged his shoulders in resignation.

The horse in place across the shaded lane, the man beckoned Mauro to the rear of the wagon where he pulled back a canvas flap.

Mauro saw a simple wooden crate. It was tied with thick hemp to the wagon's frame.

"You know what we have there?" the man asked, gesturing with his head.

Mauro looked up at him.

"A gift," he said. "A gift that you will present. *You.*"

"Yes," the boy said.

Without warning, the man lifted Mauro under his arms and hoisted him into the wagon.

Mauro hunched to avoid the rail above his head. Now sawdust covered the tops of his shoes and clung to his knee socks.

"You sit here," the man said, tapping the tattered rear panel, "and you watch the world go by."

The boy's expression was blank.

The man trotted to the barn to remove his overalls.

Mauro's mother looked at the clock above the stove and permitted herself a little grin: At this moment, her son was becoming a part of America. Her husband would have been proud; a big, gap-toothed smile beneath his walrus mustache, thumbs hooked under his suspenders against his barrel chest.

The aroma of sugar and almonds rose from the oven. The *amarena* were to serve as an expression of her gratitude for the man who had taken her son to Wall Street. She saw herself handing the pyramid of cookies to him upon their return. Perhaps he would have a story of her son's—

She realized she did not know his name.

Certain he hadn't introduced himself, she tried to recall if she had seen an errant piece of mail addressed to him. But he hadn't received any mail, as far as she knew.

A rush of worry brushed her heart. Wiping her damp hands on her apron, she was suddenly desperate for any source of his identity. His shirts bore the Arrow label, a popular brand among the men whose clothes she laundered, so that was of no—

Then she remembered the slip of paper she had found in his pocket. *The Morgan Bank*, it read. *The Morgan Bank of 23 Wall Street*. She sighed in relief. The man was known to the people of the great Morgan Bank.

L'America, she thought as she returned to work, her mind floating toward ease.

At that very moment, the man delivered the old mare and wagon to Wall Street east of Broad, at the center of the Morgan Building.

"Mauro," said the man, as he crawled beneath the canvas hood, having placed the last of the stamped notes in the postal box at the corner of Cedar Street and Broadway. "Come here, boy. Quickly."

Mauro watched while the man removed the top and side slats of the wooden crate to reveal a device made of Bessemer steel. It resembled a torpedo. A red wire protruded from a vein in its casing.

"Mauro, sit here," the man said. "That's right. On top. That's it . . ."

The boy eased himself atop the device, straddling it as if he were riding a horse.

"This is simple, son," the man said. "In a minute or so,

you will hear a church bell. Do you understand? A bell."

The man looked into the boy's round eyes.

"Yes," the boy said. "A bell. A church bell."

"Good, good," the man replied, tapping the boy's bare leg. "When the bell strikes 12, you pull this cable."

The man made a gesture with his empty hand.

"Twelve bells and you pull the cable. Understand? Twelve, pull."

Mauro said yes.

"Say it, please."

"Twelve, pull." His voice all but squeaked.

As he edged toward the rear of the truck, the man glanced at his father's pocket watch. Reaching for the canvas flap, he said, "Do your best, Mauro."

Mauro smiled. *Twelve and pull,* he thought. *Church bells.*

The Trinity Church bell struck 1.

Immediately, people began to pour from the Morgan Building, the Assay Office, the Sub-Treasury, the New York Stock Exchange, and scores of other buildings in the vicinity, moving toward restaurants and lunch counters.

On the steps of the Sub-Treasury Building, hidden behind a column adjacent to the base of a bronze statue of George Washington, stood the man with hair lighter than the color of straw, a smirk affixed to his face.

Beneath him, the Street continued to fill with people. Taxis were unable to move, and horns began to blare.

The bell struck 3.

Swelling with confidence, the man thought, *There is no system, no institution, greater than the marshaled thoughts of a singular man in the pursuit of Right.*

The bell tolled again and again, soon to 7, 8, 9 . . .

And now Justice shall be done.

The church bell struck 11. The man put the tips of his forefingers in his ears, closed his eyes, and, in preparation for the colossal explosion, hunched into his body.

But there was no explosion.

All was as it had been.

The Morgan Building was not destroyed. The executives therein had not been killed.

The unsavory crowd of co-conspirators to the folly of Wall Street continued to surge from buildings, many bypassing his horse and wagon. These included the postal inspector who had sold him information crucial to his deceit, and the German who had been vital to the construction of the bomb. He had agreed to meet them at the entrance to the Morgan Building precisely at noon.

Stunned, the man hurried down the steps.

Mauro wiped his nose with the handkerchief his mother had given him, and he struggled to return it to his back pocket. Doing so, he looked between his legs at the device, which rested on a bed of sawdust. He had been thinking of the sound of the horse as it trod cobblestone, and of the magnificent bridge that, an hour or so ago, had been high as the moon above his head.

The bells had stopped.

Dodici? he thought, having lost count.

Could have been twelve.

He shrugged. He was hungry and, in the fog of his mind, reasoned the man would not return until his chore was complete.

He looked at the red cable in his hand and gave it a hardy tug.

He was instantly blown to atoms.

A yellow-green mushroom cloud rose in his stead.

The wagon was obliterated, and the bay mare flew into the air. It landed, dead and disemboweled, in the center of the Wall and Broad streets intersection, at least fifty feet to the west.

A block away, the Broadway trolley line leaped its tracks, pinning a messenger boy beneath its wheels.

The iron bars that defended the Assay Office bowed inward.

Shrapnel more deadly than a thousand machine-gun bursts propelled forcefully in every direction. The bomb had contained thirty pounds of TNT packed beneath approximately one hundred and fifty pounds of sash weights, pieces of which landed as far away as the Trinity Church graveyard.

Riders emerging from the IRT station were greeted with a spray of viscera, and a human leg and foot landed in their midst.

A woman's severed head, hat still in place, stuck momentarily to the façade of the Morgan Building, where blood was splattered to a height of a dozen feet.

Glass and stone rained from buildings within a half-mile radius of the blast site. The windows of the New York Stock Exchange were destroyed, and several employees therein were shredded to ribbons. The American flag flying above its entrance caught fire, as did awnings throughout the district, several as high as twelve stories above ground.

Ambulance surgeons arrived to find bodies of the dead and dying strewn about. Blood pools reflected the midday sun.

Fifteen people were killed instantly. Among them was the man with hair lighter than the color of straw, who was caught full in the chest by the force of the blast.

Others died within the hour, victims of the whirling, white-hot steel bits. Thomas Joyce, Morgan's chief clerk, was violated by shards of glass from the building's cathedral windows. He was the only Morgan employee to perish, though the first floor of the building was wrecked.

Upon hearing a report that the Assay Office and Sub-Treasury had been attacked, the men of the Twenty-Third Infantry stationed on Governors Island were rushed by ferry to the Battery, from there they marched in double-time to the district, bayonets fixed.

When they arrived, they reported a stench in the air that recalled the battlefields of France. Burlap sacks placed over the blood-soaked bodies could not contain the smell of death.

The streets were swept clean overnight, as Sanitation Department employees helped police comb for clues, as well as matter to aid in the identification of victims. The smallest body parts were gathered in wax paper.

Blood was dispatched by water hose to the nearest sewer, and men took steel wool to the remnant stains.

Well before sunrise, large sheets of canvas were stretched over the glassless windows at the Morgan Building. Similarly, bunting covered the broken windows at the Stock Exchange.

Both institutions opened promptly at 9 o'clock, the appointed time. Many employees arrived dressed in bandages.

The infernal machine had exploded at one minute past noon, and the banks and exchanges regularly closed at 3 o'clock, so the terrorizing demonstration had caused only a three-hour delay in the transaction of the district's vital business.

* * *

Edwin P. Fischer, a former championship tennis player, was arrested in Hamilton, Ontario. He was said to have predicted the bombing in a series of postcards sent to various officials of government.

Mr. Fischer's brother-in-law, Robert A. Pope, said Mr. Fischer was not involved in the attack, but had known of them via "mental telepathy."

Arrangements were made for Mr. Fischer's immediate transport to New York City for questioning. The police were well aware of his erratic behavior. He had fled north to avoid being committed to an insane asylum, as per his family's wishes.

When Mr. Fischer arrived from Canada at the Grand Center Terminal, he was wearing two business suits, one atop the other, over tennis whites, on the chance that a game might opportune.

That evening, *The News*, which, as "New York's Picture Newspaper," was obligated to publish several gruesome photos of the aftermath of the attack, announced in its headlines that *Wall St. Ignored Warnings*. Another read, *Trace Crank in Bomb Outrage*. On its front page, the latter featured a photo of the troubled Mr. Fischer.

Entering the terminus of the Hudson Tubes on Church Street, the waiter T.J. O'Neal Jr. of Nutley, New Jersey accepted a copy of the paper from a newsy, but did not look at it until he had boarded the train. Then, to no one, he said, "That's not him. That's not Fischer."

The waiter reported immediately to the Old Slip police station. His statement was added to the mountain of testimony the police had already compiled, much of which only served to confuse the inquiry.

The Secret Service, the Federal Bureau of Investigation,

and Morgan's men had already decided the attack was the work of anarchists. But the New York Police Department did not agree, at least not yet. They stood by the statement that had been given to the *Evening Post*: "It may have been the work of a single criminal lunatic mind spurred on to its fiendish act by we know not what influence."

The carcass of the horse provided the clue of greatest value, and through unmitigated industry, the police identified John L. Haggerty of Finnegan & Kyle, 82 New Chambers Street, as the man who had shod it.

A taciturn man with wire spectacles and the requisite sinewy arms, Mr. Haggerty took pride in the belief he could identify any horse he'd ever shod. The condition of a horse's hoof, he said, was as distinct as a human fingerprint.

He watched while a policeman unwrapped a length of canvas containing part of a horse's foreleg, including the hoof and shoe.

"Dark bay mare. Ten years old if a day," Mr. Haggerty said, as he ran a calloused finger across the mark of the International Union of Journeymen Horseshoers. "Stood right for shoeing."

"When?"

"No more than two weeks ago."

He could not, however, identify the mare's owner.

"Never look at them," he said plainly.

Business on Wall Street closed at noon on Saturdays, marking the customary half-holiday. By 1 o'clock, thousands after thousands arrived in the district to see the site of the carnage, jamming the streets, their solemnity in stark contrast to the panic and horror of those who had been subject to the terrorizing demonstration two days ago. Women dabbed away tears as men removed their hats in silent tribute to the dead. Other visitors pointed to the hole in the surface of Wall Street and the chips in the Morgan Building façade, even as workers replaced the cathedral windows.

From the crowd emerged a panic-stricken Italian woman, her olive visage an expression of unadulterated agony, her eyes ringed red and swollen. Dressed in black from head to heel, she clawed at passersby and pleaded for help in finding her son.

At her side was Mr. Piatti, the vice principal of the boy's school. Sobbing, he was too aggrieved for purpose.

The woman cried, "My son . . . My hope. Please."

A candle peddler was retrieved and pressed into service as a translator. He was nudged amid the crowd surrounding the wailing woman.

"He is a boy. Simple," she said in Italian. "He is confused, and he is lost. You cannot tell me he is— You cannot!"

The peddler said, "Please. We wish to help you, but . . . First, did you visit the hospitals?"

"It is possible he has forgotten his name," she said, her voice a song of desperation. "He is frightened. He is just a small boy."

Mr. Piatti intervened, and it was finally understood by the crowd that the boy was ten years old and he had been treated to a day-visit to the district by a neighbor.

When her son and the nameless man had not returned by late Thursday evening, the woman reported to a nearby police station. There she had learned of the bomb attack.

The peddler tilted his head in sympathy.

After contacting the New York City police, Mr. Piatti explained, Paterson officials had come to Essex Street to examine the apartment on the third floor.

"Ah," said the peddler, nodding to the crowd.

They found it empty, save for the furniture that had been left by a previous tenant and a few discarded pages from the latest edition of *La Questione Sociale*.

TOWN CAR

BY DAVID NOONAN

85 Exchange Place

It was waiting for him in front of the building, as always, eight quick steps across the sidewalk. Black, tinted windows, minimal chrome, a little bulgy in the haunches, like a 140-pound woman in a tight dress. One of a million, utterly anonymous. But special, too, his alone, for twenty minutes anyway. This one was freshly washed; he noticed droplets of water glistening on the bumper, catching the sparkle of the traffic light on the corner. He liked that. One night the car was so dirty he sent it away and threatened to take the firm's business elsewhere. It wasn't his call to make—Hackett handled all the vendors—but the frazzled dispatcher didn't know that. He only knew he had a seriously unhappy customer screaming in his ear and a big account suddenly in play. They sent a limo to calm him down, no charge. It worked. The limo was superior to the Town Car, no question. He knew a lot of the big earners stayed with the Town Car after they made it, that whole low-profile thing. Not him. When he broke through he was getting a limo, and a retired NYPD detective to drive it and handle his personal security, one of those tough Irish guys with the blank expressions, the ones he saw in the *Daily News* all the time, escorting murder suspects out of their dreary apartment buildings in the Bronx. The car was as clean on the inside as it was on the outside, odor-free except for a hint of the driver's cheap aftershave. He could live with that. It was a lot easier to take than the greasy stench of curried goat or whatever aromatic delicacies the Middle Eastern drivers wolfed down between calls. This guy looked American, an increasingly rare thing, and he was even listening to the Yankees game.

"Eighty-third and Third, right?" said the driver, in perfect Jersey, as they slid away from the curb.

He had planned to head straight home, but now he thought he might swing over to the West Side and see Heather. Maybe pick up some Chinese on the way from that joint she liked on Amsterdam, Hunan whatever. He checked his watch. It was 10:30 already. If his wife wasn't asleep yet, she would be soon. Taking care of the twins wiped her out, even with the full-time nanny. He didn't really get that. His mother raised five kids on her own and did the old man's books every night, too. She had more energy than ten of these hothouse flowers on the Upper East Side. And she was still going strong at seventy-eight, playing tennis every morning in the jungle heat of Miami, volunteering at Jackson Memorial in the afternoon, knocking off a bottle of cabernet every night with one or another of her widow buddies. Heather would be up, of course, studying for the LSAT or doing situps or making pies or writing one of her wacky poems or meditating or organizing her rock climbing equipment or IMing with one of her eight million close personal friends. She was a jammer, and that was fine with him. The last thing he needed was a girlfriend with nothing to do, calling him six times a day, sitting in front of the TV all night wondering why he couldn't spend more time with her, carefully watering her boredom until it bloomed into glorious hysteria. Heather was too busy for that shit. He saw her three times a week, max. And forget about spending the night. She was in it for the sex, just like he was. Fucking her was like going to the gym for two hours, and that's usually where he told his wife he was.

"Change in plans," he said to the driver. "Let's head for the Upper West Side."

"Upper West Side. You got it."

Then he remembered that Heather was having her period. Or was it his wife? One of them was, he was pretty sure. Could it be both? Was that possible? He hadn't seen Heather since the Chicago trip. Or had he? Somebody had mentioned cramps recently, he knew that much. He should probably keep track of stuff like that, but then he'd have to start writing things down and that would put the whole arrangement at risk. He didn't know anyone who had a setup as sweet as his—exhausted wife on the East Side, inexhaustible mistress on the West Side, the two of them separated by the great green expanse of Central Park. And there was no chance of a random encounter because he never took Heather to the East Side and Callie, his wife, hated the West Side. When she was thirteen, some old creep in a doorway waved his dick at her and her friends as they were leaving a movie theater on Broadway. Talk about making an impression. Twenty years later, the dominant image she had of the neighborhood that included Lincoln Center, the Museum of Natural History, Columbia University, hundreds of good restaurants, and at least a dozen great ones was of a droopy penis winking at her from the shadows. He knew it was droopy because he had questioned her once in great detail about the incident. Now, it was all he could do to get her to cross the park in a limo once a year for the charity benefit the Old Man threw every fall at the Metropolitan Opera.

He sensed a change in the world and suddenly the Hudson River was on his left, wide and flat and undeniable. New Jersey loomed across the dark water, a mile away at least. A hulking tanker pushed north against the current, the white streak of its bow wave pointing the way. Manhattan was an island. He liked that. Manhattan was an island, and he lived on it. It was a great castle, surrounded by a great moat, with many kings and many more princes. It was a kingdom, full of riches and treachery, where the game was played as well as it was played anywhere in the world. And he was one of the players. And he was winning. It wasn't always pretty, it wasn't always fair, but how could anyone expect it to be? When two people wanted the same thing, one of them was bound to be disappointed. The weak would always lose to the strong, that was nature's way. If he beat someone on a deal, that was their problem, not his.

He reached across the seat to open the window—he wanted to feel the rush of air and smell the river and the summer night—but when he pushed the switch, nothing happened. He tried the window on his right, same problem.

"What's with the windows?" he asked. "They're not working."

"Short circuit, I think," the driver said.

"Can you open them from up there? I'd like some air."

"No, sorry, they're all on the blink."

"Well, that's fucked up."

"Hey, at least the AC's working, right?"

He thought about getting angry, but decided not to waste the energy. "Good point."

They stopped at a red light and through the tinted glass he could see that the car on their right was also a black Lincoln Town Car, as was the car in front of them and the car behind them. He called in the order to the restaurant, checked his e-mail, and, finally, eighteen hours after he put it on and slid it tight, he loosened his tie. It was only Monday, and the week wasn't going to get any easier, but he felt strong and in control. He put his head back and closed his eyes. Life. Was. Good.

He dozed for a bit and when he awoke they were bumper-to-bumper on the Henry Hudson, inching past the 72nd Street exit.

"Shit, driver, we need to get off here."

"Must be an accident up ahead," the driver said. "The traffic shouldn't be so heavy this time of night."

"Did you hear what I said? We have to get off here. The restaurant's at 77th and Amsterdam, then we're going to 82nd and West End."

"Could be from the Yankees game, I suppose. Jersey fans heading home, fucking everything up at the bridge."

"Hey, asshole, are you listening to me? The exit's right there. Turn the fucking wheel and get us the fuck out of here."

The driver eased the car past the exit and snugged it up against the thick stone wall that separated the highway from Riverside Park. As horns honked and cars squeezed past on the left, he turned to face the backseat.

"Don't call me asshole, asshole," the driver said.

It wasn't possible that the driver had just called him an asshole. He knew it wasn't possible because it just wasn't possible. He knew that. And yet, even though it wasn't possible that the driver had called him an asshole, the driver had in fact called him an asshole. He knew that, too. So he knew it couldn't have happened and he also knew that it had happened. Hence, his initial confusion.

"What . . . did you say?"

"I said don't call me asshole, asshole."

Now he laughed, because it was so impossible it was actually kind of funny. And then the adrenaline hit and the confusion ended and things became perfectly clear. He loved this shit, for some reason, almost as much as he loved making money. Close encounters of the fucked-up kind. His wife called them run-ins—his confrontations with waiters, parking garage attendants, the people sitting next to them in restaurants or behind them in theaters—and she hated them. To him they were like training exercises, a way to keep his edge when he was away from the office. The world was full of people who didn't keep their shit tight and he considered it his duty to straighten them out when the opportunity presented itself. The way he looked at it, he was a force for good, trying in his own small way to make the city a more organized, efficient, and civilized place by coming down hard on dopes like this driver, who thought they could say anything to anybody.

"You might as well drive straight to the unemployment office, motherfucker, because you just lost your job."

He started to dial the dispatcher, but the driver reached back and snatched the BlackBerry out of his hands. Two things about this amazed him—that it happened at all, and how quick the driver moved.

"Are you out of your fucking mind?" he said. "Give me my phone."

But the guy didn't give him the phone. Instead, with the same lizard quickness, the driver grabbed his wrist and yanked him forward. He came off the seat awkwardly and found himself kneeling, with his arms over the front seat. The driver banged on the handcuffs and shoved him back into the corner. Then a pistol appeared.

"You're going to sit still and keep your mouth shut," the driver said. "Do you understand?"

The barrel of the gun was a small black hole, deep as a well, and he couldn't take his eyes off it. What would he see if the driver pulled the trigger? Would he see the bullet? Would he see a small flame? Smoke? Anything? Was it a real gun? It looked real. The handcuffs were real, heavy and solid. What the fuck was going on?

"Are you robbing me?"

"I told you to keep your mouth shut."

"I've got eight hundred in cash on me. If you take me to an ATM I can get you another thousand or so. There's a limit on daily withdrawals."

The driver ignored him and eased back into the traffic. Was he being kidnapped? Is that what this was? But why him? He was just another trader. Sure, there were the Caribbean accounts, but nobody knew about them. Nobody. And kidnapping never worked in the States, anyway. Ever. It was a booming business in South America, but the FBI didn't put up with that Wild West shit. He rattled the cuffs. Maybe it was a joke. There was nothing funny about the driver, but that was the point, wasn't it? The more he thought about it, the more it seemed right. And he had a pretty good idea whose strange sense of humor was at work here—Christensen, that lunatic fucker. He had weird friends and he was always talking about crazy stunts, like the time he sent a bunch of hookers to his brother's wedding or the time he had one of his cop buddies pull over his ex-wife's new boyfriend and search his car with a drug-sniffing dog. The driver was exactly the kind of thug Christensen would know. They probably went to kindergarten together. "He's a great guy," Christensen would always say when he introduced one of these characters. Later on, he'd casually mention that the great guy just did a year for beating up a nun, but it wasn't really his fault because he was on acid at the time and he thought the nun was a hallucination. Real handcuffs, real gun, real criminal at the wheel—this was Christensen at his excessive best, no doubt about it. So how should he play it? He'd been pretty cool so far, and that was a good thing. There was probably one of those lipstick video cameras running. Christensen expected him to fall apart, piss his pants, maybe even cry. Then he'd e-mail the clip to everybody and they'd all have a good laugh. Well, sorry to disappoint.

"Listen, pal, I don't know who you are or who you're working for, but there's no reason we can't be civilized about this. Why don't you let me buy you a drink? There's a joint on Broadway and 97th, McGuire's. It's dark and the bartender hates everybody who comes through the door. You'll fit right in. We can sit in the back and negotiate a figure that works for both of us."

"I told you to shut the fuck up."

"Eat shit. I'm offering you a deal here." This was actually pretty great, a perfect chance to show people how tough he could be. They'd send the clip around, all right, but they wouldn't be laughing at him.

The driver left the highway at a pullout just north of 86th Street. He put the car in park and turned to face the backseat. The gun appeared again.

"You're not listening to me, douche bag," said the driver.

Jesus, where'd Christensen meet this guy? His head was the size of a cinder block and he had a lumpy scar that started in the corner of his left eye and ran down to his neck. The gun was like a toy in his big meaty hand. A bone-snapper with a rock for a heart. Born scary. Unless he was an actor.

That was also a possibility. The city was full of them, all colors and sizes. He met a few when Heather took an acting class in the Village. Losers, every one. Broke, delusional, dedicated to their art, and destined for oblivion. He used to take them out to dinner, ten at a time. Fucking babies. They ate like Teamsters. Did anything to pay the rent. This guy probably did children's theater in Brooklyn on the weekends, playing ogres and talking trees. He was good, though, really good. There was an emptiness about him, something missing, like a soul.

"Look, man—"

The driver cracked him across the forehead with the barrel of the gun. Blood gushed into his eyes and down the front of his suit. Dazed, in pain, he put his cuffed hands to his head. They came away slippery and warm.

"Oh . . . shit . . . what the fuck . . ."

"Am I getting through to you, now, asshole?"

"Christensen . . ." The blood kept coming.

"What?"

"Practical joke . . ." His white shirt wasn't white anymore.

"A joke? You think this is a joke?" The driver coughed up an ugly laugh. "Trust me, motherfucker, this ain't no joke. You made somebody very unhappy. Now you just lie there and bleed quietly."

Back into the traffic, his head throbbing. Who was unhappy? Who was this fucking unhappy? He had pissed off some people over the years, but who hadn't? Business was business. He'd been beat a few times himself. You suck it up and move on. You learn from your mistakes and let it go. You scream a little, maybe a lot, maybe you even make some threats. But that's it. You take the hit. And you try not to get beat again. There was always more money to be made.

Nobody got rough. Not really. He'd heard stories, but he figured they were just that, stories. Christ, the blood wouldn't stop. He went back over his side deals—no way this was company business—from the last couple of years. What about that Australian, Elliott? He was a hothead, for sure. But if he was going to get crazy he'd do it himself, in person, no hired help. The South Africans? The Koreans? The Russians? All had reasons to be unhappy, all had threatened him in some way. But it was mostly bullshit about going to the SEC. It had to be the Russians. They lost the most. They were the scariest. But the driver wasn't Russian. Wouldn't they use one of their own people? It was hard to think, his head hurt like hell. If he could just think it through, he could figure this thing out. He could fix it, he knew he could, if he could just get to his office, get out of this goddamn car and get to his office, make a few calls, talk to people, say the right things. He had to make a deal with the driver. That was the first step. There was $25,000 in cash in the safe in the apartment.

"Listen to me, I can pay you. Ten thousand. Cash."

"You're some piece of work, you are," the driver said.

"I know what this is about. I know who you're working for. There's been a misunderstanding. I can fix it, but I have to make some calls. I have to get out of this car. I'll pay you."

"You think you can fix this? You can't fix this. This is unfixable."

"Where are you taking me? Who are we meeting?"

"Your maker."

"Twenty thousand. Cash. It's in my apartment. On the East Side."

"Thanks for the raise. Now shut the fuck up."

"Twenty-five thousand. All yours. The Russians will never know."

"What Russians? What are you talking about? And why are you talking at all?"

The driver turned up the radio as loud as it would go, reached back, pressed the gun against his knee, and pulled the trigger. It was like being hit with a sledge hammer and stabbed at the same time. He screamed and the driver screamed with him. The people in the car next to them looked over and saw the driver screaming. Just another crazy New Yorker.

"Everybody's always talking about the Russians," the driver said. "I don't get it."

Pain now. And the back of the driver's head and the radio voices and the great steel towers of the George Washington Bridge and his bloody suit and the handcuffs and the back of the driver's head and his eyes closed and the car moving faster and his knee with the bones shattered and on fire and the car moving faster and a little dream about the river and then moonlight and then, yes, just a little better. Okay, the driver didn't want to hear it. But he was just the driver. There was bound to be another guy. There was always another guy, the guy who was really in charge. That was the guy he had to think about it. He was a serious guy, obviously hardcore. It wouldn't be easy and it wouldn't be cheap. All right, fine, whatever it takes. He could have it all. Yes, that was it. Give him everything. The Caribbean accounts, the Florida house, all of it. What the hell? Why not? He'd make it all back again eventually. And more. No way the guy turns down a deal like that. Four million total, maybe more. Not the most money in the world, but enough, a nice pile. The knee was bad, but he could live with it. Get a new one. Titanium. No problem. He'd be back on the tennis court in a few months.

They drove up the Palisades Parkway a few miles to a defunct rest area, its entrance blocked by a chain strung between two posts. The driver bumped over the curb and went around the post on the right. A hundred yards in was a small parking lot that overlooked the Hudson. There was a low wooden guardrail and ten yards beyond it was the edge of a cliff. Beyond the cliff there was nothing, just a 350-foot fall to the rocks. The guardrail had a gap where one of the crossbeams had been cut out. The driver stopped the car in front of the gap. He took a handkerchief from his pocket and wiped down the steering wheel, the gear shift, and the front seat.

"Is your boss here?"

"He'll be here in a minute," the driver said.

"Good, I need to talk to him. We're going to straighten this whole thing out."

"Glad to hear it. Now sit back and relax."

To keep the car straight, the driver rigged a piece of rope between the steering wheel and the brake pedal. He used a chunk of stone for the gas pedal and it all worked just like it was supposed to.

PART II

UPTOWN

PART II

THE QUANT

BY RICHARD ALEAS

Times Square

I t was night, and the trading floor outside Michael
Steinbach's office was empty. The TV screens suspended
from the ceiling, which had been playing CNN and
CNBC nonstop throughout the day, were turned off. But
around the perimeter of the floor, from behind closed doors,
you could still hear the rapid patter of keyboards in use.
Traders keep trading hours; hackers keep hacking hours.

Steinbach himself was a hacker, though he'd been known
to put on the occasional position himself, just to show he still
knew how. He'd written the original trading system the company used and devised the first of the company's quantitative
trading strategies, a pairs-trading algorithm that looked for
mispricings across global equity markets. Arbitrage opportunities were few, small, and short-lived—but with a powerful
enough set of computers hunting for them, you could make a
business out of exploiting the handful you could find.

And a business is what Michael Steinbach made. Starting
with a few million dollars from a single large investor, he par-
layed his original pairs-trading strategy into a billion-dollar
fund with a dozen different strategies and a staff of nearly one
hundred. Each year, the company's Human Resources team
identified the top graduates in math and computer science
from the country's best universities with the same single-

minded efficiency his computers used in locating trading opportunities on the world's securities markets. Each year, the firm interviewed several hundred prospective employees; each year, the firm made zero, one, or two offers—no more— to join their quantitative research staff. A job as a quant at Quilibrium Investment Partners, L.L.C. was a prize not easily won, nor lightly cast aside.

Which made what Simon Kurnit had to do that much harder.

He stood with one hand poised to knock on Steinbach's door, the other hovering inches away from the knob. It's not that he had any doubt about the decision he'd made—he just dreaded having to break the news. But there was no way around it.

"Yes?" Steinbach shouted when Kurnit knocked.

Kurnit stuck his head into Steinbach's office. "Is this a good time?"

Steinbach lifted his PDA from his desktop, glanced at it, and laid it down again. "For a few minutes."

Kurnit came in. Steinbach's desk was covered with papers, a mixture of computer printouts, pages torn from professional journals, and post-it notes filled with jagged scrawls. The man looked nearly as messy as his desk. His hair was nominally parted but flew away from his scalp in several directions. The whiteboard on his wall was covered with formulas and figures, and his fingers were smeared with its erasable ink. But the appearance of disorder stopped at the man's eyes, which were penetrating and intense and felt as though they were systematically peeling you apart like a lab experiment on a dissection tray.

"What?" Steinbach said.

"Listen," Kurnit began, "I'm sorry to do this—I wanted to

tell you sooner—but . . ." He raised his hands, palms up, hoping for a sympathetic nod, a gesture, something—anything—that would make this easier. But he didn't expect any help and didn't get any. "I really appreciate what you've done for me—"

Steinbach's eyes narrowed. "You're leaving."

"I don't want to," Kurnit said. "Honestly, I'm happy here, you pay me well, the work's good. If it were just me, I'd stay forever—"

"But you're leaving."

"You know Maureen's been looking for a teaching position, and it's just . . . they're hard to find in her field. NYU's not hiring and Columbia, they just, they won't hire you onto the faculty if you got your degree there, it's their policy . . ."

"You make enough money," Steinbach said. "She doesn't need to work."

"It's not the money," Kurnit replied, "it really isn't. It's just . . . she's a teacher. That's what she does, it's what she's always wanted to do. She put it on hold for me, for my sake; she spent the past five years here for me, but now . . . she got an offer from the University of Texas in Austin. It's a good offer and . . . I've got to do this for her. You understand."

If Steinbach did understand, he gave no indication of it. His face, generally affectless to begin with, was entirely blank. Except for those eyes, ticking away, trying to get under his skin.

"I've been offered a position at Blackshear. It's not as good as the job here, but it's . . . it's fine. I'll do fine. Obviously, I won't take any of the algorithms I've developed here—I hope that goes without saying. I'll start fresh there, do all new work. You've got my word." Kurnit paused. "I'm sorry to leave this place, I'm sorry to leave *you*, but . . ." He didn't have an end for the sentence, so he just stopped, looked up, and waited for Steinbach to say something. Anything.

Steinbach looked at his PDA again. "I've got a call in three minutes."

Kurnit took an envelope out of his pocket. "I don't know if you need a formal letter of resignation, but I wrote one, just in case. I'm giving thirty days notice, but if you need more— even, I don't know, sixty days—I'm sure I could get Blackshear to agree."

"Thirty is fine," Steinbach said. And he reached out across the desk. At first Kurnit thought Steinbach was reaching for the letter, but after a second he realized the man was trying to shake his hand.

He stepped forward cautiously, reached out, shook.

"Simon," Steinbach said, and something like warmth came into his voice, though it didn't sound at all natural there. "You've done excellent work for us. Without you, we wouldn't be trading warrants at all, and you know you're responsible for most of the alpha in our foreign exchange strategy. It'll be a real blow to lose you. The one thing I ask is that if anything changes, you remember you've always got a home here."

A *home*? Quilibrium offered its employees many things: the possibility of making a fortune, the chance to work in an exciting, fast-paced environment, intellectual challenges . . . but no one would have used the word "home" to describe it, and certainly no one had ever heard Michael Steinbach talk about it in those terms.

Kurnit looked into Steinbach's eyes and saw nothing there—nothing bad, nothing good. It was like looking into a computer screen after the plug has been pulled.

"I appreciate it," Kurnit said. "You've always been good to me—"

Steinbach released his hand and turned back to his keyboard. Whatever warmth there had briefly been was gone. Kurnit waited for a moment before deciding that Steinbach had, with his customary grace, ended the conversation. Well, no matter. At least he'd gotten it over with. And it could have gone worse.

Kurnit stepped to the door. "Closed or open?" he asked.

"Closed," Steinbach said.

When Kurnit had left the office and drawn the door shut behind him, Steinbach lifted his PDA again, screwed a foam-covered earpiece into his ear, and tapped a few times on the screen with a stylus. He had to let the phone ring seven times before it was finally picked up. It was only 9 o'clock, but the man sounded as though he'd been woken up.

"Perlow?"

"Who is this?"

"This is Michael Steinbach."

"Oh, Mr. Steinbach, I'm sorry." The voice woke up in a hurry. "What can I do for you?"

"Simon Kurnit just came into my office to quit. He says he's following his wife to Austin, where she's accepted a teaching job."

"Aw, jeez." Silence. "Did he say where he's going?"

"Doesn't matter. He's not going anywhere. We need him here. And there's no fucking way he's taking what he knows to one of our competitors. Period."

More silence. "What do you want me to do?"

"Kill the wife," Steinbach said.

Alec Perlow had graduated from Amherst with a 4.0 GPA,

but his degree was in English and Comparative Literature and he could no more have programmed a computer than he could have stepped off the ledge outside his window and flown. Nor did he have the mathematical skills to be a quant or the personality to be a trader. But he was smart—*Quilibrium smart,* as they liked to say in the office when evaluating a candidate (*Yes, he's smart . . . but is he* Quilibrium smart?)—and Steinbach himself came out of the interview saying they had to hire the kid. So they hired the kid. But what to have him do?

At the time, the company was small, just a few dozen people, and Steinbach couldn't launch half the strategies he wanted to, not without doubling or tripling in size. And good luck getting a quant or a trader to spend time on recruiting. So that's the job they gave to Perlow. While they were at it, they dumped the rest of Human Resources on him, too: benefits and space planning and employee relocation and, well, who the hell knew what else, but there was plenty of it, plenty of work that wasn't financial or technical but needed to get done in a firm this size. And Perlow got it done. Exceptionally well. If there had been grades in the world of business, he'd have maintained his stellar GPA.

He also excelled in another dimension, and that was loyalty. He was good at keeping his mouth shut. Everyone in the firm knew this, not least of all Steinbach. It's why they could trust him with all personnel matters, even the delicate ones.

When a trader needed to be poached from a rival shop, it was Perlow they called, and only Perlow knew about it until the news broke over AP and Reuters. When an offshore investor was in town overnight and needed tickets to a sold-out Broadway show, it was Perlow's extensive Rolodex they mined—he knew every scalper in town. And if this investor wanted a little in-room entertainment after the show, there were entries in his Rolodex for that, too.

What of the really sensitive matters, the rare cases that crossed the boundary between merely questionable and flat-out illegal? Well, Perlow was a prudent young man—no tell-tale entries in the Rolodex for men who would eliminate an employee's wife, say. But that didn't mean he didn't know such men, or that he'd never had cause to retain them.

He kept a steel cashbox in the bottom drawer of his desk, out of which he now drew ten thousand dollars in non-consecutive hundreds. One of the benefits of being a billion-dollar financial firm was the close relationships you had with all the big banks in the city. Occasional favors were traded in confidence; nothing illegal, understand, but merely agreeing not to record the serial numbers of a *de minimis* cash with-drawal, where's the harm in that?

This was the cash with which Perlow paid his scalpers and his procurers, and it was the cash that would wind up in the pocket of the man Perlow was e-mailing now, one anony-mous Hotmail account talking to another across the Internet.

New job, the message ran. *Ten men want to meet you this afternoon to discuss it, and ten more will want to talk with you next week after it's done. F&J's at 3 p.m.?*

The reply came in half an hour later: *OK*. That was all.

Perlow grabbed his coat, rode the elevator down to the street, and walked out of Quilibrium's offices into the heart of Times Square. The crowds were swarming beneath the giant computer-controlled video screens and animated signs. Fifty years ago, the signs would have been advertising singers and cigarettes and stage plays and such, but now in one direction you saw the giant Nasdaq board pouring out its endless torrent of stock quotes and in the other you saw the Morgan Stanley ticker streaming its financial data across the side of a building. Not to mention the Reuters screen and the Lehman Brothers ticker and . . . hell, even the sign in front of Toys "R" Us periodically flashed the stock prices of Disney and Mattel. This was the twenty-first century Times Square, and Alec Perlow couldn't get enough of it. Wall Street wasn't confined to Wall Street anymore, and it wasn't confined to fat middle-aged guys in suits either, with their Harvard MBAs and their secret handshakes. Now there was room for a new type of company to shake things up, as long as it had the right technology and the right people and the right contacts—and even an English major from Amherst could be part of it, if he found a way to carry his weight.

As he crossed the narrow concrete mall separating Seventh Avenue from Broadway, he saw Simon Kurnit coming the other way, a couple of folded-up cardboard packing boxes in his arms. Alec waved at him as he went past, got a smile and a nod in return. *Poor bastard*, Alec thought. *But who the hell told him to quit?*

Kurnit dragged the roll of packing tape across the top of the box, cut it off, and pressed it down. At this point, his office was basically packed—what was left were papers that belonged to the company and a few items too large to pack. He lugged the box to the corner of his office and lifted it onto the stack already there. He dialed his own phone number one-handed while uncapping a Sharpie with the other. The marker squeaked as he wrote his name and new Texas address on the side of the box.

Maureen answered on the first ring. "Hello?"

"Darling, it's me. I'm finishing up here. I should be able to leave in, I don't know, ten minutes."

"Is that a real ten minutes," she asked, "or one of those ten minutes that turn into an hour because Michael asks you to do something as you're walking out the door?"

"Michael's not here. He left early for some charity benefit. Put on a suit. Even combed his hair."

"So it's a real ten minutes."

"Yep."

"I can count on it."

"Yep."

"As in, I can order food now and you'll be there to pick it up before it's all cold and disgusting."

"Yes," he said. They had this conversation nightly, and neither of them actually meant the mock annoyance in their voices. Except when they did.

"I'm going to order Chinese, okay?"

"Sure." He snapped the cap on the marker and dropped it on his desk. "Get me beef with broccoli—no, wait, if I got General Tso's would you have a little?"

"I'll get you beef with broccoli," Maureen said, "not spicy, with brown rice. And I'll get General Tso's chicken for myself."

"I'll pick it up. In ten minutes."

"Fifteen's okay."

"I love you."

"But not twenty. I love you, too."

"See you soon," he said.

Kurnit left the office twenty-five minutes later—he hadn't meant to be late, but there'd been e-mails to answer and an exit interview HR insisted on his filling out before he left.

Fortunately, he lived close to the office, on West 44th Street near Ninth Avenue, and the restaurant was just down the block. He raced over to the place and caught his breath while the pregnant woman behind the counter sorted through a batch of bagged orders to find his.

"Beef with broccoli, General Tso?" She repeated this to herself while peering at the characters scrawled on the receipts stapled to each of the paper bags until finally she found the one she was hunting for. "Beef with broccoli, General Tso chicken. Twenty-one fifty." He counted out three bills and pocketed the change she handed back to him.

It still felt warm, for whatever that was worth. Maureen had probably allowed an extra ten minutes before calling in the order. She usually did, even when he told her it wasn't necessary, because, well, it usually was.

At the front door to his building, a squat fourteen-unit co-op with paired fire escapes zigzagging down the front, Kurnit had his keys half fished out of his pocket when a man in a black turtleneck swung the door open. He was carrying a bulging plastic garbage bag and held the door as they squeezed past each other in the tight vestibule.

"Good night," Kurnit said. The other man didn't say anything.

The building was pre-war but it had an elevator, a relatively recent addition that had added two thousand dollars to their monthly maintenance bill for a year. Kurnit stripped off his gloves and crammed them in his coat pocket as the elevator slowly carried him to the fifth floor. He still had his keys in his hand.

Normally Maureen would make it to the door before he had both locks open—the sound of the Medeco was enough to bring her running, especially when there was food and he was late. But not this time. Kurnit dropped the bag of Chinese food on the small table next to the door, hung up his coat in the closet, and locked the door.

"Darling?" he called.

He carried the food into the kitchen, popped the staples holding the bag shut, and took two large plates down from the china cabinet. Two forks, two serving spoons. He tore off two paper towels to use as napkins.

"Honey?"

He carried the plates to the table in the dining area, a corner of their L-shaped living room. He flipped on the ceiling light. "I'm sorry I'm late. But the food's not cold. Yet."

He returned to the kitchen to get the two aluminum trays containing their main dishes, the two cartons of rice, the paper-sheathed pairs of chopsticks, the cellophane-wrapped fortune cookies. He dropped it all on the table.

"Maureen? You okay?"

Finally, he went into the bedroom.

It was a week before Simon Kurnit returned to his apartment, and when he did he had to strip off the yellow police tape on the way in. The apartment was silent and dark, and he sat at the table in the dining area without turning on the light. Someone had thrown out the Chinese food and Windexed the tabletop. He could smell it.

His back ached. He had a headache, too, and he hadn't shaved that morning or washed his hair when he showered. He'd just stood under the water, barely feeling it though it was turned as hot as it would go.

The company had put him up in a hotel room—a top-of-the-line suite at the Edison with windows facing out over Central Park—while the lawyer Perlow dug up (*Find him the best in the city*, Steinbach had said when he and Perlow had shown up at the holding cell. *Not the second best, the very best)* got him straightened out with the police. He'd had Maureen's blood on him, all over his hands and shirt, and it was natural to take him into custody even though he'd been the one to phone 911, even though he was obviously distraught, even though the knife was nowhere to be found. Many husbands who kill their wives are distraught, and many of them find a way to dispose of their knives before 911 arrives.

But the lawyer, a man named Neville, Stephen J. Neville, was able to get him out, and they tucked him away in the Edison under a false name so the reporters from the *Post* and the *Daily News* couldn't find him. They found him anyway, but since he didn't come out of the building, didn't answer the phone or the door, they eventually gave up and left him alone. There were other murders to write about, after all.

Perlow testified that he'd seen Kurnit in the office around the time the murder was estimated to have taken place, and the e-mail logs supported this. Picking up the takeout food added another few minutes; a cop who spoke Chinese got confirmation from the woman at the restaurant. Then, too, there was the fact that the bedroom had been thoroughly ransacked and some large items—a DVD recorder, Maureen's laptop, her jewelry box—were missing. Kurnit told them about the man he'd passed in the vestibule, the stranger with the bulging black garbage bag, large enough to hold a DVD recorder and a laptop and a jewelry case. They either believed him or they didn't, but they let him go. He hadn't formally been charged, and Neville told him he wouldn't be.

But what did it matter? He didn't need the police to

charge him or a jury to judge him guilty. He knew he was.

Twenty-five minutes.

So it's a real ten minutes.

Yep.

I can count on it.

Yep.

He had touched the man, they had passed belly-to-belly; he'd been polite, said goodnight to him. While upstairs Maureen was bleeding to death. Or had she already been dead by then? If so, for how long? Ten minutes? Fifteen?

He'd thought he couldn't cry anymore, he'd thought this repeatedly over the past week, but he'd been wrong every time and he was wrong now. The tears ran down his face like water. His chest heaved. He made no sound. Just sat in the dark sobbing and asking himself what had been so goddamn important that it couldn't wait till tomorrow, what e-mail was worth Maureen's life.

They'd sent him flowers, the company had, and the card that came with them was signed by everyone in the office. Steinbach had written, *Take as much time as you need. You've always got a home here,* and he remembered their conversation the day he told Steinbach he was leaving. A home. A home was the one thing he didn't have, that he'd never have again.

Would ten minutes have made the difference? Would five? If he'd walked in on the man while he was filling his bag, could he have stopped him? Or would he be dead now, too, lying side by side with Maureen in that chilly basement morgue? It didn't sound so terrible to him. Not nearly as terrible as sitting here in their dark apartment, alone, afraid to open the bedroom door.

He slid the closet door open instead, ran his hand along

the coats, lifted the sleeve of one of hers, inhaled deeply. There was no smell of her, but it was her coat, it had held her once, and he pressed it to his cheek as though some residue of her might still be there. Outside, on the street five stories down, cars honked, some drunk shouted at them, life went on. In here, the radiator thumped and clanked as the heat came on, hissing. But it all sounded to him like whispers from a thousand miles away.

He counted the money in his pocket, thought about where, this time of night, he could get a quiet drink, some private spot where no one came and you could sit by yourself and if you cried a little no one would say anything. There was a bar two blocks away—he'd brought Maureen there once but she hadn't liked it, hadn't liked climbing two flights of stairs to get there and another flight if you had to use the bathroom; she said it felt like some old, decrepit, falling-apart relic from the '40s, and she was right, that's exactly what it was, it's what he liked about the place, but he'd never made her go there again. Yet she'd been there once, on the stool next to his, and if that stool held no more of her ghost than this coat did, so what? So what?

Then, when he got back, he'd brave the bedroom.

When he got back.

He locked the door behind him and headed to Frankie and Johnnie's.

It had been a speakeasy once, or anyway that's the story they told. Perlow liked it because except at theater time it was generally pretty empty. Middle of the day, you just had a few lonely retirees keeping the bartender company, and coming up on midnight you'd have the place to yourself.

At the top of the stairs, the little coat check room was

open but no one was manning the counter and the metal rod in the back had nothing on it but hangers. Perlow walked past and pushed the main door open. To the left was the bar, to the right a handful of tables where your more upscale customers could order some food with their drinks. When he'd given Mesh the assignment, they'd sat at a table so they could talk without the bartender hearing, but this time there was nothing to say, and Mesh was waiting for him at the bar.

Mesh was an older guy, well into his fifties. He still had the wooly sideburns he'd grown out when they were the hot new look around the time of the Bicentennial, only now they were white, like the rest of his hair. He had a paunch and his face was deeply grooved, and sitting at the bar in his windbreaker and turtleneck, he could've been any guy in any bar, taking home $375 a week from some union job. But he was taking home lot more than that, and they hadn't found a way yet to unionize what he did for a living.

Perlow dropped the Duane Reade bag he was carrying at the foot of the empty stool next to Mesh's, stripped off his coat, draped it over a chair back. He wasn't going to stay long, but one drink, maybe two, would give Mesh time to finish the one in front of him, settle his bill, quietly pick up the bag, and exit. They hadn't arrived together and wouldn't leave together.

The bag contained an envelope and the envelope contained the full 10k he'd promised, even though Mesh had been sloppy this time, had been seen. Perlow had wanted to dock him for that, give him maybe a ten percent haircut just to make a point, but when he suggested this to Steinbach, Steinbach had said no, that's not the way you do business. A handshake is as good as a contract, that's the way Wall Street works—billions of dollars change hands on a handshake, and if you say you're going to pay someone ten thousand dollars you don't show up with nine. You try that and pretty soon everyone knows and no one will do business with you.

Probably just as well. Guy like Mesh got unhappy with you, he might do worse than just stop doing business with you.

"What'll you have?" The bartender wiped down the spot in front of Perlow, though it was plenty clean. Just a way to keep his arm occupied, something to do while waiting for an answer.

A *beer*, Perlow was about to say, *make it a Heineken*, but the door swung open then and Simon Kurnit walked through it.

It didn't register at first. Perlow, from the office—all right, everyone at Quilibrium worked late some nights, though this late was pretty extreme. And the guy next to him who glanced up and quickly turned away—just a guy, though there was something about him. Kurnit stood in the doorway, holding onto the door, thinking, *I can't just walk out, it would be rude,* but also thinking that the last thing he wanted right now was company, was Perlow from the office, was—

Then it did register. The turtleneck. The sideburns. The face. Perlow, glancing over now at the other man, a look of panic flashing across his face. It was a moment of complete clarity. It felt to Kurnit as if he'd been walking on the surface of a frozen lake and, without warning, plunged through into the icy water beneath.

"You— You—" he said, but Perlow was facing the other way, raising his hands, saying something to the other man, who was reaching into his windbreaker with one hand, pulling out a black handgun, leveling it at Kurnit. Perlow was saying, *No, you can't shoot him, we need him,* and wrestling for the gun, one hand on the man's wrist, the other on the barrel itself, and the words "we need him" went echoing around in Kurnit's head.

He didn't move. He was rooted to the spot, watching the men fight over the gun, and it was only when the gunshot exploded in the confined space, smashing a bottle and sending Perlow backward over his stool in a spray of blood, that Kurnit found his legs again. He stumbled back against the door and fell into the hall outside as a second bullet splintered the doorframe. Getting to his feet, he scrambled for the stairs, grabbed the narrow banister, and flew down, two steps at a time, slipping, almost falling, ducking his head as he heard the clatter of footsteps behind him. He reached the landing, used the banister to pull himself through a tight 180-degree turn, and started down the steep second flight to the street.

Halfway down he missed a step. He felt his heart catch, his breath stop. He swayed for a moment in midair, tipping forward, headlong. It was suddenly silent, it seemed to him— there were no more footfalls, no shouted voices behind him, just the world tilted precariously and swinging up at him. He put out a hand to catch himself, and his fingertips raked a row of framed black-and-white photos of forgotten Irish tenors off the wall as he fell.

He felt his leg snap under him, but when he came to rest against the street door at the foot of the stairs, he was only conscious of the pain in a distant way. He was facing up, and he watched as a pair of sneakers came into view on the highest step he could see, then the legs of a pair of brown corduroy pants, then a hand holding onto the banister, a plastic Duane Reade bag hanging from its wrist. The man kept coming, picking his steps now with care. The zipped-up bottom of the windbreaker descended into view, then the other hand with its gun, the barrel pointed down at him, and finally the man's chest and face. Kurnit's heart was racing, fluttering; maybe he was going into shock. He watched the gun barrel come up and the finger tighten on the trigger and then the second pair of feet at the top of the stairs, and the second pair of legs, and the second gun, this one a long-barreled shotgun. And the man before him, the one who had murdered Maureen, the one his own company—my God—had *paid* to murder Maureen (*No, you can't shoot him, we need him*), the man who was going to kill him, too, this man spun to face the threat behind him and lost his balance and may well have died from the fall, but the blast from the bartender's shotgun didn't give him the chance.

In the hospital, Kurnit refused visitors, refused newspapers. He only turned the television on to watch *Jeopardy!*, and even regretted doing that the one time a teaser for the evening news showed footage of Michael Steinbach leaving a courthouse, Stephen Neville at his elbow.

He hesitated at the door to Steinbach's office. The cast had come off and he'd switched from crutches to a cane, but he still felt it each time he put weight on the leg, and he took a moment to arrange himself before he lifted the handle of the cane and used it to rap sharply against the wood.

"What?" Steinbach shouted.

Kurnit turned the knob and went in. He knew Steinbach was alone; his assistant had left at 5:30 and no one else had gone in during the half hour he'd been watching.

He limped across the office to Steinbach's desk, where the man waited, his face showing no expression except perhaps a trace of impatience. There was a chair off to one side of the desk, and Kurnit lowered himself into it, extended his left leg so the knee wasn't bent. It stiffened up less that way.

Steinbach stared at him, dissecting him. Kurnit stared back. He'd thought he wouldn't have the patience for this, but suddenly he found himself extremely calm.

"We're glad you're back, Simon," Steinbach finally said.

"I just want to know one thing," Kurnit said, and his voice didn't shake at all. "How could you do it? How could you possibly . . . ?"

"I don't know what got into Perlow's head," Steinbach said. "He must have—"

"No," Kurnit shot back. "No. Not Perlow. You. Perlow did what you told him to do. That's all he ever did."

"I never told Perlow to hire anyone to kill Maureen. I would never—"

"Stop it. Stop it. I'm not an idiot. You always say you hire people because of how smart they are, so how about treating me like it? I'm not wearing a wire, we're the only people here, and I want an answer. I think you owe me that."

Steinbach's eyes flicked back and forth across his. He was hunting for something. Trying to decide whether Kurnit was lying or not? He wasn't, and Steinbach apparently satisfied himself that this was the case.

Steinbach turned back to his desk, hunted briefly through one of the stacks of papers, found a recent P&L report, and tossed it at him. "Strategies you developed or worked on generated $84 million over the first eleven months of this year. You're a valuable employee."

"So . . . you kill my wife?"

"I didn't kill anyone," Steinbach said. "But speaking hypothetically? For $84 million? Let's analyze this rationally.

Put some numbers to it." He leaned back in his chair. "With her alive, we have a zero percent chance of keeping you. Remove her and your main incentive to leave has been eliminated. Now, there is some chance, call it twenty-five percent, that you decide to leave anyway, maybe quit working entirely, and there's maybe another twenty percent chance that the whole thing blows up and you find out what happened, but that leaves a fifty-five percent chance of keeping you, and those are better odds than we've had on trades that ended up making us a lot money. You tell me, what would the fair price be of an option that improved the odds from zero to fifty-five percent of keeping a man capable of generating $84 million a year? Actually—" he tapped on the screen of his PDA a few times, dividing and multiplying, "$91.6 million if you annualize. I haven't run Black-Scholes, but I can tell you it's worth a hell of a lot more than the sum of what Randall Mesh, Stephen Neville, and the Edison Hotel charged. Now, you've got to factor in the risk-adjusted cost of fighting the charges if things do blow up—as they did—and that's not cheap. And then you've got to assign some amount to the catastrophic risk, however small, of going to jail. But it still comes out an expected-value winner."

Kurnit sat in silence.

"I don't imagine you can look at it objectively right now," Steinbach continued, "but if you do look at it objectively, you'll see what I'm talking about. It's like the distressed securities business—a company's going bankrupt, the owners are behaving emotionally, you go in and price the trade accurately, and if the numbers come out positive you pull the trigger. Now, in this case it didn't work—it failed to work pretty spectacularly, in fact. But that doesn't mean it was a bad trade. It just means it was a trade that moved against us. So you count your losses and move on. I'm telling you this, Simon, for two reasons." He ticked them off on his fingers. "The first is that you asked, and you're right, you deserve a straight answer—whether you can handle it or not is up to you. The second is that I think you *can* handle it. You're angry, I understand that, but you're a rational man and extremely intelligent and I think you can put that aside and come back and be just as strong a businessperson as before."

"What odds would you give it?" Kurnit asked, and this time his voice did shake, but he didn't care. "What odds that I can come back and be a strong businessman for you?"

Steinbach considered the question seriously. "Thirty percent. Which may not be great, but it's not a trivial percentage."

"No," Kurnit said, "that's not trivial."

He got slowly to his feet. Leaning on his cane with one hand, he reached into his jacket pocket with the other. After getting out of the hospital, the first place he'd made his way on his crutches was back to Frankie and Johnnie's. He couldn't navigate the stairs, of course, but he'd called ahead and the bartender had come down to meet him. Kurnit wanted to thank him, he'd explained, and maybe the bartender would've come down for that reason alone, but he'd also told the man he was looking for someone who could hook him up; he didn't need anything like the shotgun the bartender kept under the bar, just something he could keep in the night table at home, something to give him a little peace of mind. *Not a problem*, the bartender had said, *I know a guy.*

The handgun Kurnit took from his pocket now was smaller than the one Mesh had used, and older, too, but still powerful for all that, and it frightened him to look at it, to hold it, to point it at another human being. Strangely,

Steinbach didn't seem frightened at all. A little exasperated, maybe; a little angry.

"Come on," Steinbach said. "Think about this rationally. There's zero chance that you could shoot me and get away with it. Literally zero. And what do you stand to gain?"

"A little peace of mind," Kurnit said quietly.

"Peace of mind?" Steinbach shouted. "You'll be on trial, you'll be in jail, you'll be on the front page of the fucking *New York Post*—what do you think the odds are that you'll have anything like peace of mind?"

Kurnit found himself crying again as he pulled the trigger.

"Thirty percent maybe," he said, though Steinbach could no longer hear him.

MAKE ME RICH

BY LAWRENCE LIGHT

257 W. 36th Street

Make me rich." Russ Ickes, newspaper reporter, whispered the code words into his cell phone. His heart began to thump faster. The insider trading scheme had been going so well. But things had changed.

"And?" Trip Pennypacker's cool drawl sounded in Russ's ear with the tiniest hint of impatience. You wouldn't detect it if you didn't know Trip well.

Russ felt himself starting to sweat. "Make me rich," he stammered again. He didn't understand why Trip insisted he still use the identifying code. Surely after all these years, Trip knew his voice. Russ himself would know Trip's voice from just one syllable.

"You're repeating yourself. You're calling me late, after the market close, and I'll have to use after-hours trading. That's more conspicuous. What's up, champ?"

"We have to talk, Trip." Russ could actually hear his heart. His eyes zipped around the busy newsroom. No one seemed to be noticing him.

"I'm a little tied up now." Trip had been too busy for Russ ever since they were in college. "What do you have for me?"

A squall of perspiration had erupted on Russ's forehead. He took a shaky breath and choked out the red-alert code. "Trip, there's Barney Rubble."

"Barney Rubble?" Very little ruffled Trip, the guest of honor at the unending party that was his life, but he was ruffled now. "Barney Rubble, you say, champ? What kind of Barney Rubble?"

Russ grimaced from the saltwater sluicing into his eyes and from a sudden, stinging memory. Right after college, and before he started on Wall Street, Trip and his friends had jetted over to London for a fling. During their whirlwind of intoxication and fornication, they had encountered cockney rhyming slang, where "going to the Jack Tar" meant "going to the bar," and "having Oedipus Rex with a twist and twirl" meant "having sex with a girl," and "brown bread" meant "dead."

When Russ picked up Trip and his pals from their return flight—Russ hadn't been invited to the London blowout—they were joking away in rhyming slang. The revelers, who hadn't bothered to bid hello to Russ or thank him for the lift home from the airport, suddenly started calling their driver "jam roll." Russ laughed along, as if he was in on the joke. He stopped laughing when Trip playfully told him it meant "arsehole."

Years later, when they set up their deal, Trip decreed they use cockney rhyming slang as an addition to their code, although he didn't remember many of the rhymes. Russ did. They were burned on his brainpan as if by sulfur. "Barney Rubble" meant "trouble."

"Big trouble, Trip, federal trouble," Russ whispered. His heart slammed in his chest like an industrial press about to overheat. Huge wet blobs from his forehead rained on his keyboard. He skidded his chair back from the desk. "The U.S. Attorney's office called. They want me to come in."

The flat-out uncoded statement hung spinning in the air.

Trip stayed eerily silent for a full minute while Russ listened to his hyper heartbeat. Russ was about to ask if Trip was still there when Trip said, "Come see me right now."

The familiar self-possession was back in Trip's tone. He might have been telling one of his female admirers to pay him a late-night visit. No one refused Trip.

"I'll be right over."

"Didn't you forget something?"

"What? Forget something?"

"What do you have for me?" Trip asked nonchalantly.

"A time like this, do you think that—?"

"What do you have for me?"

"I . . . Okay, Chimera Genetics. But if we're accused of insider trading—"

Trip hung up on him—to arrange, Russ knew, for the purchase of shares of Chimera Genetics. Chimera was an under-appreciated stock that had been flatlining at ten dollars for the past year, but when investors read Russ's bullish story in the next morning's newspaper, extolling Chimera's new wonder drug in final clinical testing with federal approval imminent, that would change fast. They would bid the stock price up much higher, and Trip would be there to sell his shares to them, and to skim a creamy and very illegal profit.

"Are you all right, Ickes?"

The words were like an electric shock, and Russ swung round in his chair. John Featherstone loomed above him, disdain contorting his face as though he'd bitten into bad meat. "Are you all right?" his editor asked again.

"Who, me?" Russ sputtered. "I'm fine. Fine, fine, fine." He shook his head to banish a disorienting image.

On the fifteenth of every month, outside an exclusive

and vaguely dangerous club called Inferno, Russ met Trip's business partner, Mr. Abercrombie. Abercombie, a Gothic beast of a man, would emerge from the club with a fat envelope of cash for Russ. He scared Russ witless, and seemed to know it, as he always asked the same question before disappearing back into Inferno: "Are you all right, Ickes?"

Hearing those words from his editor was an unnerving jolt. Unlike his old editor, forced into retirement now, Featherstone didn't appreciate Russ's journalistic talents, and usually treated him the way a cop does a juvenile delinquent. Concern wasn't part of the equation.

"Well, you don't look fine. You're sweating like a pig, Ickes."

"Uh, I'm not feeling well," Russ said, aware that vast wet blotches had spread from his armpits. "I better go home."

"First you're fine, then you're not—what am I going to do with you, Ickes?" Featherstone examined his waterlogged underling with gimlet eyes.

"I-I better go then," Russ said. He got up.

"Well, your column is in, and it was . . . adequate. So Chimera Genetics is about to skyrocket, huh?"

"That's what they say." Russ grabbed his Italian suit jacket from the hanger hooked to the cubicle partition. He slipped it on to hide the damp stains mottling his handcrafted shirt.

"Hmmmm." Featherstone tilted his head skeptically and peered at the reporter with the intensity of an engineer searching for a fatal structural design flaw. "Nice threads. You're certainly dressing better lately. How much did this suit cost?"

Bile rose into Russ's throat. He swallowed back the burning acid. "Uh, it was a gift. My birthday was last week. The big three-oh."

"You used to dress like you shopped at the Salvation Army."

The khakis Russ once wore were innocent of pressing and dry cleaning. Now his tailored trousers had creases sharp enough to slice a finger. "Things change, I guess."

Slumping through the newsroom, Russ passed a cluster of other business reporters near the Bloomberg machine. None of them liked him, and he suspected they were jealous of his having "Street Talk." Someone muttered, "Brain Distrust," and they laughed.

Eighteen months ago, when Russ was angling for the "Street Talk" stock tip column, he'd sought visibility by telling people he was the great-grandson of Harold Ickes, the FDR Brain Trust guy. For whatever reason—maybe for his pedigree—the paper's top brass gave him the column. But the publication had its share of nasty people, and they all had long memories, and not long ago—just after Labor Day— Russ had learned why lying to journalists was unwise. Someone on staff dug up that Russ Ickes was no relation to Harold. It was late October now, and when Russ passed through the newsroom, he ignored the snickers and walked on.

There was a bustle around the Metro desk, and Russ paused there. Another young woman—another pretty blonde—had been pushed off a subway platform onto the tracks and into the path of an oncoming train. This made it five. The murders had happened randomly at stations throughout the city, always late at night and with few witnesses. The cops had no leads. Russ thought about the trains roaring out of the darkness and the helpless figures on the tracks. A shiver went up his spine.

The air outside was bracing. It was past 8 o'clock, and the evening rush had subsided. With the sodden shirt chilling his skin, Russ moved moodily along the pavement. He had to compose himself before he saw Trip, but he couldn't slow his pounding heart.

He wandered in slow motion through Midtown, and wondered how to handle Trip. People pushed past him with purpose and places to go. So many of them were stylish and good-looking—so much like Trip.

Russ's mouth was achingly dry, and he looked down the block. He was approaching Inferno—Trip's favorite club—and he knew it wasn't just by chance. He sighed. He could use some liquid courage before facing Trip.

The beefy guard at the velvet rope wore a red greatcoat with black leather lapels. He was as welcoming as Russ's editor. "We're full," he said.

"Come on—this place doesn't get going until midnight." Russ produced a hundred-dollar bill. "Come on . . . please."

The guard regarded the bill as he might used toilet paper. "We're full."

"I was here three weeks ago." This had no impact on the guard, but Russ pressed on. "I was here with my friend, Trip Pennypacker."

The guard's eyes narrowed. "You a buddy of Mr. Cool's? He knows people here." He unfastened the velvet rope and Russ pocketed the hundred and stepped forward. The guard's face turned stormy. He stopped Russ and reached into his pocket to extract the bill.

The only other customers inside were three Japanese businessmen. The club's craggy, cavelike walls were red, and paper flames flickered everywhere. By 3 a.m. the joint would be jammed with writhing dancers. Russ ordered a twenty-dollar Scotch from the scantily clad barmaid and remembered that Saturday night with Trip.

It was only because Russ had complained that he never got to see Trip that they had gotten together at all. Trip had grudgingly agreed to let Russ join his friends for dinner at Per Se—with the proviso that Russ not give his real name or say how they knew each other. Russ sat ignored by Trip's trendy friends, and watched as a devastating blonde ran her hands through Trip's hair and her lips over his neck.

The only thing Trip said to Russ the entire evening was that the two of them would split the check. Russ's half was astronomical. Afterward, Russ tagged along to Inferno. He paid for a round of drinks—another enormous sum—and Trip and his friends vanished among the dancers, leaving Russ to get plastered by himself and at a huge price.

As he sat at the lonely bar now, Russ recognized the bartender from that night. Her little outfit was red leather. "Good to see you again," he said to her as she put the glass in front of him. "I was in here Saturday, three weeks ago."

"Great," said the barmaid, who clearly saw nothing great in Russ.

Many men would be staring at her cleavage. Russ fastened onto her bored eyes. "I was here with Trip Pennypacker."

Her blasé expression changed into something Russ couldn't read. "Trip, huh? He's your pal? You like him?'

"Trip? Sure—he's the smoothest guy I know. Handsome, smart, charming, and the girls all think he's pretty sexy."

"Yeah?" she said. "And what about you? Do you think he's sexy?"

"Me? Well, I, uh . . . Do you remember me from that night?"

"I remember—you were the little guy who bought drinks for Trip and his worshippers. Who was the bitch with him that night?"

"The blonde? Tiffany something. She's a model. He has a million of them."

The woman leaned over the bar, her breasts bulging against the red leather. "Listen," she said, "Trip has run through too many girls in this place." She made a fist and Russ guessed that included her. "And some of us are plenty pissed at him."

Russ's face burned, and his throat went tight. "Really?" he croaked.

"Really. And the thing we all learned about your pal is that Trip cares about just three things: Trip, Trip, and Trip. When the chips are down, you can count on that asswipe to be first out the door." The barmaid unclenched her fist. "Why they keep letting him in here is beyond me."

Russ swallowed hard and forced some air into his lungs. "Is it because he's friends with Mr. Abercrombie?"

She pulled away from Russ. "Don't know the guy. Never heard of him."

He fished another hundred from his pocket. "Tell me who owns the club. Is it Abercrombie? Someone else?"

The barmaid eyed the bill, then held out a hungry hand. "Just a hundred?"

Russ brought out two more bills. "Deal?"

The barmaid took the money; it vanished in the pocket of her little skirt. She shimmied her bare torso. "Some people you never want to mess with own this club, baby. So there—I've given you a valuable piece of information." The Japanese businessmen growled at her and she sashayed off. As she did, she turned back to Russ. "Better run along before I tell them you're asking questions."

If the barstool had turned into burning brimstone, Russ couldn't have scrambled off it faster. He left the club at a near run, and didn't slow until he reached the subway.

Russ looked up and down the nearly empty platform and remembered the chatter at the Metro desk. Just the kind of setup the city's latest serial killer favored, he thought. Ten yards away, a heavily pierced, waiflike woman with spiky peroxide hair eyed Russ warily. Was she thinking about the killer, too? Was she wondering if it was him? Russ shook his head. No way, he thought, he didn't fit the description.

All anyone knew about the killer was that he was white and big. No one had a clue about his motives, but several criminal psychologists opined in the media that he probably felt rejected by women and was striking back. Why pretty blondes was anyone's guess. Russ didn't know whether the guy went after peroxide blondes, too, but the pierced girl was taking no chances. She stayed well away from the platform edge—right up against the wall—as most women did these days. Pretty blondes, Russ thought, just the sort that Trip favored.

The Queens-bound train roared into the station with a hurricane rush of air. Russ stepped into the car and sat heavily on a plastic bench. The pierced girl got into another car.

As the subway rocketed into the tunnel, Russ thought about Trip and his ever-present women. He remembered the time, a year after college, when he let himself into Trip's apartment and found his friend having sex with a girl on the living room floor. Russ had stood there mesmerized until she started screaming and Trip started shouting. Trip had never before lost that famous composure. After that, he took away Russ's key. He told Russ that he didn't want to see him again; that he was tired of him. This despite all Russ had done for him: the laundry, the errands, the rides to the airport. It counted for nothing, and Russ was cast out.

Until a year ago. Then, comfortably ensconced writing the "Street Talk" column, Russ had called Trip with a proposition. Finding him hadn't been hard—Russ had followed Trip's life avidly—but getting up the courage to call was a different matter. When he finally did, Trip treated Russ like a bill collector. "Is it something quick? I'm just on my way out." It hadn't been quick, but as Russ explained to Trip how "Street Talk" could bring them fortunes, Trip had found his patience. And that old charm. Now, Trip acted as if the idea was all his own.

The train slid into the station. Russ sighed raggedly and left the car. The platform was deserted. Long Island City cleared out by nightfall. The station's old walls were as grimy as ancient evil. He trudged up the stairs. A dark forest of empty buildings greeted him. One sheet of newspaper spiraled spectrally down the deserted street. Despite the cool breeze off the dark river nearby, he was sweating again.

Russ stood before the slab of an office tower that housed Pennypacker Securities. At age thirty, Trip owned his own company. Office rents were cheap in Long Island City. Trip had leased two floors in a good building. Russ unclipped the cell from his Prada crocodile belt and, with shaking fingers, succeeded in stabbing out Trip's number. He hadn't loaded it into speed dial for safety reasons. "Make me rich," he said when Trip answered. "I'm downstairs."

"Come on up."

Russ scrawled illegibly in the book, and the wizened security guard didn't give it—or him—a glance. He took the elevator to the top floor. He had visited Pennypacker Securities only once before. Now, as then, an icily beautiful redhead met him at the elevator and escorted him back. Russ knew her name was Beatrice, and he followed her through a brightly lit area with circles of desks that resembled his news-room. Young men barely out of their teens were working the phones with demonic energy. Russ recognized one of them from that night out on the town. He had Trip's confident, preppy panache.

"Sir, this stock is about to pop," he said. "And we can get you in on it."

"The road to financial security, ma'am, is built on know-ing which stocks are hot," said another, nearly identical, young man.

"Yes, I hear what you say, sir," said yet another, a clone of the first two. "But understand I am going to build wealth for you. This is a once-in-a-lifetime opportunity."

Beatrice knocked on the open door to Trip's office. Russ peered in. The office was swathed in darkness, but he could make out Trip's silhouette. He was facing a broad window, looking out on the hypnotic Midtown skyline to the west. Russ looked too. There was the newspaper. There was Inferno. There was Russ's new apartment. So many places Russ would rather be.

A Tizio lamp clicked on. Mr. Abercrombie sat on a long, sleek sofa. The lamp, a small furnace, lit the stony crags of his broad face. He turned to look at Russ, and gave what might have been a smile. The light caught his gold tooth and it glinted. He wore a black leather jacket and a crimson tie. Monster hands, matted with hair, rested lightly on his knees, as though poised to grab. "Are you all right, Ickes?" he asked. The almost-smile vanished. "You look like you swam here."

Russ opened his mouth to respond, but no words came out. He heard Beatrice close the door behind him. He was alone with them.

Trip turned around. His sculpted hair was the color of

champagne, and that amazing grin was, as ever, a treasury of enticing enamel. His shirt had exquisite blue striping—stitched in London, Russ knew. With a dancer's grace, Trip took his seat at the steel-and-glass Boltz desk that held his laptop and phone.

"Take a load off, champ," he drawled. Russ sat in the chair in front of Trip's desk. Trip grinned at him. "Now, what's all this I hear about trouble?"

Before Russ could speak, Mr. Abercrombie got to his feet. He loomed above the desk and straightened his leather lapels. "I'll let you fellas have your talk," he said, and he stabbed at Trip's phone console with a thick finger. "Bea, baby," he rumbled at the phone, "whip up one of those cappuccinos of yours for me, okay, hon?" And then he winked at Trip and was gone.

"So, tell me all about it, champ," Trip said when the door had shut.

Russ licked his arid lips. "I told you, I got a call from the U.S. Attorney's office. They want me downtown, tomorrow at 10."

"Did they say what it was about?" Trip was supernaturally calm.

"Not a word. But what else could it be?"

How could Trip keep smiling? "Let's assume, for argument's sake, that it is about . . . our arrangement. What are you going to tell them?"

A high-pitched hysteria invaded Russ's speech. "I'm not going to admit that I'm involved in an insider trading scheme, if that's what you mean," he squeaked.

"And you're not going to mention me either, right, champ?"

"Of course not. If it comes up, I'll say that we went to college together but that I haven't seen or heard from you for years. Unless . . ."

Trip's smile blinked off. "Unless what, champ?"

"What if they have some evidence? What if they have your trading records, and see that you bought those stocks the day before the 'Street Talk' columns appeared in the paper? Then what do I do?"

Tapping a finger on the glass desktop, Trip nodded slowly to himself. "They'd still have to prove a link between you and me."

"How hard is that? I write about a stock, you buy the stock right before. Sounds like a link to me."

"They won't have my trading records, champ. The stocks and the cash go through so many cutouts and offshore accounts—the feds don't have enough accountants to even get to first base."

"But they could know that there was unusual activity in those stocks just before my columns came out. They could know that *someone* was buying or selling, even if they don't know who. They'll figure *someone* benefited."

"Sadly, champ, they will likely conclude that that someone is you. So I wish you the best of luck."

Russ's face grew slack. "What . . . what are you telling me, Trip?"

"I'm telling you, champ, that I don't want to see you again. I have better ways of making a buck." Trip favored him with another smile.

"You . . . you bastard. You ungrateful bastard!" Russ was yelling now. "Who do you think you are?"

Trip's smile took a malevolent twist. "I think you'd better get out of my office before Mr. Abercrombie comes back."

Russ glared at him. "Listen, you self-centered son of a

bitch!" he shouted. "I'll tell the feds every little last bit about you. I'll destroy you!"

"You can prove nothing. Get out."

"No? You don't think I recorded our calls? I'll give the tapes to the feds, and tell them what the code words mean. It's your voice on the other end of those calls, Trip. And we have credit card charges for the same amount at the same time at Per Se. I bought you drinks at Inferno. People there saw us together. All that sounds like a link to me."

Trip jumped to his feet. His eyes flared and his perfect lips drew back in a snarl. In all the years he'd known Trip, it was only the second time Russ had seen him lose that famous cool. A vision of the first time flashed in Russ's brain—Trip's bare back, the sweat in his blond hair. Trip smacked his hand on the desk, and the vision vanished. He was screaming now.

"You're nothing! Nothing, nothing, nothing!"

Russ gathered his breath. "Or maybe," Russ said, his voice shaking, "maybe I could gut it out and protect you. The feds can't have proof that I bought and sold those stocks—because I didn't. They can accuse all they like, but without proof . . . Maybe this is all just a fishing expedition."

Trip spread his hands on the glass desktop and trapped his ire behind a set of white teeth. "You'd protect me?" he asked.

"I would, Trip. But we'd have to be much more careful about things. And I'd need more money."

"More money," Trip repeated. He nodded to himself and drummed his fingers on the desk. Then he looked at Russ with a sly light in his eye. "We'll take it out of Abercrombie's share. I'll make an excuse about why the count is lighter. He's not that smart."

Russ's eyes widened. "But what if he objects? What if he

wants to see some proof—trading tickets or account state-ments?"

Trip laughed nastily. "The guy wouldn't know a trading ticket if it jumped up and bit his ass, and he has no clue about how the market works. I could show him my cable bill and he wouldn't know the difference. Look, if he complains, I'll tell him we're suspending operations until the heat is off. You and I will keep on with our arrangement, and I'll pass you the cash directly."

"And if, somehow, the feds *can* link us? What then?"

Trip gave a graveyard laugh. "Then we give them Abercrombie. We tell them he forced us—threatened us at gunpoint. I mean, the guy has a criminal record like a phone book. Who are they going to believe—him or us? We just have to stick together, champ, just like we always have."

Russ paused, gulping air. His vision was blurry and his voice was trembling when he spoke. "Trip, I . . . Don't you know how I feel about you?"

Before Trip could do more than raise an eyebrow, there was a rap at the door. Beatrice looked in. "Your Los Angeles call," she said.

Trip grinned and glanced at his watch. "No rest for the weary, champ. And anyway, you'd better get going. Don't want to be seen loitering around here, after all. Unless there was something else . . . ?"

Russ's throat closed up. "Nothing else," he said, then bolted through the door. There was no sign of Mr. Abercrombie, and Beatrice said nothing as he hurried by. In what seemed like no time he was in the empty subway sta-tion. He leaned back against the dirty tiles and tried to calm himself. Images of Trip reeled through his head.

He heard a low rumble and felt the building wind of an

oncoming train. He smelled something acrid and opened his eyes. He wasn't alone on the platform anymore. Mr. Abercrombie towered over him. And behind him, steaming with anger, stood Trip.

Abercrombie's massive hand closed around Russ's slender arm. "Get the other one, Trip," he said.

Trip recoiled. "Are you crazy? I shouldn't even be down here. You were supposed to take care of this yourself."

"I said, get the other arm." The fiery menace seethed out of Mr. Abercrombie, and Trip took tentative hold of Russ's other arm. Russ felt the tremble in his hand.

"What are you doing?" Russ cried as they dragged him to the edge of the platform.

"You know the feds will crack you like a walnut, champ." Trip's voice was soft in his ear. "And I just can't let that happen. I like the income stream from you, but the risk profile is up too much."

The subway train sped into the station, a thirty-five-ton, stainless steel behemoth with harsh eyelike headlights. It rolled at them with inhuman force.

The train was almost upon them when Mr. Abercrombie dropped Russ's arm and, with amazing agility for such a big man, took Trip by the throat. Trip let out a shriek and let go of Russ, who stumbled backward, away from the platform edge.

Trip's hands flailed feebly at Mr. Abercrombie. His gorgeous teeth were bared in pain and panic. Mr. Abercrombie lifted Trip from his feet and tossed him to the tracks.

The subway motorman looked up in horror to see someone stumbling off the platform. He hit the horn and then the brakes. The first car shuddered as it bumped over the body, and the cars kept rolling past amid the brakes' banshee wail.

Mr. Abercrombie took Russ by the arm again and hauled him out the turnstile and up the stairs. Russ followed the massive form numbly, along the empty street and into a black car parked in an alleyway. Mr. Abercrombie got into the driver's seat and started the engine. "We gotta get out of here."

"Trip," Russ whispered.

"I gotta hand it to you, Ickes," he heard Mr. Abercrombie say through a fog, "you had him pegged—how fucking quick he'd be to sell me down the river if he thought the feds were coming through the door. No fucking loyalty at all. I hate that. You had him pegged, all right. And that crap about the U.S. Attorney calling—that was nice touch, just like the thing with the intercom. Bea kept the line open and I heard the whole thing. You did okay tonight, Ickes—a real brain trust."

Mr. Abercrombie's huge hands worked the wheel. Sirens broke the night, coming in their direction. Russ felt water coursing down his waxen cheeks, and it wasn't sweat. Abercrombie's rumble filled the car.

"Bigger cut for everybody without Trip, and I won't have to listen to the girls at the club complain no more either. And truth is, I was getting tired of that attitude of his. *Not that smart.* Sheesh, what an asshole."

"I wanted to tell him—"

Three cop cars zoomed past, a carnival of light and noise. The black car continued toward the Queensboro Bridge. Russ sighed and Mr. Abercrombie shook his head.

"Like you said, Ickes, he served his purpose. And the way he treated you—an old friend like you—it was long overdue. It'd been me, I'd've taken care of it long ago. He had it coming, so enough with the guilt already. You can't blame yourself. Trip is brown bread. Dead." Mr.

Abercrombie glanced over at Russ. "Are you all right, Ickes? Are you crying?"

"I wanted to tell him . . ."

"Hey, cheer up, pal—everything's gonna be fine. We're gonna make mucho bucks together, you and me." With something almost like affection, Mr. Abercrombie dropped a gorilla hand on Russ's shoulder, near his windpipe. He turned and looked at Russ. "Come on, champ. Make me rich."

ROUGH JUSTICE

BY JAMES HIME

200 Park Avenue

I should be sitting here trying to figure out how to say goodbye to my wife.

Instead, I'm sitting here thinking I should have known the wheels were fixing to come off this thing the instant I spit that cough drop onto the Contessa's nipple in full view of the Hell Bitch.

That was all the omen a man could ask for.

I get to my feet and look down at Katy, all hooked up to her feeding tubes and what have you. Laid out like some old person. Instead of the vibrant and amazing young woman I married not all that long ago.

All I can think to say is, "I'm sorry, darling."

She looks at me and her eyes are wet. "Don't, Billy. Please don't."

She reaches for my hand and I let her take it and squeeze it and hold it to her sunken cheek, and I can feel her tears on my skin.

I bend down and kiss her forehead and whisper that I love her, and then I retrieve my hand and walk out of the hospital room and take the elevator down and go outside and hail a cab. I tell the driver to take me to the NYPD's Midtown North Precinct house.

That's when I see the guy walking toward me with his hand inside his coat.

I need to back up some. To the Day of the Cough Drop Incident. To what happened that afternoon.

And to what happened even before that, on the morning of the Incident.

And, come to think of it, to what happened the night before that . . . .

It happened in the Hell Bitch's office on the afternoon of the Day of the Cough Drop Incident. Half the floor could hear it and it was horrible.

It was the complete works. Screaming, invective, cussing. What a fuck-up I was. How I had embarrassed her and the firm in front of one of our most important clients, a woman with connections across the Continent. Who would no doubt tell the story of my faux pas to many extremely rich and important people, potential clients, who would make up their minds on the basis of that anecdote alone never to do business with us.

On and on it went.

I sat across the desk from her and played mental rope-a-dope. Covered my ego with a blank expression and watched the spit fly from the Hell Bitch's mouth as she yelled at me and I wondered why I hadn't had sense enough to pursue a career in dentistry. Wondered what made me think coming to Wall Street to practice law in-house at a secretive private bank was a good idea in the first place.

When she started to wind down I thought, *Well, there's no time like the present.*

I said, "Okay. For at least the fifteenth time, I apologize.

I'll write a letter of apology to the Contessa. I'll offer to have her dress cleaned. But there's one more thing you need to know. Something else happened this morning."

I told her about my ride uptown with Stu Spagnoletti, and I watched the fear and paranoia rise up in her like a fever. When I was done, her eyes were wide and her hands were shaking and she looked like a clown in some carnival of the deranged.

She stood, pulled herself erect to her full five feet, and screamed, "GET OUT! GET THE FUCK OUT!"

I was only too happy to oblige.

On my way back to my office I stopped by Frank Biallo's. I'm not even sure why. Maybe just to be in the presence of a fellow sufferer. As I got there, the guy who delivered the interoffice mail, a stooped old man who wore a blue smock and whom everybody called Sarge, was walking out and taking the helm of his mail cart.

I looked in just as Frank was fishing an inner-office envelope out of his inbox. It bulged oddly. Frank opened it and extracted a paper ball. He smoothed it out on his desk and examined it and looked up. "I guess Stecher didn't like my memo," he said.

"I have a suggestion."

"What's that, Tex?"

"Let me go to my office and call home. Then let's you and me go get drunk."

Frank hesitated. He looked at the crumpled paper on his desk. "I think maybe I'd better stay here and do some rewriting."

I shrugged. "Suit yourself, podna." I turned to go.

"Hey, Tex?"

"What?"

"You okay?"

I grinned. "Fine as frog hair."

When I got to my office I called Katy. "I'm not completely sure but I may have just gotten my ass fired."

"Oh, Billy. I'm so sorry. Maybe it's for the best."

"Maybe."

"Why don't you come home?"

"In a while. I want to go for a walk. Maybe get a drink."

"I've got good news."

"Yeah?"

"Stu already found work for Hiram. And a place for him to live."

I hesitated. "Great. What's he doing?"

"Limo driver."

"Katy? I need you to tell Carmen something and ask her to pass it along to Stu."

"What, honey?"

"Stu asked me for a favor this morning. Tell her to tell him I'm sorry, but I don't think I'm going to be able to deliver for him."

"Okay."

When I hung up I checked my e-mail. There was one from the Hell Bitch, sent after I'd left her office, telling me to be at a working group session on the Park Avenue deal the next morning at 10 o'clock. I thought, *Great. Guess I still have a job after all.*

But I knew there was no point in hanging around there the rest of the day—I was fried. I shrugged on my suit jacket and overcoat and headed out into the blizzard.

That's the night the Hell Bitch disappeared.

But for that storm I doubt there would have been any Cough

Drop Incident to begin with. So blame it on the execrable New York weather.

The morning of the Incident the snow had started at daybreak and I found myself standing on the sidewalk outside my apartment building trying but failing to hail a cab, and by that time the streets were a mess. After I'd been at it ten minutes I looked at my watch and decided maybe I'd best just walk. I was of course utterly unaware that, before the day was out, I would perpetrate a cough drop assault on a client and then endure the cussing-out from the Hell Bitch that I have already described.

A black Town Car slid to the curb and out of my building came Stu Spagnoletti, accompanied by a guy who looked like he could bench press the Brady Bunch. They were both dressed in double-breasted overcoats and fedoras and they made straight for the Town Car, but when Stu saw me he stopped and said, "Billy!"

"Stu."

"You tryin' to catch a cab? A cab, you're never gonna catch in this fuckin' weather, okay? C'mon. We're goin' uptown. We'll give ya a lift."

Stu headed for the Town Car but I hesitated.

Stu looked back. "C'mon! Get in, before your balls freeze off out here!"

I followed him into the car.

Behind the wheel was another slab of beef who looked at me in the rearview mirror. If it wasn't a hostile look then I would not particularly care to see a hostile look from this hombre. Stu leaned forward and said, "Jimmy. On the way uptown we want to stop at 200 Park." Stu looked at me. "That's where this fancy bank of yours is, right?"

I did not even want to know how Stu came by this information. "Yeah."

"Okay." Stu sat back. Adjusted his overcoat. "How's Katy? She doin' any better?"

"Thanks for asking. I'm afraid not."

Stu folded his arms over his chest and looked at me sternly. "She wants that you should be around more often. This she says to my wife."

"We've been real busy at work lately."

"This she also says to Carmen. So. Tell me about this problem of yours."

"You mean Hiram?"

Stu dropped his hands in his lap. "Who?"

"My brother-in-law."

"Naw." Stu slapped at the air with a paw that was covered in black leather. "Get to him in a minute. I'm talkin' about this crazy woman at the bank. Your boss."

I looked out the window. We were crawling up Park Avenue. If I had just trusted my instincts and walked I would have been there by now. And my throat was starting to feel scratchy. *Need to stop off at the newsstand, get some lozenges before I go upstairs.* I cleared my throat and looked at Stu. "She's just a little high strung, is all."

"High strung, huh? Show me a woman that's not. They're all outta their fuckin' gourds, you ask me. And it's made worse by this thing. This women's liberation, so-called. Now they want to be lawyers and doctors and priests and shit. They even got their own professional basketball league. It's bullshit, you ask me. I can promise you this, we ain't never gonna have no women partners in my line of work."

"What exactly is your line of work, Stu?"

"Oh, this and that, this and that. Which brings me to this other thing. Tell me about this brother-in-law of yours."

I shrugged. "We're not exactly what you'd call close."

"My wife says your wife says he's a good Joe."

"I suppose. For an ex-con."

"So the guy has done some time. Doesn't mean he's a bad person. Personally, I liked him. He and Katy, they came over for coffee yesterday."

"I heard."

"He's from some place I never heard of before and he talks funny. Aside from that, nothin' wrong with him that I can see. My wife comes to me, she says, 'Stu. Maybe you can help him out.' And I say, 'Sure. Why not?' My wife likes your wife, you know?"

"Glad to hear it."

"We're neighbors. At least we are until they're done with the construction at our house in Great Neck, see. Then we'll be movin' out."

"We'll miss you," I said, as convincingly as I could.

"Yeah. Same here. Been nice gettin' to know you some, these last coupla months."

I looked out the window and thought, *Stu, you don't know me at all and I intend to make sure it stays that way.* But I said nothing.

"So, anyway, neighbors should help one another out. Do favors. Like that. So I say to myself, 'Stu. You should help the man out, this Hiram from Nowhere with the funny manner of speech. Find him some gainful employment.'"

I looked back at him. "I'm sure Katy will be very grateful."

"Probably just minimum wage starting out. But maybe some, you know, possibility for advancement along the way."

I went back to studying the snowscape. We'd only gone as far as the lower 30s. Traffic had slowed to a crawl. I toyed with making some comment about Hiram being the first made guy ever from Arkansas but decided against it. "If he clears enough take-home pay to move out of my apartment, I'll be grateful too."

"Happy to do you a favor. Now I got to ask you about somethin' else."

I looked his way. He was studying me like a man might study the angles on a three-rail bank shot. "Okay."

"This deal you're workin' on. The air rights thing up on Park."

My ears were suddenly humming. "How'd you know about that?"

"Was in the papers."

"The fact that I'm working on it wasn't."

"All right. Have it your way, then. The Gerstens and my family, we go way back, see. And Ray Gersten comes to my old man and tells him you and this woman boss of yours are breakin' his balls with this thing. This right to back out after a year, they don't get their development plan through the P and Z. My old man comes to me and says, 'This young Texan. He's your neighbor at that nice apartment you just moved into, right? Maybe you should speak to this young man. Ask him to show a little flex on this. Do a favor for us and our old friends Ray and Ed Gersten.'"

I tried to think what to say but the humming in my ears had matured into a roar and my head felt like it was full of pea gravel. "Stu, I—"

He leaned over and put a hand on my arm. "If you could give us a little help here, my family would never forget it. Meantime, I'll talk to my people. Find something for this brother-in-law of yours to do. Get him out from under foot." Stu took his hand off my arm, pointed out the window. "I think this is your building."

I hadn't realized the car had stopped. I looked out the window and back at Stu. "Thanks for the ride."

"Don't mention it. But get back to me on this air rights thing. One way or the other. So I'll know what to tell my old man."

Fifteen minutes later I was sitting at my desk sucking on a cherry throat lozenge and staring into space. I don't remember getting out of the car or going into the building or buying the package of lozenges or going up the elevator. Somehow I had done all those things without having to think about anything other than the fact that I'd just had the arm put on me by a member of a known organized crime family concerning a real estate transaction on which I was the second chair lawyer.

The Gerstens and the Spagnolettis. Shithouse mouse.

My clients in this air rights transaction were what we euphemistically referred to as a "high net-worth family." This is Wall Street jargon for richer'n shit. You'd recognize the name if I were to mention it, but that I will not be doing. They'd made their money in tobacco and sold out long before the class-action lawyers came storming out of the sewer grates and sued that business back to the Stone Age. They'd invested a part of their fortune in Manhattan real estate, including a building on Park Avenue that had excess air rights. Rights that could, under the applicable zoning rules, support a building larger than what had been built there.

So my clients had done the smart thing and made a deal to sell these unused air rights to the Gersten Brothers, for hundreds of dollars per buildable foot, payable in part at closing and in part at substantial completion of the condo project the Gerstens aimed to construct. Condos in the East 60s, with views of Central Park West on one side and all the way to Long Island on the other. Condos with blue granite finishes and gold fixtures in the bathrooms. Condos they'd sell to rock stars and Saudi princes and captains of industry for three thousand dollars a foot if they sold them for a dime.

This was the deal that for the last three months had been my own personal galley ship, with the Hell Bitch cracking the whip.

It was Katy who gave her that name, by the way, inspired by Captain Woodrow Call's horse in *Lonesome Dove*. But her real name was Diane Martin. She was the bank's senior real estate lawyer, the woman I answered to. The woman who had taken it upon herself to ruin my life.

But back to the deal. The rescission right that Stu had mentioned was a part of the negotiations from Day One. If the Gerstens didn't get their condo development plan approved by the Planning and Zoning Commission within a year of closing, our clients could rescind the transaction—in effect, take back their air rights and return the Gerstens' purchase to them.

The Gerstens had howled about this at every opportunity. A year was a very short turnaround time at the P and Z, and their fear was that if they missed the deadline our clients would rescind the deal and sell the air rights to Trump or somebody for more money, because those rights would only increase in value with the passage of time.

But our clients had insisted on this term as a way of protecting their interest in the deferred portion of the purchase price.

I sat there, not believing the position I was in. Should I tell the Hell Bitch about this? If I did, it was sure to trigger a full-blown episode. She'd be bound and determined to go to the Gerstens' lawyer and have it out with him. She'd raise unshirted hell about this attempt to get to her through me, which would only poison the atmosphere between the two sides even more than it already was and make it harder still to get the deal closed.

On top of that, I had started to wonder about the Spagnolettis' motives. Was this simply a favor—however ham-handed—for their old pals the Gerstens? Or did they have an ownership position in the condo development? One that would make them an ass-pocket full of money if the project was successful?

I had asked the Gerstens' lawyer at least half a dozen times for a structure chart showing the full beneficial ownership of the limited partnership that the Gerstens had formed to buy the rights. The guy had done nothing but give me the Heisman.

It was going to be very hard indeed to say no to the Spagnolettis if they were looking to make money in the deal.

The whole episode had left me with a world class case of the nervous high strikes, and it just figured that when my phone rang it was the Hell Bitch's assistant calling. I lifted the handset. "Morning, Patsie."

"She has the Contessa with her and she has a question or two. Can you come up here please? And bring the closing binder."

"On my way." I popped a cherry cough drop in my mouth and stood up and pulled the closing binder down from my bookshelves and headed for the door.

We had represented a French Contessa earlier in the year when she had sent one of her gophers across the pond to buy her an apartment on Fifth Avenue. Two months and eight million dollars later, the woman owned three thousand square feet of prime Manhattan real estate. I knew the Contessa was in town and had been expecting that at some point I would get a call summoning me to the Hell Bitch's office to take her through the particulars of this transaction.

By the time I reached the Hell Bitch's three hundred square feet with commanding views up the island, I was a touch out of breath and sweating some. Made me wonder if I was fixing to take sick.

Please, God, not until after the Park Avenue deal is done.

Patsie showed me in. The two of them were seated at a conference table. The Hell Bitch was looking her most professional, wearing a blue dress that thanks to some optical illusion made her look slightly less chubby. The Hell Bitch had an on-again/off-again relationship with her grooming accessories and her makeup drawer—but today it was on-again. Her brunette hair was blown dry and combed and she'd even applied some cosmetics, not that any amount of makeup could do much for her jowly, bulldoggish aspect.

The Contessa looked like an older version of Gwyneth Paltrow. Blond hair, peaches-and-cream complexion, diamonds in her ears and at her throat and on her fingers. She was wearing a snow-white angora sweater dress that showed off a figure that might or might not have had something to do with her being royalty. She sat very erect and looked at me as a well-heeled guest might look at a doorman on her way out of her hotel.

The Hell Bitch made the introductions and I took the Contessa's hand and shook it carefully and allowed as how I was pleased to meet her. Then I held the closing binder up and said to the Hell Bitch, "What would you all like to see?"

The Hell Bitch said, "The Contessa is thinking of getting a pet and wants to see the relevant building policies."

"Got it." I flipped through the binder. "Okay. Here we are."

I walked around the table so that I was standing behind the Contessa and leaned over her and opened the binder and laid my finger along a line of text and said, "Here's what you can own without seeking permission—"

And just then the lozenge fell from my mouth. It made directly for the Contessa's sweater dress and landed on the very end of her breast. No Olympic gymnast ever stuck a better landing. A perfect ten.

Time froze.

I plucked the lozenge from the dress, and even though it was lousy with angora hair, I popped it back into my mouth and said, "—from the co-op board."

I looked at the Hell Bitch and she was staring at me with her eyes wide and a look of panic and disbelief on her face.

I said, "Maybe I should just leave you all with the binder."

The Hell Bitch said, "I think that would probably be best." Her voice was two octaves higher than normal.

I headed back to my office to wait for the inevitable Hell Bitch meltdown. Which, as I've already said, came after lunch that same day.

And which I had coming for once.

As I waited, I thought about how just yesterday, just YESTERDAY, I had for five minutes entertained notions that maybe life was going to get better around here after all.

By the time I'd left the Gulag the previous night it was almost 2 a.m., but I judged the day a good one on account of the Hell Bitch hadn't boiled over hardly at all. So with gratitude that it had gone smoothly, I sent out an e-mail transmitting the latest draft of the Park Avenue air rights P and Z agreement to the working group, powered down my laptop, slipped it into my Tumi bag, and headed for the elevators.

The firm's name is not really the Gulag, of course—that's just what us juniors called it. As I've said before, it's sort of a bank. But don't think Bank of America or Wells Fargo—it's not that kind of bank. And you wouldn't recognize the name unless your family is in the Forbes 400. Think of it as the First National Bank of No Man Is a Hero to His Valet. Because we only deal with the super-rich, and we deal with them when they're at their super-worst. Which is when they're obsessing about their money.

Along with the usual complement of bankers and traders, the Gulag has a large legal department, as big as some law firms. So that we can function as a full-service provider of all necessary services to our richer'n shit and secrecy-obsessed clients.

Which is how I'd spent my five years before the mast. Representing people who've got enough money to burn a wet mule.

I saw but one other lighted office on my walk through the dark halls of the Gulag, and I stopped and stuck my head in the door. Frank Biallo sat studying a law book, with his tie loose and shirt cuffs rolled up. He had suspenders on and he looked like a dealer in a back-room game of blackjack.

"Hey, Frank."

He looked up. His wire-rimmed spectacles caught the lights from the overheads. "Well, if it's not our token Texan and Diane's very own cowboy Friday. So, what's with this knockin' off early shit, huh? You never leave before me."

"I'm like the monkey that was fucking the skunk, podna. I've enjoyed about as much of this as I can stand. What's got you burnin' the 2 a.m. oil?"

"Memo on that transaction in Vail. Stecher wants it yesterday. So, how's your deal coming?"

"It's coming."

"And Diane? She still treating you good?"

"She's a paranoid schizophrenic with a hundred and eighty IQ who is in all likelihood demon-possessed."

"That's a bad fuckin' combination, Tex."

"But she can also get a man a managing directorship. If she doesn't kill him first."

"Or he doesn't kill her."

"Tell me about it. I sometimes think a hit would be a really good idea."

"You slurrin' my ethnicity, Tex?"

"Hell no. Last thing I need in my life is a bunch of watered-off *paisans*."

"You got that right."

"Good luck with your memo, podna."

"'Night, Tex."

"Hasta luego."

I stopped in the reception area and looked north through the plate glass windows at Park Avenue. I could just see it, way up yonder—a little building on the west side of the street, and all those beautiful air rights.

I glanced toward the sky. Clouds were moving in. Supposed to snow tomorrow, according to the weather sadist.

I missed Texas all the time but it was during the winters that I missed it most. In wintertime in New York, you see the sun maybe six hours a day and everything is gray and lifeless and depressing and the streets run with slush and even an extra fifteen pounds of clothes are not enough to keep you warm when the wind goes pounding down those canyons made by man and money.

I was soon in the back of a cab careening through the mostly empty Manhattan streets, headed for my tiny one-bedroom apartment near Union Square. The cabbie was attired in the kind of cloth headgear that has its roots in certain nomadic cultures, and he maintained a quiet and continuous cell phone conversation in a foreign tongue as he steered the cab with one hand and outside the tall buildings went by in a blur. I hung on as best I could and wondered if what I'd heard was true, that the most common cause for emergency room admissions in this town is accidents involving taxicabs.

And for aught that it was the wee hours and there were but few souls on the sidewalks, there was the ceaseless and implacable noise of New York, the cabbie mumbling and the radio tuned to 1010 WINS in the background and the sirens in the distance and the squeal of the cab's tires. New York isn't so much the City That Never Sleeps as it is the City That Never Shuts Up. So very unlike my boyhood home in South Texas where by that time of night even the coyotes have ceased carrying on and bedded down.

I got out near the corner of Fourth and 14th and paid the fare and walked through the lobby of my building, nodding at the doorman behind the reception desk. I rode the elevator to the seventeenth floor and walked down a dimly lit hall lined by doors sporting multiple locks and let myself into 17B only to find my living room couch occupied by an ex-convict from Arkansas who also happened to be my brother-in-law.

Seeing Hiram Redding in New York City at all was almost more of a shock than my system could handle. But here? In my living room? Drinking beer and watching porn with his feet up on my coffee table?

Hiram glanced my way and went back to his pay-per-view. He raised his can of Heineken in a mock toast. "What's doin', bro?"

I glanced toward the bedroom. Saw the door was closed. "Hiram? What are you doing here?"

"She didn't tell you I was comin'?"

"She hasn't said a word." I set my computer bag on the floor and shucked out of my coat and walked to the refrigerator. Opened it. I had one beer left. One beer out of the two six-packs that were there when I left the apartment that morning.

Great. I come home at 2:30 in the damn morning to find a convicted killer sitting in my damn apartment, drunker than a damn lord on my damn beer.

I took out the last beer and popped the top. Walked into the living room and dropped into a chair. "I didn't think your PO would let you leave the state."

Hiram sipped his beer. "I been a real good boy. Not so much as a parkin' ticket. I tol' her I needed to come up here, check on my little sister, since she'd took bad sick and her husband wasn't lookin' after her like he should. Even a PO is a sucker for a line like that. You always work this late?"

"If I have to." I looked him over. Prison tattoos he picked up doing fifteen in Tucker for second-degree murder. Stubble on his chin, just going to gray. Hair long and greasy and combed back. Wearing jeans and a wife beater. Alligator boots that looked to be older than he was. "You planning to stay long?"

"I might."

"We don't have a guest room."

Hiram patted the couch next to him. "Yeah you do."

"They don't know what's wrong with her, Hiram."

"She done tol' me that."

"Could be chronic fatigue syndrome. Lupus. Lou Gehrig's disease. She can barely lift her arms anymore. Has to take her food through a tube. Her immune system is for shit. She could get carried off by a cold if it was severe enough."

"She done tol' me all that too."

"Your PO has no clue where you are, does she?"

Hiram said nothing.

"Hiram? Why are you here?"

Hiram pointed at the television set. "Look at that ol' boy go. He's really givin' it to her, ain't he?"

"I'd appreciate an answer to my question."

"She said she thought I ought to meet your all's next door neighbors. They seem real nice."

"You're telling me you've met Stu and Carmen?"

"Me and Katy had a cup of coffee over yonder this evenin'. That Stu is one funny sumbitch. He talks like some guy in a gangster flick."

I took a drink and thought, *Jesus H. Christ.*

When I was done with my beer I slipped as quietly as I could into the bedroom. Undressed and got into bed. Listened to my wife's breathing. I used to be able to tell by how she breathed whether she was asleep or not. Anymore, I had no clue.

She ended the guesswork by saying, "I was planning to tell you, Billy. It's just that he showed up a week earlier than I thought he would."

"You could've called me at the office."

"You hate it when I call you at the office."

"I like it better than I do walking into my apartment and finding Mr. Murder-Two drinking my next-to-last Heineken."

"There's nothing for Hiram in Arkansas. I've been talking to Carmen about him. She thinks her husband can help him out."

I turned on my side, tried to see my wife's wasted shell of

a body by what little light there was from the clock radio. "Katy, I hate to be the one to tell you, babe, but that is a real bad idea."

"Why?"

"Because the Spagnolettis are mobbed up to high heaven, is why."

"You don't know this."

"Katy. Sweetheart. Everyone knows this."

"Carmen has talked to me some about their family businesses. They sound very legitimate to me."

"What businesses would these be?"

"Importing. Or exporting. Or something. I don't know the details. Carmen says Stu will try to get Hiram hired on, doing some kind of work, maybe over in Queens."

"Christ."

"You're too cynical, Billy. You weren't that way when we met. You were sweet and trusting. This city, the bank—that woman—they've changed you."

I leaned over and kissed Katy on her sunken cheek. "Well. I reckon. Now you should get some sleep. We both need some sleep."

"Okay."

But it was awhile before sleep carried me off that night.

Only to awake the following morning to a day that would start with a ride with Stu Spagnoletti, be punctuated by the Cough Drop Incident and a museum-quality Hell Bitch meltdown, and end with the Hell Bitch herself disappearing from the face of the earth.

The morning after all that happened we met for our 10 a.m. working group session on the Park Avenue deal, and that's when we noticed we were short one Hell Bitch. When she hadn't shown by 10:30, I left the conference room and chased her assistant down by phone. "Patsie, have you heard from Diane?"

"No. I haven't seen or heard from her since last night when I called a Town Car for her just before I left."

"Can you try her at home and on her cell, please?"

After that I had no choice but to go back in the conference room and get the meeting started. They were all there but the Hell Bitch, and by that I mean the Gerstens, their lawyers, and my client's representative, Manhattan celebrity broker Donnie Dominick.

The Gerstens' lawyer started right in about the Hell Bitch not being there.

"Where is she, anyway?"

"I honestly couldn't say. Her assistant is trying to track her down now."

The lawyer laid his pencil down on his stack of deal documents and crossed his arms over his chest. "Without her, we really can't get much done, can we? I mean, unless you're prepared to assure us that you speak for both her and your client."

We all knew what he meant by this. *Any deal we make with you, she's just gonna un-make at the next meeting, hotshot. Why should we waste our time?*

I looked at Donnie. He shrugged. I could tell he agreed with the Gerstens' lawyer.

"You want to reschedule?"

"Maybe we should."

Nods all around, and we broke up with plans to meet the next day.

Only, the next day? Still no Hell Bitch.

And at that point, I really had no choice.

I crossed my fingers and took control of the deal and gave

the Gerstens' lawyer the assurances he was looking for. Then I worked around the clock on the damn thing to resolve all the open issues, including the rescission clause.

Four sleepless days later, three things happened: I closed the Park Avenue deal; the Hell Bitch turned up graveyard dead, stuffed into a refrigerator in a vacant lot in the Bronx; and Katy was rushed to the hospital with full-blown pneumonia, damn near dead herself.

A week after they found the Hell Bitch's body, I was taking a break from my vigil in ICU at Presbyterian, headed down to the cafeteria in search of caffeine, when two NYPD Homicide detectives badged me by the elevators.

"Your office said we would find you here," said the older one, a short guy with a face like a basset hound, whose name was French.

"We're working the Diane Martin case. We wanna ask you a few questions," said his partner, a tall guy in spectacles with a prominent nose whose name was Reston.

"Can we do it over coffee?"

"Sure."

Five minutes later we were down in the cafeteria sipping coffee and French was talking to me while he consulted his notebook. "Ms. Martin's assistant says she called her usual Town Car service to pick her up the night she went missing. We checked with them, and they say they got that call all right, but then they got a second call canceling the car. Ms. Martin's assistant said she made just the one call, the first one, so we're wondering if something hinky went down.

"Anyhow, Ms. Martin was seen by one of your colleagues getting into a Town Car at the west entrance to 200 Park at approximately 7:30 that night. George and me, we been all over this city talking to limo drivers who picked up at that spot that night. Yesterday we found a guy, says he remembers seeing Ms. Martin get into a car. He remembers her because he drove for her once and she lost her temper at him."

I sipped my coffee. "She had a short fuse."

"Our guy said he got a look at her driver when he got out from behind the wheel to open the door for her. The guy who was driving for her that night, he looked different."

"Different how?"

"Different as in not clean cut like your typical chauffeur who drives rich lawyers around. Our witness sat with a sketch artist and this is what the two of them came up with."

He reached in his pocket and pulled out a piece of paper and laid it on the table.

Looking back at me was a perfect likeness of my brother-in-law, Hiram Redding.

French said, "You ever seen this guy, Mr. Carson?"

I swallowed hard and looked the cop in the eye. "Nope."

"You sure?"

"Yep."

He nodded and peered at his partner. "We understand from talking to some of your colleagues that you had a nickname for the victim."

"A nickname?"

"A way of referring to her. Could you tell us what that was, please?"

"The Hell Bitch." My voice came out a little squeaky. I cleared my throat and said, "I called her the Hell Bitch."

"Not a very nice way to refer to somebody, is it?"

"It was a joke. Like I said, she had a temper. And she wasn't afraid to use it. It was just a joke."

"We talked to a Mr. Biallo in your office this afternoon.

He says you once said you thought maybe it would not be such a bad idea if someone was to kill Ms. Martin."

"I was kidding. For chrissakes—Frank knew I was just kidding."

"Doesn't seem all that funny now, does it?"

"No."

"Do you know how she died?"

"I heard she was shot."

"Once. In the back of the head." The cop made quotation marks with his fingers. "'Execution style,' like they say in the papers. You know a Mr. Stu Spagnoletti?"

"He's a neighbor of mine."

"You were seen getting in a car with him the morning the victim disappeared."

"It was snowing. I needed a ride to the office. He offered. I accepted."

The cop tapped the sketch with a forefinger. "You sure you don't know this person?"

"Positive."

"Okay." The two cops stood to go. "Before we go—"

"I know. You don't want me to leave town."

The two cops looked at one another. Then French said, "I was gonna say, we just want you to know, we hope your wife gets better soon."

With that they turned and walked away.

When I knocked on his apartment door, Stu answered it himself.

"How's the little woman doin'?" he said.

"Better. She's regained consciousness and the doctors say they think she's gonna make it. Thanks for asking. Now I have a question for you."

He shifted his stance and crossed his arms over his chest. "Okay."

"Did you have Diane Martin whacked?"

"Who is Diane Martin?"

"My boss. She was murdered last week."

He shook his head. "I don't know what you're talkin' about."

"She wasn't showing the flex you and the Gerstens wanted to see in the air rights deal. Maybe you decided she was the problem and that she needed to be gotten rid of. Knowing that I would take the lead in negotiating the deal once she disappeared and that I would come up with a reasonable compromise—with something we Texans call 'rough justice.' A deal that works for both buyer and seller, even if it's not perfect for either one. Which is just exactly what happened."

"Good for you."

"You're telling me you had nothing to do with her death."

"I'm tellin' you I don't know what you're talkin' about."

"Where's my brother-in-law?"

A shrug. "Gone."

"Gone?"

"He worked a couple days drivin' people. Then called in. Said he missed Arkansas. Was goin' home."

"Stu?"

"Yeah?"

"New York is a city with apartments by the hundreds of thousands. What made you pick this particular one to relocate to while your place in Great Neck was being redone? How is it that you happened to pick this very apartment, just a couple weeks after I started working on the Park Avenue air rights deal?"

Stu looked at me for a long moment. Then he walked back in his apartment and closed the door.

"Shithouse mouse," I said to the closed door.

I went to my apartment, got out Katy's address book, and tried every phone number she had for Hiram. No answer at any of them.

By this time my head was seriously spinning. I sat in my living room and looked out the window at a lowering sky that promised yet another winter storm before the night was out. I sat there for a long time, thinking.

It was full dark when I grabbed my overcoat and headed downstairs again.

On my way through the lobby the doorman called to me, a little sheepish. "Oh, Mr. Carson?"

"Yeah?"

"Thought you'd want to know, sir. A couple of detectives were in here before, asking me to look at a sketch of a man. He looked just like the man who stayed with you and your wife a couple weeks ago."

I nodded. "Great. Thanks."

Katy is awake when I get back to her hospital room. I pull a chair next to her bed, and brush her hair off her forehead and kiss her. "Hey, babe. How you doing?"

I get back a weak smile. "I'm feeling okay."

"Honey? I need to ask you something."

"Okay."

"Where's Hiram?"

Her face grows serious. "Sweetheart, I have no idea. I haven't seen or heard from him since he moved out."

"I talked to Stu today. He said Hiram went back to

Arkansas."

"Oh."

"The police say a man who looks like him picked up Diane Martin the night she disappeared."

"She's not the Hell Bitch anymore?"

"Katy. I need you to tell me what's going on here."

She looks away. When she turns back she has tears in her eyes. "Stu heard me talking with Carmen about her. How awful she is—how crazy and paranoid and how she keeps you down. How you're really a better lawyer than she is. A more reasonable person to deal with."

"God Almighty."

"Carmen said it was a shame and Stu said not to worry—that so much worry would only make me sick and there was no point in it. He said that this is New York, and people come and go all the time—to new jobs or new careers, or sometimes they, you know, get hit by a bus. Something like that. I didn't argue with him."

"You didn't argue with him?"

Now she's crying in earnest. "I said that would make me happy. Oh, babe, I was half kidding, but, my God, she treated you so badly. I just wanted her out of our lives."

"Christ, Katy. Where did Hiram fit in?"

"I'd told Carmen about him. She said I should invite him to come to town. She said Stu might be able to find something for him. Something that would let Hiram make a little money, so he wouldn't have it so bad back home."

"Stu found something for him to do all right."

"Oh God, Billy. I had no idea what she was talking about. Really and truly."

"I gotta go to the cops with this, Katy."

"Do you have to?"

"Katy. The cops are gonna think I brought Hiram to town to cap Diane. And you know why they're gonna think that? Because Stu set it up to look just that way."

I sit listening to her cry, knowing I need to go.

Knowing I need to go now.

Knowing I need to say goodbye to my wife and go dime out one of the most dangerous men in New York along with my asshole brother-in-law.

I stand and say, "I'm sorry, darling."

Two minutes later I'm walking out of my wife's room, the back of my hand still wet from her tears. The sound of her voice as she pleaded with me still in my head. The taste of her skin still on my lips.

I speak to the cabbie but he makes no move to pull away from the curb. And as I watch the guy in the overcoat walk toward me, I think about my wife lying in her hospital bed and hope that Carmen will see to it that Stu does right by Katy, maybe with some of the money his family will make off the Gerstens' condo deal.

And I suddenly realize that the City That Never Shuts Up is completely silent, that there is no sound to be heard at all, no chattering cabbie, no radio traffic report, no jackhammers in the street, no sirens, no blaring horns, no drunken laughter, and the guy keeps coming with his hand in his coat and now he pulls out his hand and there's something in it that's dark and heavy and he makes straight for the cab window and what I next hear in this first ever moment of total silence in this town is glass exploding and the quiet deadly cough of a silenced gunshot.

THE CONSULTANT

BY PETER BLAUNER

1313 Avenue of the Americas

A s soon as she wedged her way off the crowded elevator on the forty-fifth floor, pregnant belly swathed in a navy Anne Klein duffel coat, with a sticker from the security desk on the lapel, she noticed the charge in the atmosphere. A mood of muffled tension and high-wire efficiency pervaded the reception area with its Oriental carpet, copies of *Billboard* and *Variety* arrayed on the coffee tables, and works of contemporary art hanging on the mahogany-paneled walls.

"Can I help you?" A receptionist with honey highlights in her hair and a small gold stud in her nose spoke to her from behind glass.

"I'm Nancy Arthur. I'm here to see Scott Locasio."

"Have a seat, please."

She went over and sank into a black leather sofa, her feet aching, her eyes drawn to a painting of a seated screaming man surrounded by a cage of lines. She studied it carefully, telling herself it couldn't possibly be the original version of the Francis Bacon she'd written a paper on back when she was an art history major.

"He'll see you now." An assistant in stilettoes as thin as ice picks came striding up the hall, carrying herself with a kind of daunting confidence meant to convey a sense of both her own importance and the visitor's provisional status.

Nancy struggled to her feet and followed her past a row of mounted platinum records and movie posters, feeling that familiar hummingbird flutter in her gut. *Come on, you can do this. Don't be such a girl.* A great oak door opened onto a sweeping godlike view of northern Manhattan, a perspective that made the trees of Central Park look like the current occupant's private garden and filled her with an uncomfortable mixture of envy and awe. Its majesty was only slightly undercut by the presence of a Styrofoam backboard in the corner and the brutal thump of hip-hop coming from a pair of four-foot-high Altec Lansing speakers.

"So you're supposed to be the new coach, huh?" He spoke without taking his eyes off his computer monitor. A stocky, thick-necked young man in charcoal double-breasted pinstripes, with a pair of black suede Bruno Magli loafers insouciantly up on his desk. "No disrespect," he said. "But if it was up to me, you wouldn't even be here."

"And why's that?" She sat down before him without being asked, trying to stake a claim and accommodate herself to the deliberate thuggishness in his manner. A lot of them were like that these days. The new breed, who wore flashy jewelry to the office, listened to misogynist rap, and left copies of *Maxim* on their desks, in full view of their pregnant guests.

"I don't think I need it," he said matter-of-factly. "When I took over as head of worldwide media last year, this company's stock was in the toilet. Now we've got three CDs in *Billboard*'s Top Ten, four of the top-rated shows on the networks, and the top-grossing game system in the country for the last three weeks running. Nothing wrong with the way I'm doing my job."

"So why do you think the board hired me to work with you?"

He finally took his eyes off the monitor, to give her the once-over.

"I guess somebody thinks I need a little 'seasoning.'" He made little quotation marks with his fingers. "They want me to work on my 'sandbox skills.' Apparently, Scottso might have hurt somebody's little feelings when he took over. Like that has any relevance."

"And you don't think it does?"

"Revenues have been up every quarter since I came in. All these Ivy League bitches with their Harvard MBAs and their Yale degrees wouldn't know a hit if it came up and bit them in the ass. Things needed to be shaken up. A couple of dishes got chipped along the way? So fucking what? I never knew this industry had so many pussies."

She tried to cross her legs, knowing that she was being tested here. *Pussies. Bitches.* The language of intimidation. If you protested, you were barred from the boys' locker room. But if you put up with too much, you were a doormat for life.

"So you're the only one with balls around here, I guess," she said flatly, letting him know she could play if she really had to.

He snorted in contempt. *"You're the only one with balls,"* he mimicked her. "Listen to you. Like you're going to tell me about my business? And where'd you go to college, Princeton?"

"I did my graduate work in organizational psychology at the University of Michigan." She started to stick her chin out and then caught herself. "Why is that important to you?"

"Organizational *psychology*." He looked like he'd just licked a cat. "That's like a tofu hamburger, isn't it? What are you? You're not in business and you're not a real shrink. Who do you think you're kidding?"

She felt the little form squirming and kicking inside her, not wanting to let on that she'd asked herself the same question at least once a week for the last twelve years. She wondered if he somehow knew this was the biggest account she'd ever landed. Twelve years of patiently handing out business cards, trying to spread her name around, billing for less than she was worth, trying to build on each of her little success stories. Twelve years of holding hands with brusque, socially underdeveloped executives who needed a coach to keep them from alienating colleagues and damaging their companies.

"Well, my understanding is that I have a mandate to work with you on your management skills," she said, trying to sound firm. "And I usually don't get called in if everything is hunky-dory."

He fidgeted a little, his left loafer waggling on the edge of the desk.

"But how the hell can you understand my position? Have you ever even run a business?" He paused for effect, hoping to humiliate her. "I've got fifteen hundred people answering to me worldwide and I bet you can't even balance your checkbook. And now you're going to walk in here and tell me something I don't already know?"

She had the sensation of finding herself pressed up against a cold wall. If she let him push her around now, she'd never gain his respect. Her eyes moved across the office, searching for something that would put them on more even footing. When everything else failed nowadays, she could usually make her pregnancy into a conversation piece, sometimes even a bond she could share with other women and family-minded men. But there were no photos of children here. Just shots of several different silicon-enhanced stripper-types accompanying him on Cancún vacations, fishing expeditions in the Florida Keys, and autographed photos taken with members of Bon Jovi and various sports luminaries she didn't quite recognize.

Instead, with mounting unease, she found her gaze drawn to a life-sized cut-out in the corner, the figure of a barrel-chested man in a tuxedo with a picture of her client's face imposed on the top.

"What's that?" she asked.

"Whadayya mean, *what's that?* It's the Don."

"The Don?"

"Whaddaya, kidding? The Don. *The Don!*" He looked incredulous. "Don Corleone. From . . . *The* . . . *Godfather.* Maybe you've heard of it . . . ?"

He smiled as if he was addressing a child with special needs, and she nodded, mildly embarrassed, not daring to let on that somehow she had reached the ripe age of thirty-eight without ever seeing that particular film.

Oh, of course she'd heard of it. She even vaguely remembered her older sister and her middle school friends whispering and giggling about some tawdry bit of business on page twenty-seven of the novel it was based on. But the truth was, the story had never interested her enough to actually sit down and watch it, even though most of the men she worked with referred to it as some kind of sacred inviolate *Ur*-text. All those dark muttering codes and oaths of masculinity, all those silly posturing threats from a bunch of frat boys. She could never take it seriously, even when her husband begged her to watch it with him.

"Ohhhh, so *you're* the Don," she said.

He looked pleased, perhaps hearing an undertone of admiration that she had not really intended.

"What have I ever done to make you treat me so disrespectfully?" he mumbled. "Had you come to me in friendship, then this scum that ruined your daughter would be suffering this very day."

She froze in alarm, until she realized he must have been reciting lines from the film.

"You sound just like him," she said.

Who was in this movie anyway? Marlon Brando? Al Pacino? She was more partial to films about women triumphing over adversity. *A League of Their Own. Pretty Woman.*

"I better." He laced his hands behind his head. "I must've watched it two, three hundred times with my old man."

"Really?" She pretended to be impressed.

"Well, whaddaya want? You grow up in Bensonhurst, it's like learning the Pledge of Allegiance."

"Sure. A rite of passage."

She watched the way his body language changed as he began to talk about it. How his feet finally came off the desk and he sat forward in his seat a little, looking her in the eye for the first time.

"You ever wonder . . . ?"

He'd started to ask an earnest question but stopped himself, not sure if he was quite ready to show her any kind of deference yet.

"What?"

She saw him wrestle with an idea, his eyes narrowing as he tried to pin it down, a flush of boyish pinkness rising in his cheeks.

"Did you ever really wonder why Kay left Michael?" he asked.

She steepled her fingers, as if it was a question that had long troubled her as well.

"Well, why do *you* think Kay left Michael?"

She watched him for cues, seeing that she'd set off a circuit of associations. He looked down at a shrink-wrapped CD that had been lying on his desk and scratched at the edge of the cellophane with his fingernail.

"I don't know," he said, turning pensive. "She acts like she's shocked when she finds out what he does for a living, but c'mon—like she didn't know already from being at the wedding and seeing his father? What business did she think they were in, State Farm home insurance?"

"Maybe she just came to realize he wasn't the man his father was," she said glibly.

He looked as if he'd just been slapped. You could almost see the outline of a palm print on his cheek.

"Why'd you say that?"

She shrugged, not having really meant anything by it. But of course he was going to react. A therapist getting a rise out of a client by bringing up his parents was like a cook turning on a stove. If it didn't occur to you, you were probably in the wrong business.

"So are you saying that if Michael could've learned to be strong like the Don, he wouldn't have lost his family?" he said, again reading more into her words than she'd put in.

"Well, what do *you* think?"

In the course of just a few seconds, he seemed to have transformed from a truculent executive to a parochial school boy working up the nerve to raise his hand in class.

"Let me ask you something," he said quietly. "And if you tell a soul I asked you this, I swear I'll throw you out the window."

"Okay."

"If I hire you, can you teach me organization principles according to the Godfather?"

"Can I . . . ?"

"Can you be a wartime *consigliere?* That's what I'm asking."

She weighed her answer as she looked around the room, calculating that there were at least six pieces of furniture present that would probably cover a year's mortgage for their "classic six" co-op on the Upper West Side. The guy who took care of the plants in the office was probably making as much as she was. She tried to fight down her growing resentment, reminding herself that she was supposed to be here to help. Then she remembered a line from a spunky Meg Ryan comedy she'd loved a few years back, something Tom Hanks quoted from *The Godfather*.

"I'm ready to go to the mattresses," she said.

He grinned. "*Bella*."

Two nights later, she lay sideways on the living room couch, watching Diane Keaton stand helplessly on the threshold as one of her husband's henchmen closed the door in her face and the closing-credits theme swelled.

"Because he's a beast," she said.

"What?"

Her husband Mark, shaggy-haired, unemployed, and banished to the club chair at some point after the murders of Sollozzo and the police captain, looked up bleary-eyed.

"It's because he's a beast," she explained. "That's why she'll end up leaving him. Plain and simple."

"So you're not going to take this job?"

"Of course I'm going to take this job. Are you kidding? Did you see what our mortgage rate went up to today? We *need* this job."

He pulled a well-thumbed copy of *Maximum PC* out from under his buttocks, having just noticed he was sitting on it.

"I thought you couldn't stand this guy, Scottso."

"But now I *get* him."

"I don't know." He yawned and scratched his stomach. "How can you help someone you don't like?"

"Because unlike some people, I'm willing to do what it takes to . . ."

She stopped herself from saying more, sucking in her lip. No point in flaying him again for being out of work for two months. It wasn't *entirely* his fault that his little software start-up collapsed so soon after she got pregnant. If she wanted to marry a master of the universe, an industry leader, a true tycoon, she could have gone for some Wall Street lifer or some Cro Mag alpha-male type, like Scottso, instead of settling for her college boyfriend.

"Well, just as long as it's strictly business, I suppose it'll be fine," he said, holding the magazine in front of his face as if she hadn't wounded him. "You're a pro."

Larry Longman, head of the TV division, was a nervous man who always needed to be doing something with his hands. If he wasn't squeezing a ball or fingering a pen, he was shooting his cuffs and making a half-closed fist, like he was holding a pair of dice.

"I think I have a good relationship with Scott," he said. "I only have good things to say about him."

Nancy nodded, already hearing something in his voice the way a police officer would hear gunshots from two blocks away. "I understand, but I want to assure you that everything we say here in the evaluation process is anonymous. He's not going to know where it came from."

"Well, not that I *would* say anything negative, but how do I know that?"

He rearranged the pens and paperweights on his desk, touched his computer mouse, and tugged on the fat end of his tie.

"You can trust my discretion. I wouldn't have much of a reputation in the consulting business if I couldn't guarantee anonymity when I'm interviewing different people in a company to do a 360-degree evaluation of an executive."

"True." Larry rubbed his palms together. "*True.* But couldn't he still guess who your source is when he reads your report? I mean, if somebody's talking about how he treats people in the TV division, he's going to know it's me, isn't he?"

"You have my word that I'll protect you by disguising your comments." She smiled. "I mean, we all have the same goal here, which is to improve overall performance for the company."

"Right. *Right.*"

He reshuffled his pens, fingered his cell phone, smoothed his tie, and shot his cuffs again. She made a note to herself, seeing how much of a disturbance Scottso could cause without even being present in a room.

"So why don't you just start off by telling me a little about Scott's management style?"

"Well . . . obviously, he's very, very bright . . ." He made the half-fist again and began shaking it, as if he was getting ready to throw the dice. "And very, very energetic . . ."

"*But . . .*" She leaned forward, as if she was trying to see something smoking under the hood.

"But . . ." The fist tightened. "Some people sometimes feel a little shut out of the decision-making process . . ."

"He can be autocratic," she ventured, making it a statement rather than a question.

"*Definitely.*" He nodded, emboldened, beginning to trust her a little. "Some people might even call it arrogant. Rude. *Bullying.* Not that that's always a bad thing . . ."

"It's better to be feared than loved," she said.

"That's funny." He fumbled for his rubber ball, looking startled. "Scott's always saying the same thing."

Michael Corleone was plotting again. On the screen, Al Pacino was playing it cool, all steady sunken eyes and coiled posture in a coat black as crow's feathers, as he carefully explained to hot-headed Frank Five Angels what he wanted done to Hyman Roth for his treachery.

"*There are many things my father taught me here in this room,*" he was saying. "*He taught me: Keep your friends close, but your enemies closer.*"

"Amazing," said Nancy, sitting up on the couch.

"What?" Mark looked up from studying the tech column in the *Wall Street Journal.*

"The way he takes power, by using people and turning them against each other."

"You know, I don't think you're supposed to admire him." Mark folded the paper over. "He had his brother-in-law killed at the end of the last movie."

"I know, but he's so . . . *controlled.* The way he takes care of his family."

"Sounds like you're falling in love," he said, watching the movie again. "Maybe you're spending too much time on your client. He's starting to rub off on you."

"Maybe you need to start working again."

"Ouch."

"Well, it's true. Did you see what the prime rate went up to today? I don't think we'd be struggling with the mortgage if one of us was willing to be a little more ruthless sometimes."

She lay back again, immediately regretting her sharpness with him. Still, it *was* true. Why couldn't he be a little stronger, a little more deliberate, a little more cold-blooded like these contained and quietly decisive men on the screen? After all, he had a baby of his own coming, a family to take care of.

She was beginning to understand what men like Scottso and Mark saw in these films, but also how short they fell of the image. They all thought they could be the Don, but really they were Fredos and Sonnys, either too weak-willed or too impulsive to hold onto power. They lacked the necessary detachment, the patient willingness to stand in the shadows letting events play themselves out until the right opportunity presented itself.

"I want you to open an account," she said.

"*What?*"

"You heard me. I want you to set up an account, in your own name."

"What's this about?"

"Just do what I'm asking you for once. Okay? Is that too much for you?"

"You know, you're getting kinda bossy all of a sudden, Mama." He reached over and touched her stomach, seeing if the baby was moving. "Am I going to end up sleeping with the fishes before my son is born?"

"Don't tempt me." She pushed his hand away.

Scottso threw the evaluation report down on his desk, almost hitting a platter of tea and cookies his secretary had brought in, his face starting to redden.

"Fucking Larry Longman," he said. "It took him about two seconds to try to stick a knife in my back."

"You're jumping to conclusions," she answered in a carefully modulated voice. "You're focusing on trying to guess who said what in the 360s, instead of concentrating on the more substantial analysis of your management style. Do you really think that's helpful?"

"I *know* it was Larry, because he had his assistant call about the reservations for the Michael's meeting the other day." He fumed, staring out the window. "It's just like the Don says—*whoever comes to you with this meeting, he's the traitor.* He's trying to organize a coup with the other division heads. Those fucking Harvard MBAs can't stand taking orders from a guy from Bath Avenue."

She felt herself hang back a bit, like Robert DeNiro in the tenement hallway with his gun, waiting for the Black Hand to arrive.

"Don't you think that sounds a little paranoid?"

"Don't tell me I'm paranoid," he said. "Do you know how many of these fuckers are gunning for me? Do you know how bad they wanna see me fail? I worked my whole life to put myself in this chair by the sweat of my balls. And I'm not going to let some little chardonnay-pansy bean counter who can't stop playing with his pens slip a wire around my throat."

She tilted forward, clasping her hands before her, studying him closely. "And so what are you going to instead?"

He looked startled. Not so much by the question itself, but by the way she was asking it. Calm, without judgment, and not completely unsupportive. Clearly, he'd been expecting something else from her.

"Well," he said quietly, "to tell you the truth, I was thinking of making a move on him."

"You mean, you were thinking of getting rid of him."

He slowly nodded, assessing the gravity of what he'd just told her and then watching for her reaction.

"You gonna tell the board about that?"

"That's not my role here." She held him in a level gaze, imagining that if she stayed this way long enough her cheekbones would start to rise and her eyes would move back into her skull the way Al Pacino's did.

"You know, I can't figure you out." A smile tugged at the corner of his mouth. "I thought you'd try to talk me out of it."

"It's your business. I'm just the consultant. All I'm asking is if you're prepared to deal with the fallout. It's like Michael killing the police captain and Sollozo. You have to be prepared for all-out war afterwards."

"Jesus." He ran his tongue under his lip in admiration. "Is this what they teach you in organizational psychology?"

"You said you didn't need a psychologist," she reminded him, reaching for one of the cookies. "You needed a wartime *consigliere*."

He slapped his desk, pleased with himself. "You know, somehow I knew we were going to be *paisans* the minute you walked into this office. Something about the way you handle yourself. We're coming from the same place. You sure you're not Sicilian?"

"Just when I thought I was out, they pull me back in!"

Mark unfurled the business section so loudly that Nancy almost missed the gleeful way Al Pacino, older but more feral, tore into the line.

"Will you keep it down?" She rolled over from doing her exercises in front of the set, the baby due in less than six weeks. "I can barely concentrate here."

"I don't know why you're even bothering with the third one. I told you the thrill was gone after *Godfather II*."

"I still want to see how it ends."

"You know how it ends. Gangster movies never have a happy ending." He folded the paper in half and looked at it closely. "*Whoa*. Your guy's stock is taking a major beating here. What's going on?"

"Total bloodbath. I thought I told you." She raised her head, attempting to catch a glimpse of her feet. "Scottso tried to fire the head of the TV division and put his own guy in, but it just united all the other factions against him and caused a mutiny. They had a meeting the other day that left entrails all over the conference room."

"And where does that leave Scottso?"

"Hanging by a thread, if you ask me." She gasped, trying to lift her legs, feeling the baby move down a little further.

"And that doesn't reflect badly on you?"

"Not my fault if someone decides to self-destruct. Besides, nothing wrong with a little shake-up now and then. Like Clemenza says, it helps get rid of the bad blood."

"I think you're turning into the Godfather."

"What a thing to say to the mother of your unborn child." She raised up on her elbows, frowning. "If I was a man, you'd be high-fiving me and buying me a beer."

"If you were a man, I wouldn't have married you."

She started practicing her breathing again, trying to decide if she should feel bad. A nice girl wouldn't act this way. On the other hand, a nice girl might not be able to keep her family from going into debt a month and a half before her first child arrived.

"So, are you still shorting that stock?" she asked.

"Not every single day, but I did a few trades on Wednesday."

He pinched the roll of belly flab he'd been developing in sympathy lately. "I'm worried about playing it too close to the edge."

"As long as you keep the trades small and use your own last name, there's not going to be a problem."

"It still makes me uncomfortable." He reached back, trying to get at an itch between his shoulder blades. "Betting against the company where your wife's supposed to be consulting."

She gave him a long look, silently deciding that he would stay home after the baby was born and she'd go back to work right away. He'd find out about that later. Fredo didn't make the big decisions in the family.

"Go get me an orange, will you?" she said. "This kid's sucking the calcium right out of my bones."

She was wearing a $2,500 shearling coat from Searle and a pair of fur-lined Coach boots when she came to see Scottso the next week. He was busy at his desk, having been given an hour to clear out, while a security officer stood at the door making sure he didn't take any material belonging to the company.

"Scott, I'm so sorry. I came as soon as I heard. Are you going to be all right?"

He looked at her once, shook his head, and reached across his desk for a stack of CDs.

"Ah, sir, you're going to have to leave those," said the security officer, waiting to escort him out of the building. "Those are property of the company."

"You believe this?" Scott's lip curled. "I signed half the artists on this label—I was in the *studio* when they cut these—and now they won't even let me walk out of the office with a disc it cost about three cents to make."

"I know how hard this must be." She nodded. "But I'm sure you're going to land on your feet once this is all over."

"Yeah, no thanks to you."

He snatched a picture of himself with John McEnroe off the corner of his desk and put it in the cardboard box at his feet.

"Do you really think it's that useful assigning blame at this point?" she asked.

"Who else am I supposed to blame—*myself?*"

"Well, some people would take this as a time for self-reflection . . ."

"Oh, you're good." His nostrils flared. "You're really good, I'll give you that. I just can't figure what your angle was."

"I don't know what you're talking about."

"Sure you don't. Like you didn't wind me up and play me off against Larry Longman on purpose."

"Oh Scott, come on . . ."

"Just tell me one thing: Were you working for Larry or was there someone on the board gunning for me?"

She turned away as he lumbered toward her, crossing her arms in front of her stomach.

"There was no one else," she said. "You wanted a war, so you got a war. Wars are messy."

He reached out and fingered the soft collar of her jacket, the knuckle of his thumb lightly brushing her cheek.

"I know it was you, Fredo," he said almost tenderly. "You broke my heart."

"Oh, come on, it's not the fall of Havana." She pulled away from him and started toward the door. "Act like a man, Johnny Fontaine. What's the matter with you?"

"Jesus." He made his eyes into slits. "What'd you do, memorize the dialogue?"

"And that's not what you wanted?"

He gave her the wounded uncomprehending look of a lover betrayed.

"I don't understand," he said, following her. "Why'd you do this to me? Did I ever hurt you? Just tell me that. Why would you do this to someone you don't even know?"

"It was never anything personal, Scott." She stopped on the threshold. "It was strictly business."

PART III

MAIN STREET

THE DAY TRADER IN THE TRUNK OF CLETO'S CAR

BY MARK HASKELL SMITH

Los Angeles, California

Fuck me, man. What is Cleto talking about? I can't understand a word. He's just barking all mad dog at me, spit flying from his mouth, sweat dripping from his big shaved head. He's pissed. I can tell. His shirt is off and he's pounding his chest with his fists, slapping the tattoo of the two skeletons buttfucking over his heart. He keeps saying stuff, but I don't know what it means. He knows I don't speak Spanish.

Naldo and Ramón. Those fuckers. They just rolled up on me and next thing I know my nose is broken, my bottom teeth are sticking through my lip, and I'm clotheslined by the driveway. Seeing stars. Really. Little bursts of light, like flashbulbs.

Amigos, what the fuck?

There must be some mistake. It's me. Russell.

I want to say something but I can't get any air. I think my jaw is broken too.

Cleto yelled some more and they stopped kicking me. Fucking Naldo and his cowboy boots. He kicked me so hard it feels like I have exit wounds. I'm pretty sure I broke a rib. Maybe two. And my shirt. Shit. My tofu festival T-shirt. What are they thinking? It's collectible, man. The tofu festival only comes once a year.

I'm trying to tell them this as they pick me up off the ground. But they can't hear me. It was a mistake only taking one year of Spanish in high school. If I could *habla*, I'm sure we could work this all out.

Naldo is holding me up, but I can't see much. Something's wrong with one of my eyes, like it's dislocated. No, it's my neck. I can't hold my head up; it just bounces around like those stupid bobblehead dolls you get at Dodger Stadium. I can't control the bobbling. It bobbles left, then right, then back. Bobble, bobble. I see the ground, the street. There are bright dark blotches on the pavement. My blood. Naldo's boots. Bobble, bobble. The wheels of the car.

Why can't I control my head?

Cleto helps me out. He grabs my hair and lifts my head up so I can see him. I start talking, but it just sounds like gargling. There's too much blood in my mouth. That can't be good.

Cleto looks me in the eye.

"You are gonna fuckin' die, *hijo de puta*."

I try to explain. Doesn't he understand that it's just a little correction? The market does this all the time. In another month everything will be back where it was, maybe higher. It's certainly no reason to do anything drastic. Everyone, KLD Research and Analytics, Price Target, the Jaywalk Consensus, they all said *hold*. Not sell. Hold.

Hold on tight, everything will be all right.

I try to explain this to Cleto, but my mouth won't work. I sound like a cow. I'm mooing. Cleto looks at me and shakes his head.

"Throw this piece of shit in the trunk and let's go."

Now he speaks English?

Naldo and Ramon pick me up and throw me in the trunk

of Cleto's car. If I wasn't already numb from the beating, that would've hurt. Naldo leans in and smiles at me. I try to talk again. Weren't we friends? Didn't I tell you to invest in Genentech (NYSE: DNA)? Didn't you double your money when Caterpillar (NYSE: CAT) split?

Naldo whispers some advice in my ear: "Don't bleed on Cleto's car, *ese.*"

Then he shut the lid.

It's dark in the trunk. I go fetal. I can't help it. There is no other way to get comfortable. I suppose that's the point. They're trying to teach me a lesson. I shouldn't have hesitated. I should've made the trade, taken a small loss, protected the nut. Okay. I get that. But it's not like it's a washout. Not like that stupid computer stock I had. Cleto's money is safe—well, as safe as it can be.

I wish I could explain it to him. It's not like I had him in volatile stocks. I didn't put his money in junk bonds. I mean, c'mon man, Time Warner (NYSE: TWX), Cisco (NASDAQ: CSCO), Eastman Kodak (NYSE: EK), these are not dogs we're talking about. They may not be blue chip, but they're blue chip*ish.* Right? They took a dive. Okay. I see that. But it's not like they're over. He's got seventy grand in Microsoft (NASDAQ: MSFT), for fuck's sake. It'll all bounce back; he just has to be patient. Stocks go up, stocks go down. It's what they do. Cleto needs to relax and enjoy the journey, think of it as an "E" ticket experience—the Cyclone at Coney Island, the Colossus at Magic Mountain, Mr. Toad's Wild Ride—it's supposed to be fun.

I feel the car shake to life. The big V-8 under the hood rumbles awake and the steel body trembles like it's actually afraid of all that power. I'm not really a fan of muscle cars; the gas mileage is terrible, the cost of insurance is ridiculous, but they do look cool and it's fun to cruise around with the top down at night.

I'm also not really a fan of the monster bass tube sub-woofer he had installed in the trunk. My back was pressed up against it when it kicked in and it felt like Naldo's boots had somehow reached through the trunk to paste my kidneys a few more times. The fucking rivets are buzzing and popping, trying to escape the metal with each thump of the kick drum and snap of the bass. It sounds like a beehive of pissed-off steel. What the fuck is Cleto listening to? Oh shit. I know this song. It's "Frijolero" by Molotov.

No me digas beaner,
Mr. Puñetero.
Te sacaré un susto
por racista y culero.
No me llames frijolero,
Pinche gringo puñetero.

Naldo once translated this song for me. It's roughly, *"Don't call me beaner, you fucking racist asshole."*

Is he playing the song for my benefit? I think he is, and this kind of hurts my feelings. I don't deserve that. I'm not a racist and I never called him a beaner or anything else like that.

I thought Cleto was my friend.

I didn't start out as a day trader. I didn't even know what a day trader was. I came to Los Angeles to be a screenwriter. Well, honestly, I came to Los Angeles to be a director. But the easiest way to becoming a director is to be a screenwriter first.

That's the way it works. You write a couple of hit movies that someone else directs—some guy with a ponytail who wears jeans and drives a Porsche—and then it's your turn. Pretty soon you don't have to write the scripts, you sit in your Hollywood Hills home and give the writer notes over the phone while some aspiring actress gives you a blowjob, then you hike up your jeans and get in your Porsche.

Of course, now that I say it, now that I know better, it sounds hopelessly naïve. But what did I know? Nothing. I was fresh off the bus. Now I understand how it works. I've wised up. I have learned the one important truth, the most absolute vodka-clear truth about Hollywood. I'll share this with you, but honestly, I hate to sound like one of them, you know, the wannabes that never quite made it. So try not to think of me as bitter. I'm not.

The big stinking truth with a capital T is that no one in this town—and I mean not one single living person—gives a flying fuckadoodle-do about you, your script, and whatever talent you think you might have. They don't. Deal with it.

But I didn't know that when I came to town. I figured it might take a few years, but one day I'd have the jeans, the ponytail, the Porsche, and a three-picture deal. I was clueless and hopeful and staked with a small inheritance I got when my grandpa died.

I didn't really know my grandpa that well. When I was little he used to take me fishing for catfish. You know, where you glob that bait on the hook—the bait that looks and smells exactly like fresh dog poo—and throw the line in the river with a big sinker on it. Then you wait for the catfish to swim up to your big stinky piece of shit in the murky bottom of the river and eat it. Then you just reel 'em in. It's about as exciting as taking out the trash.

My grandpa would fry the catfish when we got home, but I couldn't eat anything that liked to eat shit. Sorry. Just not for me.

After I went to high school I kinda lost touch with him, and after college I didn't even get a Christmas card. But then he was dead and he gave me over a hundred thousand dollars in his will. That cash was my screenwriting fund. I could stay in my apartment and just work. Like a real writer. No day job to distract me.

In fact, the only real distraction I found was this website by Mandy LaFrance. She was a Tulane University co-ed who liked to cruise the French Quarter for guys to blow. Mandy was awesome. She didn't even take the guys into the bathroom. She'd just drop to her knees in a crowd and go to it, then she'd post the pictures and a kind of play-by-play description of these fellatio sorties on her website. I was in love with her. Not like really "in love." She had a boyfriend; he was the guy who took all the photos of her sucking cock. When I say I was in love with her, it's more that I admired and respected her audacity, her gumption, her take-no-prisoners attitude. She was like the opposite of a catfish. A barracuda, maybe. Plus, I liked to look at the pictures and beat off.

There. I *said it.*

But who could blame me? As a busy screenwriter, I didn't have time to go out on dates or maintain girlfriends—there would be time for that after I was famous, then I'd be out at the Tropicana or the Skybar, all those kinds of places. But in the beginning I needed to stay in and work.

I did this for about a year, hardly spending any of my money, but eventually I realized that it was dwindling, it might actually run out before I got an agent and a six-figure paycheck. So I took a weekend workshop called the

"Millionaire's Club." It was supposed to teach me how to make my money work for me. Like it was an employee.

I don't think I got much out of the seminar. Really. I didn't want to get all tied up in real estate and evicting old people and bidding on probate cases. That had *bad karma* written all over it. But I was intrigued by this day trading idea. You know what I mean? Like, how hard could it be? You buy a stock at a certain price, wait for it to go up, and then sell it. Buy low, sell high. A monkey could do it.

I didn't know much about investing. I still don't. I know nothing about the market capitalization of companies, their enterprise value, or the P&E trailing. I mean, really? What the fuck is P&E trailing? I can't read a five-year historical EPS growth rate. I don't even know if you're supposed to. But it didn't matter. I was making money. Lots of it. And I didn't have to shave, get dressed, or leave the apartment. It was a lot like screenwriting.

Cleto stopped the car. Thank God he stopped the music; my fucking ears were bleeding. I don't know how long we've been driving. I think I kind of blacked out for a minute or two.

I can feel the bruises on my legs and ribs and back and face and arms. They're big and hot and fuck do they hurt. I need to pack my body in ice, man.

I can hear them talking outside. I hope they know that I've learned my lesson. I have. Totally. It's ingrained. I will never take my eye off the market again. Ever. That's the lesson I learned. You look away for a heartbeat—Mandy had met some guys from a fraternity at the University of Texas and she was flashing the "hook 'em horns!" sign while she serviced them—and the market will fuck you right up the ass.

It occurs to me that I still have my cell phone. I can call

Cleto. Maybe that's the best way to do this. Not face-to-face where tempers flare and misunderstandings turn to violence, but detached—calm and cool—like businessmen. I dig it out of my pocket, thank God I got one of those flip phones and it didn't get smashed, and open it up. I've got Cleto on speed dial.

It's ringing.

I get his voice mail.

I'm still having trouble talking, my lips have ballooned up like the Michelin Man, I try very hard to enunciate.

"Dude, it's Russell. Look. Sorry, man. Let's talk. Okay? I'll make it up to you, man. C'mon. I need to go to the hospital. Let me outta the trunk."

I could call 911. But what would I say? I don't know where I am, I don't know the license plate number of Cleto's car; how could they find me? And I don't really want to confess to laundering money for a drug smuggler. Then Cleto would be really mad.

Those "Millionaire Club" guys were right. Having your money work for you is exciting. Totally. At first, I couldn't take my eyes off it. I'd start the morning with a buy—you know, five thousand shares of Millennium Pharmaceuticals (NASDAQ: MLNM) or something, watch it go up a dollar a share, then sell. *Bam!* Five thousand bucks. Get a couple different stocks going, and I'm like a juggler, keeping all the balls in the air until it's time to strike. It's totally cool. And for some reason I have a knack for it. I just know when to sell. Sure, some of it is luck. I know that. Though sometimes it's instinct. Luck and instinct. That's my formula for success.

But after a while I realized that I was paying too much attention to the market; all day my eyes glued to the computer screen, watching those stocks go up and down. Making trades, taking profit. It was turning into a job.

To help me get back on track with my writing, I took a class at UCLA extension. The teacher was some kind of action-movie hotshot who checked his BlackBerry every ten minutes, but he was very encouraging. He really liked one script I wrote, an alien-invasion romantic comedy—think *Sleepless in Seattle* meets *Invasion of the Body Snatchers*—and said he thought it had a lot of potential. He encouraged us to start a writers group. You know, like a support group.

So me and these guys Dave and Victor from the class joined Wendy and Pasha from another class and started one.

It's not difficult to start a writers group. You buy a six-pack of beer, a six-pack of Diet Coke, and one of those raw vegetable and dip platters from the supermarket, hide your dirty clothes, and you're ready to host a literary salon. You don't need to be Dorothy Parker or Gertrude Stein. I wasn't. And Dave, he hardly even picked up his dirty gym shorts off the floor when we had "group" at his house—that's what we called it, "group"—and there was always a funny smell in the air, kinda like cheese.

The meetings were fun. We'd talk about our work and our struggles trying to break into Hollywood. We'd help each other with ideas and talk about agents we'd heard about and stuff like that. This was when I was optimistic. When I thought success in Hollywood was just a screenplay away. This was before I learned the big stinking truth.

One night it was my turn to host and I decided to go all out. I'd had a particularly good day trading. I managed to jump on an IPO and ride it like it was a wild bull. It was crazy. A couple of times I thought about jumping out, taking a solid profit, and calling it a day. But something told me to hang in—that sixth sense I told you about—and despite various ups and downs I managed to triple my money, turning twenty grand into sixty grand and then getting out seconds before the closing bell rang.

You fucking know I was feeling good. I bought some white wine from this little shop on Colorado Boulevard and a large shrimp and crab claw platter from this Japanese fish market in Glendale. I went to a Cuban bakery and got empanadas stuffed with spicy chicken and pastries filled with guava and cream cheese. In other words, I went out of my way to be a great host.

I was the only one in the group who didn't have a regular day job. Dave and Wendy both worked as assistants, Victor worked at Book Soup, and Pasha was some kind of textile designer. Everyone was talking about their various jobs, the humiliations that they suffered on a daily basis, and finally Wendy asked me what I did.

I told them it was hard to explain. When they pressed me, I turned on my computer and show them my portfolio, trading strategies, how the software worked, things like that. They were more impressed by my day trading than by the first fifteen pages of a Spanish Civil War epic—imagine Tom Hanks as a volunteer in the Abraham Lincoln brigades captured and befriended by Javier Bardem as Franco—and that's all they could talk about. Pasha even stayed after group to help me clean up, and for the first time in over a year I didn't end my night looking at pictures of Mandy LaFrance blowing Bourbon Street; I spent it in bed with a slightly pudgy Indian girl with beautiful eyes.

That's how I met Cleto. Not by banging Pasha—that turned out to be the best part of the whole day trading thing: It got me a girlfriend. You know day trading, it's sexy, kind of dangerous, but it's also responsible. You're investing money. It's like a very grownup thing to do. That impressed Pasha, and once she spread her legs, that was it, we were an item.

It was Victor who caused the problem. Cleto was Victor's cousin and Victor couldn't keep his mouth shut. Cleto had a bunch of cash he wanted to invest, but he couldn't exactly put it in a bank because he'd earned it "under the table." I guess I was naïve, but when I met him he just seemed like a nice, hardworking Mexican man who was trying to make a better life for himself just like everybody else who comes to this country. Later I learned that he'd earned his money selling drugs. What can I tell you? I'm a moron.

Anyway, at first I said no. I didn't want the responsibility. What if I lost Cleto's nest egg? Then what? He goes back to Oaxaca peso-less? But when Cleto opened that gym bag stuffed full of hundred-dollar bills, well, I couldn't resist. I mean, he was giving me ten percent of the profit.

I thought they were going to leave me in here to slowly roast to death. But now Cleto's started up the car and we're moving. Air is circulating. I can breathe again. He's popped another CD in and now it's some kind of salsa—no, wait, I know it. It's Ozomatli.

Ozomatli is blasting in the trunk.

I like this much better. It's happier, bouncy, and has a horn section. Maybe Cleto's mood has improved.

I take out my cell phone and try again. Still no answer; maybe he can't hear it ringing over the music. It's too loud in the trunk to leave a message so I hang up.

I guess you could say I got greedy. I could've stuck Cleto's cash into a couple of über-safe stocks and called it a day. All he wanted was for me to let them ride for a year or two, then sell them, pay the taxes on the gains, and give him a nice clean cashier's check. But I thought about that and realized, you know, *what's in it for me?* Ten percent of the profits if the profits are small is like hardly worth my time. I'm not risking my neck to make a couple hundred bucks when I could make thousands, right? Doesn't make sense. So I gambled a little. I suppose, in retrospect, I should've diversified . . . took some conservative positions. That's what they call it.

But you know what I thought? I thought, *I don't take conservative positions in bed with Pasha, why should I take 'em with Cleto's money?*

You know? You gotta break some eggs to make an omelet. I wonder if I can explain it to Cleto that way. Do they have omelets in Mexico?

Finally the car's stopped. We've been driving for hours. I tried to call Pasha but I'm not getting any reception. Where are we?

The trunk lid opens and it's bright. I feel like the Moleman or something. If the Moleman had the living shit kicked out of him. The sun is searing my eyeballs and I can't seem to blink. Naldo and Ramón pull me out of the trunk. Fuck. *That hurts.* I can hardly stand up. My body's stiff like I'm filled with concrete. My legs don't work at all and my pants are wet.

"You pissed your pants, *ese.* Cleto's not gonna be happy about that."

What do they expect? How long was I in there?

I try to talk. "Where are we?"

I look around. We're up in the mountains. Out in the woods. I think I've been here before. Cleto used to come up here and practice shooting. There's an outdoor gun range. It was fun. They taught me how to shoot. I look around for Cleto, but I don't see him. I see my car parked next to the road. Maybe that's it. Beat me up. Leave me in the woods to drive myself home.

"C'mon, *ese*, let's go for a drive."

I nod. But I don't know if I can drive. I'm not feeling too good.

Naldo and Ramón put me in my car and start it for me. That's nice. But I can't put my seatbelt on because I think my arm's broken. I try to tell them this, but they're not listening.

"Drive safe."

They put the car in gear for me and now I'm moving. I guess this is better than being in the trunk. I'll drive to the hospital. I'll call Pasha. She'll visit me. She loves me.

As the car goes over the lip of the cliff, takes a hard bounce, and nosedives toward the canyon floor, I close my eyes. I don't want to see it. I feel weightless, floating, like when the roller coaster comes up from a big dip and just crests the rise before it starts to go down again. It's that little gap of suspense, the dead air between songs on the radio, the frozen moment between exhaling and inhaling, the nervous pause between the order and the execution.

FIVE DAYS AT THE SUNSET

BY PETER SPIEGELMAN

Lethe, South Dakota

Lethe, South Dakota. Not much to it. Not much more than a wide place at the end of an off-ramp—a frozen, flinty afterthought to the interstate, just right for gassing up, taking a leak, and heading out again. Not much to see besides the filling station and the quick-mart, the Sunset Motor Inn, the plow barn for the county road crews, and the Lethe Lounge next door. No reason to hang around.

"Not unless you're lost or out of luck," the desk clerk had said. She was maybe twenty, and her pimpled face was round and sort of vacant, but she'd got it exactly right. I made up a name and paid cash for the room.

There was no particular reason I stopped in Lethe—no particular draw it had over any of the hundred other shitholes I'd driven through in the past week, and nothing about the peeling paint and blistered plywood of the Sunset that was especially tempting when I pulled off the highway that first night. I hadn't planned on anything more than a few hours sleep and maybe a shower, but when morning came I couldn't get out of bed.

I don't know how long I lay there, listening to the wind in the light poles, fingering the thin sheets, and smelling the mildew and my own sour breath. There was a constellation of brown stains on the ceiling, and if I squinted they looked like the outlines of the states I'd passed through. Jersey, Pennsylvania, Ohio, Illinois. Blind panic, fear, anger, and, as I crossed the Mississippi, a floaty, detached kind of feeling. It was a funny buzz—like a contact high but more fragile. It vanished like smoke whenever I thought of Mia.

The sun had crawled right to left across the window shade by the time I managed to reach for the remote. I channel-surfed until I found CNN, and watched what passed for news until someone knocked at the door. It was the pimply girl, wearing a coat like a sleeping bag and carrying a can of Lysol and an armful of dingy towels. I pulled on some clothes and let her in. Then I went to the Lethe Lounge.

It was a cinder-block bunker with a satellite dish on the roof and chicken wire on the windows. Inside was nighttime, and the smell of beer, cigarettes, fried potatoes, and piss. There was a jukebox near the door, and a pool table and pin-ball machine in back. I hadn't seen the cruiser in the parking lot, and I almost bolted when I noticed the state trooper at the bar. Sweat pricked on my forehead when he turned to look, and my knees went soft, but then he turned away, no more interested in me than the bartender was.

I took a deep breath and slid onto a stool and ordered a Coke. I looked at the TV mounted on the wall, and—miracle of miracles—it was tuned to CNBC. I sipped my Coke and watched, and after an hour a piece about the bank came on. It was nothing new, a summary of the story so far—*Rumors of Trading Irregularities at Ketchum Leeds; Ketchum Stock Plunges as Management Confirms Derivatives Losses; Widely Held Ketchum Shares Imperil Pension Funds; Fed Considers Bailout Plan for Ketchum.* A parade of talking heads came next, pre-

222 // Wall Street Noir

dicting doom and disaster all around—for Ketchum management, for shareholders, for anyone who'd ever used a piggybank. And then there was Carter Strickland.

It was a night shot. A square-faced, forty-something fratboy climbs from a black Town Car in front of a green office tower—the Ketchum Leeds headquarters. Snow falls around him and camera flash flares off his forehead and gelled blond hair. A chorus of questions rises, and Strickland—somber and determined—pledges to get to the bottom of things. I smiled and wondered when the last time was he'd worked past dark.

Then the final headline—*Ketchum Derivatives Guru Sought*—and a grainy photo on the screen and my stomach clenched. Without thinking I touched my chin. I'd lost the mustache and the little beard outside of Chicago, and I still felt naked without them. *Derivatives guru.* I shook my head.

I watched CNBC until the bartender changed the channel to bull riding, and after that I watched the place fill up with highway department guys and cowboy truckers and a parade of assorted shitkickers. I switched from Coke to Scotch, and sat motionless on my stool until a rangy guy with a three-day beard staggered against me. He wore a red baseball cap with *Reno* printed on it, and he squinted and looked me up and down. His eyes caught on my L.L.Bean boots, my corduroys, and my North Face parka, and he bared a row of yellow teeth.

"You from the coast or from back east?" he asked. His voice was deeper than I expected. I made a noncommittal noise, and the guy squinted harder. Something knowing came into the yellow smile. "Well which is it? San Fag-cisco, or Jew York City?" I looked at the narrow, knobby face and the tobacco-stained lips, and felt my throat close. The rangy guy put a finger against his pitted nose and pushed it to one side. "Don't bullshit me," he whispered. "I kin always sniff it out." Before I could answer, or even swallow hard, the bartender rapped heavy knuckles on the counter.

"You buying, Ross, or just standing around?" he said to the rangy guy. His voice was flat and rumbling, and he reminded me of the football coach at my high school. Maybe he reminded Ross of something, too, because he ordered a Bud and walked away as soon as he got it.

"Asshole," the bartender muttered, and shook his big bald head. "You want a refill?"

I told him no, and left. The air was like a knife in my chest on the way back to the Sunset, but I stopped in the parking lot anyway, and looked up at the night. There were no stars, just low gray clouds, like a pot lid pressing down.

On my second day in Lethe, I went looking for a newspaper. What I found at the quick-mart barely qualified: two-day-old copies of USA Today, week-old copies of something called the Eagle Recorder, and a stupefying array of gun and tit mags. I bought a muddy coffee and a USA Today and went back to the Sunset, where I leafed through the business section. I stopped when I got to the story about me.

The article was brief: authorities expanding their search for Paul Dillon, managing director at Ketchum Leeds and head of its lucrative hybrid derivatives trading desk, in an ongoing probe of falsified profits at the venerable bank. Blah, blah, blah. The picture was the same blurred headshot they'd been showing on television, and below it was a photo of the place I was last seen—my apartment building. There was a slim woman out front, with long dark hair, who for a wobbly instant I thought was Mia, but wasn't.

There was a knock on the door, and the pimply girl was there again. I added the business section to the stack of papers I'd collected since New York, and left.

The Lethe Lounge was empty, and CNBC was on the box again. The bartender was loading beer bottles into a cooler and looked up when I came in. His forehead wrinkled in recognition.

"Coke?" he asked.

I shook my head. "A Bud."

He pulled one from the cooler. "If you want lunch, you're early."

I took a long drink. "I can wait."

He shrugged and tossed a thumb at the television. "You want to watch something else?"

"This is fine," I said.

A lacquered blonde was interviewing an edgy-looking guy in a dealing room somewhere. The edgy man was talking about another broad sell-off in equities—led again by financial stocks—but I wasn't listening. My attention was on the background: the long, crowded rows of desks, the well-dressed bodies hunched over keyboards, the dense mosaic of glowing monitors, the chirping telephones, the muted rumble of a thousand urgent conversations—all the low-gear chaos and white noise of money made and lost.

It hauled me back to my first day on the Ketchum Leeds trading floor, on the interest rate swaps desk. Eight years ago, and it still made my face hot. I could barely figure out how to work the telephones that morning, much less make sense of what the traders were talking about on the calls. Everything I learned in b-school seemed to blur and slide and wash away, until all I heard was meaningless sound and I was covered in sweat. When the senior trader who'd been saddled with me asked if I had questions, I choked on my embarrassment and shook my head no. He pursed his lips and raised an eyebrow, and we both knew I was lying.

I deciphered the phones eventually, and the vocabulary, too, but I'd never escaped the feeling of that day—of being two steps behind everyone else, of never being the first, or even the second, to see the bud of an opportunity or the tip of an iceberg. Of being in over my head. Two mortifying months later, the senior trader took pity on me, and put me down in front of something that sat still when I looked at it— something that made sense to me—a spreadsheet.

It was a pricing model—a collection of formulas that determined the value of the instruments we were trading, and let us mark our positions to market every day, and calculate our profits and losses. At least that's what it was supposed to do. The trader was convinced it was fucked-up somehow, and low-balling his P&L.

"Some dick from accounting came by last week with an IT guy who didn't know a discounted cash flow from his asshole. They swear up and down they were just tweaking it, but now I don't believe the numbers."

I pored over the spreadsheet for two hours, and every time I glanced up the senior trader was looking at me. The problem, when I found it, was a subtle one—a change in how the yield curves were being built—and it wasn't so much a glitch as a more conservative approach to valuing our swaps. I explained it all to the trader, who listened without expression and smiled when I was done.

"They think I'm a little too aggressive," he chuckled. "Now change it back." And I did, without pause or question. It added 108 grand to that month's profit, and the senior trader grinned wider. It was Carter Strickland's test, and I had passed.

"You want some?" the bartender asked, and brought me back with a jolt.

It was the lunch special—brown and lumpy. It was a long way from the Four Seasons, but the beer and coffee needed something to hold them down. I nodded and he dropped a ladleful into a bowl and set it on the bar and picked up the remote.

"Enough of this," he said, and changed the channel to ESPN. They were covering the trade of a reliable closer and two journeymen right-handers for a big-hitting catcher and an aging first-baseman whose wife was a country singer. The bartender shook his head.

"Fucking Cubbies," he sighed. "Every year the same thing—always a master plan."

"You know what they say about plans."

"What's that?"

"That everybody has one—until you hit 'em in the face."

"Mike Tyson, the great philosopher, right?"

I nodded and looked up. I saw the bumper sticker over the cash register—*Bleed Cubbie Blue*—and the Sammy Sosa bobblehead with the chipped nose next to it. The bartender followed my eyes.

"Never missed a home opener," he said.

"You have a lot of patience."

"What else can you do? Eventually they'll get it right."

"Optimistic too."

He shrugged. "You do what you can with the cards you're dealt, and you hope for something better on the next go round. The important thing is to stay in the game, right?"

"That's the plan."

He put the remote on the bar and went in back. I pushed my food around and flicked the channels. There was a cop show rerun on TBS, with world-weary detectives and an arrogant prick of a suspect who'd be a pathetic wreck by the end. I kept surfing.

I stopped at the fashion channel. It was something about making perfume, and I wasn't sure where the show left off and the commercials started, but I watched anyway. I was looking for Mia. I knew there was little chance of seeing her—she'd only been on that once, and it was months ago— a documentary about aspiring fashion designers. Still, I looked. I remembered how nervous she'd been the night before it first aired, her over-caffeinated engine amped higher than usual.

"They're going to make me look like an asshole, I know it. That's what they do on these things. Either that or I'll come off as a babbling idiot. Or maybe both. And they probably won't even show the clothes. That cocktail dress is one of my best things, and I bet they cut it out." She got nine minutes and fifty-one seconds of screen time, total—more than anyone else—and no one looked better.

Strickland had introduced us a year and a half ago, at Milk & Honey. She was raising money, and glad to see anyone who would pick up a check. I was looking for the usual— a model to fuck—and though she'd never made it on the runway, Mia looked the part: tall and pale, with a glossy wing of hair across a naughty, sulky face. I'd fronted the cash for her fall line, and for the spring one afterwards, and six months back she'd given up her apartment and moved into mine. I wondered how long it would be before someone asked her to move out again. Probably around the time my monthly maintenance check didn't show.

A knot rolled through my gut and I pushed the bowl away. The perfume show ended and another one, about eyeliner, began. I called into the kitchen for the check.

I was crossing the lot at the Lethe Lounge when a rust-scabbed pickup turned too fast off the road. It churned up stones and a cloud of icy dust, and its rear end slewed wildly. I jumped out of the way. A big guy in a blue parka with an American flag patch on the sleeve fell out of the passenger side and stumbled into the bar. The driver paused by the door and looked back at me. He took off his red cap and waved.

On the third day I bought maps. The quick-mart had more of these than it did newspapers, and I got ones for points north, south, and west. I bought a twelve-pack of tallboys and a bag of pork rinds, too, and carried it all to my room. I turned on the TV and spread the maps on the bed and opened a beer.

I'd had no plan when I left New York—nothing besides getting as far as I could from the office and from the questions that'd been growing like barnacles on my trading desk ever since that fucking auditor, DiMarco, had come around. But now I was running out of country. A couple of days driving and I'd hit water, and then what? South to Mexico? North to Canada? Or maybe straight on through, into the Pacific.

I opened another beer and stared at the roads and dotted borders. Lines and colors braided into impossible knots, and the place names began to squirm like bugs. I rubbed my eyes and jabbed at the remote. The channels flew by like towns through a train window, and after a while it made me dizzy. I grabbed my coat and the pork rinds and went to the Lethe Lounge.

There was a dented gray van in the lot, and a blue parka with a flag patch on the sleeve hanging on a barstool inside. A big guy was working the pinball machine and drinking a beer. The bartender was leafing through the sports section of a newspaper. I slid onto a stool and he eyed the pork rinds.

"There a problem with these?" I asked.

He shrugged. "Not if you finish them fast. You want a Bud?" I nodded, and he opened the cooler. I looked at his newspaper. The *Chicago Tribune.*

"Where'd that come from?" I asked, and dug into the chips.

"They have it at the store sometimes. I read it online, but the real thing's good when you can get it."

I offered him the bag. "Any more trades?"

"Just rumors," he said. He reached in and ate a chip.

I pointed to the paper. "Mind if I look?"

He slid the paper over and went into the kitchen. It was the local news, sports, and arts sections—no business. I folded it and pushed it aside, and the big guy from the pinball machine knocked an empty beer bottle on the bar.

"Hey, Mickey," he called, "lemme get another."

"In a sec," the bartender answered, and the big guy looked at me. His face was lined and freckled, with scars around the eyes. His teeth were gray, and the smell of cigarettes and asphalt rolled off him. He looked at the newspaper and back at me and frowned.

"You a Chicago boy, like ol' Mick?" he asked. I shook my head. "No? But you from the city somewhere. What the hell you doin' out here?"

Mickey came out and pushed a beer in front of the big guy. "What else do you need, Len—more quarters for the machine?"

"Sure," Len said, "quarters." He put two bills on the bar, but kept staring at me. Mickey gave him change and he went away.

"Friendly," I said.

Mickey frowned. "You want to keep away from him. From his buddy Ross, too." I thought back to the guy in the red cap, waving in the parking lot.

"Why? They don't like strangers?"

"Something like that," he said, and looked up as the door opened. A girl came in, awkward in a coat like a sleeping bag. The pimply girl from the Sunset. She unzipped the coat and went behind the bar.

"Sorry I'm late, Pops," she said. Mickey nodded and she went into the kitchen.

"Your daughter?" I asked.

"Yep."

"You run the motel too?"

"I own it, like I own this place."

I ate a pork rind. "How'd you end up out here?"

He shrugged. "Company early-retired me, and I always wanted to buy property out west. I didn't necessarily have this in mind, but the 401k didn't go as far as I planned."

"You like it?"

He took my empty beer bottle and replaced it with a full one. "Keeps me in the game. What about you?"

"Me? I'm headed west."

He nodded and produced the remote from under the bar and turned on the tube. He started surfing through the channels and stopped when his daughter called from the kitchen. He left the remote by the chips.

The box was tuned to Court TV, a grimy video—the interrogation of a scrawny teenage boy by two big cops in a bleak white room. I took a long pull on my beer. The cops were shouting and pacing, and the kid had his head in his hands. He was saying something about a girlfriend. I picked up the remote, but my thumb froze above the button as the kid's voice broke.

I knew it was only a matter of time for me. I'd tossed my cell phone in a trashcan in Altoona, but eventually I'd run out of cash and have to use a credit card or an ATM, and that would be it. Then it would be me in a room somewhere, with my head in my hands. *How did you do it? How long was it going on? Was anyone else involved?*

How long wasn't easy to nail down. When, precisely, did panic become a plan? When did I pass through the gray zones of deniability—the honest mistake, the error in judgment, the pardonable miscalculation—and into the pitch black? Hard to say, but fixing that spreadsheet for Strickland was the first step. He'd shined that too-wide smile on me, dropped a big hand on my shoulder, and promised he'd square everything with the accountants. Then he'd christened me with a nickname, and made me what he called his go-to guy for numbers.

"You've got a feel for the models, P-Man, and before we put up any new ones, I want you to check them out—make sure everything is copasetic."

I was stunned. Relieved, of course, that he wasn't canning my ass, and wildly flattered—but stunned. I'd protested—that I didn't have the experience, that I knew the math but not the markets—but Strickland didn't care. He winked and spoke in a stage whisper. "Don't worry about it, P, nobody else around here knows what this stuff is worth either. Anybody asks questions, you throw some math at 'em. If that doesn't scare 'em off, you send 'em my way."

He took me out for drinks after that, a blurry bar crawl that ended nine hours and a dozen lap-dances later at the Platinum Playpen. Everyone knew him there, and I can still see the colored lights shining on his teeth, and the glitter and sweat on that stripper's tits. He took me back to the Playpen four months later, when he was starting up the hybrids desk.

"It'll be a different gig—more of a boutique business. The guys we're trading with need customized stuff—derivatives to hedge against ice in Orlando, or too much rain in Napa, or pipeline problems in Kazakhstan. It's exotic shit, each time a one-off, and we can charge big premiums and still have them lining up. Assuming, of course, we can price things right. That's where you come in, P-Man. And who knows—if the business takes hold, maybe we can get you back to trading. It's more cerebral than what we're doing now—more up your alley."

I'd been handed my first bonus check by then, and though it was hefty for a numbers guy—enough for a new Beemer and a down payment on a Tribeca loft—it was nothing like the monsters the traders took home. I wasn't inclined to argue.

After that, things went according to Strickland's plan: We built it and they came. And they paid. They bitched about it, but in the end they paid. Actually, there was bitching all around at first—from customers about our pricing, and from our own accountants, who were antsy about our mark-to-market calculations. *Too aggressive*, they said. *Overly optimistic*. But whenever anyone came around with questions, I followed Strickland's advice and dazzled them with bullshit. The complexity of the models intimidated eighty percent of the worriers off the bat, and they went away nodding wisely, as if they had a clue about what I'd said. Anyone more persistent I referred to Strickland, who worked his hale-fellow mojo and somehow turned their doubts into soap bubbles. Maybe he took them to the Playpen.

As profits mounted, less and less mojo was required, and the questions all but vanished amidst high praise and promotions. In two years' time, riding an ever-growing wave of revenue, Carter Strickland became head of the entire dealing room. Two years later he became president of Ketchum Leeds.

And me, I held tight to his coattails. Strickland hadn't been jerking me off about trading again, and a few months after we opened for business I had a book of my own to run. This time I knew how to work the phones. I made managing director at the end of our first year, and when he moved up to take over the dealing room, I took over the hybrids desk.

It was a steep climb, and not without its bumps. There were months when the P&L slipped, but never two in a row—Strickland wouldn't allow it. When trouble loomed, he'd saunter over to my desk, drop a hand on my shoulder, and invite me to his glassed-in office. We'd prop our feet, drink espressos, and shoot the shit about his latest vacation, his latest car, or his latest wife, and when we'd exhausted the chat and the coffee, he'd sigh and say the same thing.

"Numbers looking a little hinky, don't you think, P-Man? Maybe you oughta check the models—see if something needs goosing." After which we'd stroll back to the dealing room and I'd take up my keyboard.

There was never any talk of my leaving the desk—not when Strickland took over the trading floor, and not when he stepped up to run the whole bank either. Somebody had to do the goosing, after all. And besides paying for a bigger loft, the house in East Hampton, and Mia and her line of clothes, the seven-figure bonus checks made staying behind easy to take. At least until DiMarco.

I took another drink and gagged on the warm beer. On

TV, one of the cops pounded the table. His partner shook his head and asked more questions, and the kid slumped lower in his chair. I thought about the maps on the motel bed and my car, icing over in the parking lot, and about throwing my stuff in the back and driving off. Mexico, or maybe Canada. I tried to remember where I'd put my car keys. In my coat pocket, maybe. Inches away, but too far to reach.

I slept late on the fourth day—past noon, and through the pimply girl's knock on the door. I awoke in my clothes, on top of maps and surrounded by beer cans. There was a car chase playing silently on TV—a minivan rolling down an empty highway, five cop cars and the shadow of a helicopter in pursuit. My head was full of road salt and pieces of a dream. DiMarco standing over my desk, holding a report and tapping it with a boney finger. There was a smug, triumphant look on his librarian's face, and a noise like static whenever he opened his mouth. Mia at the beach house, making blender drinks and laughing. Her hair was up, and her long neck was pale and damp. Her hands were bandaged, and there were red streaks in my margarita. Mia and Carter Strickland at the Playpen, bite marks on her breasts and colored lights shining on his big teeth.

My bones were like lead, and it was all I could do to lever myself up and into the shower. I stayed there until the dry heaves subsided and my skin was a savage red, and it was night by the time I set out for the quick-mart. I picked up a Snickers, some beef jerky, and another six of beer, and I was looking at the magazines when the state trooper came in. He bought coffee and a sandwich that he heated in the microwave, but he didn't even glance down the aisle while it cooked. Still, I waited until he'd pulled out of the lot to pay for my stuff. My hands were shaking when I paid the clerk, and he gave me the eye when he handed back change.

"What are you looking at?" I said. He frowned and shook his head.

Even with every light on, a brown twilight was the most I could manage in my room. I turned on the radio and found the one station that wasn't static. An angry guy was talking to an angrier guy about weakness and depravity on both coasts. It was drivel, but I wanted voices.

I opened a beer and turned on the TV. It was tuned to the game show channel—a show from the '70s, with puffy-haired people in bad clothes. The contestants were paired with celebrities, though I wasn't sure who was who. The point of the thing was one player guessing a secret word from clues given by his partner. *Condiment; spicy; hotdog . . . mustard!* Much applause followed.

I downed my beer in one swallow, and eyed the host. Something about him—the unlikely tan, the wide forehead, maybe the teeth—reminded me of Carter Strickland. I pictured Strickland in an ugly plaid jacket and too-wide tie, smiling, nodding, directing the game. I worked a strip of jerky in my back teeth, and thought about our last meeting.

It was in his vast office at the top of the tower. The shades were up and the river was bright and hard-looking in the morning light. The trading day hadn't started in New York, but the big monitors on his wall showed the action in London. Strickland was scanning his e-mail, and I closed the door.

"Don't give me more of that *relax* crap," I said. "It's all I've heard for weeks, and this guy still hasn't gone away."

He ran a palm over his slick hair and smiled indulgently. "He has questions, that's all. Give him some answers, and this thing will run its course."

"*Run its course?* He has questions about the models, Carter—the fucking pricing models. And this guy is no lightweight—he's half a dissertation away from being *Doctor* DiMarco. The formulas don't faze him. He's down in the guts of things, and he's looking at P&L going back Christ knows how long."

He kept smiling. "Is he?"

"Fucking right he is. So get him promoted, get him fired—take him out and get him laid for all I care—just get rid of him."

The tanned brow crinkled. "Come on, Paul, you know how the game is played. The man has a job to do, and it wouldn't look good if people thought I was trying to stop him from doing it. It wouldn't look appropriate."

"*Appropriate?* What the fuck does that mean?"

Strickland smiled wide and shook his head like I was an idiot nephew. "It's the optics of the thing, Paul, just the optics. Let it work itself out. It'll be fine."

I don't how long I stood there with my mouth open. Long enough for Strickland's secretary to come in and remind him of a conference call and usher me into his waiting room. She disappeared back into his office and shut the door behind her. I ran my hands through my hair.

Optics? Work itself out? And what's with Paul—*what happened to* P-Man?

I looked down at his secretary's desk, and at his appointment book, open on it. I flipped the pages back, week after week—and there they were. Early breakfasts, late lunches, drinks and dinners—*DiMarco, DiMarco, DiMarco.* Since before the audit started. I went to the street from there, and didn't even stop at my desk.

What's the secret word, Carter? *Scapegoat,* maybe?

Fallguy? How about *fucked?* Yeah—that's it—definitely *fucked.*

More clapping on TV. A woman with heavy eye makeup was showing a flair for the game. *Antlers, slipcover, clandestine—* she got them all with just a hint or two. I couldn't recall her name but I recognized her from a sitcom that ran when I was a kid, and I was pretty sure she was dead. Her hair was dark and wavy, and it reminded me of Mia's.

I'd almost told her a hundred times, but always managed to convince myself the timing wasn't right. This weekend maybe, at the beach—or next month, when she's finished with her show. Maybe on the trip to Bali, or maybe after. Maybe over dinner. There would always be another, better moment.

The truth was, I was looking for a sure thing and Mia wasn't it. Her moods were too volatile, and could whip from elated to dismal three times while her coffee cooled—and she traveled way too light. A bag of clothes, another of shoes, and she could leave on a whim. Sometimes, when I woke up next to her, I was surprised to find she hadn't left already. Then I'd remember the dump she'd been living in and the firetrap that used to be her workshop, and I'd think of her shiny new studio and her plans for her next line. Who knew what she'd do if I told her they were built on sand?

Still, there were times I'd nearly risked it. In the cab, coming back from some club in Brooklyn, when she put her fingers in my hair and whispered in my mouth. In bed, when she looked at me like she was reading tea leaves. Walking home from dinner, when she took my hand and put it in her pocket. Each time I told myself, *Don't lose this,* and, *Hold on.* Each time I told myself to speak, but never said a word.

The last time was on the day I left. The car was running

and I punched her number on my cell. I was going to tell her everything, and ask her to pack a bag, but when I heard her voice, I saw her and Strickland at Milk & Honey on the night we met. They were talking and smiling, and suddenly there was something conspiratorial in their laughter. She knew it was me on the line, and she said my name again and again. I switched the phone off and drove away. What's your secret word, Mia? I couldn't begin to guess. The woman on TV scored again. *Mystery; riddle; puzzle—enigma!* Much applause. I drank my last beer and picked up my coat.

There were trucks in the lot of the Lethe Lounge, and the smell of exhaust on the cold air. Inside, a layer of cigarette smoke was gathering at the ceiling. There were customers in back, playing pinball and pool, and a stock car race on TV. I took a stool and ordered a double Scotch. Mickey poured it and put it down in front of me.

"How're you doing?" he asked. "Still in the game?"

"Sure," I said, and he went away.

I drank my drink and watched the cars become a loud blur around the bright track. The sun and flags and noise reminded me of absolutely nothing, and it was very restful. When Mickey came back, my head was on the bar and he looked worried. I sat up and waved my glass at him. He just stood there. I waggled my glass again.

"I thought this was the international sign for *give me another fucking drink.*"

Mickey shook his head. "Not for you."

I wiped my chin with my sleeve. "What—I have to listen to some bullshit bartender wisdom first?"

His eyes narrowed. "The only wisdom I have is: Go back to your room and sleep it off."

I slammed my glass down, loud enough to turn heads.

"What happened—you all of a sudden run out of advice? A couple of days ago you were chockful—crap about *plans* and *staying in the game* and who I should keep away from."

Mickey's face darkened. "Keep your voice down," he rumbled. "Anyway, you're not looking for advice."

"The fuck you know—nobody needs advice more than I do."

"You need it, but drunks don't listen."

"Try me."

"Fine," he sighed. "I don't know what you're playing at, but it's slow right now. What do you want advice about?"

"About staying in the game. I want to know what the point of it is."

"Staying in the game? It's an expression, that's all—like *hanging in there*. It means sometimes things get hard, but you keep trying. You tough it out."

"I know what it means, for chrissakes—my question is: Why bother?"

He rolled his eyes. "What's the alternative—whining about life all day? Laying down and dying? I don't think so. I think you stay in the game."

"And if the game is rigged? If you just can't win—then what do you do?"

Mickey sighed. "This is what I get for talking to a drunk. I should know better by now."

"I'm serious—what do you do?"

"What else can you do except keep trying?"

I laughed. "That's sucker thinking—it's what gets people spending their welfare checks on lottery tickets. I'm talking about when the serious fix is in—when it's a stacked deck. I'm asking what if you *know* there's just no way to win?"

He squinted at me, and took his time rubbing a cloth

over the bar. "Then maybe I'd try to change the game—try to get a little something back. See if I couldn't get even, and then get out."

I leaned over the bar and took hold of Mickey's arm and whispered to him, "Getting even—I like that. But *how*, Mickey—how do you do it?"

He jerked his arm loose and shook his head. "You need to lie down."

The door opened and a crowd came in and Mickey moved off. The cigarette smoke grew thicker and bodies jammed the bar, and I was pushed sideways and then away. I ended up at a table in a corner, thinking about getting even and about getting another drink. I wasn't there long when a wiry hand gripped my shoulder. I looked up at a knobby face, a row of yellow teeth, and a red cap.

"I owe you a drink from the other night—for being a prick. What're you havin'?" I looked at his hand on my shoulder, and at the twin lightning bolts tattooed across his knuckles. He squeezed harder. "What's the matter, pard—you don't want to drink with me?"

"Scotch," I said.

He brought back two doubles, two beers for himself, and one for his pal Len, who brought along three other guys whose names I never got. They stood around the small table and blocked out the light. They let Ross do all the talking, and they took their eyes off me only to glance at one another and exchange narrow smiles. I knew I should be scared, and a part of me was, but another part was thirsty. And the rest of me—the biggest part by far—could barely pay attention to any of it.

Two doubles became two more, and two after that, and the room was now a smear of noise and smoke and sweat.

The circle of bodies around the table grew tighter and darker and like a cave, and only Ross's questions made it through the gloom. He kept repeating them—again and again—and they stuck like splinters in my head. *Where're you from? Where're you headed? Why'd you stop here? Who's expecting you?* His voice was raspy and intimate, and his face was close to mine. His breath was like a barnyard and the questions kept coming, and all of a sudden it seemed important to have the answers. I worked up a sweat trying, but every time I reached for one, it wriggled away.

"Who's expecting you?" he asked again, and Mia's pale, fretting face rose up and I started to cry. There was laughter in the cave, and someone dropped a hand on my shoulder and put another shot glass in front of me. I downed it and choked, and the world began to slide. I was covered in sweat, and I knotted up inside, from the chest down.

"Jesus, Ross," someone said, "he's gonna boot." Then there were arms under mine.

"Come on, pard, you need air."

Hands pushed me along, and the cave became a tunnel. I stumbled to the end of it, out into the frozen night. I staggered against a dumpster and emptied myself in a bellowing retch. I kneeled against the dumpster, shaking, and when I looked up there were stars in the sky.

"Holy shit," a voice said, "the fucking guy gave birth."

There was laughter and a hand on my collar and Ross's voice. "Come on, pard, a little ride will fix you."

I didn't want to move, but the hand pulled me up. I tried to hold onto the dumpster, but the hand pried my fingers loose and pulled me across the parking lot to a dented gray van. A door slid open and someone took my arm. I looked up at the stars.

"Climb in, pard," Ross said, but I didn't want to. I yanked my arm away and pushed backward.

"I have to make a call," I said. My voice sounded hollow. "I have to call Mia."

"Sure," Ross said, "I got a phone in here."

Hands grabbed at my coat, but I spun away and stumbled. "I want to talk to Mia."

"Who the fuck is Mia?" someone said.

"Maybe it's his mother—like Mama Mia."

There was laughter, and another voice shouted: "He don't look Italian!"

More laughter, and still another voice. "She can't come to the phone anyway—she's in the can, giving head to Lenny." Louder laughter, and someone had my arm.

"I want to talk to her," I said, and I threw my elbow back. It hit something soft, and for a moment everything went quiet. And then the walls came down.

Rocks, stones, big boulders—in my face, my gut, my balls. I was on my knees, on my stomach, curled up with my arms around my head. There was blood in my mouth and in my eyes, and nothing but ringing in my ears.

Then there was a sudden boom like thunder and the sound of breaking glass, and it all stopped.

"Jesus Christ, Mickey—what the fuck's with you? That's my goddamn windshield." It was Len's voice.

There was another sound—a mechanical slide and click—and Ross's voice, nervous.

"For chrissake, Mickey, put that thing down."

"Just as soon as you drive away, you and your pals."

"C'mon, man, we're having a little fun is all."

"Have it somewhere else, and with somebody else."

"Christ, Mick, he's just a drunk."

"He's my drunk, Ross."

I heard shuffling and someone spit on me, and then the space around me cleared. I saw the sky, and Mickey and his daughter standing over me.

"Can you walk?" Mickey asked.

"Sure," I said, and I passed out.

I woke in my room on the fifth day, surprised to be anywhere at all. In the mirror, my face was cut and skewed, like a shredded document glued back together but with pieces gone. And the rest of me, from what I could see, was no better. Someone had gotten my clothes off, but I still smelled like smoke and vomit and burnt garbage. I hobbled to the bathroom to piss, and when I did, it was dark and felt like a wire going through me. I stood at the sink and ran water on my hands. It stung in the cuts, but it was nothing compared to the pain in my throat, which felt like lye, and the pain in my head, which felt fatal.

I climbed into the shower and let the water boil me. After a while, heat overcame pain and I washed myself three times. Then I boiled myself some more, while memories of Strickland and our last meeting rose from the steam—the smiling face, those teeth, *you know how the game is played*. His face and voice mixed with scraps of the night before—the circle of men, Ross's questions, and Mickey's words. *Get even and get out*. After a longer while, I smiled. I was still a shambles—brittle, scrambled, full of broken glass—but my mind felt clearer than it had in weeks, in years maybe. I finally had a plan.

There was nothing complicated about it: good lawyers, a plea bargain, whatever testimony they wanted, and then a book deal. It wouldn't be easy, and it would cost me every cent I had and more, but I knew I could make it work. The very first step, even before the lawyers, was to call Mia. I needed to talk to her—to hear her voice and tell her everything. And then I needed to get the hell out of this dump and back to civilization.

I turned off the water and wrapped a towel around me. I hobbled from the bathroom, and that's when I noticed that my clothes were gone. Not just the stuff I'd worn the night before, but everything—underwear, socks, shoes, all of it. And not just my clothes. My bags were gone, too, and my wallet—even my stack of newspapers. I went to the window. No car.

"Motherfuckers." I picked up the phone and was listening to silence in the receiver when the door opened. Mickey came in, followed by his daughter and an icy wind. I shivered and put the receiver down.

"They robbed me, those bastards. They took everything."

Mickey sat in the only chair. His daughter closed the door and leaned against it. I tied my towel more tightly.

"Plus, the fucking phone's not working," I said. Mickey nodded and I took a deep breath. "You saved my ass last night, and I owe you big time. But I need your help again. I've got to get out of here—and in a hurry—but those fuckers cleaned me out." Mickey nodded some more and looked around the room. "I'll pay you back for everything," I added.

"Sure you will," he said, and smiled. "But it wasn't Ross that cleaned you out." His daughter opened her big coat and produced a newspaper. It was the *Philadelphia Inquirer*, the business section, one of the papers off my stack. I sat on the bed. My face was throbbing, and when I touched it, my fingers were dotted with blood.

"You don't look much like your picture," she said.

I peered at Mickey. "What the hell is this?"

He shrugged. "It's getting something back."

My throat was tight, and I had to force the words out. "Getting what?"

Mickey smiled. "Two weeks ago, I had four hundred thousand in my retirement account. Not as much as I thought I'd have at this point—not as much as I would've if my old company hadn't messed with our pension fund—but with the income from this place and the bar, it was enough to keep body and soul together. At least until you came along."

"What did I—"

"The money was in a fund that bet big on bank stocks. Stupid of them probably, and probably stupid of me to invest, but it was doing fine until you. Now it's all but gone."

My head was spinning, and I couldn't seem to get any air in my lungs. I looked in the mirror and for an instant I thought I saw Mia behind me. "And what do you want from me—money?"

The pimply girl took her hand from the pocket of her big coat. There was an ugly black gun in it, and an ugly smile on her face. Mickey shook his head sadly. "For starters," he said.

TODAY WE HIT

BY MEGAN ABBOTT

110 W. 139th Street

Her mother taught her there could be something lovely in the way a rainbow would arc through a tub of soapy water, even as the smell pinched her nose and her hands cracked red from the bleach, from a hundred splinters off the cracking wood of the mop handle. A thousand rainbows could span that tub now and she wouldn't bat an eye.

And there he was, how many paychecks for that almond-green felt derby of his, telling her once more that he would soon be covering her broken hands in rose milk and fine perfumes, a bauble for every bleach-brined finger.

"Say it all you want, my man. But that won't make it so," she said, looking out the browned window, the fading orange light streaking the building tops.

He laughed. He always laughed and it was charming once, that gentle burr, the lilt of the islands twisting through it like a stick of peppermint.

He had taken his hat off and unfastened the very top button on his coat. The room was hot and she herself, laid up all day with an awful pain, had settled on the bed so he might have the chair in the corner that came with the faintest breeze. Wearily, she opened two buttons on her dress, buttons tacky to the touch with the awful thick in the air, and reached for her hand fan, the one he bought her at the curio shop on Pell Street.

"I've walked this road before, my man," she said to him. "I won't walk it again without something more than a honey promise."

Over the past year, she'd said it to him ten, twenty times or more. And he'd always nod, even laugh, and never press the point. And that ease, the kindness in it—sometimes it brought heat under her eyes when she thought about it and she hated him for it. How dare he do that to her, bring that out in her when he'd yet to make money enough to put more than a paper fan from Chinatown in her cracked hand.

He could hardly wait to get to her apartment that night. He ran the last seven blocks, crosstown. They had a date and he'd told her to wear her good dress, the one she called "Alice blue," because they were going to celebrate something and he was taking her dancing. He wanted to see her twirl in that dress. He wanted to see her smile when she looked at him, which hadn't happened in some time.

But she wasn't wearing the dress and didn't want to go out. She felt sickly and had missed work and was worried she'd be dismissed. Her hip had started up again, a relentless throb. Four months back she'd been burned, the cook accidentally spattering hot sugar on her. When they tried to brush it off, the skin came with it. She missed two days of work and had been lucky to keep the job. But the hurt kept starting up again, twitching under her skin and then blazing by the end of a long day scrubbing, knees to the floor.

He knew she must be feeling very poorly. Before, she'd never reclined on the bed in his presence, never even let him three steps past the doorway.

Looking at her arranged there like a wilted flower, petals spread forlorn, he knew it would be an uphill battle, but he had much to tell her, much to make her understand. Everything had changed for him, for both of them, since the day before. He needed to make her see because it would mean he'd finally be worth her time, *her closed-off heart.*

There was a brightness in his eye that night, but she'd seen it before, on him, on other men. She'd long ago stopped letting the brightness spark off her. There was no dividend.

"I want you to see it," he was telling her. "I want you to see it like I did. Like seeing the face of God himself. You realize it's been there all along. You just didn't know how to look."

She turned away from him and remembered. Something long ago was visiting her, something from before he started calling, before any men started calling. She was standing, a long-limbed, long-necked eleven-year-old, before a large window display at Blumstein's on 125th Street, a rippling row of summer dresses in every color—peacock blue, canary yellow, the deep orange of summer tea on a windowsill. It was as if they were moving in the June breeze, drifting on some clothesline, and if she reached out she could touch the soft linen.

Finding herself struck by the memory of it, she forced herself back. "It's just another policy game," she said, shaking her head back and forth on the pillow. "That's all you're talking. There's ten policy bankers in ten Harlem blocks and none of them making a slim dime anymore."

"This is different," he said. "Let me show you how." His voice like sugar on a spoon, crackling in her ear. "Let me show you."

* * *

He'd been working at No. 37 Wall Street for almost a year, evening to sunrise, and had yet to see more than a handful of souls. All those gray-hatted, gray-faced men in their Arrow collars and polished brogues had long dispersed by the time he arrived, all off to some elegant drawing rooms in tall brownstones or Fifth Avenue apartments, in stately buildings dripping with white trim like wedding cakes, or to dinner at Sherry's, Lobster Newberg, sweet bread in terrapin, jelly rubanée, and cigars, or train rides to homes on Long Island with stretches of lawn that seemed to end somewhere across the ocean.

And there he'd be, in the empty husk they left behind each day, boot to bucket. But he never minded any of it.

Nights, 2, 3 o'clock, he'd sit at one of the brokers' desks, each night a different one, slippery walnut top, elbows on green felt, fingers spread on the ledgers. He'd sit there in his bleach-specked trousers, his worn work shirt. He'd sit there and he'd read. He'd read the newspapers, one by one, the *Wall Street Journal*, the *Times*, the *Evening Journal*, the *Herald*, the *World*, the *American*, everything he could find. And he'd think. He'd wonder about the broker who sat there all day, probably ten or fifteen years younger, a seersucker-suited youth, lazy from summers in Newport, a winter's month in St. Augustine. Did that man, that mere boy, know the hard majesty of numbers? Or did he stare dreamily out the window and ponder gossamer, the winsome heiress with whom he danced at the previous night's Mayflower Ball?

Well he, he wouldn't waste a minute at that desk. And hell if he was going to do his reading in the janitor's closet. He had a right to be at that desk. He knew none of those brokers saw the numbers float miraculous. Sometimes the digits felt so alive they were shimmering things he could roll across his knuckles like his granddad with his lucky gold piece.

He never doubted his purpose, his reason for being there, for making the long way down to the tip of the island five days a week. After all, he'd been waiting a long time, since coming out of Boys High School in Brooklyn twenty years before. He'd worked as a bellhop, a short-order cook, four years in the Navy, near seven more as a hotel porter, and he could certainly push a mop on those fine marble floors a little while longer. To him, it was like a running leap. And if he ever felt a flicker of uncertainty, he'd pull a worn piece of paper from his pocket. Copied from a periodical, it read:

> *Immense power is acquired by assuring yourself in your secret reveries that you were born to control affairs.*

Because he had a plan he was working on and he could, with a pure heart, promise her that, if she would just wait a little longer, they'd both be gliding across their own marble floors by New Year's and wouldn't she like to be a June bride anyway?

That night with her, the plan was no longer shimmering on the horizon. It was trapped in his belly and he could feel it when he laid his hand there, when he rested his hat over it.

When she heard his news, he assured her, she would feel the pain soften and dissolve and she would want to put on her Alice-blue dress and tie a ribbon in her hair and be ready to dance all night, because everything had changed and he would tell her why.

She almost didn't want him to tell her. She knew how he

could talk, first like butterflies flitting softly against her ear, and then, as the story, the idea, the promise would build, a music so lovely, so deep and bone-stirring, and then she'd have to work so hard to keep that hardness inside her. That tightness that had protected her for a year or more with this man, protected her from yet another disappointment—one man forgot to say he had a wife and newborn baby down in Baltimore, one man forgot to tell her he'd just signed up for a hitch in the Merchant Marines, one man forgot to say his mother wouldn't like to see him with a colored woman on a public street. Or, worst of all, the ones who wanted to stay around but couldn't—couldn't hold a job, or got so beaten down by hard labor it was all they could do to keep from jumping off the Willis Avenue Bridge.

Please don't, she wanted to tell him now. But telling him even that would be showing him something, and she was determined to show him nothing.

So she listened.

He wouldn't rush. He knew he had to take her through it step by step so she could experience it as he had.

My girl, he said, it was just last night at old No. 37. Finished with floors five through fifteen. Every long corridor swept and mopped, every waste basket emptied, the candlestick telephones polished, the standing ashtrays shaken out and filled with fresh sand. The smell of Dazzle bleach and carnauba wax heavy in the air.

He was standing in the closet, pouring bleach down the sink drain.

It came in a flash, his whole destiny flickering before his eyes, like a newsreel unspooling. A jittery image of himself, a Borsalino bowler on his head, Malacca walking stick in his hand, a topcoat of finest Italian wool, standing in an elegant drawing room with tall curtains and chandeliers. And pieces of gold, they were funneling down from the top edge of the screen, the ceiling, the sky, twirling like long sparkling ribbons in front of him and through his hands, his fingers, and to the carpet beneath him where it massed in enormous piles, a pirate's booty out of a child's picture book.

It came to him like that.

It was like St. Paul, wasn't it, a mop standing in for a horse hoof. And standing there, he laughed like a drunken fool, teetering and spinning like a top because it was all there, waiting for him. He just had to take it.

It was all the clearing house totals, you see. Published each day in the financial press.

He'd kept the pages with each day's totals in stacks tied with string. They sat in the corner of the basement next to the bags of salt. He'd kept them because he liked to watch the turn, the tilt, the romance of the rising and falling totals. He'd kept them for reasons he hadn't known before but knew now.

Carrying those papers, strings slipped over his fingers, he walked to the mahogany-walled warren of the floor's head broker, Mr. Thornton, the one who proudly displayed a photograph of himself astride a powerful horse, polo mallet in hand.

He sat at Mr. Thornton's desk, pulled out a scratch pad and pencil, and went to work.

He sat there, a pile of ginger nuts, a few stray cigarettes to fire his mind, paper and grease pencil in hand. He knew it would work, had known it back in that closet. But he wasn't taking any chances. He would play with those numbers all night, making sure . . .

* * *

"I sat at that desk," he told her now, "and time passed like two beats of my heart and then it was dawn. My hands covered with ink, dear lady, and I felt drunk as a preacher, and just like a preacher, kissed by God, because I knew. I knew."

When he told her this, she felt like she was fighting him off, heel of hand to chest, knees tucked high, and it was hard, because he looked lit from within, a Midas in a felt fedora with the voice of a soft-tongued minister with a pure, pure heart.

Even as she fought, however, she felt the something tight inside her, the thing she kept fitted tight and compact inside her all day every day, start to loosen, the hard bolts that held it together giving way slowly and falling. And she hated this feeling because she knew the tightness and it kept her and it was all she had.

When he talked, he used his hands, which were graceful, lithe, delicate, didn't fit with his round face, his big barrel chest, his heavy lidded eyes. When he talked, he created pictures for her, with his hands, with his silver-toned voice, the way he kept his eyes on her and at the same time some imagined place over her left shoulder where, he assured them both, a shimmering future lay. A future beckoning them, artlessly.

Once it was . . .

Then it was . . .

Now it would be . . .

She looked at him, at his eager eyes flickering, daring her to come and join his dream like it wasn't a dream at all but a thing you could lay your hands on and feel under each finger like the ropy filaments on a mop.

The only thing that's real, she kept telling herself, is the pain in my curved back. No, she wouldn't join that dream. He hadn't earned the right. Didn't he know all that was real to her was her five dollars a week plus bus fare? Didn't he see he'd have to put her hands on something more than a fancy man's story to make it matter for her now? She was twenty-eight years old, twenty-eight years too old for the soft-tongued promises of handsome men leaning over her tired bed.

It's not enough anymore, she told him. It was once but not anymore. I have to be able to lay my hands on it. Can you do that for me? Can you make it real?

I can, he said. My dear, I can.

"So what did you figure out down there in that closet? A way to beat the bankers?" she said, forcing a toughness in her voice. "You think you're going to make a fat pot on the stock market with your handful of dollars a week?"

He shook his head. "I'm not *playing* the market, my girl. I'm *making* a market."

"And what's for sale in your market, my man? What are we buying?"

"Same as Wall Street. A glimmer down the road."

She shook her head. "Don't tell me you're just talking about another numbers racket." When she met him, he was a runner for a policy game, taking bets from hotel customers. "I don't make time with racketeers."

He smiled and rose from his chair, walking to the edge of the bed. "It's no racket. It's honest as your furrowed brow, m'lady. It's a true thing."

"Sounds to me like you're just talking another numbers game, fat chances and day wages down. *Bolita* all over again," she said, still shaking her head. She told him how her auntie had played every day for years, a penny down each morning and hit five dollars once in a blue moon. They drew the numbers at the cigar store, pulling numbered ball bearings from a sack behind the counter. Sometimes Auntie took her for the drawing and sometimes she was the one chosen to pluck the ball bearings from the soft muslin pouch that made her fingertips smell like sweet tobacco.

When Auntie needed that operation on her neck to take out the swollen tumor the size of a large lemon, she had no money to pay for it. The charity hospital took her instead. Everyone said the doctor who removed it smelled like apple jack. She died the next morning, her face gray and frozen. She could picture her auntie's face now, the awful way the skin pearled along the bones, like wax.

Not three months later, word spread that the smiling cigar store owner had been rigging the numbers for years, palming duplicate ball bearings on days when it suited him. Before anything could happen, the store was shuttered up and he was long gone. Someone thought they spotted him on the platform at Pennsylvania Station, getting on a train to parts south.

A lot of the *bolita* bankers closed up shop after that, one after another. "When I played the game, that lady was a virgin," one of them said. "Now she is a whore."

He smiled when she told him this. He'd been hoping she would take him to just this point. It was what it was all about.

He recalled his favorite teacher at Brooklyn Boys High School, dark-eyed, timid Mrs. Koplon, who stayed after school with him, who filled the blackboard with glorious clouds of numbers, the chalk dust swirling around their heads.

And now he began talking softly, gently, just like Mrs. Koplon. Numbers aren't just what you have or you don't have in your pocket, bus fare or shoe-leathering it, steak on a fine plate or canned hash, he told her. Do you want to see what they can do? Because they have a power, my dear, if you let them work their witchery. Do you want to see what we can make them do?

Of course she did. Of course. But she said nothing.

He reached into his pocket and pulled out a handfull of coins gathered from his second job, porter at the Hotel Walcott four days a week.

He let them slip through his fingers onto the bedspread beside her. A penny, a nickel, a dime.

The coins resting there, shimmering a little with each breath, each faint twist of her body as she raised it to see them better, to see his hands fluttering over them.

He sat down on the bed beside her. She let him. This was something.

"What are the odds, my girl? Tell me now. What are the odds you draw that shiny liberty-head?"

"One in three," she said, barely a whisper. "One in three."

"So you'd play?"

"I'd play. Sure. I'd play."

"So in a three-digit number game, what are the odds of picking the right three numbers?"

"I don't know. I don't know that," she said, not meeting his eyes.

"You pick a four first. How many ways can you go wrong?" he asked, tender like the man at post office when she was small, the one with the whiskers who never made her wait in line, and together they counted. She lifted one finger to his, raised hands, fingers spread, and they counted.

"Nine," she said. "Nine," she said again.

"So pick your three numbers. What are your odds?" he repeated. Taking her hand in his, in the soft center of his palm, he spread three of her fingers over three coins.

She let her fingertips graze the coins. Turning her body, she could feel the crisp edges of the sugar burns beneath the cool.

"One in 999?" she ventured.

He nodded, so pleased with her, this girl, pulled from school by her mother at age thirteen to go to work at the Loth Fair & Square Ribbon factory before it shut down.

Reaching down, he lifted the newspaper that stood like a flag in his coat pocket. He held it folded in front of her and pointed to smudgy columns:

Exchanges: *$823,411,011*
Balances: *$ 97,425,366*

With his grease pencil, he'd circled the 2 and 3 in the first figure and the 7 in the second figure.

"The rules will be simple," he said. "They'll never change. The numbers in those three columns make up the number that pays that day. So today, it'd be 237. You play 237 and you hit it. The big time."

Pointing to the columns again, he said, "The totals create a random number each day, my girl. And it's published in the daily papers everyday for all to see. Do you see how that changes everything?"

"Because the game can't be fixed," she said, even as she tried to imagine a way it could. Tried to imagine a way to make him wrong. "You can't rig the numbers."

My, was she fast. He knew she would be. It was why he'd waited so long for her.

"That's why this is different," he said, but they both recognized what he was really saying: *That's why I'm different.* "No drawing of numbers, no silky hands slipping favorites behind the counter. And you don't need to spread the word about the winning number. You don't need any operation at all except to collect and, when someone hits, pay out. I'll pay 600-to-1 to those dear souls who hit."

"Not 999-to-1?"

"No," he said with a loose grin that made her eyes unfocus, her feet arch. He was very close to her on the bed and she could smell tobacco and ginger, and she could feel his weight shifting her, sinking her toward him.

"It's all so simple," he added, almost a whisper, as if to himself. "And yet someone needed to think of it. And now they have."

"I'd never play those odds," she said, her breath slightly fast.

"You wouldn't," he smiled. "Not you. Nor me, my girl."

He flicked one of the coins with the tip of his finger. It flipped over on her belly, sending a wave of soft heat all the way up to her nostrils. He flicked another, and then one more.

"But lots of fine, warm, striving folks would," he said. "For a promise."

He set his hand down on her torso, each coin pushing into her. His hands on her, his warm palms pressing the coins cool onto her skin.

We all want a promise, she thought.

"And here's why," he said, and they both looked at the coins on her skin. "And here's why."

But it wasn't just that. She knew that it was the same for them as it was for every cleaning lady, line worker, porter, janitor, seamstress, who would put coins down for the clearinghouse racket; it wasn't these thin scales of copper, bronze, silver, gold. It was the promise. It was grander than that, and they were smarter. It had to mean more, didn't it? Yes, she told herself. It was the promise. And what could be hard and mean about a promise?

And she could feel it and she rested her hands on his and they interlaced and, in the pockets between their braided fingers, she could still see that liberty-head glint.

And she smiled and kept her eyes fixed down on that flash of mercury because it was the most real thing she'd ever known, this hard-struck illusion. It would be real for them.

Legend has it that Casper Alexander Holstein, Harlem's "King of Policy," invented the clearinghouse totals racket while sitting in a janitor's closet amid mops and brooms. J. Saunders Redding wrote in 1934 that Holstein "combined the prosaic traits of a financier with the dizzy imaginative flights of a fingerless Midas," recounting how he was studying the clearinghouse totals late one night when the idea "struck him between the eyes [and] he let out an uproarious laugh and in general acted like a drunken man." Within a year he owned "three of the finest apartment buildings in Harlem, a fleet of expensive cars, a home on Long Island, and several thousand acres of farmland in Virginia." A generous philanthropist, Holstein became one of the foremost patrons of the Harlem Renaissance. His luck, however, would run out. By the late 1920s, Dutch Schultz had wiped out all of Harlem's policy bankers and seized control of the numbers racket. As Claude McKay wrote, "And the 'clat in the atmosphere, which formerly made Harlem hum like a beehive, went out of the game forever."

When Holstein died in 1944, the headline read: Former Policy King in Harlem Dies Broke.

THE BASHER

BY JASON STARR

Hoboken, New Jersey

Before 9/11 and after the millennium, when most of the dotcoms became dot-bombs, I got fired from my job as a Java programmer. To say I left Delivero.com on bad terms would be an understatement. It took two security guards to get me out of the office in Jersey City, and if the goons hadn't shown up I probably would've killed Alan Silver, the CEO. Although Silver was too much of a coward to admit it, he fired me for one reason and one reason only—because his wife had a thing for me. He saw her hitting on me at the holiday party, and after that he used every excuse he could think of to get rid of me—lack of motivation, poor interpersonal skills, not a team player, tardiness. Yeah, right. It was because his slutty trophy wife wanted my body. That was it. End of story.

The job market was tight back then, with so many Net companies folding left and right, and it didn't help that I'd left Delivero on bad terms and couldn't get a recommendation. I'd made some money on stock options, but Silver, that cocksucker, had canned me right before annual bonuses were given out, costing me about fifty grand. I explored a lawsuit, but the lawyers I talked to either told me I didn't have a case or wanted to charge me up the wazoo. After several months out of work, I was starting to go through my money and needed a source of income, so I became a full-time day trader.

I knew I could make big money in the stock market. Yeah, I know, who didn't feel that way in the '90s, right? To hell with baseball; trading stocks had become the new national pastime. But for me, it wasn't a fad. I had a knack for picking winners, spotting trends, and timing the market, and I felt like I could clean up if I put my mind to it. I wanted to take this thing seriously. I converted the bedroom of my condo in Hoboken into a home office and moved my bed out into the living room. I opened a few online trading accounts, bought all the state-of-the-art software and an Aeron chair to sit my ass down on, and I got to work.

At first I had good days and bad, mostly bad. My instincts were good, but sometimes I got too cute, tried to hold onto positions to make big scores, when I knew I should've been conservative and gotten out. Though I never held positions overnight, so I didn't get burned after 9/11. Actually, the market volatility after the attacks worked out great for me and I made big money on the swings up and down. I made more money going short than going long, and seemed to have a knack for spotting the stocks that were in deep shit. One day I decided to stop going long altogether and only sell short. It turned out to be one of the best decisions I'd ever made.

I was a natural short seller. It fit my personality, I guess— I was good at spotting the bad in things. I knew when a stock was going to tank before any jackass analyst did, and I knew how to profit from the situation. And with all the Internet crapola out there, spotting trouble wasn't exactly a chore. Net stocks were still trading at astronomical prices and I rode the suckers all the way down to bankruptcy. Some of the companies were such obvious losers that I broke my rules about not holding positions overnight and went short long-term. I wasn't an idiot—I covered with options so I couldn't get burned on the upside, but that rarely happened. It seemed like there were an endless number of dotcraps going belly-up and an endless number of opportunities to cash in.

In early 2002, when Bush and his boys were bombing the shit out of Afghanistan, I made my first million. But at that point I didn't really care about the money. It was all about the action, about being right. Although I could've afforded some-place bigger, I stayed in my one-bedroom in Hoboken. I almost never went out; what was the point? The things I gave a shit about were the stock market and making money. I saw my friends less and less and I'd never been much of a family guy. I used to have girlfriends. Nothing long-term or serious, but I was a good-looking guy and when I went out to a bar or a club I had no trouble meeting women. Like Silver's wife. Sometimes I thought about calling her up and taking her out and trying to nail her just for the hell of it. I could've, but the truth was I wasn't interested. Sex just didn't do it for me anymore.

I spent more and more time online and less time sleeping. It got to the point where I was spending eighteen to twenty hours a day staring at my computer screen. If I wasn't making trades or doing research I was posting on stock message boards. My comments were always negative, always designed to inflict maximum damage on the companies I was shorting. I attacked management, put negative spins on positive news, and even wrote outright lies—anything I could do to help crush stock prices. I posted under multiple names—partly because the board monitors on sites like Yahoo and Motley Fool kept kick-ing me off, and partly because I wanted to create the impression for newbies following stocks that there was massive negativity about the companies. Still, everyone eventually knew who I was. I guess my posts had a style to them or whatever, because I became one of the most well-known stock bashers on the Internet.

My favorite stock to bash, without a doubt, was Delivero. Part of it was personal. I wanted revenge. I wanted to take Silver down, for him to feel some of the pain I'd felt when he fired my ass. But I also truly believed that the company had despicable business practices and was a perfect example of everything that was wrong with Wall Street. Somehow the piece of shit had managed to stay in business through the height of the Internet bloodbath, though its stock had plummeted from a high of eighty-four to around six bucks a share. Even when I was working for them, I knew their business plan was smoke and mirrors.

They wanted to be a competitor of Kozmo.com, that other brilliant company that thought delivering Ben & Jerry's and VHS movies by bicycle was the wave of the future. The problem was that Delivero had no real growth plan and they were burning cash. They'd had a few awful quarters where their numbers didn't come close to analyst estimates. But every time the company was in dire straits they'd raise more money in a new stock offering or announce a new "partnership," and somehow the shares managed to tread water, even go up. I'd post like crazy on those days, about how Silver and his cronies were criminals and deserved jail time, but the idiot longs would circle jerk themselves, going on about how Delivero's stock was going to a hundred a share and how I was the world's biggest moron.

It got to the point where I felt like I was the most hated man on the Internet, and the disgust toward me was probably the most glaring on the Delivero message boards. There was a lot of bad blood on those boards from suckers who had gotten in when Delivero was in the stratosphere and were desperately waiting for the stock to go back up. Yeah, like that would ever happen. They ganged up on me, called me a loser, a retard, the village idiot—every name imaginable that could get through the web filters. A lot of the idiots started calling me a "paid basher" and claimed I'd been hired by hedge funds to bad-mouth stocks all day. One nutcase claimed he knew for a fact that I received five cents for every negative post I wrote. It amazed me how angry I could get these guys, but I liked it too. I knew that in order for me to make money as a short, I needed jackass longs on the other side of my trades, and I thanked God there was no shortage of fools among Delivero's investors.

As the months went by, and it seemed like another Net stock/ex high flyer from the '90s went under every day, Delivero somehow stayed in business. The company was like a cockroach that you stamp on ten times but still won't die. It had to be a combination of luck and pure stupidity from the delusional longs living in fantasyland who continued to buy the company's worthless shares—there was no other explanation. It was so obvious to me that Delivero wasn't in the business to make money—they were in the business to deceive stockholders. The company expanded to other cities, made new partnerships, floated more stock, and issued other bullshit PR releases to make the stock price go up. Then insiders, especially Silver, sold at every possible opportunity. Dipshit longs claimed that the sales were planned, part of the execs' normal retirement plans—yeah, right. They believed that, there was a bridge I would've liked to sell them. Every three months I listened to the webcast of Delivero's quarterly results and got nauseous as Silver, in his pompous, know-it-all voice, fed his crap to gullible analysts. Some dork from

Morgan Stanley or Citigroup would ask Silver why he was lowering estimates for the next fiscal year and he'd go on about "new strategies going forward" and "adapting to the current landscape," never answering the question, of course. Did the analysts give a shit? No sirree. They had their own agendas, pumping up garbage stocks like Delivero with their *Buy* and *Strong Buy* ratings to keep their clients happy.

When the WorldCom scandal hit, I thought Delivero would go down the toilet too. I was so positive that the company was history that I got out of all of my other positions and shorted the shit out of the stock. It had been trading in a recent range of four to six dollars a share. I profited on the short-term moves downward and covered on options when the stock ticked up. And everything I made, I plowed back into my long-term short position. Every morning when I woke up, I went online and checked for news on Delivero. I knew that one day the Chapter Eleven announcement would appear. It was only a matter of time.

Meanwhile, since I had no other stocks in my portfolio, I was able to focus full-time on my bashing of Delivero. I started posting at least five hundred times a day on various message boards. I attacked the business model of the company and its deceitful accounting, but my messages also became more personal, more focused on Silver. I wrote about how incompetent he was and about how he had an alcohol and drug problem. I posted that he was into child porn, that he had ties to Al-Qaeda, that his trophy wife was a transvestite. I knew my posts came off as bizarre and irrational—that was the point. I wanted to incite rage, to stir the pot—and it worked like a charm. There was no end to the number of longs who got sucked in and started arguing with me. Their posts were even nuttier than mine. Wannabe investors would visit the Delivero message boards and see all of the wacky posts from the longs and get the impression that a bunch of lunatics were investing in the stock.

I knew Silver read the message boards, or had employees who did, and would find out about my posts. I also knew that when I started focusing on his trophy wife, he'd know it was me posting. This was my intention. I wanted him to know who his enemy was, that it was me who was out to get him. It would make my ultimate victory even more satisfying.

Some longs—including Silver himself, for all I knew—now responded to my attacks by saying that I had a hidden agenda, that I had to be an irate former employee or have some other vendetta against the company. People put me on "ignore" and tried to block my messages, but I had multiple IDs and was unstoppable. I knew that my posts were having an effect, that I was influencing the stock price. On days when I wrote my most scathing attacks, the stock almost always dropped and I profited. I felt like I could manipulate the buying and selling on a whim. It was just a matter of how often I posted and how effective my bashings were. But there was no doubt that I was in total control of the company's fate. If I wanted to change my position and go long I could've driven the stock up to twenty dollars a share in one month.

My new goal was to demolish the stock with my most furious attacks yet, to go for the kill. And I got some huge help one morning when Delivero issued a major earnings warning before the market open. The same analysts who had been cheerleading the stock for years finally woke up out of their fucking cocoons and reduced their ratings to "hold" and "sell," and the stock opened down over two points. I cashed in big time on a day trade but I didn't put the moolah in the bank, into money heaven; instead, I shoved it into my margin account and upped my short position even more. Armageddon for Delivero was on the horizon and I stood to make millions.

I increased the frequency of my postings. Sometimes I stayed up all night to influence foreign investors, and one day I set a personal record of one thousand posts in a day. Delivero's stock was continuing to tank, sinking to under two dollars a share, and I knew it was all because of me.

Then a registered letter arrived at my apartment. It was from Delivero's lawyers, threatening a lawsuit if I didn't stop bashing the company. Silver was just trying to intimidate me, and I sure as hell wasn't going to let that happen.

A week later, as the stock price continued to drop, I started getting threatening e-mails. They were from anonymous addresses, but I knew Silver was sending them. All of the notes basically said the same thing—that I'd better stop bashing or else. Some got more explicit, warning me that I'd lose limbs or die in pain.

I considered calling the police, but I was afraid of what might happen if I did. There were detailed records of me bashing Silver's stock and I began to fear that I could go to jail for libel for some of the things I'd written.

I didn't respond to any of the notes and stopped my onslaught, hoping the thing would die down on its own. Then, one morning while I was sitting at my PC, a brick shattered my window and almost hit me in the head. I looked outside and saw a black car speeding away, but I couldn't catch the license plate. I didn't bother calling the cops, figuring that Silver would just deny responsibility, try to make me look like the bad guy.

Then I left my apartment that Sunday afternoon to get a haircut and returned to discover a message spray painted on my bedroom wall:

DIE MOTHERFUCKING BASHER DIE

I decided enough was enough. I was surprised that Silver had gone this far, but I remembered that he'd always had a temper, screaming at employees and firing them on a whim—hell, he'd fired me for no legitimate reason—and maybe the stress of his company going under was getting to him and he was snapping. How the hell did I know what was going on with him? All I knew was that he was starting to threaten my personal safety and I had to take some action.

Years ago, after an attempted break-in at my building, I'd bought a gun for protection. I decided I'd go talk to Silver face-to-face and try to get him to back off. If he caused trouble, started threatening me again, I'd show the gun, just to scare him and make him think I was more psycho than he was. I knew that beneath all of the tough talk, Silver was a big pussy and I could intimidate him easily.

The next day, Monday, I drove to Silver's house in Bernardsville. They should've called it Snootyville. When I was working at Delivero I went to a company picnic in Silver's backyard. It was one of the biggest, most expensive houses on a block of big, expensive houses. He probably blew three million bucks of stockholders' money on it.

I waited in my car in a spot near his driveway. I figured he'd leave the office at around 6 or 7 and the drive from Jersey City to Bernardsville would take about an hour—an hour and a half with traffic. But at 9 o'clock there was still no sign of him. I knew he wasn't out of town because I'd called his office earlier from a pay phone and his security said he was busy in a meeting. He was probably out with a client, making one of his bullshit deals.

Sure enough, at a little after 10 o'clock, his red Porsche

pulled into the drive. The garage door opened and the car went in. I got out of my car and walked fast toward the garage. Silver got out of the Porsche. He looked like crap, like he'd aged ten years, but he still had that pompous, my-shit-doesn't-stink quality he'd had when he fired me, and I remembered how gleeful he'd seemed that day, as if showing me the door was giving him a big fat boner.

When Silver saw me I knew he recognized me, even though he pretended not to. I told him I knew what he was doing, trying to terrorize me, and it wouldn't work. Then he squinted, acting like it was all starting to click for him, and then he fake smiled, pretending he wasn't scared shitless, but it was obvious he was. It was great watching him squirm.

He claimed he had no idea what I wanted from him and said a lot of other shit, trying to calm me down so he could have a chance to escape into the house and call the cops. I told him I wasn't playing games and I took out the Glock. I have no idea why he grabbed at the gun, what he was trying to do. Maybe he didn't know what he was trying to do either; maybe he just panicked. Who the fuck knows? We struggled for a few seconds, at least it seemed like seconds. Inches away from the man whose company I'd been bashing for years, I hated him right then the same way I had when he called me into his office and told me I was being let go. *Let go*, like I was a fucking fish he was tossing back to sea. I remembered how I could've killed him that day, and how I'd always wished I had, and then the gun went off. He fell onto the concrete next to the Porsche, blood spilling out of his chest.

I ran like hell. When I got into my car, I heard a woman screaming—maybe his slut wife—but I was pretty sure I got away before she saw me or the car.

The drive back to Hoboken was a blur. I still don't know

how I made it without getting pulled over, because I must've been speeding my ass off.

The rest of the night I was in a state of total panic. Even if no one could identify me, I knew I was going to be an obvious suspect. I'd been bashing Silver for years and all of my posts were online for the world to see. Toward dawn, I started packing. My only chance was to leave the country.

I went online to see if there was any news about the murder; it was all over the Internet already. Because of fear and uncertainty about the future, Delivero's stock was tanking in the pre-market, down below a dollar a share. It was like a dream come true—it had become a penny stock. I put in an order to cover my short position at the market open. I stood to make about four million dollars. I just hoped the authorities didn't freeze my accounts before I could have the money wired to me in Mexico.

Then I checked my e-mail and almost passed out. There was a new message from one of the e-mail addresses that I'd suspected Silver had been using. The note read:

DIE IN PAIN ALONE YOU COCKSUCKING BASHING ASSHOLE

I stared at the screen for a few minutes, realizing the huge mistake I'd made. It wasn't Silver who'd been harassing me. The real scumbag was probably one of the hundreds of people I'd pissed off with my bashings.

I was a mess for a while, then I got even. I went to the Yahoo Delivero message board and rubbed it in to the dumbasses who were giving me all their money. I was in the middle of one of my best posts ever when the cops started banging on my front door.

PART IV

GLOBAL MARKETS

PART IV

THE ENLIGHTENMENT OF MAGNUS MCKAY

BY JOHN BURDETT

Bangkok, Thailand

And the harlots will go into the kingdom of God before you
Matthew 21:31

WALL STREET, NEW YORK, MONDAY, FEBRUARY 28, 2005

Magnus McKay, alpha male, writes: *Lalita, teelak—that does mean "darling" in Thai, right?—I miss you. I know this sounds ridiculous, but those two short moments we spent together have touched something inside of me. I'm going to bring you here as soon as possible, if I can't find an excuse to visit Thailand next week (I'm working on it). Will you wait for me? Magnus.*

He sits back in his executive chair to rub his jaw, then he stands up to look down on the ants bundled up against the cold on the Street.

He is not officially the senior partner of Weisman, Constant and Draper, so they had to give him the second corner office. Nevertheless, here we have power expressed through space: seven hundred square feet, two sets of windows. He'd chosen the crimson trimmings to go with his famous suspenders, the rest he'd left to the interior designer.

Musing: Does his draft e-mail hit the right tone or not? Hookers are no different to everyone else, right? You adapt human resources techniques to make them feel special, and if they're good you give them a glittering prize to aim for. Not that Lalita's performances in that seedy short-time hotel had been in any way deficient. To tell the truth, he hasn't stopped thinking about her for the past three days.

Reminiscing with twinges: She was beautiful, far too beautiful for that cheap go-go dive where he found her, quite by accident. He had been with Samson Lee's main man in Thailand, Tallboy Yip. Normally, McKay would never take his pleasure so down market, for, as a frequent traveler to Bangkok, he had joined the best, most discreet, and most expensive of the city's brothels; but Yip, who these days was almost as wide as he was tall—with thick degenerate lips in a lived-in mug—owned low-life tastes.

McKay had been on the point of making excuses and going back to his hotel, when he'd seen her gyrating around that stainless steel pole on the revolving platform with all the other girls, her long black hair reaching to the small of her back. When she passed by the second time he deliberately smiled at her. On the third turn she deliberately smiled at him. Within the law of contract his offer had been accepted: They had a deal. He bought her a triple tequila because she asked him to.

His first thought had been to use her merely as an excuse to lose Tallboy, for he was not really in the mood, having sated his lust in a threesome the night before. He paid her bar fine after ten minutes of talking to her, then said goodnight to Yip with a lecherous smirk which Yip appreciated: Uncontrollable lust was always an acceptable reason for cutting a drinking bout short. Magnus had let her lead him up a set of squalid stairs to the room, following her perfect body from behind. He watched her undress automatically in front of him; long hair covering dark-brown nipples when she stood up straight to face him; he noted that she was smiling with just the right amount of shyness. Should he have her after all, or should he merely pay her modest fee and leave without taking his pleasure? She saw his hesitation and went to work on him. Magnus McKay, veteran womanizer and whoremonger, had never known anything like it. He gave her a hundred-dollar tip. She took it in the spirit it was meant: a symbol of his intent to return for more.

The next night had been his last in Bangkok and he really didn't have time for her; but he made time for her anyway, between checkout and airport. It was uncanny, she seemed to know more about his libido than he did. It was magic, no other word for it. This time he gave her five hundred dollars: serious money. They talked briefly, like business people, about the possibility of her making regular visits to New York at his expense: say once a month, business class. She immediately undertook to get a passport, as if she had been expecting such an offer. They exchanged e-mail addresses. That was only three days ago.

He checks himself in a crimson-framed mirror behind his chair. He knows how Thai girls like her think: a *farang*, a foreigner, a lawyer who works on Wall Street, a forty-one-year-old bachelor in perfect shape who could solve her financial problems and those of her family with one flash of his platinum credit card.

A fool would succumb to narcissism, remind himself what an incredible catch he must be for a Third World hooker (tall, slim, handsome, rich, charm-enhanced American); but Magnus knows better than that. Hunting is what makes him run. In work he hunts for money, in women he hunts for that extreme performance which you only extract from a girl who believes she has found the answer to her prayers and a meal ticket for life. Magnus would play that white knight role perfectly, and, if *she* played *her* cards right, he would certainly give her the golden handshake when he grew bored. Hell, he probably *would* solve most of her financial problems, how much could it cost? Twenty grand, fifty at most? In the old days he'd spent that on crack in a week, and she was *better* than crack. Another twinge forces him to wrench consciousness out of his groin chakra.

Back facing his computer, he clicks on *send*, logs off of his personal account with Yahoo Mail, and, switching with ruthless discipline to his work mindset, returns to his business e-mail.

His sorting technique is primitive but appropriate for his practice: Anything not concerning the Thai-Chinese businessman Samson Lee, no matter how grave and weighty, he forwards to his numerous assistants; anything touching on his master, no matter how trivial, he works on himself. He knows he is Lee's slave, but so what? It is symbiotic. Lee simply could not survive in the U.S. without a lawyer of McKay's cunning and ruthlessness, for he is perpetually hounded by all the usual suspects: FBI, CIA, DEA, Inland Revenue. Samson Lee thinks McKay some kind of blue-eyed magus, for Magnus always finds a way out of the apparently watertight traps these agencies lay for his client. Magnus has lost count of the jams he's gotten Lee and his five sons out of, frequently risking his career. But that is the deal. Roughly thirty percent of the firm's income comes from the Lee family and nobody, absolutely nobody in the firm, so much as speaks to Lee's *secretary* without McKay's prior knowledge and approval. Samson Lee is the reason McKay got the second corner office.

Checking his solid gold Longines watch: 7:35 in the

morning, which is the time Samson Lee likes him to start. In Bangkok it is twelve hours later, she's probably started dancing already in that seedy bar, nearly naked in a G-string and flimsy bra—though sometimes she starts late. It is just possible she is sitting in an Internet café hoping to hear from him. In response to more prodding from his loins, he logs on again to Yahoo Mail. Yep, there it is, a message from Naronsip Wiwatanasan, a.k.a., Lalita: *Yes, teelak means darling in Thai. Yes, I am waiting for you. Can you send me a photo?*

A cool positive? McKay smiles. That's exactly how he would have replied if he had been in her position. Clearly, she is a master of the game, like him. The secret to McKay's success: He never fools himself; lawyers are whores too.

As it happens, his laptop includes a digital camera. He takes a snap of his face turned slightly to highlight the manly strength of his jaw, and zings it off to her.

Just then the laptop telephone beeps. This is McKay's secret number which he gives out to no one except Samson Lee. Lee has an Asian addiction to video conferencing.

McKay's only important client appears on the monitor, looking a lot more Chinese than Thai, with eyes so slit McKay wonders how any light ever gets in there: a vast moon face with near-circular wrinkles, small flat nose, cheap off-the-peg sweater.

"I can't see you," Lee snaps. McKay switches the movie camera function on. "That's better."

"Good morning, Mr. Lee," McKay says with a big, bright, yes-I-do-love-to-suck-your-bum smile. He tried using "Samson" once at the beginning of the relationship, but it didn't work for either of them. Lee is very conservative in the Confucian tradition. His sons are his slaves and his daughters marry whoever he tells them to marry. The Lees are certainly a centralized family, if not a close one.

"You're going back to Bangkok on the next plane," Lee says.

McKay maintains self-control, at the same time congratulating himself on his usual good luck. He is simply one of those hyper-neat guys who kind of constellate everything around them so that, even without his thinking about it, events conspire to conform to his will. The journey is twenty hours plus, and he can probably get on a flight that morning if he kicks ass. In other words, Lalita—naked—will be servicing him again in less than a day.

Keeping a straight face: "Certainly, Mr. Lee. What's the problem?"

Lee looks directly into his digital camera. By making certain adjustments on his laptop McKay can enlarge those heavily lidded eyes until they almost fill the screen. He's done this many times, out of curiosity. It never makes any difference. Even magnified as much as ten times, Lee's eyes still have no life in them.

"It's wet," Lee says.

McKay pales somewhat and experiences a hundred-and-eighty degree mood swing. Maybe his luck isn't so good today, after all. Wet?

"Well, now, Mr. Lee . . ." McKay begins.

"I already know what you don't do," Lee says.

This is a reference to something McKay witnessed at the beginning of their relationship. Shaken, he found a way to explain that it was very counter-productive for Lee to implicate his main and most trusted lawyer-fixer in that kind of thing. Lee had agreed, to his relief.

McKay doesn't mind bending the rules for a benevolent billionaire, but he is not a sadist. Like every successful man and woman on the Street, he believes in dictatorship by the filthy rich, but as a civilized American he sees himself as a benign despot.

Question: Who am I? Where do I come from? Where am I going?

Answer: I have not the faintest idea, my culture forgot to tell me.

Yes, he has a sensitive side. Both parents were pious English Literature teachers martyred by the functional barbarism of these times. Without respect, money, power, or direction, they both hit the bottle. When they started having fist fights, they all knew the barbarism had won. His father jumped from a high window and his mother, unable to live without him, took an overdose.

In a nutshell, whatever kind of crook he was at heart, he was totally white collar. Whatever kind of crook Lee was, it was not white collar. That was why Lee was so rich: He took the barbarism all the way, sucked it all up. Even Magnus didn't know how much dough Lee had. Officially, only thirty percent of the trillions of trillions of dollars washing around the international banking system every minute was illegal drug money, but that was certainly disinformation designed to keep the sober majority from panicking. The true figure was probably more than fifty percent, perhaps as much as seventy. Maybe everyone worked for Samson Lee without knowing it? Maybe that was why they would never legalize recreational drugs? Nobody loves Prohibition more than Al Capone. If not for criminalization, Lee would be selling secondhand automobiles.

"I still don't do wet," McKay says.

"The Spics have grabbed my son Hercules," Lee says, as if relating an irritating but predictable occurrence.

McKay's heart sinks: war. "I'm very sorry to hear that, Mr. Lee, but I don't see—"

"Emerald Buddha Corporation," Lee says. "Forty-nine percent. Sign before you get on the plane, or I'll FedEx the docs to you in Bangkok if you prefer."

McKay knows Lee is watching his face closely on the giant monitor hanging on a wall in his Long Island mansion. McKay knows Lee saw him swallow immediately on hearing the name. The EBC is Lee's respectable front. Well, it is only semi-respectable since it smuggles illegal Buddha heads and other priceless icons stolen from Ankor Wat, but Lee keeps it scrupulously apart from his other businesses. It is his "face" for official America, and as such he's been obliged to spend quite a few tens of millions on stock, which is not exclusively Khmer, but includes some museum-quality jade pieces; they look identical to world-famous missing items, once the property of the last emperor of China. McKay has hinted more than once that a good way for Lee to reward his extra, secret, and professionally life-threatening efforts on behalf of his master would be for Lee to simply hand over a chunk of EBC stock. McKay knows Lee has been keeping EBC for a rainy day, when he will ask McKay to go even deeper into hell as his legal representative. Well, today it's raining.

McKay doesn't know he's been holding his breath until he breathes out: Did the man say forty-nine percent? That is worth about twenty-five million, but the best of it is: The little firm actually makes a very healthy profit, averaging more than sixteen percent net per year of stock value. Sixteen percent of twenty-five million is four million. That would almost exactly triple his average yearly income. He supposes he will get drunk or something to see him through Tallboy's elaborate vengeance strategy, whatever it is. He sure will need a night with Lalita afterwards, though.

"Okay," McKay says, "but why?"

"Because I can't go myself and Tallboy is losing it. He has tactics but no strategy. He spends his time drinking whiskey and screwing whores. He doesn't have your discipline. You don't have to do anything—he'll take care of the wet side— you just have to tell him when to start, when to pause . . ." Lee himself pauses at this point to lick his lips ". . . and when to stop."

"I see."

"I want Hercules back alive, not sliced up like a lump of salami. If he's dead or crippled his mother will never stop bitching."

"I understand that," says McKay. Then, as an after-thought: "Which Colombian did you grab after you heard they'd grabbed Hercules?"

"The kid brother," Lee says, and logs off. Secretaries will take care of the rest.

OFF SOI 4, SUKHUMVIT, BANGKOK, MONDAY, FEBRUARY 28, 2005
Lalita has the Internet café print a copy of McKay's picture to take to the clairvoyant monk at Wat Tanorn, then logs off. A little overwhelmed by the events of the past few days, she slumps in her chair to think for a moment.

It was her sexual frigidity that was getting her the sack from the go-go bar, before McKay burst into her life. Customers had started to complain. Her technique, pre-McKay, had consisted of apologizing that she was menstruat-ing, so would a hand job do for tonight? Usually she got away with it, counting on the customer's guilt and pity, but some of the old hands had caught on to her and complained to the mamasan. The mamasan, a good Buddhist, had been kind in suggesting that Lalita was just not cut out for this type of work: Why not serve behind the bar? Lalita would have loved to work behind the bar, but there was the problem of her mother's cataracts—she would be quite blind in three months if Lalita did not pay for the operation, not to mention her father's heart condition and her younger brother's boarding school fees. Girls who worked behind the bar made three hundred dollars a month, max. Girls who were good at selling their bodies made nearly a thousand dollars a month. Lalita wasn't making anything like that, but not because she wasn't attractive. She looked outstanding, everyone said so, and at the beginning men had almost lined up for her. Then word got around that she loathed sex, which was true. When she couldn't avoid intercourse she would lay on the bed more or less inert and let him get on with it. Girls like her can make a man impotent, one of her customers had explained in exasperation.

"Listen," the mamasan had said, "there's one thing you can do. It only works for girls like you, because any man with sense can see you're no natural to the Game, to say the least. So you find the best prospect you can, give him everything he wants from you, and allow yourself to fall in love with him so you don't have to keep faking it. Nine times out of ten the *farang* will fall for you too and marry you or at least take care of you and your family for a few years, which is a lot better than selling your body in a bar."

How to fall in love? She shared a room with three other girls, all from Lalita's home village near Surin on the border with Cambodia. Together they spoke in a dialect of Khmer, which made things feel cozy and happy. The three others knew all about Lalita's problem with sex, for they told each other everything. After her little chat with the mamasan, Lalita had gone home to her friends and burst into tears. It was so frustrating. If only she could open her legs and screw with exaggerated abandon like the others, she would be able to save her mother's sight and her father's life and her brother's future in less than a year. Nong, her best friend, realized that a radical solution was called for.

"I know what you're going to say," Lalita replied. "You're going to say that I should aim for one special guy and give him everything so he can't live without me—but I don't have a clue how to do that."

"That wasn't what I was going to say at all," Nong countered. She took a DVD out of her handbag and inserted it into the DVD machine they had all bought together. It was Japanese hard porn, very professionally produced with unusual camera angles. As Nong had guessed, Lalita had never seen hard porn before. Of course, Lalita knew what other women did for their clients from the general conversation, but she had never actually seen a woman in action like that, really working the john. It made her feel sick and she told Nong to turn it off. "No," Nong said, "you're going to watch it to the end."

"Now what?" Lalita asked when the movie finally ended in an unconvincing crescendo of groans and moans, the girl's face dripping with his goo.

"Now you're gonna watch it and watch it and watch it, and you're gonna make sure you get every move, and then you're gonna figure out how to refine it because you're much more sensitive than that whore in the movie and a lot smarter, so when you've got the idea you can easily do better than her, depending on the john's personality. And then you're gonna ask yourself how many tequilas you need to do that. And then, because no way you're gonna be able to keep up that kind of performance night after night, you're gonna—"

"Find the right john and lock him in," Lalita supplied.

"Right," said Nong.

So it all pointed to luck after all. For luck you need an expert. The monk at Wat Tanorn was from Surin; he spoke to her in her own Khmer dialect and liked to discuss the rice harvest and other agricultural matters.

"The sow under the house is pregnant," she told him, "due in a week's time."

Phra Tanatika knew Lalita's mother and father, both of whom were highly respected: poor but devout and dependable. Nobody wanted to see her mother go blind, or her father die, if it could be helped. In other words, he had to balance spiritual duty with community service. He tried to use his gift of clairvoyance wisely, in a way consistent with spiritual evolution. Lalita never told him she was a prostitute; she didn't need to.

"I'm having trouble making ends meet but I do work in a field where I meet *farang* men quite a lot, and I'm wondering if astrologically this is a moment when I can expect to meet my Number One, or someone close to it," Lalita explained.

"Tell me again your date and time of birth?"

In Thailand everyone uses the Chinese horoscope, with some Hindu flourishes. Lalita was born in the year of the metal rabbit. This meant that although sensitive, smart, and more than a little inclined to freak out when life got tough, she nevertheless had about her a persistence, even a stubbornness, which no one ever saw except *in extremis*. Then there was the hour of her birth, which in the young was at least as important as the year. Phra Tanatika was impressed with her dragon rising. It was tremendously well aspected at this moment and he told her so. But when she looked up at him, there was something else in her eyes, something that made him very sad.

"This isn't easy for you, is it?"

"No," Lalita admitted.

"You have to be careful. You might not know it, but at this moment you wield extraordinary power, especially over men. And as we know, the world is balanced by duality. The other side of the coin is that you will have to give something from your heart."

"Enthusiasm?"

"More than that," the monk said, still feeling slightly depressed, for he was beginning to get serious signals concerning her future. "Look, I'll give it to you straight. The man you are going to meet in the next few days is, well, someone who can help you much much more than you think, but the only way to really keep him is to give him something special."

"What's that?"

"You already know."

The monk, divining with little effort that Lalita was one of those pure souls who tend to take sexual love far more seriously than is healthy, decided to tell her about an interesting recent event. Soon after his alms round a few mornings before, when he had been eating the food his flock had prepared for him, he saw the astral body of Old Tou, whom he knew to be on his deathbed. Old Tou had led an averagely debauched life—a great womanizer in his youth, an alcoholic as he grew older, just another lost, self-centered soul. Phra Tanatika had watched in fascination while Old Tou's astral body ent   ody of a puppy who had just been born to

one of the temple dogs. The puppy didn't have a name yet, so
Phra Tanatika called him "Tou."

"We copulate because karma forces us to," the Phra
explained with a smile. "Like Old Tou, everyone needs a body
to inhabit—that's all it amounts to. Humans make love for
exactly the same reason dogs do."

Lalita smiled at the story and felt a great fondness for
Phra Tanatika, for she saw he was trying to take the edge off
of her problem with sex. Surely he was right: It was just an
agricultural function, why did she take it so seriously?

"What can I do to help my karma along in this regard and
find the right man?"

"Imaging," the monk promptly replied. "You make an
image in your mind of the kind of man you could give everything to—then when you see him you will know him."

Which is exactly what she did. Every night before she
went to sleep, every morning when she woke up, she painstak-
ingly built up an image of a *farang* man to whom she could
happily give her heart and body and enthusiastically perform
all those dreadful things that Japanese whore was doing in the
porn video.

The image she built up in her mind was surprisingly
detailed: tall, slim, handsome, probably American, wealthy, a
strong jaw, beautifully dressed in expensive casual clothes,
with a telltale look in his eyes that most men don't have: the
look of a conquering dragon, to go with her own inner dragon
which very few people ever saw. She even imaged his favorite
color: crimson.

All that happened over the past week. Now she is taking
Magnus's photograph to Phra Tanatika at Tanorn,
using the sheet of paper as a makes   the hot,

steamy bus that costs only two baht because there is no air-conditioning.

"Is this him?" she asks the monk. Phra Tanatika stares at Magnus's picture, complete with crimson neck tie and suspenders. What he sees there he dares not tell her.

"What do *you* think?" he asks her. "Is it him or not?"

"I'm sure it is," says Lalita.

"Then it is your karma, you cannot alter it."

When she leaves, the monk looks after her with a worried expression. He knows that we humans are in reality a spaghetti junction of intertwined influences, called samscaras, from previous lifetimes. Some of the samscaras we bear date back to reptilian lifetimes and simply lie in wait indefinitely, like tics, for an opportunity to assert themselves, even in the most pure and gentle souls.

BANGKOK, BY THE CHAO PRAYA RIVER, TUESDAY, MARCH 1, 2005
Magnus watches while Tallboy and a dozen Thai men set up the giant plasma TV monitor in the warehouse in Bangkok's Chinatown, near the river. Every now and then Tallboy receives a call from Colombia on his cell phone. Sometimes he's the one to make the call to Colombia.

"How's your link?" Tallboy asks. "Everything in place?"

Tallboy is talking to his opposite number in the enemy camp, but practical issues force a polite, even genial tone. War will resume as soon as they have fixed the glitches.

"I know, the technology is never as advanced as they claim, there are always problems. How good is your satellite link? I mean, you're on the top of some stone age hill in the Andes, right? I'm in the middle of a modern city, so most likely you would be the one with the problem, right? Okay, let's do another trial run."

The giant screen, hung on the back wall of the warehouse, is joined to a box of technological tricks from which a dozen cables emerge. A Sony digital movie camera points at an empty gurney. When a technician flicks a switch, the screen fills with a kind of energetic fuzz, billions of pixels in some chaotic state.

"Tell me something," Tallboy says into his cell phone, "you got rain over there? Looks like rain on the screen. No, wait, okay, we're receiving you. Shit, you weren't supposed to start yet."

Lacking Tallboy's finesse, the Colombians have already pointed their camera at Hercules Lee, who is tied to a chair and gagged and looking very sick.

"Is Samson linked in to this?" Magnus asks Tallboy.

"Sure," Tallboy says, looking worried.

"Better bring in the kid brother," Magnus tells Tallboy.

"Right."

Felipe Maria Jesus González Escaverada is swarthy, unshaven, in his late twenties, cuffed hand and foot. Maybe they tranquilized him, or simply beat the hell out of him already; he's not fully conscious, anyway. But Magnus knows Tallboy has adrenalin and testosterone on hand: If necessary, the kid brother could be very alert in seconds. The boys dump the kid brother onto the gurney and strap him in with hospital-style restrainers. Now the screen splits: One half is Hercules Lee looking very sick on some hill in the Andes, the other half is Felipe Maria Jesus González also looking very sick strapped to the gurney in Bangkok. In Colombia they are watching the same split screen.

"Ready?" Tallboy asks.

"*Ready.*" The thick Hispanic accent booms over the sound system.

Tallboy looks to Magnus for strategic advice: What do I do now?

"Ask if they're ready to talk. Tell them what a childish waste of time this all is—waste of money too. It's ridiculous in this day and age."

Talking into a microphone, Tallboy repeats what Magnus has said, word for word.

"*It's a matter of honor,*" the Hispanic voice says from the speakers.

"It's a matter of two little kilos of coke," Tallboy corrects. "What's to get macho about? Are you in business or do you spend all your time playing with yourself?"

"*Don't get cheeky, flatnose.*"

"At least I don't have a whole forest growing out of my nose. Do you grow coca in there?"

"*You're not a man. Men do not talk like that. Only boys, women, and Chinks.*"

Tallboy, fuming now and picking up a pair of pliers: "Okay, I'm starting with the left ear."

"*Me too,*" says the Hispanic voice.

Magnus cannot stand to watch. This is a preliminary skirmish; no new stage in the negotiations will be reached before both victims are properly softened up with a few minor body parts ripped to shreds, gags off, screaming the place down. McKay needs a drink, preferably where he will not hear the screams.

He leaves the warehouse and passes between ten of Tallboy's men who are on guard outside. Magnus knows the area and heads toward the river. Small shops sell beer, basic provisions, and cigarettes. Magnus buys a pack of Marlboro Red and a can of Singha beer. He checks his watch. His experience with these kinds of negotiations suggests that a good ten minutes of terror on both sides is needed before anyone starts to see sense.

Halfway through his cigarette, he hears a sound both muffled and tremendous, then the sky above the river lights up for a moment, illuminating the water, the opposite shore, his hand holding the can of beer, and the face of the old lady who owns the shop. Little stars rise and dance amidst the acrid stench of plastic, the crude fragrance of petrol, the primeval aroma of burning wood. He stands and turns to watch the conflagration, less than a block away, quickly diminish to a massive blaze.

With the lightning reflex of a pro, Magnus realizes he misjudged the timing. Obviously the Colombians knew the location of the warehouse, and as soon as Pablo Escaverada, the godfather, decided the torture would have to be taken all the way, he preferred to kill his own kid brother along with Tallboy Yip and his men. He still held Hercules Lee, of course, and therefore had brilliantly gained the upper hand in the incomprehensible war.

Badly shaken: How the hell did a bunch of Colombian bums find out a secret address in Bangkok? Fighting an adrenalin rush: He needs to hide. If the Escaverada family know about the warehouse, they must know about him too. Maybe the bombers saw him leave the warehouse and know he's still alive?

He calls Lalita on her cell phone. They'd had no time to make love, but he'd paid her bar fine, so she was in the hotel room waiting for him.

"Get the hell out of there right now," Magnus says. "Just get out right now."

They meet at On Nut Sky train station. He tells her things have gone terribly for him. He doesn't go into detail and she is too smart to ask. He tells her she is not to worry, he still has plenty of money and will look after her, but she must help him. He will pay whatever she wants for a week or so totally out of sight, out of play.

Lalita does not seem overly put out. Sure, she knows a place: her home in the country, near Surin, right on the Cambodian border.

He waits while Lalita calls her parents, tells them she is coming to see them with her fiancé. After all, these are respectable, pious country people, no way she can turn up with a man unless she is at least engaged to him. Magnus doesn't mind. He guesses enough dough will settle ruffled feathers at the end of the day. Things are difficult, but not so difficult he would consider marrying a Third World whore.

Or would he?

THE FARM, FRIDAY, MARCH 4, 2005

It is interesting, Magnus muses after a couple of days, how an environment can change one. Lalita's parents' house is quite big, a wood structure on concrete stilts on a couple acres of land in a flat hot dry region that owns a peculiar beauty. Tall trees break up the landscape; to McKay's astonishment, elephants graze in fields. Wild-looking young day workers with cloths tied around their heads, bundled up against the sun, race by in the backs of pickup trucks from time to time. Monks from the local wat make alms rounds at dawn. Lalita, her near-blind mother, and her seriously ill father take food out to the road every morning to offer to the monks. Lalita has explained that sex is out of the question. McKay has already gathered this from the fact that there are no rooms in the house, only one vast space upstairs where all domestic business is conducted, save cooking which takes place under the house where the sow lives. Yet surely they could find a way? Only by going through a Buddhist ceremony, Lalita tells him firmly. Lawyer McKay notes that she is not talking about anything legally binding.

In the meantime, he gets in touch with Samson Lee via a cheap cell phone, using one of a dozen SIM cards that Lalita has purchased for him. McKay will use each SIM card only once. A second cell phone fitted with the twelfth simcard he puts aside exclusively for Lee to use to call him.

"*Better stay where you are for the moment, till I sort this out,*" was all Samson Lee would say on the first call. "*It may take awhile. Don't tell me where you are, just tell me if it's secure for a month or two.*"

"Month or two?"

"*This will take some time.*"

"Did they kill Hercules?"

"*Of course they killed Hercules, what was left of him. His mother's seriously pissed.*"

McKay absorbs this information while, from an upstairs window, he watches Lalita's mother pick rice. It doesn't look so hard. You simply pull up a clump of the plant from the wet earth, bash it against the side of your foot, and chuck it in the basket. It's hot though: The landscape turns into a mirage soon after sunup. And it cannot help to be almost blind. The old lady works mostly by feel.

On the second call on the second cell phone the next day, Lee tells him there is a whole gang of Colombians still in Thailand. They bribed the cops in advance, so no one is looking for them except Lee's people. Lee's people, though, have connections with senior police that go very deep. As a matter of fact, Lee is connected to almost everyone important in Thailand. The Colombians, who only had the know-how to bribe minor cops, are still at large, but they will find it difficult to leave the country. Magnus is probably not in imminent danger, he just needs to keep his head down until the Thai side of the war is won.

Magnus has to rethink his situation. A week in the country might be quaint, in a pinch, but a month or more is a different ballgame. Especially without sex. With the increased emotional need which is a function of insecurity, McKay finds it difficult to keep his hands off Lalita. Images from those two incandescent times he slept with her provoke almost continuous arousal. What to do? Furtive fumbling at night, or during the day when her parents are working the fields, is out of the question—Lalita has made that clear. On the other hand, he dares not take her to a hotel in Surin, not so much because the Colombians might be looking for him (though they might be), but mostly because Samson Lee would surely find out and Magnus is supposed to be incognito. McKay doesn't want to enrage Samson Lee at a time like this.

So what about a quaint Buddhist ceremony, as Lalita more or less suggested? Probably Lalita, considering her profession, will understand his pragmatism: get married Buddhist-style in order to make his sojourn in the country that much easier. Using his lawyerly knack of expressing himself in positive terms whilst playing down the counter arguments, he subtly lets Lalita understand that he will accept a Buddhist marriage with her, on certain terms which could be summarized as voluntary sex slavery on her part. He is not sure they are quite reading from the same hymn sheet, but does it really matter? He'll take care of her and her parents, he really will solve all their money problems with a wave of his platinum Visa card. He knows you don't get nothin' for nothin' in this world, and he is genuinely grateful to her. The way he puts it, the whole deal sounds eminently reasonable, although he's not sure she's fully understood his complicated logic in English.

He's no sooner given this heavily nuanced "yes," than her father appears as if from nowhere to discuss Lalita's sale price. Her father is only a couple of years older than McKay, but to McKay he looks about eighty.

McKay has very little cash with him, but in Surin he can use his credit card to get money from an ATM. Except that he cannot go to Surin. To his astonishment, he realizes he can probably trust his fiancée. In these circumstances, the old man's fee of fifteen thousand dollars for his beautiful daughter's body for life does not seem unreasonable. (Maybe he'll keep her indefinitely, a twenty-two-year-old sensual feast waiting for him in a sarong in the country—why not?)

Lalita rides to Surin in back of a pickup truck, and by using a number of ATMs manages to extract fifteen thousand dollars. Out of curiosity, McKay calls his bank to check: Yep, she took out exactly the agreed sum, not a penny more.

Next day, nine monks appear in their saffron robes, form a semicircle, join themselves together with a length of white string, and start chanting in Pali, while Magnus and his bride kneel with their palms held together near their chests for what seems to McKay like an inordinate period of time. Indeed, he is so tired from keeping his hands up after the first hour, and so bored with listening to the incomprehensible Pali, and at the same time so determined to show he has the stamina of any Thai man, that he is not paying very much attention to Lalita.

Like most Thais, Lalita understands quite a lot of Pali, thanks to the cultural influence of Buddhism. She knows that Pali is a dialect of Sanskrit, which is perhaps the only language on earth wholly dedicated to the sacred. Like most people in the world outside of the West, Lalita assumes that everyone, even McKay, has a God-shaped hole in his head, otherwise he could not be human at all, could he? She also assumes that the monks' words are having the same effect on him as they are on her.

Of course, she knows he does not consciously understand anything, but this is a magical moment and these words are sacred. So sacred, indeed, that she finds she is undergoing that religious experience which she has always known would come to her sooner or later. Quite simply, this is the happiest day of her life and she has quickly forgotten the rather legalistic caveats that McKay tried to impose on their union. Indeed, as invariably happens when a soul begins to awaken, the spiritual experience is so powerful that she simply drops her former identity like a set of old clothes. Miraculously, but not unusually, she is able to forget she was ever on the Game. After all, as far as her community is concerned, in one smart move she has become a rich, respectable, powerful, married woman.

She enters a trance while the monks recite ancient texts concerning the sacredness of marriage, the intrinsic part it plays for lay people on the eight-fold path, the importance of the tiny beam of light at the center of every human soul that is like an authentic splinter of nirvana, and how much stronger we become when we are able to join with another in total commitment and faithfulness, and how we need this strength for that crucial and terrifying moment when at death we enter the transitional state called "The Other Side." They end by reciting the duties each spouse owes the other, particularly emphasizing fidelity and honesty.

When the monks are gone, Lalita explains to her parents the strange *farang* inhibition about privacy: Basically, Magnus wants them to consummate their marriage alone in the house. After a short discussion, McKay forks out another three hundred dollars for her parents to go stay with her father's brother, who lives up the road, for a week or so.

Now he can finally achieve what he has been planning since New York. A week is a long time for a millionaire to postpone gratification.

Afterwards, he tries to stifle his disappointment, tells himself it is early days and there has been a breakdown in communication somewhere along the line. She used none of her tantalizing tricks at all, employed none of those spectacular techniques which had been haunting his libido for so long. On the contrary, she made love to him with unstinting adoration in her eyes and the functionality of a country girl who wants to make a baby.

Laying on his back, controlling himself, not looking at her, smoking a Marlboro Red, McKay uses his softest, most charming tone. Smart attorney, he makes his pitch as a man with a problem: Due to an appalling childhood he is hopelessly promiscuous and favors threesomes. He would like for her to work on him with another woman, especially since he knows that Thai prostitutes often prefer threesomes and he has no doubt she has often done that sort of thing in the course of trade. There are plenty of whores for hire twenty miles away in Surin, right?

Somewhat preoccupied with his disappointment, he fails to notice a stiffening in her arm which lies across his chest. Staring at the ceiling, he does not notice a sudden contraction in her pupils or the tightening of the muscles around her eyes.

Changing the subject, Magnus asks her if she can get him some opium to help him pass the time (he does not say: *in this godforsaken hellhole*). He's heard it is easily available in Cambodia, so logically there must be some importation, no?

Lalita nods: Yes, she can get him some.

"We can make out on it—wouldn't that be fun?"

"Yes," she says, looking away, "that could be fun."

Of course, they do not make love on opium. She shows him how to prepare the pipe, as the old crone in the village where she bought it had shown her, and after a few puffs his mind takes a quite different direction. After five pipes he is in a trance which lasts eight hours. When he comes around he decides that opium is definitely his new recreational drug of choice. It is incredible: a lot more civilized than crack and therefore more suitable for one's middle years. He has spent eight hours in a fascinating dream world where he lay on the king-size bed from his Manhattan apartment, except that the bed floated in a dynamic, light-filled space and Magnus was able to travel to different stars and back at will, on his magic bed.

While Magnus is in his opium trance the next day, Samson Lee calls on the special cell phone. Lalita tells Lee that McKay has gone out for the day. Lee speaks to her in Thai and tries to convey, in coded language McKay would understand, that the war is won on all fronts. The bodies of twenty-three horribly tortured and mutilated Colombians have been found by Thai police, following a tip-off, somewhere on the border with Mayanmar; at the same time, someone who shall be nameless informed the DEA of the exact location of the Escaverada family's main jungle factory. He tells her to tell Magnus to watch the international news or buy a newspaper. In any event, McKay must get the next flight to New York, Lee has some urgent matters for him to attend to.

Lalita watches CNN at a shop in the village and sees how a massive haul of cocaine has been retrieved from a certain factory known to be the property of the Escaverada family, who have all been taken into custody except for those who died in the battle, which happens to be most of them: A combined Colombian government and U.S. operation had mobilized more than five hundred men. However, the godfather, Pablo Escaverada, is still at large; indeed, according to intelligence he has been traveling overseas for some time, running his operation by cell phone and e-mail.

Lalita is able to guess, from tone and manner, what kind of Thai-Chinese Samson Lee must be. She now has no doubt that Magnus is in reality Pablo Escaverada, a business partner of Lee, for sure, on the run from international law enforcement. Lalita doesn't tell McKay about Lee's call when he comes around.

For three and a half days Lalita keeps McKay opiated while she waits for the sow. Whenever he comes down from his opium trips, she has a fresh pipe prepared and ready for him, and off he goes again. She has no way of knowing that in his disembodied state he sloughs off all carnality. He wants to tell her he has discovered that he genuinely loves her, from the bottom of his heart, but he never gets the chance. Finally, she knows by the unusual grunts that the sow has started to give birth.

As soon as the first piglet pops out, she takes it tenderly in her arms and climbs the stairs to where Magnus lies on a futon on the floor. With grim stubbornness working her jaw, she takes a large roll of agricultural plastic to lay out next to him, then rolls him over onto it. She turns up all the corners and edges, so that it forms a kind of shallow pool. Then she removes the gold Longines watch from his left wrist and lays it next to the piglet, which she lays next to McKay; or rather, next to McKay's body, for as we know, Magnus himself is off on some celestial frolic, where we must join him briefly to get his side of the story.

THE OTHER SIDE, TUESDAY MARCH 8, 2005, AROUND NOON

McKay, who after only three days has developed a measure of expertise in the manipulation of his opium dreams, has discovered that it is not only the bed which is under his control: On the contrary, the *whole dream* is at his command. This is the total-immersion virtual world that computer scientists hope to achieve in maybe fifty years time; opium smokers have been visiting it for thousands. His new and favorite trick is to expand until the bed is a structure of stardust and he is as big as the universe.

Today, unaware of Lalita's strange arrangements, McKay has once again expanded his astral body until he is almost perfectly absorbed by the great, luminous Inner Kingdom. Then something odd starts to happen. A door stretching from Saturn to Andromeda appears in the sky with the words *Other Side* hanging on a sign above it. McKay notices millions upon millions of people entering this doorway and cannot resist following them.

On the other side of the door, things are not so idyllic. The great football crowds of bewildered souls are engulfed by terrible whirlwinds consisting of samsaras from all the lifetimes those souls have lived through. A large number of the newly dead are overcome by powerful currents, which lead them into the bodies of animals and insects. To his surprise, he watches a highly respected Supreme Court judge, who must have died that very hour, turn into a scorpion. The more developed reincarnate as humans, usually in some situation of tedious drudgery and/or reckless debauchery. Only one or two escape the spiritual tsunami to rise to the challenge of an intense beam of white light shining above the appalling chaos. McKay is not one of these. Although his commendable clarity of mind enables him to see without self-deception, his lifelong commitment to undiluted self-indulgence makes it impossible for him to resist the turgid currents. Then, all of a sudden and with an overwhelming relief that makes him cry, he sees his gold Longines watch, which appears magically before him in gigantic form. He flies toward it as if toward salvation. Too late, he sees the trap. Struggle though he might, he is sucked into a warm, smelly, squealing body.

MEANWHILE, BACK ON THE FARM

Lalita has opened all the major veins and arteries that she can penetrate with a kitchen knife, and while her husband bleeds to death, she caresses the piglet whose name henceforth will be Magnus McKay and presses his Longines gold watch against the wriggling creature until she is quite sure McKay's soul has found its new lodging. She ties a crimson ribbon around each of the piglet's legs, so that she will not get him mixed up with the others, then gives him back to his mother to feed.

She has been terribly torn, right to the core, but she is finally at peace. Her torment consisted of the conflict between her undeniable need to possess him forever and the equally pressing need to kill him because he was a depraved monster who deceived and abused both her and the Buddha's holy monks. This is resolved now. Pigs live at least ten years and she will have him with her constantly for that time. Using McKay's platinum Visa card and the ATM code he gave her, she takes out as much as the account will allow on a daily basis, until she is rich enough to pay for her mother's cataract operation and her father's quadruple heart bypass. She also makes sure she can pay for her young brother's school fees all the way to post-graduate level, and for herself to retire from the Game and live contentedly in her native land for the rest of her life. Her first and most pressing expense, though, is to bribe the local cops. Fortunately, she has known them since childhood, so once a sum has been agreed upon, they conclude that the *farang* died of bird flu.

When Magnus McKay the Pig finally dies, she will have had enough time to arrange for his transmigration to a more long-lived creature: perhaps an elephant? Marriage is forever, right?

BONUS SEASON

BY HENRY BLODGET

Shanghai, China

W hen you were right, all was well in the world. The air seemed clearer, the future brighter, and the forest of roof-top construction cranes stretching west over the Huangpu a symbol of limitless opportunity. When you were wrong, however, as Emerson Jordan was now, a knot tightened in your chest, the Shanghai skyline just looked polluted, and your dubious future condensed to a red number at the bottom of your screen.

"It'll come back," a voice on Jordan's left said.

Jordan prayed that, for once, Fishman would be right.

They had $400 million in a yuan-baht derivative, a bet that this afternoon's Ministry of Finance meeting would send the yuan to the stars. Two hours earlier, when the markets had briefly lurched their way, Jordan had fantasized about ending his year with a ninth-inning grand slam. Up $80 million, he had rehearsed the final pitch he would make to Stack that night, after Stack had been softened by hours of hosannas from Reingold and other visiting New York brass. He had also considered taking the easy money, quitting while he was ahead. But he hadn't, and now this was no longer an option.

As the red number blipped lower, the tightness in Jordan's chest crept outward, and the scroll-wheel of his mouse grew damp with sweat. He had worked hard on hiding the stress—the lip-pinching and fetal slouching of the early years were long gone—but he couldn't do anything about his palms. Wiping his hands on his pants, he glanced out the windows, where the smog had thickened to an ugly brown soup in the afternoon sun.

Should he cut and run? Even down $120 million—the latest bulletin—he was still up on the year (barely). Yes, the timing was terrible—mere hours before Stack finished the numbers and made the final decisions—but as of now, he could still make a case for a solid number. If he hung on, though? In the space of an hour, the trade had wiped out most of that year's gains.

"You think they know something we don't?" the ever-helpful Fishman asked. "Maybe some bastard in New York has a direct line into the meeting?"

Jordan suppressed an urge to smash Fishman's face into his keyboard. But it was possible—especially here, where the same bigwigs who plotted policy placed trades on their BlackBerries. But that was what Stack was for—Stack, Mr. China, Mr. *Guanxi*. Stack had made his calls. Stack had signed off on the trade.

Two minutes later, after a tantalizing uptick had falsely raised his hopes, Jordan was down another $20 million. The knot in his chest now extended into his arms, stomach, and legs. All traces of the morning's optimism were gone, replaced with the conviction that this new frontier was a land of pirates and thieves, that he'd lost his touch, that he was about to lose his job. A trader's primary task is to manage emotions, and—irony of ironies!—he was actually thought to be good at it. An entire year's work draining away, Jordan pushed his chair back and rose to his feet.

"Where are you going?" Fishman asked.

Jordan ignored him.

Stack's office was off the far end of the floor, a glass box that jutted from the building like an observation platform. To get to it, Jordan had to walk past no fewer than fourteen trading desks. In the middle of a trading day, there were only two reasons to see Stack: you were making a killing, or you were getting killed. As he walked, Jordan tried to maintain his poker face—his *Stack* face—but he knew he wasn't fooling anyone. On the contrary, on this day of all days, he imagined his fellow traders quietly celebrating, thinking that Stack's erstwhile boy wonder had finally blown himself up, leaving more for everyone else.

The entrance to Stack's imperial suite was guarded by two secretaries: Clara from Hong Kong and Lauren from New York. Neither seemed surprised to see him. Jordan nodded to both, then walked past into a dim, windowless corridor. As always, the door to Stack's office was closed, leaving Jordan with nothing to do but stand helplessly in the gloom. Sometimes Stack made you wait seconds. Sometimes minutes. Sometimes, rumor had it, an hour or more. Today, thirty seconds after Jordan arrived, the door clicked softly and swung open.

Stack's office had been designed for maximum impact: a sensory deprivation trip through a dark tunnel followed by an assault of light and space—as though you had burrowed into a cave and emerged on the side of a cliff. The office was two stories high, walled by 270 degrees of floor-to-ceiling glass. Not content with the knee-weakening vertigo this instilled— and eager to fully embrace the over-the-top carnival spirit of the new Shanghai—the London-based architects had added another special feature: a translucent floor. It supposedly employed the same technology as photosensitive sunglasses, except in this case (and others), Stack retained control. On Stack's desk was a box with the usual knobs—temperature, lights, AV, etc.—one of which allowed him to modify the clarity of the glass. If Stack wished, he could set the floor to "clear" and watch visitors discover what it felt like to negotiate while hovering 870 feet above the wide streets of Pudong.

Jordan, no fan of heights, had developed a method for dealing with the floor: From the moment the door swung open, he stared Stack straight in the eyes and never looked away. In the early days, Stack had observed this and, surprisingly, had responded by turning the floor as dark as onyx whenever Jordan arrived. It was a subject of debate on Jordan's desk whether Stack had done this out of respect for Jordan's trading prowess, or, as Jordan suspected, because Stack had liked him. In any case, in recent months, as Jordan's market wizardry had faded, Stack had dispensed with this gesture and now left the floor as clear as glass.

"Sorry to bother you, Alan," Jordan said. "We have a problem."

Stack nodded. The back wall of the office, the one behind Jordan, held six enormous screens, allowing Stack to monitor every trading position in the firm.

"The rumors in New York are that the Ministry has voted to maintain its current stance," Jordan continued. "But I think the rumors are wrong."

"Any new information?" Stack asked.

"Just some b.s. fed to the wires," Jordan said.

"Who's on the other side?"

"Draco, I think," Jordan answered, referring to a massive New York hedge fund. "Most of the wire quotes came from their shills."

Stack nodded again, almost imperceptibly.

The meeting was over. A hundred and fifty million was real money, even for Stack. If Jordan took the loss, it would hit Stack too. And yet, as always, he had reacted as though receiving a weather report.

Back on the trading floor, Fishman stood up when Jordan approached, so agitated that he seemed about to shout across the floor.

"We're down two hundred now," Fishman hissed, as Jordan slid back his chair. "Two hundred fucking million."

"You'd be a terrible poker player, Fishman," Jordan said, trying to maintain a Stacklike demeanor. Despite his efforts, the number was a kick in the chest. They were now down for the year. He was going to get blown out the door.

Fishman shut up, thankfully, but the market didn't stop falling. Ten minutes later, they were down $240 million. Then 280. Word spreads fast on a trading floor, and Jordan's conviction that he was getting famous increased with every downtick. The glances, the murmurs . . . Finally, ten minutes after Jordan returned from Stack's office, a light on his phone flashed: Stack. Jordan stabbed at the button.

"Double it," Stack said. Then he was gone.

Double it? Jordan's heart raced. The loss was huge now, even for Stack, but it wouldn't kill him. Stack could take the hit, fire Jordan, cover his ass. *Double it?* No matter who Stack had called, no matter what he had learned, nothing was certain. It was no mystery why Stack sat in that translucent office and Jordan in a dime-a-dozen swivel chair.

Jordan turned to Fishman, who looked like the defendant in a murder trial.

"Double it," Jordan said.

"Are you crazy? Stack said double it?"

"*I* said double it," Jordan said. So Fishman did.

* * *

It wasn't a *baijiu* headache, fortunately, but three hours of sake at the Japanese-themed year-end banquet had gone to work on Jordan's head: a pinpoint throbbing pain, gradually increasing in intensity, just forward of his right ear. The waiters were pouring tea now, offering hope of a recharge, and Jordan knew he would need it to get in a final word. Fifty feet away, at the power table, Stack was still joined at the hip with Reingold and Zhu.

"Rumor has it Reingold's mainly here to kiss Stack's ass," Fishman said, catching Jordan looking, referring to Steve Reingold, the head of Global Sales and Training. "Apparently he's no longer the shoe-in for the CEO job."

"Oh?" Jordan said. Fishman's main attribute was that he was plugged in.

"Apparently, Beston seduced a couple of the board members over the past month," Fishman continued. "He's tight with Stack. The board is worried that if they pick Reingold, Stack will bolt, taking most of us with him. Reingold's probably here to suck up to Stack, make sure he can keep him."

"I thought Reingold had it sewn up," Jordan said, feigning ignorance.

"So did everyone else," Fishman replied. "But Beston crushed his numbers this year, and now he's persuaded everyone he can hang onto Stack."

"May the best man win," Jordan said.

"And may we all get paid in the meantime," Fishman added.

Fishman grabbed the sake bottle and, for the umpteenth time that evening, refilled everyone's cup. Then he stood up and raised his own. "The night is as yet an embryo," he proclaimed to the four junior members of the desk, trying to channel some frat lingo in a sad attempt to bond with them. "But before we move on, I would like once again to toast our fearless leader, Mr. Emerson Jordan, without whom we would all be living in *hutongs*."

"To Emerson!" they shouted.

Jordan nodded his head in gratitude, embarrassed, hoping Fishman would leave it at that. But Fishman had been working up to this all evening.

"Those of you in fixed-income land," he continued, louder, nodding toward six members of the emerging-market bond desk at the other end of the table, "may not be aware of the absolute *killing* that was made on the forex desk this afternoon. And to be sure that you show the proper deference to the god among men in our presence this evening, I would like to—"

"Thanks, Fishman," Jordan interrupted, raising his own glass. "What Mr. Fishman means is that, once again, the Shanghai team at Whitney Gilman wiped the floor with every other division at the firm, and we should all drink to that."

"To Shanghai!" ten of the twelve voices at the table concurred. They drained their glasses, set them back on the table. Then an eleventh voice, previously silent, chimed in.

"What I heard," Joseph Wilson said, from the other end of the table, audible even over the cacophonous conversation of the banquet hall, "was that our resident 'god among men' got himself in a bit of a fix this afternoon."

In the instant silence, Jordan looked down the table at Wilson, who was still holding a full cup. Jordan felt a stab of humiliation, and hoped Wilson wouldn't take it farther.

Wilson was drunk, drunker than Jordan, drunker than most of them. His desk had had a bad year—the second in a row—and everyone knew that unless Stack made him a charity case, Wilson was done. That was why Wilson's people were whooping at Fishman's lousy jokes—they needed a lifeboat. Tomorrow, when Jordan's team was getting their numbers, Wilson would be packing up the wife and kids and heading back to New York.

Making a scene now would only add to Wilson's disgrace: a bitter has-been hastening his transformation into a never-was. Jordan wasn't eager to hear the rest of whatever Wilson had to say, though—no doubt something to the effect that Jordan was just an empty-suited puppet on Stack's string—and he especially wasn't eager to have his team hear it. He stared at Wilson, readying himself for the verbal punch. After a few seconds, however, Wilson backed down.

"To Whitney Gilman," he said, raising his cup into the air. "And to the forex desk, for riding out the storm."

"To Whitney Gilman!" the table roared, in enthusiasm and relief.

A few minutes later, after chugging a cup of tea, Jordan made his move. He had hoped to catch Stack alone, but Stack was still glued to Reingold and Zhu. The banquet was over, the crowd was dissipating, and the three were now standing at the head table, waiting to follow everyone else to the door. Jordan worked his way across the room, as confidently—and soberly—as possible.

"Mr. Reingold, Mr. Zhu, I'm sorry to interrupt. I'm Emerson Jordan. I run the currency desk. I just wanted to say goodnight to Alan." Turning to Reingold, he added: "It's a pleasure to see you again, sir. We met last year in New York."

"I remember," said Reingold. "And I gather you had another good year."

"Well, thanks, yes, we did," Jordan said. "But we had help. Especially this afternoon."

As he said this, Jordan nodded toward Stack.

"I hear you made a stirring comeback," Reingold said, smiling. "Have you met Mr. Zhu?"

"I haven't yet had the pleasure, sir," Jordan responded, shaking the hand of the billionaire real estate mogul everyone assumed was one of Stack's key *guanxi*. "You're quite a celebrity on the trading floor, sir."

"It's a privilege to do business with the firm," Zhu said.

"Thanks for stopping by, Emerson," Stack said, speaking for the first time. His tone was courteous, but it was also a kiss-off.

Jordan was going to respond with a play for time, when Reingold jumped in: "Yes, thanks for stopping by. X.D. is giving us a ride back to the Hive. Why don't you come along?"

It had been a rough early afternoon, but since then, Jordan's luck had taken a turn for the better.

X.D., as Mr. Xiaodong Zhu was known (a concession to foreigners' inability to pronounce even the simplest Mandarin), was chauffered around town in a forty-two-foot stretch Hummer—the kind, Jordan reflected, that only drug dealers and rap-stars would be caught dead in back home. The Hummer had two PC-equipped desks, fully reclining seats, a fifty-inch flat-panel HDTV, and a lounge. In addition to the driver, it was staffed by a steward, who navigated, checked traffic via the government-sanitized Internet, refilled the mini-bar, and, at every stop, brushed grime off the car with a feather duster.

On board the Hummer, the four men settled into the lounge, and Zhu's steward opened a bottle of Laphroaig, pouring four glasses. Zhu reached for one, raised it toward his guests.

"I have promised to show Mr. Reingold my car," Zhu said. "Before I do, however, I would like to toast Mr. Jordan."

"Here, here," said Reingold.

Jordan considered playing along, but decided not to risk it. "I'm sorry?" he said.

"One of my companies was overweight with baht this morning," Zhu explained. "We needed some time to convert before the Ministry meeting. Without your help, we'd never have gotten out."

"I see," said Jordan, even though he didn't.

"Thanks to your efforts," Zhu continued, "some folks in New York temporarily concluded that the Ministry wasn't going to relax the peg. Unfortunately for them, this conclusion was wrong."

"All's well that ends well," Reingold said, raising his glass.

So that explained Jordan's temporary $280 million loss—and the near–heart attack that had accompanied it. Stack's contacts had floated rumors to grease Zhu's wheels—and Draco had fallen for them. No wonder Stack had been so cool. Remembering the depths of the afternoon's panic, the walk of shame across the trading floor, the conviction that an entire year's worth of work (and, likely, his job) had vaporized, Jordan once again felt the heat of humiliation flood into his cheeks. Would it have killed Stack to let him in on the game? This must have been the story that Wilson had threatened to spill at dinner—that the currency desk's 'god among men' was so blind that he didn't even see he was a pawn.

Zhu slipped out of his seat and headed forward, with Reingold following. As plush as it was, Zhu's Hummer was no more luxurious than the G5 in which Reingold had just floated across the Pacific, so its interior could hardly have been of interest. But Zhu's conglomerate had paid Whitney

Gilman $172 million in fees that year, so if necessary, Jordan knew, Reingold would lick the tire treads.

Zhu and Reingold's departure left Jordan alone with Stack—the moment he had been trying to engineer all evening. To Jordan's annoyance, however, Stack took the opportunity to check his BlackBerry. As Jordan watched Stack scroll through e-mails, he took another sip of his Laphroaig, felt its warmth radiate outward from his throat and stomach, emboldening him.

"Well, that certainly sheds some light on this afternoon," Jordan said, aggressively.

Stack stiffened ever so slightly, and his thumbs stopped working the BlackBerry keys—a reaction that, for him, was almost frenzied.

"All's well that ends well," Stack said, without looking up. In the long, infuriating silence that followed, Jordan took another swig of Laphroaig.

"Speaking of ending well," Jordan said, "I—"

"This is not a good time," Stack shot back, again without looking up.

"Well, can we talk before the final decisions are made?" Jordan asked.

"They've already been made," Stack said. "And this is not a good time."

"When—"

"It's not a good time," Stack said again, sharply, suddenly looking straight at Jordan. "And the politics in New York"— at this, Stack nodded toward Reingold, who was hunched over a computer with Zhu in the belly of the Hummer— "have made this a challenging year."

Stack returned to his BlackBerry, leaving Jordan to chew on this—and to chase it with another belt of Laphroaig. So

Stack was going to fall back on the "challenging year" crap? He was *Alan Stack*—not some dime-a-dozen managing director—surely he could do better than that. Maybe the bonus pool was just fine and Stack was hoarding most of it for himself. That was what some of the sleazier managing directors did: duped their people into thinking that the department had gotten stiffed, then kept the lion's share.

Jordan's indignation was getting up a good head of steam when a bolt of fear arced through him. Maybe there was another explanation for Stack's frigidity. Maybe Jordan's name was already on the execution list. It was Reingold, after all, who had invited Jordan on this last supper of a limo ride. Maybe Stack just didn't want to break the news to him tonight.

"We aren't the only game in town anymore," Jordan said, a feeble threat, and one that, to his embarrassment, sounded as awe-inspiring as a mouse squeak.

"We're the *best* game in town," Stack replied, still engrossed in his BlackBerry. "And we are only as good as our team."

Stack stopped short of pointing out that *Jordan* was only as good as his team, a pulled-punch that, in another mood, Jordan might have appreciated. In his current mood, however—drunk, over-caffeinated, and deep into his Laphroaig—he wasn't grateful. Instead, he felt shafted and exposed. And he was still feeling that way another Laphroaig later, when they reached their destination.

The Hive was a ninety-seven-story needle two blocks from the glittery Pearl TV tower in Pudong. It had been designed to symbolize industriousness and dedication—to facilitate work, to honor work, to *beatify* work—and it did this by eliminating the need for its inhabitants to do anything but work.

Many of those who worked in the Hive, including Jordan and Stack, also lived, shopped, ate, worked out, and drank there. The lower third of the building housed condos. The middle third restaurants, grocery stores, health clubs, night clubs, and the only mid-building heliport in the world. (The best tables in the sixty-third-floor restaurants hung above the heliport's doors, so diners could watch executives nip to and from the airport and Hangzhou like bees.) The top third held the most expensive office space in Shanghai.

Such was the Hive's self-sufficiency that the year-end banquet was the first time Jordan had left the building in over a month. He usually used the main door, in the building's west lobby, overlooking the Huangpu. When Zhu's Hummer pulled up that evening, though, it was to the southern lobby, which existed exclusively for VIPs. The instant the vehicle stopped, the doors opened and two valets reached upward with white-gloved hands.

Reingold got out first, followed by Stack and Jordan. Inside the Hummer, Zhu nodded goodbye as the steward cleared the Scotch glasses and wiped down the table. A valet swung the door shut, and the Hummer pulled away.

Reingold led them across the lobby to the elevators. He paused in front of them and turned to Jordan. "Nice to get to know you, Emerson."

"Thank you, Mr. Reingold," Jordan replied weakly, having persuaded himself that he was done.

"X.D. gave me this to give to you," Reingold added, reaching into his jacket pocket and pulling out an envelope. "Another token of his appreciation. He looks forward to seeing you again."

Jordan took the envelope. The elevator door opened, and Reingold and Stack stepped in.

"Goodnight, Emerson," Stack said.

"Goodnight, Alan," Jordan replied, wondering if he would ever see him again.

Alone in the lobby, suddenly aware of how drunk he was, Jordan fingered the envelope Reingold had given him. He opened it and found a key card, the kind used to operate most of the elevators and doors in the Hive. The card bore no markings, nothing to indicate what it provided access to. Jordan stood in front of the elevators for a moment, examining the card. When the doors opened again, he decided what the hell and stuck it into the slot.

The doors closed and the elevator began to ascend, but the screen displayed no floor numbers, so Jordan had no idea how high he rose. Higher than his floor, certainly, high enough that his ears popped and his booze-addled brain fought back a wave of seasickness when the elevator finally decelerated.

The doors opened to reveal an unfamiliar foyer, one that looked as though it had been airlifted from a Victorian exhibit in an art museum. The room was furnished with ornate chairs and lamps, Impressionist paintings, and—Jordan did a double-take—a fireplace with a crackling fire. On the far wall was an antique desk, behind which stood a Caucasian woman Jordan had seen somewhere before.

"Good evening, Mr. Jordan," she said, as Jordan stepped out of the elevator.

"Um, good evening," Jordan responded.

The woman crossed the room to shake his hand. "I'm Sarah Lewis. It's a pleasure to meet you. Mr. Zhu asked me to look after you. Follow me, please."

She led Jordan through a door and down a hallway, the parquet floor creaking under her shoes. At the end of the hall, she slid a key card into the slot beside a door, then held it open for him. By now, he had a good idea of what to expect inside.

Zhu's fantasy boudoir wasn't your average bordello bunk room. Rather, it was a four-room suite, complete with a stocked refrigerator, six-foot bar, seventy-two-inch flat-panel TV, 500-thread count sheets, and, surprise surprise, a plexiglass Jacuzzi mounted in a floor-to-ceiling glass wall.

"If you don't like heights," Sarah said, while giving him a tour of the bathroom, "I recommend the jets."

After showing him around, she lifted the TV remote off the bedside table and held it up.

"If you would like company," she said, "click here to bring up our interactive catalog. We would be happy to accommodate any special needs."

A video hooker catalog—nice touch. Despite this innovation, Jordan felt a wash of disappointment. He was enjoying the company he already had.

"What button do I press to ask you to have a drink with me?"

"We don't have a button for that," Sarah Lewis replied. "And I don't drink on the job. But if that's one of your special needs, I'll be happy to pour you one."

"I have a lot of special needs," Jordan said, smiling.

Since joining Whitney Gilman, Jordan had made it a practice to wake up every morning at 4:55 a.m. He did this seven days a week, on the theory that it had a self-regulating effect on his evening activities. The theory was flimsy—the evenings went on no matter how exhausted he got—but one positive side-effect was that after eight years, Jordan no longer needed an alarm clock. To reduce the risk of falling

back to sleep, moreover, he had instituted a policy of standing up the moment he awoke, an aggressive maneuver that
often left him grasping for support as blood drained out of
his head.

In the predawn blackness, Jordan awoke and stood up.
This time, the brain drain was so severe that he slumped to
his knees. Head hanging, palms flat on the rug, he thought he
was going to black out, but he kept still and the feeling
passed. After several deep breaths, his strength returned, and
he lifted himself to his feet—at which point he remembered
where he was and why he felt so bad.

The "where" was Zhu's fantasy pad, high up in the Hive.
The "why" was the lack of sleep and the fact that he was still,
indisputably, drunk. Head pounding, Jordan glanced at an
easy-chair, the last place he remembered being. The glasses
were gone (Lagavulin for him, water for her), as was the
jacket draped over the back of the chair. Looking down, he
discovered that his clothes were gone too, replaced with silk
boxers. He hadn't undressed—he was pretty sure of that. He
also didn't remember browsing through Zhu's video catalog.
But someone had removed his clothes and tucked him into
the bed. And the same someone, he discovered after some
shaky steps to the closet, had hung up his suit, shirt, underwear, and socks.

In the darkness, Jordan picked up his wallet, keys cards,
and BlackBerry from the bedside table. Reflexively, he
checked the markets and headlines—New York had closed
higher—along with his e-mail. In the seven hours since the
end of the banquet, eighty-six e-mails had accumulated in
his inbox, mostly blasts from the research and trading desks
in New York. This was a good sign: He hadn't yet been
canned. He scrolled down the list, looking for anything time-

sensitive, and was about to toss the BlackBerry on the bed when he found her note.

From: Sarah Lewis.

Sarah Lewis. Seeing her name brought everything back. Just a few hours earlier, he remembered, she had expertly accommodated (some of) his "special needs," needs that Zhu's catalog would only have exacerbated, needs that often intruded in times like these. Despite her repeated attempts to excuse herself, he'd kept asking her to stay. He had even, pathetically, insisted on her watching *Casablanca* with him, in the hope that it would kindle something. (It hadn't—and he had fallen asleep during the flashback sequence.) Now, he clicked on the e-mail, and the message filled the screen.

Hope you slept well, it read. *Sorry you missed the end.*

Very personal. No Mr. *Jordan,* and a tantalizing vagueness too. What "end" was she referring to—the movie or the evening? The note gave Jordan hope that, magic key card or no magic key card, he would see her again.

Thought you should see this, the note concluded, adding a link to a video file.

Jordan clicked the link and sat down on the edge of the bed, having no idea what to expect. As the file loaded, he glanced toward the windows. The BlackBerry's luminescent screen reflected off the dark glass, a glowing spot of blue among the lights of a predawn Shanghai.

The video began to play, and at first Jordan couldn't tell what he was seeing. Then the image brightened, and he realized it was the view from an elevator security camera. The elevator doors opened, flooding the image with light, and a man in a suit got in. He inserted a key card into the console, stepped to the back of the elevator, then turned around and looked up toward the camera: Stack.

The image jiggled as the elevator began moving, and after twenty seconds jiggled again as it came to a halt. Then the doors opened and Stack walked out.

The scene switched to a waist-level shot of Stack emerging from the elevator into a familiar Victorian room with impressionist paintings and a fire. Recognizing the setting, Jordan's heart began to race. Had they taped him too? Had the whole Zhu fantasy thing been a setup? Stack approached the camera, reached out to shake the hand of a woman who appeared in the foreground. (Sarah? Jordan couldn't tell.)

Next shot: an empty hallway. The woman appeared, walking past the camera—Jordan still couldn't see her face—and Stack followed behind. At the end of the hall, they paused in front of a door. The woman inserted a key card and opened it. They both disappeared inside.

Jordan had a queasy notion of what was coming next: a video of his boss in action—a sight he wasn't anxious to see. He'd also broken out in a sweat. What had *he* done last night? Was he sure it wasn't something worth filming? Why had Sarah sent him this, anyway? Was it a warning?

The scene switched again, and for a moment Jordan was confused. Instead of the Zhu fantasy suite, the room looked like a classroom, with the camera looking out from what would have been the blackboard. The room was empty except for the teacher's desk and a single pupil, a pretty girl of perhaps eleven or twelve, seated at a desk in the center of the frame. She was dressed in a black skirt and white shirt, the ubiquitous uniform of Japanese grade-school students. (First the banquet, and now this—did Stack have some sort of Japan fetish?) The girl appeared to be copying something from the blackboard: She would look up, look down to write in her notebook, and look up again.

The classroom door opened, and the "teacher" walked in—and Jordan's fears were confirmed. The girl stood to bow low to Teacher Stack. Stack strode toward the front of the classroom and sat at the desk, his back to the camera.

Jordan felt sick. Was this a standard option in Zhu's video catalog—or one of Stack's "special needs"? Was this how his hyper-cool, hyper-professional boss spent his leisure hours—indulging in power-trip kiddie fantasies?

The girl stood beside her chair, head bowed. Teacher Stack rose, picked up a fistful of papers from the desk, and began shaking them at her. He was yelling now, his head and shoulders jerking as he barked. Jordan had never known Stack to so much as raise his voice, so this alone was startling. Stack moved toward the girl, who remained motionless with her head bowed. He stopped in front of her, still yelling. Then, of course, she dropped to her knees.

A moment later, Jordan was on his knees too, beside Zhu's luxurious toilet. He gagged, his hands gripping the bowl, and a Scotch-flavored flame surged up his throat. He swallowed hard, closed his eyes, waited for the next heave. It came, and Jordan expelled it, spraying the porcelain brown. Head hanging, hand groping upwards, he found the handle and pulled. The toilet flushed white, splashing Jordan's face with cool water. He stood, staggered to the sink, and turned on the tap. He plunged his hands into the stream and doused water on his burning cheeks. Then he leaned on the counter and let water drip from his chalky face into the sink.

Images rushed through his head, one after the other—power fantasies that even Stack himself might have warmed to: Jordan as ninja, Jordan as heavyweight champion, Jordan as axe murderer, Jordan as righteous gunslinger. Had he been sober and rested, he might have realized that it was more than just the video fueling his fantasies, that his resentment toward Stack had been building for years. And it might have occurred to him that he hadn't been fired yet, that he could have misread Stack the night before, that twelve hours— twelve drunken hours—of reeling year-end emotions weren't worth betting a career on. He might have realized that *some* pictures were worth a thousand words, but others weren't worth the hard drives they were stored on. But Jordan wasn't sober, and he wasn't rested, and he wasn't thinking any of that. Instead, as the water dripped away, his churning emotions condensed into a single, simple concept: payback.

Turning from the sink, Jordan strode back into the bedroom and picked up the BlackBerry. Several years earlier, when e-mail scandals had temporarily terrorized Wall Street, a techie friend had taught him how to send e-mails with untraceable return-path information. Thumbs clicking frantically, Jordan logged off the network, logged in again as an administrator, and returned to the e-mail. He copied the video file into a new e-mail. In the "Subject" field, he typed *A Message From Alan Stack*, and then skipped to the "BCC" field. From a pull-down menu, he selected *Global Sales and Trading*, a distribution list that included some 11,000 Whitney Gilman professionals worldwide. Then he pressed *send*.

What does it feel like to walk into your own execution? Jordan was sure he was about to find out. Seven hours earlier, after escaping from Zhu's lair and returning to his own Hive pad, he had sent Fishman an e-mail implying a hangover and asking him to take over for the morning. Then he had unplugged every communication device he owned and crawled into bed. When he awoke, just after noon, he had remembered the Stack e-mail and been hit with a bolt of terror and regret: What had he done?

He had considered camping in his apartment, but figured that, in the event they hadn't yet traced the e-mail, this would be a dead giveaway. So, he had showered, dressed, and headed for the trading floor. Now, as Jordan approached the desk, he was glad to see that little had changed. Fishman leaned toward him.

"You're not going to believe what you missed."

"Do tell," Jordan said, steeling himself.

As Fishman told it, the e-mail had hit Whitney's trading floors like a bomb, blowing an otherwise ordinary morning to smithereens. No one knew where it had come from, but the Australia guys had opened it first: A bizarre pederastic-sado-fantasy in which Stack fucked a schoolgirl on a teacher's desk. Within an hour, the video had bloomed on a thousand desktops in Singapore, Hong Kong, Moscow, Paris, London. The administrators had caught up with it, finally, ripped it off every server in the firm, but not before some bastard had posted it on the Internet. The networks had it now, and had been showing clips all morning, along with profiles of Whitney Gilman and headshots of Stack. The Shanghai government had demanded an apology, as had the Japanese government, and everyone was expecting a similar demand from Beijing. The firm's Executive Committee had called an emergency meeting in New York in the middle of the night. And Stack! Poor Stack. He'd been picked up by the police at his apartment that morning and taken in for questioning. No one had seen him since.

As Fishman's story unfolded, Jordan felt like a kid who

had tossed a cigarette in a garbage can and burned down a city. The knot tightened in his chest again, and his hands dampened with sweat.

"You've got to see the video," Fishman concluded. "It's some sick shit. I'll send you the link. Oh, and Reingold's been calling you."

"Reingold?"

"He's holed up in Stack's office, doing damage control. One of Stack's secretaries keeps calling."

"What does Reingold want with me?" Jordan asked, his heart pounding like a kettle drum, sure that this was it.

"Got me," Fishman said. "Give her a call."

Hand shaking, Jordan dialed Stack's number. Lauren answered, confirmed that Reingold wanted to see him immediately. Now getting fired seemed like a dream scenario— he'd be lucky if he didn't get *jailed*. Jordan stood up and set off across the trading floor, a dead man walking.

The translucent walls and floor in Stack's office were dark, the only light coming from a strip of glass behind the desk. Reingold was in Stack's seat, surrounded by the heads of Asia Wealth Management and Investment Banking, along with the regional general counsel, the head of HR, and the head of PR. Of course the lawyers and HR folks were there: Reingold would need witnesses. Security guards were no doubt waiting just outside the door.

As Jordan entered, everyone was staring at a speaker-phone in the middle of the desk. Reingold looked up.

"Karl?" he said to the speakerphone. "Emerson Jordan has just walked in."

Karl, Jordan assumed, was Karl Eichenwald, Whitney's CEO.

"Hello, Mr. Jordan," said Eichenwald's disembodied but

unmistakable voice. "Glad you could join us on this fucking peach of an evening."

"Emerson," Reingold said, "we've got a situation here, so we'll be brief. Other than myself, I believe you were the last one to see Alan last night. I've told everyone how we rode back from the banquet together. After that, Alan and I went upstairs for a nightcap, and then Alan headed off—to his apartment, I thought. Did you see Alan again last night?"

So they were going to interrogate him first. Interrogate him, find out what he knew, then shoot him.

"No," Jordan said.

The general counsel jumped in.

"Was he behaving normally on the ride home? Was he drunk?"

"Not that I noticed," said Jordan.

"Any idea where the video was shot?"

Jordan's heart skipped. "No," he lied.

"Any idea who would have sent this video around?"

"No."

"Well, whoever it was ought to be fried alive!" Eichenwald's voice boomed. "Stack's in need of some serious therapy, but whoever spammed this thing around has fucked the rest of us. Issue the statement. I'll do a press conference in the morning."

"I'm not sure that's wise, sir," the general counsel said. "We haven't authenticated the video. We haven't interviewed Stack. We haven't even gotten all the basic facts."

"*Authenticated the video?*" Eichenwald boomed. "What the fuck is there to authenticate? The head of our Asian trading organization is on four networks banging a twelve-year-old!"

The speakerphone chirped as Eichenwald hung up.

"Well, I guess we're done," another voice said through the speakerphone, one Jordan didn't recognize. "Thanks for the rapid response. Can't say I agree with the Chinese about living in interesting times."

"Hopefully, they'll be less interesting in the morning," Reingold said.

The speakerphone chirped several times in succession: the rest of the board disconnecting.

Reingold looked up. "Thanks, everyone."

The executives rose and filed past Jordan toward the door.

Reingold stood up and walked toward him. "There's one other thing we need to discuss," he said. Jordan's heart raced again, as Reingold placed a hand on his shoulder. "I have to go apologize to Shanghai's mayor on the firm's behalf, so I don't have much time. I've spoken to most of our big clients this morning, including X.D. I've explained the situation, told them that, regardless of what happens, they'll be in good hands. And they will be."

Why the preamble? Jordan wondered.

"No matter what else happens," Reingold continued, "Stack's done. For now, he's on administrative leave, but I suspect he won't be coming back. We need a new head of Asian trading. And I'm looking at him."

"Excuse me?" Jordan said.

"The press release will be on the wire in ten minutes. Eichenwald has already approved it. He wanted me to congratulate you on his behalf. Our clients are happy with our choice—they're ready to help you however they can. X.D., especially, would be eager to hear from you this afternoon."

"I'm not sure what to say," Jordan replied, meaning it.

"Give it time," Reingold said, patting Jordan's shoulder

again, turning toward the door. "Congratulations, Emerson. I'll be out of your new office this afternoon. Enjoy it. And don't let me down."

For the first time in his life, it seemed, Fishman wasn't completely in the loop. He had been busy, though, thinking everything through. When Jordan sat down, still in shock, Fishman was positively bursting.

"So, is Reingold on cloud nine, or what?"

"I'm sorry?" Jordan said.

"You've just had a private meeting with our next CEO," Fishman said, "a man who until this morning was an also-ran."

"What do you mean?"

"Remember Beston? The heir apparent? Well, the reason Beston made the late surge to the front of the CEO lottery was because of Stack. Stack had lost confidence in Reingold, and threw in with Beston. But now Stack's toxic, and everyone who ever knew him is running for the fumigator. There's no way Beston can distance himself. So that leaves Reingold, the man who was suspicious of Stack to begin with. He's our new CEO."

"Interesting," Jordan said, his heart pounding again.

"Yes," said Fishman. "And I have a feeling we're going to be seeing a lot of him."

"Oh?"

"Rumor is he's got a girlfriend in the Hive. An American—Sarah Something. Lives upstairs. One of the bond guys runs the StairMaster with her in the gym, and he saw her coming out of Reingold's apartment this morning. Now, Reingold can fly his jet-copter into the heliport, take a couple of meetings, and then bang away all night long. How's that for convenience? Doesn't even have to leave the building."

Jordan sat frozen, ostensibly watching headlines tick up the screen.

"And you want to know the kicker?" Fishman continued. "I just talked to a buddy of mine who's obsessed with that Stack video. Has been playing it again and again, all day long. He has all this fancy equipment, and he says that he's pretty sure the thing's a fake. The first part's okay—that's Stack riding up the elevator, shaking the woman's hand—he's sure of that. But the kiddie porn thing? In the whole sequence with the girl there's only one shot where you see Stack's face, and my buddy doesn't think it's really him. Says he's blown it up to the pixel level, and he thinks Stack's face was cut-and-pasted from the first part, the elevator segment. Something about the angle—looking up when he should be looking out. In any case, he thinks Stack has been framed."

"Where did the sex part come from, then?" Jordan said, feeling sick.

"My friend thinks it's from some dime-a-dozen porn flick, the kind piled eight feet deep in Xiangyang Park."

"And Stack?"

"Stack's toast. He'll rot in prison until they finally let him call a lawyer, and even then he won't be able to do much. It's not like the folks at the embassy are clamoring to save him, not with that horrific video going around. He'll get off eventually—if my friend can spot a fraud, the forensic gurus can too—but it won't be anytime soon. R.I.P., Stack. Meanwhile, I wonder who they're going to get to run things around here."

Just then, as Jordan watched, a Whitney Gilman press release blipped onto the screen.

EVERYTHING I'M NOT

BY LAUREN SANDERS

Tel Aviv, Israel

T en. *Counting backwards*
Middle of summer and Tel Aviv's wilted to its roots.
But a deep chill cuts through Ben-Gurion. Outside
the tarmac steams, monstrous 757s nose-to-nose with mili-
tary planes, security everywhere. Look matronly, I'd been
told: Former combat soldiers comprise airport security, and
everyone knows the army's stocked with mama's boys. I'm
wearing a long floral skirt, loose-fitting T-shirt, sensible
shoes, purple beret covering my head like a religious woman.
The band of my skirt is soaked.

One security officer approaches a man a few people
ahead of me, who presents his passport, Israeli, and the back
and forth begins. I make out a few words . . . *Nothing . . . I go
to travel . . . Paris.* Closer to the checkpoint, I fear the religious
drag might be all wrong; everyone hates the orthodox. I take
heavy breaths, heart like full magazine fire, counting backwards . . . *ten,* exhale, *nine,* exhale, *eight,* exhale . . . a technique from my days on ice, those last few minutes before
pushing off when you're led into position based on a coin
toss. Random. Waiting for a signal, the gunshot, and it's do or
die. Counting was the only way to clear my head. Still is . . .
four, exhale . . . *three,* exhale . . .

A soldier moves into another line full of tourists, careful

to keep the nose of his M16 to the left. The IDF has an arms code peppered with words like *humanity* and *dignity*. Soldiers respect their rifles. No solace as they advance, and I know I'm doing something I shouldn't be doing, and probably for all the wrong reasons: guilt, loyalty . . . My father says all people are motivated by sex or money. As a teenager, declaring myself the opposition, I'd float examples to ruin his theory, and ask about, say, nuns. "Sex," he replied. "God is sex." The president (can't remember which one): "That's too easy, Jen. Watch the State of the Union. See the way the idiot smiles, rolls his fist, senators, dignitaries, special guests sitting and standing like puppets, the eyes of the whole world on him up there at the podium, and you know he's doing it all for the friggin' lead pipe in his pants."

My father is crude in a way that can delight as much as disgust. He knows the feeling of hundreds of thousands of eyes on him, the lead pipe. He's made me what I am today, standing a few travelers from interrogation, limbs on alert, stuffed with enough stolen information to detain me in the Holy Land—and not how I'd like it. I start the count all over again, *ten*, exhale . . .

Nine. The conference (five days earlier)
She finds me at the bus depot, grabbing my arm as I'm about to board the shuttle in the thick, dusty parking lot. "What are you thinking?" She pulls me back, lemony rose scent eclipsing burning fuel, vegetable oil, falafel. "You make it so hard to see you with those drab clothes. I have to find you, don't I?"

She's got loose brown curls, dark skin, and freckles. Lips like a blow pop. Israeli women might be the sexiest in the world. Utterly brazen and comfortable in their skin.

"You look much better than I thought," she says, leading me to a creamy white sports car. A little Honda. "You don't photograph well. And the stories make you so hard and serious. But you're okay. *Ma?* . . . What? What's the problem?"

I nod. "Nothing, I—"

"Why are you standing there? Open the door."

"Are you from the conference?"

A quick stare, candied lips cracking slightly. "Get in," she says.

As a child, I could recite the exact number of city blocks to my father's office. I knew when the streets got skinnier, the buildings taller, where we'd come upon the World Trade Center. My father hated the towers from the moment they went up, said they blighted the district. His revenge was buying up souvenir T-shirts and dumping them into the river, buying because he would never rob anyone of their livelihood—not if they were making less than he was. Week after sunny week, cotton shirts bobbed around lower Manhattan, from above resembling a wispy cirrus cloud, said my painterly mother, who like all of us mourned when the police caught up with him. That was the first time he made the cover of the *New York Post.*

Wall Street begins with an old church and ends at the river, the New York Stock Exchange its sire. My father liked being near the exchange, though he rarely visited the floor. He'd made a name shoveling his family's millions into venture capital and private equity, ideas thrilling him more than commodities. The family had traded in dry goods, which seemed as remote as amber waves of grain, you don't hear much about dry goods anymore. My father claimed his was the tallest building on the street, and maybe that's why he hated the towers. From his windows, you could see past the

Empire State Building, out to the row houses in Queens and Brooklyn, airports and wetlands, industrial New Jersey. "Take a look at my *shtetle*, Jen," he said, lifting me up high and despite his tight grip on my hips I felt dizzy, the drop so far and only a thin pane of glass between me and the end. I read somewhere that people who work on high floors in offices are more likely to have affairs. Something about the thin air and subliminal sense of danger keeps them keyed up. Like driving through a city on pins and needles.

"Always there is so much traffic," Gila says, as we inch along Ha-Yarkon. She'd given me a few hours to relax at the Sheraton, read through the conference literature. The government had invited me to present on international philanthropy. Once I was a competitive speed skater; now I spend my days handing out the family's money, though many of my father's assets have been frozen since he disappeared. "The people of Tel Aviv, they like to go out, dress well, eat well . . . They don't let much get in the way. The city is full of pride. Always they compare it to New York City—of course, most people who say this have never been to New York City. But they are very cosmopolitan and alive. Makes a lot of traffic."

"If I were an urban planner," I offer, for a moment actually considering it, "I'd invent a city without cars."

"Hold on." Gila smiles, then turns off the main boulevard, steadying us through venous streets, tourists left lagging beneath the palms. For me, Tel Aviv has always conjured Miami Beach with its concrete terraces, salty-dog air, and long, languorous summers, hotels shooting up against blue-green water . . . and Jews. All the little old ladies who argue with you in supermarkets and eat dinner at 5 o'clock. But a few generations have given the natives their own look, a tougher dark skin, mirrored in the metallic skyscrapers shooting up around the flat white boxes, many of them historic. The city's also got its own twin towers, though they're fraternal: one rectangular, one round, and still they smack of tragedy.

We pull up in front of a coastal bar in Yaffa, the old Arab port, now low on Arabs, high on cafés. Inside Gila signals a man in a gauzy black linen suit who kisses the air next to her cheek two times as Israeli men do and bows reverently, then leads the two of us to a secluded outdoor table overlooking the black-and-white waves, tiny lava lamps strung along the patio, chairs like ice cubes. Very chic, Gila says. She orders a clear liquor that clouds when you add water. I wanted a Coke but with the waiter in front of me say Scotch, neat. I am not supposed to drink, a little wine with dinner, but . . . Gila's studying the way I lift my glass and swallow, as if she knows.

"You must be tired," she says. "I hate flying over the Atlantic. Small flights, sure, but anything more than two hours . . . I try to set my watch two days before to the new time. Sometimes I take a little hashish, a pill. I have a pill if you'd like."

I say no thanks, order another Scotch. Gila tells me she learned to fly planes in the army, often winged undercover into Lebanon, Syria, Iraq on fact-finding missions. There were no female fighter pilots when she served and she was training in psychological warfare. I ask what's psychological warfare and she says strategy. You study your enemy, learn his mind, his methods, so you can defeat him. I say dumb American things like "wow." I ask when she served, trying to guess her age, and she says between the *Intifadas* . . . mid-'90s? She's younger than her talk, younger than me, and though she's posturing I am enjoying our conversation, the thick winds coming off the sea, slow songs from the '80s, American. *Chic?* I ask if she was ever in combat.

She shrugs, "Every day I am in combat."

"I meant in the army."

"Ah, you have romantic thoughts about the Israeli army." She smiles, I believe. Hard to tell with her. "Americans think, *Women serve, they let the gay people in, everyone's on reserve, it's egalitarian,* but it's really so much macho bullshit."

"My brother used to say the same."

"What?"

"He came over here to serve."

"You have a brother?"

"He's dead." I blurt this out so fast I'm stunned. I don't share personal information easily, if at all. Gila's face ices over, and that's exactly why. When you drop bombs, you've got to clean up the debris. "It wasn't here, happened a little later," I nervously add. She is silent for a long while, then shakes her head. "I had no idea."

"Well, it's not something for the bio."

Staring beyond me, as if she might not have heard me or might have but despises the levity, so damn American, she repeats herself. *She had no idea.* Around us, others laugh, converse, provoke, and we're stuck in the silence . . . until her phone coughs up a symphony.

I jump slightly. "Sorry."

She purses her lips, raises a forefinger, shakes her head. "No." All of this one seamless gesture before she fishes the yammering phone from her bag and checks the number, her face a declarative sentence. I feel feverish.

Gila doesn't take the call but says we must go. She has work still for tomorrow. It's been a long night, we agree. Then silently leave the café.

* * *

Eight. Why I don't drink

Late into the night, fueled by Scotch and jetlag, wishing I'd taken her pill, then playing out worst-case scenarios—you betray a lover, cause an accident, someone's death, your own, *why am I doing this?*—the way I'd practiced in rehab, when counting wasn't enough . . . I Google her. Gila Zyskun is a common name. I find the conference website. She's on the staff list, no picture. Beyond that, a roulette wheel of possibilities: graphic novelist, advertising executive, espionage consultant, entomologist, rare-glass collector, government bureaucrat, teenage chess champion. I flip on the TV: CNN: I'm old enough to remember the network's coming of age during the first Gulf War. At twenty-three, I was here with my brother and felt the fear of Scud missiles pointed at damp, wintry Tel Aviv, the smell of gunpowder over the Mediterranean, people trolling the streets in gas masks, the orthodox lobbying for expensive masks to fit their beards inside, the anti-Semitism rabid in this seaside town. Tonight there are hard-luck stories of those displaced by the pullout. I'm captivated. Sleep experts say Thomas Edison revolutionized insomnia when he invented the lightbulb, extending the day into oblivion, to say nothing of TV sets and wireless Internet. I throw open the curtains and stare out at the charcoal waves to remind myself it's nighttime, a few hours away from the conference, and I am so small.

Seven. Slacking off

Gila Zyskun shows up the next morning at the Sheraton in a tight miniskirt, curls still wet, maroon-tinged sunglasses, balancing coffee in tall paper cups like martini shakers. She'd called from downstairs, said take your bathing suit, we're going to the beach, be fast. Though my day was slated for panels and prospecting, I'd fallen asleep thinking about her, the way her pinkie nail grazed the rim of her cloudy glass, her tall tales of moonlit reconnaissance—*government bureaucrat? entomologist?*—and while it's impossible to visit this country without thinking of my brother, our stay at the kibbutz, all the fig trees we'd planted, the hash in Dahab, I wish I'd left him out of it. Loose lips sink ships.

That was a propaganda campaign during the Second World War: how the gossipy women back home could fuck up troop movements over a cup of coffee.

In the lobby, Gila hands me a caffeine cocktail, says she thought it would make me less disoriented. "I'm juiced up already," I say, but it tastes very good.

"There is never too much coffee. That's why Israel has so many cafés. We take coffee sitting down; it's hard to find anywhere with paper cups. Starbucks couldn't make it."

"I thought the politics drove them out."

"Everyone always assumes politics, sometimes it's just life," she says. We are walking through the parking lot. It's already hot and my bones are jumpy, expectant. I see her Honda a few cars off. "It's my turn now for a question," she says, as we split, each to our own side. "Why did you stop skating?"

Her lock clicks open like a shot. "Did I tell you that? When—"

"You don't remember," she shrugs, pulls open her door, still looking at me over the roof. I remember drinking a few Scotches and telling her my brother was dead. Not much more. "Jetlag is very powerful. Once after a terrible rocky flight I married a man I just met."

"Married? You don't seem the type."

"I'm not."

She dips beneath the roof, slams the door. Beyond the parking lot, frothy waves tumble into the beach, already too crowded. Years ago I watched a woman dive from the top of this hotel. Saw bodies on the beach hive together, as if in a disaster film—tourists, police, men in fatigues—but it was too late. The Sheraton is a tall building and she'd landed on concrete. People couldn't fathom it. Even in a land where soldiers caressed their guns in restaurants, poised always to shoot, and Arab children threw rocks at tanks (this was before the era of suicide bombers), nobody wanted to believe a pretty young woman—Dutch, no less—would throw herself from a building. But sometimes everywhere you look is death.

Inside Gila's car, I let the cool leather vanquish me. We are going to a beautiful place, she tells me. Private, she says knowingly. We can swim, have lunch at the spa, even return for the afternoon sessions. Nothing is too far from anything else.

Israel is paved with primitive two-lane highways. Marc and I hitchhiked everywhere, once he'd had enough of the army and quit. He left me frantic messages, begging me to come, just don't tell the old bastard—my father had arranged the army after the cops seized fifty pounds of mushrooms from Marc's apartment, Hefty bags full of them. The old bastard was capable of tectonic shifts in time and space, could bend the law with one phone call. He'd been prospecting in Israel since the Six-Day War, helping to modernize the desert ravaged for centuries by explorers and asylum seekers, his belief in the land holy, rehabilitative. The Jews would make a man of my brother. But my father underestimated Marc's resistance, and though I was about to begin aggressive training for my second Olympics, the one I'd fantasized about every day since flopping Calgary, I left the country to be with my brother. I never qualified.

At the beach, we climb up on big rocks and lay out a few towels. Gila has come prepared. She says I can change into my suit but don't worry about the top. It's European style. The water is a shallow green today, like a drained emerald. I don't want to be topless in front of her, plagued by an atavistic terror of shared hotel suites, locker rooms, shower stalls: You're afraid to look but more afraid to *not-look* too hard. But you get good at pretending. We lie next to each other absorbing the day, talking easily.

When she stands and rolls her arms through the holes of her gauzy shirt, I don't want to go. We have a reservation, she says. A seaweed wrap before lunch.

To be wrapped I must take off all my clothes, hand over my body to the experts. Gila lies next to me, naked, and I'm *not-looking* because this is what women do. These thoughts surprise me. Nothing about my life now is closeted. Ours is a concealed terrace, sunny but embedded in a cool granite fortress, a fleet of leafy green plants on the floor. Bodies wrapped, our eyes are covered with plastic goggles and faces rubbed with a sandy cream. Years ago I took a mud bath in the Dead Sea, let the salt hold me up like a million tiny fingers. It's impossible to drown, Marc said, and I felt light as a souvenir T-shirt in the East River.

Every so often a young woman sprays gentle streams of water, moistening the seaweed. I feel like an eel. A happy little eel falling in and out of sleep, relaxed in way I can't remember ever being without drugs.

"Hello, Jen."

I rip off my goggles. My father's standing in front of me, and Gila's disappeared. Bisected by cubist rays, he's light and dark and larger than ever. I sit up slightly, afraid to crack my cellophane cover. "What are you doing here?" I ask, and he smiles—obviously the wrong question: Gila Zyskun is a rat.

"It's great to see you." He lights a cigarette, leans back against the granite. "I miss you. I hate being so out-of-pocket."

"Don't bullshit me, Dad. Everyone's going crazy looking for you. I've got lawyers harassing me, not to mention the feds . . . What makes you think they're not tailing me?"

He smiles. "What's it they say? Everyone's got a doppelganger."

"Shit! I should have known, the minute I heard Israel—"

"Let's face it, your brain's just not wired that way," he says, dispirited I'm not the canny apprentice he'd always wanted. He shifts in the piercing rays, and I see stars, I think, I'm dizzy. I cup a hand against my forehead, twist my neck up into the sun, and our eyes meet, the stars really millions of tiny gnats, and I'm suddenly shamed, the contours of my body wet and shiny, hidden but not, the theory of latex. "Put on your clothes," he says. "We're having lunch."

The early settlers survived on tilapia, my father tells me, as we're served colorful plates of fish, hummus, pickles, pink radishes, tomatoes and cucumbers diced infinitesimally small, what they call salad. Tilapia is peasant fish; the kings ate trout. We sit on another terrace, this one also scooped into the side of the mountain but with a long dining table. We squeeze together at one end, a waterfall rushing behind us, the air cleaner and cooler than it should be on a sticky summer day. My father eats voraciously, in between bites signaling staff to bring us more food, wine, his laptop, bantering as if it hasn't been nine months since we've seen each other.

"More fish?" He pushes a platter of smoked trout under my nose. I roll my eyes and break off a piece with my fork.

"Sorry about you and . . ."

"Barbara."

"Right . . . Never liked her. How's your mother?"

"Come on, Dad."

"She's my favorite, you know that."

"She's living in the mountains with Lionel. They're into race horses and Fresh Air kids. And what's going on here?"

"What?" he says, palms open, shoulders up like Gila's, innocent as the state of Israel . . . *What, what did I do?* We're staring but it's hopeless: I can take him down with one look. He exhales deeply, pours another glass of wine, and the tale flows from his mouth like something out of the Old Testament. I am not in Israel for a conference. He needs my help.

Six. The kite

My ride back to Tel Aviv comes in a small sport utility vehicle with tinted windows, the driver, Moti, a stout, surly man with no neck. When I ask where's Gila, my father steels and I know there are things he's left out of the story, things too indecorous even for a man on his fourth wife, and I want to spit in his over-tanned face, but count . . . *ten*, exhale, *nine*, exhale . . .

At the Sheraton, they still believe I am here for a government conference. "*Shalom, Shalom!*" they greet overzealously, asking how my day went, was there anything I needed. No, nothing, thank you, I'll be in the gym. Forty-five minutes on the elliptical trainer gets my heart up, though I hate pumping in place, you lose the gorgeous expanse of speed. It's your everyday corporate hotel. The gym is well equipped. In my room there are movies in English, bottles of water, free wireless, plush pillows, and a feathery comforter that reeks of stale anonymous sex. I climb under the covers and check my e-mail, when a window pops up on my screen. I'm not set to receive instant messages, but there she is: *Meet me at the bar in Yaffa.*

Backdropped once more by the Mediterranean, the gurgling lava lamps, '80s lounge music, I let her apologize. "I shouldn't even be here," she says. "It's dangerous."

"What's the danger?"

"I know he told you."

"He said you were lovers."

Caught sipping from her cloudy glass, she holds the liquid against the roof of her mouth, lowers her chin slightly, swallows. My neck is hot, back hot, eyes burning white, it's all the confirmation I need. "He is a very interesting man," she says.

"He's a thief."

We are silent for a moment, then she says it started as business. Says she'd been researching for him in New York, angling her way into other VC companies and investment banks, helping him figure out who was backing what, how he could bridge the right startup then liquidate it before his partners knew what hit them. Much of it was legal, she says, there's no law against misrepresenting yourself nor using information obtained in bad faith. He made many enemies and far too much money for his tax returns—and here's where his story gets nebulous. For years he'd been skimming profits and funneling them into Israeli accounts; before the towers fell you could do this under the radar. She liked his mind, she says, even the way he ordered meals was tactical, and he was audacious in business, could convince investors an empty shell of a company was hot issue stock . . . What was it like growing up with that? Big, I say, everything about him was enormous, even his absences.

Her phone goes off, that damn score, Beethoven maybe, blaring like a nervous breakdown. She looks at the number, a revelation in those few seconds, embarrassed. "Hello! Hello!" she says, some intimacy to it. "Nothing, really . . . I'm in the car . . . Sure . . ."

Up she goes, and I'm grateful. Cell phones: how one can ramble across from another at a table, uncivilized on any level, particularly dicey when it's my father's lover and he is on the other end and we are out late.

You learn over the years when people are holding back. Afraid to jump in, they extend, obfuscation teasing night-caps, long anecdotes. Should we walk along the beach? she says. The water glows in moonlight. They say it's phosphorus . . . or the remnants of oil spills. The soldiers are not far away. You get used to them. Gila drops her bomb: After the army she was recruited by Mossad. She helped develop new technologies for the field and learned how to gather information, a commodity as valuable as dry goods once were. But disillusion quickly set in, she hated politics, and she took her skills to market. She is what they call a kite.

I kick off my sandals, feel the sand between my toes as we stroll. "So *you're* the thief."

"I am simply pulling together data, same as I used to for Mossad. If I have to tell a story or rearrange things to get what I want, it's what I do. Stealing, I don't know. I think you must want the thing before you can steal it."

"You're as delusional as he is. If you take something that's not yours, it's stealing. You just give him the out if you're caught, he can shrug, *What? Who is she?*"

I touch her arm, slow us down. She is a brisk walker.

"What?" she says, then turns away, utterly still for the first time since we met. The chatty one in her skirts, glasses without frames. This woman who's maybe romanced members of Parliament and worked her way into corporations with ten levels of security. She raises her head slightly, eyes reflecting moonlight like a raccoon's. "In Mossad I learned to be more cunning than anyone at the table, to think out of the box. We were bold, risky, we had no choice. We created systems that could detect a heartbeat ten feet outside of a tank, all kinds of surveillance devices tapping into databases, and still we killed so many wrong people. Where do you put that? There's no place for it. But money, it makes more sense. People think—"

"Stop it with the 'people think,' okay, I'm not interested in your little philosophies."

"Then what interests you? From what I can tell, nothing."

"That's not true, you have no idea." I hear my voice crack, blood coursing under my skin, Gila steady as a newscaster. She is so much like my father: clever, manipulative, "audacious," everything I'm not. I work this through in less than thirty seconds, while she's *not-looking*, trust me, I know *not-looking*, and then I'm babbling about the sea, the stars, how different this country is from the one I'd traversed with Marc, and somehow we're conversing again, bumping into each other slightly as we walk. Desire always gets me by the throat first. Then elsewhere. The various twitches and pulses. But the throat . . .

She walks a step in front and takes my arm. "Shhhh."

"I—"

"*Regah, regah!* Do not speak a word, don't move!" She sits me down, then disappears into the sand, up over the board-walk. Left in shadows, I wish I were armed with something other than a BlackBerry. Fear and desire share a path to the heart. I count backwards until she appears, stuffing a shiny object inside her shirt—definitely not a BlackBerry. "It's nothing, just him."

"Who?"

"He often has me followed."

I realize she's talking about my father. "Sounds like you two have a great relationship."

"Come, we'll take you to the hotel. I must go to him."

Five. Old habits die hard

At the Sheraton, she drops me without a word, and I know my father's on to me. I twist open a midget bottle of Scotch and suck it down in one sip, lying back on the lonely com-forter. Hotel beds make me want to come, but this time it's more. Gila Zyskun is not like any of my father's lovers, though she asked about them. At first they liked to care for me, be my best friend. Some insisted we "go shopping," a ridiculous activity. Gila laughed, she hated shopping too. The few he married stopped trying. A hand on my arm, she under-stands, her father had been a notorious philanderer, a general, and that's all we need, so different from those who'd endlessly probe, *How did it feel?* in the name of love. Like my father, I have failed every relationship in my life, but Gila doesn't care, says we're more alike than different. I come so fast it's clear: I don't trust me either.

Four. An unbelievable story

The three of us have lunch at an upscale Russian restaurant

in Herzliya. This is diamond money, my father says, tapping his thin, manicured finger on the crisp white linen. Marc had the same fingers, long and elegant, a few neat black hairs above each knuckle as if they'd been perfectly embroidered. You wouldn't think such pretty hands capable of such mischief.

My father divulges the plan over bowls of creamy pink borscht, blinis, caviar—comfort food, he says. On Sundays, as a boy, his father took him to visit Russian relatives in Brighton Beach and on the way home they ate lunch. He misses New York but won't endure a trial. "I'll die first," he says, and he's not joking. Gila says he carries vials of hemlock, at any moment ready to cut out on his own.

The plan is simple. I am to take a jump drive to Paris and deliver it to an associate, who'll move the contents accordingly. Simple until I know how I'm carrying—"It's small and thin," my father says. "Undetectable as a tampon. And there's something else you should know."

"Don't bother her with that," Gila says, worried, I think. Spying has taught her to be stoic, controlled.

"She has to know, everyone's on edge. The police are being extra-vigilant."

"It'll just make her nervous."

He glowers at Gila, then me, knows something's up, maybe? Her concern warms me, then nurtures paranoia: *What if this conversation is staged?* "Look, Jen, there was trouble here recently. Something like twenty companies were busted for spying on each other . . . It's an unbelievable story. One day out of the blue, this mystery writer calls the police and says parts of his unpublished novel are appearing all over the Internet and they trace it to a virus planted on his computer—"

"No, not a virus," Gila interrupts. "It was a Trojan horse, you know that."

"Same thing."

"No, it is not the same, the Trojan is much smarter, you have to invite it in. Tell the story right or don't tell it. Already, you leave out that he was writing with his wife, they were a team, but the son-in-law was related to the wife."

"He was after the husband, trying to humiliate him."

Voices raised, the vein under my father's left eye pulsing, Gila's long neck coiled, they argue back and forth about who did what and when, a slick coat of oil congealing over the untouched blinis. The gist: Upset over his breakup with their daughter, the former son-in-law hacked into the mystery-writing couple's computer with spying software, mining whatever he could and releasing it on the Internet, at times altered to sully the man's reputation. He'd also sold his Trojan to a number of private detectives who used it to spy for their corporate clients.

"They were very sloppy," Gila says.

"Israel has one of the most competitive business climates in the world," my fathers says.

"They left a trail longer than a rocketship to the moon."

"Without that writer—*writers*," he winks at Gila, "they would have been fine, which is the takeaway here: Don't mess with the family."

"What's on the drive?" I jump in, speaking loudly, as much to topple their excitement, the current between them, as to figure out what I'm in for. They angle toward me, my father no doubt wondering how much to divulge, whether it'll make a difference. Everything I own, he says. No need to elaborate, it can't be legal, and though my father's gall shouldn't stun me, throughout my life I've been his foil, I am slightly taken aback that he'd sacrifice me for his crumbling empire.

Gila excuses herself to go to the restroom, silencing my father and me as we stare, traces of her lingering, the afterglow. He sighs, "Did she tell you she worked for Mossad?"

I nod.

"She's come up with things you wouldn't believe if you saw them in a James Bond movie. Can't imagine what I'd do without her. She's amazing."

"Oh, I know."

"What's that supposed to mean?"

My own version of the Israeli shrug: "*What?*"

"Don't do anything stupid, Jen." He cuts a fork into a hardened blini, me down to fourteen. "This is disgusting . . . Hey!" He barks a few words of Russian at the waiter, lights a cigarette, and we're eye to eye.

"I'm not sure I'm going to do this for you," I say.

"Then you might as well drive a stake through my heart."

Gila returns as the waiter sets down another set of plates: blinis, chicken, salmon, chilled shots of vodka. "More food?"

"I take care of my people," says my father, stubbing out his cigarette, then piling his plate. We eat together, talking of a gentrifying Tel Aviv, how to smoke a fish . . . through much of it, her toe tickling my ankle.

On the way home, Gila and I go shopping. We park off Allenby and walk to the *shuk*, but there's nothing to buy. I wanted metal stalls with Oriental rugs, hookahs, *kaffiyehs*—years ago I'd bought one like Arafat's in solidarity with the opposition. But now it's just jellied sandals, cheap jeans, underwear, plastic sunglasses. Global capitalism run amok. Sensing my disenchantment, Gila takes me down a block to a bustling street fair. We stop and listen to a woman with eyes like caverns busk a Hebrew folk song, the refrain a desperate *Anee rotzah, Anee rotzah (I want, I want)* . . .

After my mother left, my father stayed late at the office. He'd fall asleep on his couch, then take long walks through the Fulton fish market, bargaining in the coldest hours for the catch of the day. Mornings we'd find men in thermal sweatshirts with grizzled faces and thick leathery fingers being served soft boiled eggs in tiny silver cups, strips of bacon, thick slices of toast dripping with butter, and my father, upon noticing Marc and me shyly hovering in our pajamas, beamed, "See how they taste it, it's like they've never eaten an egg!" I have inherited his romance of the working class, a propensity for self-aggrandizing acts of tenderness.

Gila raises the corner of her mouth at the singer. "So horrible," she says. I agree but toss a few coins in her sack, and we move silently, flanked by artists in canvas tents hawking jewelry, ceramic pots, stained-glass icons. A mime tries to engage us in faceplay, but we break away, walking toward the sea.

"You put that Trojan horse on my computer," I say finally.

"Not that one . . . Mine is much better," she says proudly.

"How long have you been spying on me?"

"For a little while only. We had to make sure you would come."

"And here I am," I smile. This time she holds it but has to go. Before dropping me off she tells me to keep my computer on.

Three. The ballad of the Trojan horse
Myth has it the Greeks won the Trojan War by sneaking their army into a giant hollow horse and rolling it into the city of Troy for the grand pillage. Gila stuffed her soldiers into "con-

ference" files I'd blithely downloaded but swears there is no danger, my data is safe with her. It's not the data I'm worried about. After midnight, my hotel room dark but for the computer screen, we talk through tiny windows:

—*are you in love with him?*

—*interested, sure . . . but love?*

—*you have to understand, young men are filled up with themselves, they have nothing to say but who they are*

—*he's more than twice your age*

—*this means nothing to me, if you saw him in action you'd understand*

—*that's twisted and disgusting*

—*in business . . . you have a dirty mind*

—*better than dirty money*

—*he said you wouldn't understand, you were too serious and wouldn't respect who I am in this world, and for some reason I want to show you you are all wrong*

—*i'm waiting*

—*it's more complicated than you think*

I'm typing a response when the phone rings, then

—*pick it up*

Static on the other end, what sounds like a recorded message: "Go to the window and undress, then turn on the TV loud enough to be heard. Put on your clothes in the bathroom and crawl low to the door . . ."

I do as I'm told, slipping out the back stairway that empties onto the beach. Gila Zyskun is downstairs in a Fiat with black windows.

We drive over a bridge out toward the desert. She can't promise we're not being followed but has a friend in real estate. Development is rampant on the outskirts of Tel Aviv, technology still booming. Here they move systems to market faster and cheaper, there's no time to waste. She tells me my father cycled some of his dirty money into backend machinery for electronics, computers, smart bombs. Gila drives quickly, every so often sipping from a bottle of clear liquid, then handing it to me. It tastes like licorice and motor oil, and I'm drinking again, better than *not-drinking*. Yemenite disco on the CD player, we drive through poorly lit highways, long past the Bauhaus curves into a half-baked lot with multiple excavations, two cranes dipped like gazelles. She pulls up in front of a trailer, shuts off the car. I reach for her. She stops me, says she must go in first, five minutes later, me. Five excruciating minutes in a hot, dark car, lights in the distance tingling like space saucers, half expecting my father to beam in beside me, defiance fanning desire. You have to want the thing before you can steal it, and I *want, I want! Ten,* exhale . . . *nine,* exhale . . . a bang, loud click . . . *the trigger?* I scream. But it's just the car door, Gila's return. She covers my mouth and drags me into the trailer. Locking the door behind her, she clicks on a portable lantern, and we're in musty shadows.

"You lost count or something?"

I steady myself against the faux-wood paneling, then burst out laughing.

"*Ma?* What? You don't believe me, but you don't know how many people are after him. This is no joke."

"Gila—"

"You think you know—"

"Shut up." I step forward and grab her by the shirt. It tears. She closes her eyes. I push her against the cardboard wall. Her lungs floating up and down, I run my hand along her ribs under the holster. "Take this off," I say, ordering the way I like, sensing it's what he does. She unbuckles the leather strap, gun bouncing against the flat carpet, then rips off her shirt. I step back to look—gold ring through her belly button, compact breasts, neck like an expensive vase, all hot issue—then open onto her, my tongue flicking her nipple as my hand slips under her skirt, fast and cheap.

"We have only two hours," she confirms, clamping down on me, and for two hours we dive in and out of blissful waves of fucking.

Two. Drinking from my father's cup
The next morning I call the emergency number my father'd given me. Okay, I'll do this thing for you, Dad, I tell him, but then we're even, you can't ask me for anything else. I hear him talking to someone on the other end . . . *her?*

"I had a feeling you'd come through," he says, holding a beat, "for me."

A few hours later he arrives at my hotel room with two men in heavy cologne, tight gelled hair, black T-shirts, and perfectly creased jeans, so obviously bodyguards. Used to be brown leather jackets tapered at the waist, accentuating how puffed-up they were in all the right places. I kissed one once to see if his lips were as robotic as the rest of him: They were. A few weeks later he was gone.

"Nice laptop," my father says, eyeing the screen I've kept up all morning waiting for her, as if he's also expecting someone to come galloping through on the Trojan. "Personally, I hate Macs."

He removes his silver cigarette case, and though I point to no-smoking symbols all over the room, he lights up. Rules are superfluous to him. A decade ago, when Republicans in Congress tried to ban flag burning while civilians sued cigarette companies for hooking them on cancer, my father had American flags stenciled on his Dunhills, so he could burn old glory every time he lit up. Libertarian to his bones, he abhors too much government and too little personal responsibility. In other words, he's been very lucky. He's smoked for five decades, survived two heart attacks, is crammed with plastic tubes under his ribs, and outside he's Dorian Gray—he's been done, of course, a few slices around the eyes and chin, and keeps his finely cured mane a dark, distinguished gray. We all know the story: Something's got to bear the scars. He lies back on my bed, defiantly kicking up his feet, and puffs, the edge of his cigarette curved down like a retired dick, and I hate how sex seeps into every inch of me. He spills on the carpet, deliberately. I unwrap a glass, take it to the bathroom, and run the tap.

"Let me tell you something, Jen," he shouts from the bed. "Time is an invidious mind fuck. You look around one day and everything's unfamiliar. All these people working for you, they're little womblets, your favorite suit's hopelessly out of date, rings don't fit, and even though you're getting fat, and I'm talking way beyond love handles, it feels like you're evaporating."

I hold the water glass in front of him.

"Your brother was lucky," he says, and I feel a hole opening in my chest. "There's something to be said for pissing away the whole damn thing."

"He was twenty-five. He drove into a mountain going ninety miles an hour, and don't pretend you don't know why."

"He was never that bright."

Chest throbbing, the glass in my hand shakes. "Why do you have to be such an asshole? You almost had me feeling something for you."

"What? The kid was born with one testicle, couldn't read until he was eight . . . He might have been retarded."

I throw the water in his face.

"Hey!" he shouts, sitting up and shaking a few drops from his hair. The bodyguards step toward me but he warns them off. "Listen to me: Whenever you went away, he slept in your goddamn bed, his head on that little monkey thing looking like— Serena always said you two acted really weird together."

"What are you saying?"

"Maybe there's another side of the story where I'm not the villain, maybe it's you."

"Fuck you!" I stammer backwards, then regain my footing. "And fuck this . . . And you know what? I fucked your girlfriend last night."

He stands up, towering over me, and gives his head a final shake. A bead of water hits my nose like a razor. "Jen, Jen, Jen," he says, "do you think I'm stupid? You think I don't know what's going on here? Why do you think—" He slips forward, punches his right hand against his heart, eyes squeezed together tightly, then through gritted teeth to one of his bodyguards: "You need to get me somewhere."

Oldest of the three competitive skating sports, speed skating is the most misunderstood. It lacks the glorious partnerships that give figure skating its connubial thrill, compounding defeat with total psychological annihilation. Gone too is the vicious orgy of hockey, players so convinced they're one organism they think nothing of slamming their stick over the head of the opposition. Speed skating, especially long track, is more psychological. You study your enemy, learn her mind, her methods, so you can defeat her. But when it comes down to it, you're out there circling those three thousand meters of ice alone.

I am outside Tel Aviv, perhaps not far from where I heedlessly entered Gila last night, in a hospital waiting room with Dan the bodyguard. We sit together looking at Israeli magazines, CNN. On screen, an orthodox woman with a New York accent cries, *"Never did I think I'd live to see my country take away my home!"* Dan nods in agreement, calls government officials Palestinian sympathizers, trying to enlist me in this opinion, but I've heard how the settlers steered their Trojan horses, sometimes carting possessions into Gaza under cover of night, and once you're in, well, my father might say possession is nine-tenths of the law, if I hadn't laid him flat on his back. Or perhaps it was her, lips dripping enough to sink a fucking fleet—how else would he have known . . . unless they'd planned it. I can't figure out who's playing who, I'm not that bright, but this country has a way of raising the stakes.

I bury my head in my hands, feel a palm on my back, Dan whispering, "Don't worry, you'll get used to it," and though I'm not sure what he means, I let him rub my shoulders until the doctor comes out.

He won't shake my hand, he's orthodox, but in Hebrew says the rabbi will be fine. "His heart is strong, the hardware is doing its job, perhaps he ate something."

"The rabbi?"

"Of course, he is first a father to you."

"I'd like to see him."

One. If I were a suicide bomber
Anyone here will tell you it's easier getting out than in. But decades of terrorism have refined suspicion of air travel into policy. After the towers fell—the first and only time I remember seeing my father truly unhinged, he knew so many people who worked on high floors, and his lawyer and best friend, Chuck Birnbaum, had been finishing up a cozy breakfast at

Windows on the World with a young woman who was not
Chuck's wife—America turned to Israel for lessons in airport
security. But nobody takes seriously questions from U.S. air-
line workers about whose hands might have fondled their
luggage, not even the interrogators. At Ben-Gurion, men
(and the odd woman) trained in espionage do the asking,
randomly swapping questions to make even the most sea-
soned traveler squirm.

When they finally get to me, I'm as wilted as the city outside and long past counting. For the past hour, I've tried to forget I am a Trojan horse, crammed with hot accounts and reg-
isters where two nights earlier Gila's heated tongue had
trailed, the spoils of my father's dirty little war, and perhaps it's
his dream of dying in the Holy Land, how sickly and unkempt
he looked in that hospital bed despite the doctor's assertions
as he clued me in: I am carrying the key to every one of his
off-shore accounts, decades of profits gleaned from his years
on Wall Street and reinvested all over this tiny country, even
in the settlements, which pleased neither the Israeli government nor the opposition—how did he ever talk me into this?

"Who is taking care of your children?" a security officer
asks in English, after checking my fake passport and itinerary.

"My sister-in-law," I shrug, suitably religious, maternal,
uxorial. "She knows how difficult it is for me to leave my
family."

He nods, mama's boy through and through, and part of
me thinks it's too easy, this is El Al, and another part feels
like skating, feels like sex, the world heightened into a short
incandescent stretch, and maybe that's the big secret of
crime: It's exhilarating. The officer flips again through my
passport, then slaps it back and forth against his palm. "Why
are you carrying only one bag?" he asks.

"It's all I need."

"No gifts for anyone?"

"I'm cheap."

He smirks, and I am through security: mule, liar, my father's emissary, feeling closer to him than I can ever remember, but he's warned me—there are undercover security people on every flight.

In the passengers' lounge, I open my computer and tap into the Internet, hoping for a sign, but . . . Just before Marc and I ended our trip, I fell apart. There'd been an older woman from Britain (she was all of thirty-five!) who cornered me on the roof of the hostel with a view of the boardwalk, the beach, the muddy brown Sheraton. Up on the roof from where we'd watched the pretty Dutch girl dive to her death, this woman came up behind me, slipped her hands around my stomach, down my inner thighs, and squeezed. "If we were stranded on a desert island together," she whispered, "these are what I'd eat first," and I fell hopelessly in love. We snuck away to the Sinai together, leaving Marc to put together the pieces, and when we returned several days later, she unceremoniously took up with a Palestinian dishwasher, dragging him up to our rooftop parties, kissing him flagrantly in bars haunted by travelers, as if she'd started eating from my heart. As the years move on, I remember less and less of her, can barely reconstruct her face, while Marc looms large: one of his graceful hands gripping my shoulder, he smiles, "Even the old bastard's got better taste than that."

My flight is called over the loudspeaker. I shut the laptop and walk with a group of religious women to the gate, feeling somber. I know Gila is my father's girlfriend, know she's probably betrayed me, yet I walk seamlessly through the gate comforted she's part of the data snug inside me. It's only when I'm in my seat, looking out the window at the green army planes, that I spot her standing on the tarmac in her miniskirt, sunglasses on top of her head, arguing with a soldier. She raises a fist in his face as if she's about to pound, tears streaming down her cheeks, and I'm looking, then *not-looking* so hard it's worse. A stake drives through my gut: My father is dead.

DUE DILIGENCE

BY REED FARREL COLEMAN

Tegucigalpa, Honduras

Trisha Tanglewood didn't bother with the safety card in the seat pouch in front of her, nor did she bother listening to the flight attendant's sonorous reading of the evacuation procedures. Her disdain was neither an expression of fatalism nor boredom, but of familiarity. Ms. Tanglewood knew more about commercial aircraft than most human beings who didn't actually design them for a living. It was a safe bet she knew more about the 737-700 than the pilot at the controls of the updated Boeing, certainly more than the cabin crew.

"Excuse me . . . Kathy," she read the flight attendant's winged name tag, "can you tell me, are these engines GE CFM56-7B26s or 27s?"

A blank stare washed over Kathy's face. Trisha might just as well have asked her for the gross national product of Burkina Faso.

"I'll make sure to ask the pilot," Kathy said, recovering nicely. "Enjoy the flight."

It was silly, she knew, harassing flight attendants this way, but it comforted her.

"Ladies and gentlemen, this is Captain Saunders on the flight deck. Just wanted to let you know we'll be taking off in just a couple of minutes here. We'll be cruising at an altitude of thirty-six

thousand feet at a speed of approximately five hundred and fifty miles per hour. The weather's pretty clear between here and Tegucigalpa, so we anticipate a fairly smooth flight. If there's anything we can do to make your trip more enjoyable, please let one of the cabin staff know. Once we get to cruising altitude, I'll be back on with you. Until then, enjoy the ride. Flight attendants, please prepare the cabin for departure."

"You seem to know a lot about planes," said the man in the next seat.

Trisha started—usually on top of everything, she hadn't even seen him there. She just hadn't been herself lately. No, that wasn't really true. In spite of the self-confidence and competence she wore like armor in the halls of Paisley Shutter, Trisha had, since her father's death eleven months before, been functioning in a state of psychological vertigo. An executive at Sikorsky had once told her that flying a helicopter was like playing the piano while balancing one-legged on a basketball. She hadn't quite gotten it the first time she heard it. These days, she understood it perfectly.

"I said, you seem to know an awful lot about planes," he repeated.

She looked at the man. He was forty-ish, ruggedly handsome, with a square chin and lined face; a refugee from Marlboro Country. He had a mouthful of straight white teeth and shiny, silver-gray hair like her father's. She noticed too that he had his armrest in a death grip, and that his speckled blue eyes darted nervously to and from the cabin window.

"I do indeed," she said. "And there's not a lot to worry about, so try and relax."

"You a pilot or something?"

Trisha laughed. "Or something."

"What's that mean?"

"I'm an investment banker," she said, as if that explained something.

The man nodded. "I'm Pete Dutton, by the way." He removed his hand from the armrest and offered it to her.

"Trisha Tanglewood." She briefly shook his hand. He had a firm grip and a surprisingly dry palm.

"Pleasure to meet you, Trisha." He tipped an invisible hat.

"Yes, a pleasure."

"How is it that a banker knows so much about planes?"

"I spent seven years analyzing the aircraft manufacturing industry—the last two years as chief analyst."

"Really?"

"Really. If you'd like to discuss the relative merits of this aircraft as opposed to, let's say, the Airbus A320, or why some airlines prefer Pratt & Whitney power plants over GE or Rolls Royce, just let me know."

"No thanks. Too much knowledge makes me even more unsettled," Pete said, trying to smile and failing. "I already have enough trouble thinking of jets as gas tanks with wings."

"Well, that's essentially correct; wings *and* seats."

"Great. You're a real comfort."

As if on cue, the pilot wound up the turbofans and the jet began its urgent rumbling down the tarmac. Then they were off, gradually leaving Miami behind and beneath them. Trisha could see the near panic in Pete's face as the servos repositioned the flaps and the bottom seemed to drop out of the starboard side of the aircraft, the captain turning west into the setting sun. In her own way, she was just as unsteady.

She had gotten what she thought she had wanted, a kick up the ladder. No longer could she hide herself in the shadow of tail fins or rotor blades. Trisha had been forced out of her cozy titanium, aluminum, and carbon fiber womb. The whole manufacturing sector was her gig now, all of it, everything from baby bottles to ball bearings, from farm equipment to pharmaceuticals. The days of simple, seamless trips to Seattle and Toulouse were no more. She was far less familiar with her new arena, an arena with a distinctly Third World flavor.

Trisha knew she was good at managing herself and her career. She was more than good, she was superior, and had handled her small team deftly. Problem was, the team had grown exponentially. And as much money as was at stake in aircraft manufacturing, it was penny-ante compared to the whole manufacturing shebang. *Shebang*, she thought, *what a silly word*, but her dad had used it all the time. He was full of quaint phrases and cowboy wisdom. Even now she had trouble accepting he was gone. Other than her job, he had been all she had. He would have been so proud of her. Remembering him, his crooked smile, his rough good looks, the day he gave her her first saddle, Trisha looked past Pete Dutton and out the window into the deepening night. And she found her eyes drifting back toward Pete's face.

He seemed an interesting man, polite and unafraid to show vulnerability. She could count on one finger the number of male colleagues who would have dared display fear in front of her. On the Street, fear was weakness and weakness was death, and you never let it see the light of day. You battened it down, you plowed it under. You swallowed that bastard whole.

"Ladies and gentlemen, the captain has turned off the seatbelt sign, so you're free to move about the cabin. However, when you are in your seat, we'd like it if you could keep your seatbelts on. The captain has also indicated that you may use all approved electronic devices, such as laptops . . ."

Trisha already had her tray table down, her Dell out of its case and booting up before the flight attendant had gotten past the first sentence of her announcement. She called up the file marked MM/ZIPS/H.1. Six months earlier Paisley Shutter had been retained by Mega-Mart, Inc., one of the world's largest big box retailers, to look into the feasibility of acquiring PriceStar, Inc. PriceStar was an undercapitalized, debt-heavy, second-rung player in retail space, but the one big asset it possessed was its offshore textile plants. Their profit margin on their in-house clothing lines was the envy of the industry. And now that takeover talks had progressed from flirtation to third base, Trisha was going down to Honduras to make sure all the numbers that her team had given her checked out.

She owed due diligence not only to Mega-Mart, but to herself. Partnerships at Paisley Shutter didn't get handed out like Halloween candy, and especially not to women. In fact, Trisha Tanglewood was the first woman under the age of forty to have even sniffed a partnership. Some of her male colleagues had warned her off making the trip at all. They were full of sage advice and playful chiding, but she understood the old-boy code better than they suspected. Her taking this trip not only made her look good, it made them look bad— worse than bad, lazy. Like her dad used to say, "If the crows're gonna caw anyhow, you might as well give 'em a reason." *Fuck 'em!* was the way they said it on the Street.

"Christ, how do you deal with all those figures?" Pete spoke up, peering at her screen. "Gimme anything more than three digits either side of the decimal point and I'm befuddled."

Reflexively, Trisha slammed her laptop closed. She did it with such force that passengers from surrounding rows snapped their heads about to see what had happened.

"Whoa—sorry about that," Pete said. "I didn't mean to peek."

"It's okay," she lied.

"No, it's not. It was rude, and my momma schooled me better than that." He pressed the call button.

Trisha didn't know what to think but said nothing.

"I'm sorry to bother you," Pete said when the flight attendant arrived, "but is there an empty seat somewhere? The lady wants to do her work and I'm afraid I'm disturbing her."

"That's not necessary," Trisha said. "I'm fine."

"Well, that's a good thing," said the flight attendant, "because we're out of empty seats. Will there be anything else? . . . No? Enjoy the rest of your flight."

There was a moment of awkward silence before Pete stood up and moved to the front of the cabin. Trisha's face burned. She felt like an idiot, but what could you do—paranoia was standard equipment in her line of work, like a cell phone or a BlackBerry. How many deals had been poached by someone shoulder surfing at a Starbucks? How many times had she done it herself? Mistrust came with the territory.

Jesus Christ, Trisha wondered, what had happened to her? Where was the girl who'd won those blue ribbons for her trick riding back home in Wyoming? She stared out at the stars and thought of her father, and of Dancer. They were once the two most important things in her world. Dancer was a roan, and to Trisha, the most graceful animal on God's earth. She had been too young to remember her mother's death, and Dancer's was her first encounter with grief. Now everyone who mattered was gone. Suddenly there was little solace in her new title, and little protection in her paranoia.

"I hope you'll accept this in the spirit of reconciliation,"

Pete said, catching her off guard once again. He carried two plastic glasses filled with champagne.

"Where did you—"

"Ssshhhh!" He winked, sitting back down. "It's a secret."

"But how?"

"I make this flight twice a month, usually up front. Let's just say the flight attendants and I have an understanding. Cheers."

They drank and Trisha found her face forming a smile. It was an unfamiliar feeling.

"I'm sorry for overreacting," she said. "Paranoia's an occupational hazard."

"The fault was mine, but no more apologizing. Deal?"

"Deal."

They shook on it. Trisha held onto his hand a little longer this time. This silly encounter was the first relief she'd had in months. She even felt a bit of a buzz. This man had that rare quality of both relaxing and exciting her.

"What do you do that you're down here twice a month?"

"I'm sort of in HR."

"Human resources? Who with?"

"I'm on my own, really—a consultant."

"A headhunter?"

"Sort of. It's a little more complicated."

"Interesting?"

"Challenging, more like. Now, what about you—you do a lot of business travel as part of your mysterious banking business?"

Trisha laughed. "No mystery—just visiting clients. And, yes, I travel a lot, though not to Latin America before."

"You like it—the travel part, I mean?"

It was a simple question—a throwaway question from

one stranger to another, to be answered without thinking—but it brought Trisha up short. New York, Seattle, Toulouse, Tegucigalpa—they were, she now realized, all the same to her. One airport, one Town Car, one conference room, identical to all the rest, and how different really was her apartment from a hotel room? Did she mind the travel? What the hell else was she going to do with her life? What else was there to it? It took her nearly a minute to answer.

"I don't . . . It's . . . it's part of the job," she said finally. Just a few words, but she felt as if she'd said too much. She wanted to look away, but those speckled blue eyes held her own.

Dutton nodded. "It wears on you after a while, though, doesn't it? The strange food, the strange smells, the money, the language—everything's an effort. And there's always something to look out for. The water, local customs, the neighborhood you're in—you're always on your guard, and especially down here. You can never just relax. You can never rest."

Trisha Tanglewood felt her throat close up and her eyes start to burn, and she managed to wrench her gaze from Dutton's to the inside of her champagne glass. She took a sip, and then a full swallow. Dutton put a hand on her arm, and she flinched.

"You all right, Trisha?" His voice was a comforting rumble. "I didn't put my foot in it again, did I? You looked so sad for a minute there—homesick almost."

His eyes found Trisha's again, and she felt utterly exposed. *Homesick?* Didn't you need a home for that? For Trisha, home was where the money was—Hong Kong, Tokyo, the fifth circle of Hell, wherever—it washed around the world, and she followed in its wake. Suddenly her life in New

York seemed so empty and insubstantial—all her acquaintances spectral and hollow and half a step from spinning into space. Certainly the men she saw were no anchors—their main concerns had to do with finding the hippest new proxies for the size of their dicks. She was sick to death of their *finest this* and *most exclusive that,* and she swore sometimes, if she heard another word about the hottest new anything, she'd scream.

The scariest part was that it had taken a total stranger to recognize the sadness in her. Sure, there had been condolences when her father died—the *Take-as-much-time-as-you-need* speech from the senior partners, and the *Let-me-know-if-there's-anything-I-can-dos* from her colleagues. But it was all pro forma—the thing that one did, like mucking the stalls at day's end. And here was this total stranger . . .

"My daddy died about a year ago," she found herself confessing in her spontaneously returned Laramie accent. "My momma died when I was little, so it was just me and him forever."

"Sorry doesn't come close, does it? Listen, I'm gonna be in Teguze for about a week, and it's a city I know pretty well. Why don't you let me show it to you, or at least take you to dinner? I'd like to hear about your daddy, if you wouldn't mind sharing."

No! "Dinner would be lovely," Trisha heard herself say, "but I've got to go north for a day or two, and then—"

"I understand," Pete saved her from the awkward explanation. "You've got that mysterious business to do."

Trisha managed a smile. "Not so mysterious."

Pete smiled back and took out a business card. He scrawled a number across the back. "You can reach me at this number anytime. This way there's no pressure if you change your mind, and at least we had a pleasant flight together."

Trisha looked at it. It wasn't so much a business card as a calling card. There was his name, a Miami phone number, and a cryptic e-mail address on heavy beige stock. No company name, no snail-mail address, no title. Trisha studied it, hesitating, wondering if she should return the courtesy. He noticed her pause, and let her off the hook again.

"No card necessary. Remember, no pressure."

After two more glasses of champagne, Pete Dutton drifted off into sleep. For her part, Trisha went back to her work, occasionally twirling Pete's card in her fingers and smiling. Yes, he reminded her of her daddy, but there was something else about him, something sweet and comfortable, but also a little bit elusive. She liked it. The boys on the Street all fancied themselves masters of the universe, but disarmed of their Pings and their squash rackets they were a relatively impotent bunch. *Impotent* was the last word she would associate with Pete Dutton. When she put his card away on final approach to Toncontín International, Trisha noticed she was more than a little wet.

If anyone wanted to see where all those textile jobs from Georgia and North Carolina had gone, they'd just have to hop a plane from Tegucigalpa to San Pedro Sula in the northwest of Honduras. That's where Trisha Tanglewood spent her first two days in-country, and where PriceStar, Inc. had its main textile plants, or *maquilas*, as the locals called them. But PriceStar was just one of many firms to set up shop in the free trade zones. Driving in from the airport, Trisha saw Oshkosh B'Gosh, Maidenform, Hanes, and Wrangler factories, and more than a few South Korean and Taiwanese plants. Mile after mile, the long, low structures slid across her car window, and by the time the driver pulled up to the largest of the PriceStar buildings, Trisha had begun to think of the whole country as one big free trade zone. But vast as these plants were, Trisha knew, and as fixed in the landscape as they seemed, they'd empty out tomorrow if it suddenly became cheaper to work in Thailand or Tibet. It was simply smart business.

If she didn't know better, Trisha would have thought San Pedro Sula was the patron saint of inertia. There seemed to be shackles on the hands of the clocks as she ground through two days of meetings with her team and the PriceStar executives. She was struggling to pay attention, and found herself thinking that maybe her colleagues in New York had been right. You could pore over the same spreadsheets in Manhattan, and with a lot better air-conditioning. By 3 p.m. on her first day, Trisha was almost regretting making a show of her meticulousness.

As a matter of courtesy and protocol, she strolled the factory floor with the Honduran operations manager, a PriceStar exec, and a Paisley Shutter analyst named Ellis Quantrill. Although he was a member of her team, Trisha wasn't terribly fond of Quantrill. Just thirty, WASP-ishly handsome, and bred for success, Ellis fancied himself quite the shark. He made no secret of his desire to go very far, very fast, and at any cost . . . any cost to others. She'd seen his type before, the eaglet hatched first who pushes its brother out of the nest. What Ellis hadn't learned yet was that there is always a bigger eaglet. Always.

Their relationship was rocky from the start. At first, Ellis had tried to be the teacher's pet—solicitous and deferential to the point of obsequious. Then he'd tried to make himself her indispensable ally and coconspirator—always ready to share a confidence, always fishing for one in return, and always the latest in rumors, speculation, and snarky political gossip from across the firm. When neither approach had gotten him far, he'd taken a different—riskier—tack: coming on to Trisha at the golf outing last May. He'd kissed her hard on the mouth behind the pro shop at the country club in Armonk, and Trisha laughed in his face. On reflection, she realized she'd have done better to slap him. That was the peculiar thing about Ellis's type: They'd eat dogshit to get ahead, but not if anyone was watching. Personal embarrassment was intolerable. From that ill-fated kiss forward, Ellis Quantrill had put Trisha Tanglewood in his crosshairs. She knew it, and he knew she knew it.

The factory was clean and modern. Most of the machinery was new, and what wasn't, was perfectly maintained. The workers sat in neat rows, and they moved quickly. Still, the production area was terribly noisy. There were a lot of hand gestures and head shakes, and very little speaking. Near the end of the tour, Ellis tapped Trisha on the shoulder and shepherded her into an empty break room. *Christ*, she thought, *what now?* Some new ploy to curry favor? Was he going to profess his love this time? That would be a novel approach. They took off their ear protection.

"Noisy, isn't it?" he said.

"What do you want, Ellis?" Trisha enjoyed being curt with him.

"Just a quick word about tonight."

"What about tonight?"

"We've set up a thing this evening—"

"Whoa, whoa, whoa—the only thing I'm doing tonight is getting in my bed by 8."

Ellis grimaced in mock pain. "It's set already. No

clients—just you and the team, for drinks, dinner, more drinks—very casual. You know the drill."

"Christ, Ellis, why the hell didn't you run it by me first? I can barely keep my eyes open as it is; no way I'm going to—"

"I know you're beat, but it's important to them. I don't care one way or the other myself, but these guys have been down here for weeks now, working sixteen-hour days. A night out with the new skipper—a chance to let their hair down, maybe collect a few attaboys—it'll mean a lot to these kids." Trisha shook her head, but Ellis was undeterred. "And it won't hurt you, either, to build some support amongst the rank and file—a little grassroots loyalty." She kept shaking her head, but more slowly. Ellis gave her one his ironic frat-boy grins, and a tone to match. "Come on, chief—don't pussy out on me. Have another coffee, and be a man."

Fucking Ellis, Trisha thought, and forced a thin smile in return. "I'm back at the hotel by midnight, or it's your ass."

Trisha had only the lowest expectations when it came to enforced camaraderie, but—while she wasn't about to suckle Ellis Quantrill to her bosom—she had to admit that the evening wasn't horrible, at least not to start with. The Paisley Shutter team that had worked so hard on the Mega-Mart–PriceStar project assembled in an Asian restaurant that featured a mix of Thai, Korean, and Japanese foods. A bizarre setting in the midst of northwest Honduras, to be sure, but just one more blur to set atop all the other blurs that had become Trisha's over-caffeinated day. Someone—Ellis probably—knew that she rode, and the team presented Trisha with a miniature saddle, smaller than her cell phone, as a souvenir. It was an exquisite piece of local craftsmanship, and it was even Western-style. Saki and champagne and local beer flowed freely, and Ellis made a point of keeping his distance. Trisha caught just glimpses of him, and only now and then. She appreciated his restraint.

As things wound down, the men in the group did the Cuban cigar thing, while the women gathered around Trisha to give her the lowdown on shopping and restaurants back in Tegucigalpa. Trisha found herself engaged by the conversation and felt something like her old self again. It was the longest time she'd gone without thinking of her dad in months.

"But there's one thing," Pam Richter, a junior analyst, said, her voice turning suddenly serious. "When you're in Teguz or anywhere in-country, you don't want to—"

"Come on, Pammy, don't spoil the evening with this shit," chided Maggie Wilson, a five-year Paisley Shutter vet. "It's nonsense and Trisha's only going to be here a few days."

Trisha waved away Maggie's concern. "No, go ahead, Pam," she said.

"It's not safe for American women to walk the streets alone in certain parts of the cities, especially after dark."

"Why only American women?" Trisha asked.

"Baby thieves!" Pam blurted.

"What?"

"It's a Central American urban legend. You know, like the one back home—about a couple who snatch a kid in Toys 'R' Us and change his clothes in the bathroom and dye his hair. The baby thieves myth is even bigger here, and in Guatemala too."

"I've never heard that one," Trisha said. "I only know about the poodle in the microwave."

"Well, boss, here the myths and legends are a little more . . . um, radical. Here the story goes that rich American women fly down, pick out their babies, have the mothers executed, and ship the kids back to the States to raise as their own."

"Jesus Christ," Trisha breathed. "That's . . . horrible."

"It's also a load of crap," Maggie said. "Whenever the government feels threatened, or the economy takes a hit, they spread these rumors around. The good old U.S. of A. still makes one hell of a convenient scapegoat. And it's not like our government hasn't screwed with folks down here before. The trouble is, the rumors linger even after they've served their political purposes—and especially in the poorest areas."

"That's why it's not safe," Pam said, and then she read her boss's face. "Shit, I freaked you out, didn't I? I'm sorry to have mentioned it. I . . ."

Trisha managed a smile. "No, that's okay—and I appreciate the heads-up. I'm just tired is all. Maybe we better call it a night."

But it wasn't all right. Pam's story had somehow brought all of Trisha's vertigo and sadness rushing back, and the alcohol had only made things worse. Trisha stared at the table, and at the tiny saddle she'd been given, nearly lost amidst the empty glasses, overflowing ashtrays, and sodden napkins. At some point it had acquired a tiny rider—a stiff-limbed man made from skinny plastic straws. He was tilted and reeling, barely hanging on above a puddle of Scotch, and Trisha felt very much the same. She looked up and saw Ellis Quantrill standing ten feet away. He raised his cognac to her, a mischievous smile on his face. Had he been listening? No, she thought, it was just booze and paranoia.

Back at the hotel, she took a long hot bath. Her thoughts kept drifting to Pete Dutton, and after a while her fingers drifted to her pussy. She masturbated over and over again, imagining any number of ways Pete Dutton might have her, or she him. Her orgasms were as intense as if the sex was real, and it scared her a little. She found she liked being scared, that it heightened her climax and took away some of her sadness. She found his card in her purse and placed it on her bedside, but didn't call the number.

She still hadn't called thirty-six hours later, when a plane returned her to Tegucigalpa. Trisha had the driver take her straight to the hotel. The sky was turquoise blue and cloudless, but the streets of the capital city spread out before her in a muddy blur. She was exhausted and headachy. The traffic noise mixed with colors around her, the colors merged with indistinct shapes, and pretty soon the whole world was sliding away. She couldn't focus on anything, and she found herself filled with . . . what . . . homesickness? She missed her old job; she missed her dad; she even missed Tommy Skilling, the first boy she'd let slip a hand into her panties, in a car on a roadside just north of Laramie. She hadn't thought of him in years. She opened the door to her hotel suite and her world came back into focus.

There on the desk sat a spectacular arrangement of orchids, and a single white rose. The card read: *No pressure. Pete*

She finally made the call.

Later, at the PriceStar *maquila* on the outskirts of Tegucigalpa, Trisha felt fully awake for the first time since Miami. Both her own people and the PriceStar execs noticed the change, though they weren't necessarily happy about it. The woman who'd struggled to keep the drool off her chin during the sessions in San Pedro Sula was spitting out questions like a Gatling gun. And if the answers didn't come as rapidly in return, she did not hide her displeasure. Even Trisha recognized she was being hard on everyone, but she was enjoying the high of her own adrenaline, and fuck 'em if they couldn't take the heat.

The morning smelled of spilled champagne, orchids, and sex. Pete's flavor still lingered in her mouth, with grace notes of herself. And she was gloriously sore. Pete had been everything she had imagined, and more. He seemed to see right through her, to read her, and somehow he'd known exactly how far to push things and just when to draw back. The real surprise, however, had been her. For the first time in years she'd held nothing back—not her hungers or her fantasies or her screams. Dinner was great. Maybe. She realized she couldn't remember a thing about the meal.

Pete was gone. There was no surprise in that. He had warned her he had early business, but that he would take her to dinner again tonight, if that's what she wanted. *If she wanted!* At the moment, it was all she wanted. When she left the suite, Trisha placed a twenty-dollar bill in an envelope for the chambermaid. Given the state of the bedroom, it might not have been enough.

Walking past the reception desk, the clerk got her attention.

"Miss Tanglewood, *por favor*. We have a message for you," he said, handing her a note.

The note was in English, but very cryptic: *If you want to see how PriceStar makes such profits, come see the real factories.*

There was an address, which Trisha showed to the clerk. He did not try to hide his worry.

"This is not a place for a . . ." he searched for the word.

"A woman," she offered.

"For anyone, but especially for an American. It is a slum. Very dangerous. Very dangerous."

"Okay. Thank you."

Trisha took a deep breath and gathered her thoughts. It was late in the game for this kind of bullshit—fucking late. There'd been questions up front about how PriceStar, a chronic underachiever by all other measures, had managed to outperform its competitors when it came to the profitability of its in-house label, and for a while there'd been whispers of unsavory labor practices. But those kinds of rumors—of child labor, beatings, virtual slavery—always circulated in trade zones like this, and PriceStar had checked out. At least, that's what Ellis and his team had assured her, and they'd been on the ground here for weeks. No one had even hinted . . .

"Damn it," she whispered. This had to be investigated—that's what due diligence was all about. But she couldn't very well ask the PriceStar execs about it, nor could she ask anyone on the Paisley Shutter team—she wasn't about to give one of them, especially not Ellis Quantrill, a chance to shred their way out of this kind of fuck-up. If there was a fuck-up. She put the note in her purse and called the only person in Honduras she could trust.

"They're called *cuarterias*," Peter Dutton explained, driving his rented Jetta through the narrow streets. "It means *rows* in English. They're these long tracts of wooden buildings with tile roofs, dirt floors, and connected rooms. Usually six or seven people to a room."

"Oh my god."

"It's rough, but they're good people. We'll be okay."

"Why did the desk clerk warn me that this was a bad place for Americans?"

"Well, there's the obvious reason. Money. They're good people, but they're sometimes desperate too."

"And the baby thieves myth," she said.

"Yes, that too. It's bullshit, pardon my French, but these are poor people with no education."

"I understand."

"Can we change the subject?" he asked.

"Please."

"Last night was . . ."

"Yeah, I know, Pete. For me too. I've never felt like that before." His face reddened, and that made her smile.

"Here we are," he said, rolling to a stop. "You ready?"

"Let's go."

Before they got five feet, Trisha stopped and pointed at the noisy gas generator right outside the door they were about to enter. "What's this for?"

"You'll see soon enough."

Pete Dutton had tried to warn her she might not like what she was about to see, but words were inadequate to the task. Inside, ten girls—the youngest about eight years, the oldest about fourteen—dressed in filthy, frayed frocks, were ankle-tethered with leather straps to sewing machine tables. Most of the girls kept their heads down, unfazed by the man and woman who had come through the door. One girl—bony, with a harelip and the most haunting brown eyes Trisha had ever seen—stared with frank curiosity. This did not go unpunished. A squat man with a cloudy left eye, who stank of alcohol even above the smell of urine, snapped a switch across the harelipped girl's hands.

Pete locked a hand on Trisha's forearm. "Don't do anything," he said. "Let me handle this."

Dutton called the man over and whispered something to

him. Cloudy Eye grunted. But when Pete slipped a twenty-dollar bill in his hand, his mouth split into a gapped brown-toothed grin. He stepped outside.

"We have five minutes," Pete said.

"Her!" Trisha said, pointing to the harelipped girl.

That evening the sex was more intense, if less satisfying. Trisha had gotten so mind-numbingly drunk that she barely remembered asking Pete to hit her as he rode her from behind. In fact, it was only when she looked in the dressing mirror and noticed the palm-shaped bruises on her flanks that she recalled making her demands. She brushed her fingers across the bruises. The pain had been only a temporary fix. The weather outside had deteriorated, as if to match her mood. The skies were eclipse dark and a biblical rain threatened to drown the city. Trisha would have welcomed the water over her head.

"Something's come up," she said to Susan Blum, her assistant in New York. "I'm taking the day to handle some loose ends. I'll call everyone here. By tomorrow, we should be back on track."

Even as she spoke, Trisha could not get her head around what the harelipped girl had told her and Pete. Her name was Linda, and she was twelve. She was the eldest of six children, the daughter of a whore who had no idea who the fathers were of any of her children. Recently, her mother had gotten very sick. So about three months ago, the whore had "sold" her eldest child into pseudo-slavery. The girl worked fourteen-hour days and made a few *lempira* per piece. None of the clothes she sewed had labels, but yes, a man from PriceStar occasionally came to talk to Jorge, the cloudy-eyed overseer who sometimes made the girls fuck him.

"I am a smart girl," Linda said through Pete. "I may be ugly, but I hear things, I see things."

But Trisha had no proof. She could not stop a multi-billion-dollar deal based on the word of an abused twelve-year-old Honduran girl. She needed something real, something tangible, something to bring to the firm. Even then, she wasn't quite sure it would do any good. These sorts of deals have a kind of self-sustaining inertia, especially this late in the process. Trisha had explained to Linda that she needed proof.

"Okay," said the little girl, "I understand. You come to my house tomorrow night and I will bring your proof. Other girls, too, to tell their stories."

Trisha had reached into her bag to give money to Linda.

"No! No! Not now!" the girl shouted in English. Then in Spanish to Pete, "Jorge will just take it. Bring it tomorrow night. Bring money for all the girls."

When she clutched Trisha's hand and kissed her fingers, Trisha found it hard to take a breath.

The rain had gone from biblical to drizzle. Pete picked her up in front of the hotel at 9:00. Trisha got in the backseat. There was someone in the front with Pete. He was a bulldog-faced fellow of thirty with red skin, thick arms, and flat affect.

"This is Paolo," Pete said. "He works for me. He'll have your back. He speaks perfect English. Right Paolo?"

"Very perfect. The best," he said in an accentless monotone.

"What about you? Aren't you—"

"I wish I could, but I've got business of my own to handle. And besides, the two of us in that area at night . . . We'd attract too much of a crowd. The wrong kind of crowd. You'll be much safer with Paolo. Trust me. No one is apt to fuck with him. Isn't that right, Paolo?"

"They wouldn't dare."

Please, please, Pete, forget your business. I'm scared out of my mind. I'll do anything if you come with me. I'll do anything . . .

"Okay," she said.

They drove into the mountains that surrounded the city. Trisha was numb, frightened about getting into a situation over which she would have very little control, but remained silent. When Pete turned off the main road and into a neighborhood of *cuarterias*, it was hard for Trisha to know if these were the same slums she had been to the previous day. Places, times, dates . . . It was all starting to run together into another indistinguishable blur.

"It's right over there," Pete said, pointing to a shabby door as he rolled by. "I'm going to leave you and Paolo off at the end of the row. I'll be back for you in . . ." he checked his watch, "half an hour, tops." He reached over the seat and squeezed Trisha's hand reassuringly. "You'll be fine. Paolo will see to that. Right, Paolo?"

"I'll take good care of the lady."

"Good," Pete said. "I'll be right back in this spot in a half hour."

Paolo and Trisha got out of the Jetta. Pete beckoned Trisha to his rolled-down window. She knew he wanted her to kiss him, which she did with little enthusiasm, the rain pelting her cheeks. He smiled at her when their lips parted. There was, she thought, something disquieting about his expression. Then, as she watched his taillights disappear, Trisha shook it off. It was her own discomfort, she thought, projected onto Pete.

"Let's go," Paolo urged, placing his meaty hand around her bicep.

Paolo didn't bother knocking and just pushed back the shabby door to the harelipped girl's house. The inside was lit by a string of bare bulbs. The tamped-down dirt floor was not muddy, but was dark with moisture. The room was crowded and noisy and smelled of a sickening mixture of wet garbage and feces.

Linda sat on a crude bench, a young baby wrapped in a blanket cradled in her twiglike arms. There were children of varying ages all over the place, the older ones staring at Trisha and the big man at her side. The younger ones cried or played, happily ignoring the strangers. There were adults too, mostly haggard old women, probably not nearly as old as they looked. There were a few younger women as well, but no one, in Trisha's estimation, who looked like the whore who had sold her child into a life of slavery and rape.

"Ask her where her mother is," Trisha told Paolo.

He did as she requested and translated the answer. "She's out sucking strangers' cocks for some *lempira*."

Some of the women laughed. Trisha failed to see the humor.

"Okay, ask her if these are the girls and women who will talk about PriceStar."

"Yes," Linda answered herself.

Again some of the women laughed. Again Trisha failed to see the joke.

"You have the money?" Linda asked in perfect English.

Trisha removed an envelope which contained five hundred American dollars in twenty-dollar bills.

"Let me see it, touch it," Linda said in Spanish. Paolo translated.

Trisha Tanglewood slowly removed the cash from the envelope and placed it in Linda's bony left hand. Linda

showed the money to the baby in her arms and cooed something in the child's ear. Then, when she was done, she looked
up at Trisha. On the harelipped girl's face was a cruel, almost
feral smile. It made Trisha's blood run cold. She could feel
herself blanch, feel the strength run out of her through the
soles of her shoes and seep slowly into the shifting wet earth
under her feet. All the individual sounds in the little room
became a muted ringing in her ears. A wave of nausea
slammed into her and she nearly fainted.

Linda's malformed lips and darting tongue shaped words
which Trisha's eyes read but could not understand. They
repeated the words again and again. She was shouting them.
Now everyone was shaking their fists at Trisha, shouting, but
the shouts just blended into the ringing. Somehow Trisha
found the strength to ask Paolo, "What are they saying?
What are they saying?"

Paolo turned to look Trisha right in the face. His flat
affect seemed to vanish, replaced by a broad mirthful smile.
"Baby thief. They're calling you baby thief. Run!" he
screamed. "Run!"

In a quieter *cuarteria*, no more than a mile away from where
Trisha Tanglewood was now running for her life, Peter Dutton
was taking cover and comfort in the house of a sixteen-year-
old whore. He found her disappointing. Even at sixteen she
was so experienced as to be robotic, but he let her finish what
she had started. He needed at least another five or ten minutes. He wasn't much for regrets, but he had really enjoyed
fucking the broad from New York. What she lacked in expertise, she made up for in enthusiasm. A shame, he thought, to
waste that kind of talent.

When he finally came, he yanked the Honduran girl by

the hair to make sure she swallowed. He couldn't abide spitters. He zipped up and threw two twenty-dollar bills onto the damp earthen floor. She smiled at him with more feeling than she'd displayed the whole time he'd been there.

The skies had opened up once again, and as he closed the driver's side door, Pete could hear the cries of *Baby thief! Baby thief!* spreading through the slum like an airborne virus. Not a soul noticed as he drove off into the blackness.

Trisha kept herself in great shape, and she'd gotten a good lead on the mob. Unfortunately, a good lead when you have no idea of where you're going, or the terrain you're going on, or what lurks around the next dark corner, is of limited value. Suddenly, a searing pain tore through her left shoulder. *A rock! Shit, they're throwing stones. They're going to stone me to death!* Trisha picked up her pace, but to no avail—the next rock caught her square in the jaw. Only adrenaline and her instinct for self-preservation kept her legs moving, and then only for a few more steps.

She toppled face-first into the mud, and into the netherworld between consciousness and coma. Things she heard, things she felt, all seemed like they were happening to someone else. She could sense her body move with each kick, but the pain was remote. Above her, buried in the clouds, she heard the roar of an ascending jet. She could not distinguish what kind of aircraft. It suddenly occurred to her that the flight attendant, Kathy, had never gotten back to her with the answer to her question. It's funny what you think about. Then something bounced violently against her skull and the world turned a silent shade of black.

* * *

A few hours later, Peter Dutton met with Ellis Quantrill at a prearranged spot on the road to Toncontín Airport.

"Is it done?" Quantrill wanted to know.

"Like you wanted, painful and nasty. It's going to be hard to identify her. I got the call a few minutes ago from my man confirming it."

"Excellent. That's the other forty grand, plus expenses," Quantrill said, handing over a sleek leather attaché case.

"Boy, she must've really pissed you off."

"I don't think that's any of your affair. Now, I've got to go and act shocked. Goodbye, Mister . . . ?"

"Dutton will do," he said, walking to his car. "And remember, if anything should happen to me in the near future, I've seen to it that you'll go in a manner far worse than Miss Tanglewood. My colleagues will make it last much, much longer."

"Are these sorts of threats really necessary?"

"Due diligence, Ellis. Due diligence."

ABOUT THE CONTRIBUTORS:

MEGAN ABBOTT is the author of three novels, the Edgar-nominated *Die a Little*, *The Song Is You*, and *Queenpin*; and a nonfiction study, *The Street Was Mine: White Masculinity in Hardboiled Fiction and Film Noir*. She lives in Queens, New York.

RICHARD ALEAS is the author of *Little Girl Lost*, which was nominated for both the Edgar Award and the Shamus Award for Best First Novel, as well as its sequel, *Songs of Innocence*. By day (and under a different name), Aleas is a managing director at a $25 billion investment firm that *Fortune* magazine once called "the most intriguing and mysterious force on Wall Street."

PETER BLAUNER is the author of six novels, including *Slow Motion Riot*, which won an Edgar Award for Best First Novel, and *The Intruder*, which was a *New York Times* bestseller. He lives in Brooklyn with his wife Peg Tyre and their two children. His most recent book is *Slipping into Darkness*.

HENRY BLODGET lives in New York City.

TIM BRODERICK was born and raised on the southwest side of Chicago, and currently lives on the northwest side with his wife and identical-twin daughters. His first book, *Something to Build Upon*, was published by Twilight Tales, and his graphic novel/mystery series *Odd Jobs* can be found at timbroderick.net.

JOHN BURDETT, a native of England, is a former lawyer whose practice ranged from barefoot counseling in the tough suburbs of Southeast London to high finance in Hong Kong. He is the author of various novels, including *Bangkok 8, Bangkok Tattoo,* and *Bangkok Haunts.* He lives in Bangkok, Thailand.

REED FARREL COLEMAN is the Executive Vice President of Mystery Writers of America. His sixth novel, *The James Deans,* won the Shamus, Barry, and Anthony Awards for Best Paperback Original of 2005. The book was also nominated for Edgar, Macavity, and Gumshoe Awards. His short stories appear in several anthologies, including *Dublin Noir, These Guns for Hire,* and *Hardboiled Brooklyn.*

JIM FUSILLI is the author of the New York City–based Terry Orr series, which includes *Closing Time, A Well-Known Secret, Tribeca Blues,* and *Hard, Hard City,* which was named Best Novel of 2004 by *Mystery Ink* magazine. He also writes about rock and pop music for *The Wall Street Journal.* His book on Brian Wilson and the Beach Boys' album *Pet Sounds* was published in 2005 by Continuum.

JAMES HIME is the author of the Jeremiah Spur novels and has a thirty-year relationship with Wall Street as a tax lawyer, real estate capital markets expert, Internet entrepreneur, and, most recently, the CEO of a bioscience company.

LAWRENCE LIGHT, the Wall Street editor of *Forbes* magazine, has won many journalism awards. He is the author of *Too Rich to Live* and *Fear & Greed,* the first two books in the Karen Glick mystery series, about a financial investigative reporter.

DAVID NOONAN, a senior editor at *Newsweek*, is the author of the nonfiction book *Neuro* and the novel *Memoirs of a Caddy*. He is currently at work on a second novel.

TWIST PHELAN, commodity futures trader and former plaintiff's trial lawyer, is the author of the legal-themed Pinnacle Peak mystery series, each featuring a different adventure sport. Her investment advice to would-be day traders? "Go to Las Vegas. You'll lose the same amount of money, and the drinks are free." Find out more about Twist and her books at www.twistphelan.com.

STEPHEN RHODES is the pen name for Keith Styrcula, a fourteen-year derivatives specialist who is the Chairman and Founder of the Structured Products Association. He is the author of two suspense thrillers, including *The Velocity of Money*, which has been translated into four languages. "At the Top of His Game" is an excerpt from his forthcoming novel, *Spontaneous Combustion*. His career on Wall Street includes senior roles at JPMorgan, CSFB, and UBS.

LAUREN SANDERS is the author of two novels: *With or Without You* and *Kamikaze Lust*, winner of a Lambda Literary Award. Her short fiction and nonfiction have appeared in many publications, including *Book Forum*, *American Book Review*, and *Time Out New York*. Sanders is coeditor of the anthology *Too Darn Hot: Writing About Sex Since Kinsey*. She lives with her partner in the nation of Brooklyn.

MARK HASKELL SMITH is the author of *Moist*, *Delicious*, and *Salty*, as well as an award-winning screenwriter. He lives in Los Angeles, where he invests in short-term tequila futures.

PETER SPIEGELMAN is the Shamus Award–winning author of *Black Maps, Death's Little Helpers,* and *Red Cat,* which feature private detective and Wall Street refugee John March. Mr. Spiegelman is a twenty-year veteran of the financial services and software industries, and has worked with brokerage houses and central banks in major markets around the world. He lives in Connecticut.

JASON STARR, winner of the Anthony Award and the Barry Award, is the author of eight critically acclaimed crime novels, including *Cold Caller, Nothing Personal, Bust* (cowritten with Ken Bruen), and his latest thriller, *Lights Out.* Before turning to fiction writing, Starr was a financial reporter, writing for magazines such as *Financial World* and *Crain's New York Business.*

Also available from the Akashic Books Noir Series

BROOKLYN NOIR
edited by Tim McLoughlin
350 pages, trade paperback original, $15.95
*Winner of SHAMUS AWARD, ANTHONY AWARD, ROBERT L. FISH
MEMORIAL AWARD; Finalist for EDGAR AWARD, PUSHCART PRIZE

Brand new stories by: Pete Hamill, Arthur Nersesian, Maggie Estep,
Nelson George, Neal Pollack, Sidney Offit, Ken Bruen, and others.

"*Brooklyn Noir* is such a stunningly perfect combination that you
can't believe you haven't read an anthology like this before. But trust
me—you haven't. Story after story is a revelation, filled with the requisite sense of place, but also the perfect twists that crime stories
demand. The writing is flat-out superb, filled with lines that will sing
in your head for a long time to come."
—Laura Lippman, winner of the Edgar, Agatha, and Shamus awards

MANHATTAN NOIR
edited by Lawrence Block
257 pages, trade paperback original, $14.95
*Two finalists for EDGAR AWARDS

Brand new stories by: Jeffery Deaver, Lawrence Block, Charles Ardai,
Carol Lea Benjamin, Thomas H. Cook, Jim Fusilli, John Lutz, Liz
Martínez, Maan Meyers, Martin Meyers, S.J. Rozan, and others.

"A pleasing variety of Manhattan neighborhoods come to life in
Block's solid anthology . . . the writing is of a high order and a nice
mix of styles."
—*Publishers Weekly*

LOS ANGELES NOIR
edited by Denise Hamilton
360 pages, trade paperback original, $15.95

Brand new stories by: Michael Connelly, Janet Fitch, Susan Straight,
Héctor Tobar, Patt Morrison, Robert Ferrigno, Neal Pollack, Gary
Phillips, Christopher Rice, Naomi Hirahara, Jim Pascoe, and others.

Los Angeles Noir brings the ethos of Chandler and Cain filtered
through a twenty-first-century, multicultural lens . . . a literary trav-
elogue from the Chinese mansions of San Marino to the day spas of
Koreatown to the windy hills of Mulholland Drive, the baby gangsters
of East Hollywood, the old money of Beverly Hills, and the struggling
working class of Mar Vista.

D.C. NOIR
edited by George Pelecanos
384 pages, trade paperback original, $14.95

Brand new stories by: George Pelecanos, Laura Lippman, James Grady, Kenji Jasper, Jim Beane, Ruben Castaneda, Robert Wisdom, James Patton, Norman Kelley, Jennifer Howard, Jim Fusilli, and others.

GEORGE PELECANOS is a screenwriter, independent-film producer, award-winning journalist, and the author of the bestselling series of Derek Strange novels set in and around Washington, D.C., where he lives with his wife and children.

CHICAGO NOIR
edited by Neal Pollack
252 pages, trade paperback original, $14.95

Brand new stories by: Neal Pollack, Achy Obejas, Alexai Galaviz-Budziszewski, Adam Langer, Joe Meno, Peter Orner, Kevin Guilfoile, Bayo Ojikutu, Jeff Allen, Claire Zulkey, Andrew Ervin, M.K. Meyers, Todd Dills, Daniel Buckman, Amy Sayre-Roberts, and others.

"*Chicago Noir* is a legitimate heir to the noble literary tradition of the greatest city in America. Nelson Algren and James Farrell would be proud."
—Stephen Elliott, author of *Happy Baby*

NEW ORLEANS NOIR
edited by Julie Smith
298 pages, trade paperback original, $14.95

Brand new stories by: Ace Atkins, Laura Lippman, Patty Friedmann, Barbara Hambly, Tim McLoughlin, Olympia Vernon, Kalamu ya Salaam, Thomas Adcock, Christine Wiltz, Greg Herren, and others.

New Orleans Noir is a sparkling collection of tales exploring the city's wasted, gutted neighborhoods, its outwardly gleaming "sliver by the river," its still-raunchy French Quarter, and other hoods so far from the Quarter they might as well be on another continent.